I0602879

THE DEVIL'S HOUR

EAGLE BROTHERHOOD SERIES

KAT LE VEQUE

OLIVERHEBERBOOKS

AUTHOR'S NOTE

They call themselves the Eagle Brotherhood.

We've all got 'that' group of friends. People we've bonded with that just 'get' you and you get them. Whether you bond over common interests, or a job, of even just mutual friends, we've all found that connection at one time or another.

Same with the Eagle Brotherhood.

It started with five Americans. They were young, brilliant, idealistic, and met during a semester abroad. When I first wrote this series, many years ago, it was originally called the American Heroes series. It was supposed to be about guys who knew each other as young men, but who went on to live their own lives and have their own adventures. Ordinary guys in extraordinary circumstances was how I described it. There were only five in the beginning, but somewhere along the line, we added two Brits as 'honorary' members. There are actually more books slated to be written, but I just haven't gotten around to it yet. One of the Eagle Brotherhood — Nash Aury — even has a sequel mostly written to his book, so this is really a series that has a lot of growth potential. And why not? It centers around men who are honorable, chivalric, and end up facing some really stressful and, in a few cases, dangerous situations. Some explainable, some not. That's the fun of it.

But it all had to start somewhere.

Each Eagle Brotherhood book starts out with the same *"How it began"* preface so you, as the reader, knows where these guys connect because they don't appear in each other's stories. It's a rather interesting connection, but one that opens up the hero of each tale — and eventually the heroine — to one heck of a story. These guys are connected to me as much as to each other.

They really are a true brotherhood.

I hope you enjoy the stories in this series because they were a labor of love to write. You don't have to read them in any particular order:

The Burning Hour
The Sunset Hour
The Secret Hour
The Unholy Hour
The Devil's Hour
The Killing Hour
The Ancient Hour

Happy reading,

AQUILA FRATRUM

Seven men.
Each with a story to tell.
Welcome to the world of the Eagle Brotherhood.

Years ago, five Americans on a semester abroad met at the home of their sponsor in Yorkshire, England. They were taking the same course at the University of York, including the son of their host. But it wasn't the course in International Law that bonded them. It was an incident from that time, something that happened on a dark and stormy night in an alley behind a bar in York called *The Calcaria.*

It is something that changed their perspectives forever.

These days, the men who once called themselves the *Aquila Fratrum* or the Eagle Brotherhood — a name based on the Americans who were military-based at that time — have gone forth in their lives. They are men in normal, everyday professions who succeed in extraordinary things. Their paths aren't smooth, and they aren't perfect, but they understand more than most that life is never about the smooth or the perfect. It is about the imperfect and the difficult. It's even about the unexplainable.

And, above all else, light overcomes the darkness.
Aquila Fratrum.
Ordinary men who have lived extraordinary circumstances.
And the women who love them.

HOW IT BEGAN
MORE THEN TWENTY YEARS AGO, THE CALCARIA, YORK

MICK MCCONNELL, PROPRIETOR

"Beck." A big man with a crown of auburn hair spoke with a drunken slur to his words. "Beck. *Seavington!*"

The blond Californian on the other side of the table, who had been half-lidded as he watched a group of women across the darkened room of the pub, jerked at the sound of his name as if he'd just been slapped.

"What?" he said, looking at the man with the auburn hair. "Christ, Phipps. Can't you just leave me alone for a minute?"

Archer Phipps struggled not to laugh. "Why?"

"Because you're breaking my powers of concentration, you ass."

That broke the table out in snorts of laughter. The man seated next to Beck, big and blond and with a mega-watt smile, put a hand on Beck's shoulder.

"What in the hell are you concentrating on?" he said, leaning over to see what Beck might be seeing. When he spied it, he gestured. "Over there?"

Beck full-on pointed to the women across the pub. "There."

"Those?"

"*Those.*"

"Well... what are you trying to do by staring at them? Just go talk to them."

Beck scowled at the man. "Because I'm trying to lure them with the power of suggestion, Trevor," he said. Then, he looked around the table and pointed. "It works. Colt over there has a laser stare. He doesn't even have to say anything — women know what he's thinking just by the expression on his face. Isn't that right, Sheridan?"

Colt Sheridan, clean-cut and square-jawed, waved an annoyed hand at the man he'd spent nearly every day with for the past six months. "Some of us don't have to be obvious," he said. "Look at Nash. All he has to do is give them one of those sexy, down-home expressions and they're falling all over themselves. I don't have anything on him."

Across the table, Nash Aury, the quiet and diplomatic sort with a Louisiana drawl, laughed softly. "It's all in the face," he said, gesturing to the big dimples in each cheek. "I don't have anything y'all don't have, but we don't have anything that Serreaux has, so maybe we should just give it up and let him take the lead."

The group looked over at Ethan Serreaux, a man with a French parents even though he was born in America. Dark-eyed and dark-haired, he looked like he'd just come off the pages of a men's magazine. When he saw that the entire table of semi-drunks was looking at him, he smiled lasciviously.

"*Belle fille,*" he said in his best Maurice Chevalier impression. "*Asseyez-vous sur mes genoux et dites-moi à quel point vous me voulez.*"

Everyone burst out laughing except for Beck, who slowly banged his forehead on the table. "You sound like Pepe Le Pew," he said. "Shut *up!*"

More laughter, most especially from Archer and the last man of their group, a giant of a figure who wasn't part of their academic group. Fox Henredon was in the process of obtaining his Ph.D. in Archaeology with an emphasis in Egyptology from Oxford. In fact, he'd come back a few months ago from a dig near Aswan and when he visited his best friend from grade school, Archer, he'd come across the Americans temporarily housed in Archer's pad. He'd gotten on so well with them that they'd made him an honorary member of their group. But not just the group — of their secret society, as well.

Aquila Fratrum.

The Eagle Brotherhood.

The whole secret group was really meant as a joke, but the basis of it — the honor, the patriotism — they took seriously. Three out of the five Americans had come from Annapolis and all five of them were majoring in International Law, hence the purpose of the semester abroad course. Archer was taking the same course, and he'd been the host house, and given that they were all within a few years of each other age-wise, they'd all bonded over common likes, common dislikes, and a passion for adventure.

It was a guy gang like no other.

But tonight, they were drinking to the group that would soon be separating. The course at the University of York was finished and the Americans would soon be heading back to their native lands, but promises of reciprocal visits had abound all evening. Nash, in particular, had invited everyone to New Orleans for the holidays because his family, having made their money in sugar, had a massive house that could accommodate everyone. Beck, Cord, and Colt had already committed to it, but Ethan had family obligations he needed to get out of. Archer was trying to figure out how to break the news to his parents, who were possessive of his time, while Fox was on the verge of committing. He'd never been to New Orleans and a street named after liquor intrigued him. As the Brotherhood planned their next gathering, Beck stood up from the table.

"I need to find the loo," he said, looking around. "Where is it? Back behind the bar?"

The problem was that he was drunker than the rest of them

and probably not in great shape to find anything, so Cord stood up next to him.

"Back in the corner," he said. "Come on, little brother."

He had Beck by the neck, pulling him back behind the bar where there was a dark corridor that led to bathrooms and the kitchen. The term 'little brother' was essentially referring to Beck's age because he happened to be the youngest out of their group. But he was also the toughest. Beck Seavington could out-fight anybody, Fox included, and Fox had participated in underground fight clubs during his earlier college days. He'd won money at it, too.

But Beck's fists were quite lethal.

The Navy wanted him that way.

Cord went with Beck so he wouldn't get into any trouble. Cord was an enormous man, having played football, and the rumor was that he was being scouted by the NFL. He wasn't a fighter by nature, but no one was going to test of man of that size. He'd just push the scrapper, Beck, in front of him, anyway, and let the career Navy man do the damage.

Every group had a scrapper.

It smelled like stale booze and bleach back here and the door to the men's room was locked. Beck rattled it but it remained fixed. With a heavy sigh, he looked at Cord.

"I can't wait," he muttered.

Cord tipped his head in the direction of the door to the alley out back, which was next to the kitchen door.

"Outside?" he said.

Beck nodded, which nearly threw him off balance, and charged through the back door. Cord followed him and they ended up in the dirty, damp alley behind the bar. It smelled worse out here, like garbage and animals. There were crates against the wall, broken down cardboard boxes, and little else. There were two ends to the alley, but they were standing closer to the end that dumped out onto the street where *The Calcaria* was located. Beck was looking for a discreet place to relieve himself when the back door smacked back on its hinges again, spilling forth the rest of their group.

"I think we're done with this place," Archer said, rubbing his eyes because the alcohol was messing with his vision. "There's another pub down the way called Valhalla. Let's go there."

Beck had found a spot behind some crates. "Are the women more proactive there?" he asked. "I mean, will they actually come up and talk to you? I don't think my mind control is working."

Archer grinned. "Do you seriously want a woman that approaches you?" he said. "The wooing of a woman is an art, Beck. You don't want some nervy woman up in your grill, do you?"

The others snorted in agreement. Ethan and Nash were by the back door, leaning back against the wall, as Colt went to stand next to Beck. Fox went to stand with Cord, maybe as a lookout since they really shouldn't be pissing in an alley, when three men suddenly appeared from what was a small walkway between buildings. It was dark, so no one really noticed, until one of the men walked up behind Colt and put a knife to the man's back.

Then, everything changed.

The drunken, happy mood was gone.

"Easy, big man," the man said. He was short, with a dirty jacket, but the knife he'd produced was quite large. "If you want to keep your kidney, you'll relax, mate."

Everyone froze — Ethan, Nash, Archer, Fox, Cord, Beck, and most of all, Colt. But his features never changed expression, even as he felt the prick of cold steel against his right kidney.

"If you're looking for money, you're too late," he said steadily. "We're coming out of the bar, not going into it. We've spent our money."

The man in the dirty jacket grunted as his friends also produced big knives. "Somehow, I doubt it," he said. "We were watching you inside. I think you're from money, so you've got more where that came from, Yank. I think all of you have more."

With that, his friends began to move. One of them was heading for Ethan while the other one was heading for Archer. The group, as a whole, instinctively started to back away from the men approaching, but Fox refused to budge. At seven inches over six feet, he had that luxury of being stubborn.

"You blokes really think you're going to rob guys who are twice your size?" he said incredulously. "You're either incredibly stupid or way too overconfident."

"I'll go with stupid," Cord muttered.

Fox quickly agreed with him. "Stupid, for sure," he said. "There are seven of us and three of you. You may be able to take out a couple of us, but there are five of us left who will break your fucking necks. Are you ready for that?"

That brought some pause to the man's companions, but the man in the dirty jacket poked Colt enough to draw blood.

"Give me your fucking money!" he hissed. "Another word and I'll cut a hole in this man big enough to stick my hand through!"

Colt didn't even flinch when the man jabbed him. He kept his right hand up while his left once reached into his pocket for his wallet. But as he was doing that, and the other two men with knives were advancing on Ethan and Archer, no one happened to be watching Cord.

And that would be their fatal mistake.

"*Quaere ferro scopum tuum*," Cord suddenly mumbled. "*Oboedite mihi!*"

Inexplicably, the man holding the knife to Colt's back jerked. He jolted. His hand flew up and the big blade he'd been forcing on Colt flew up and into his own throat, straight back through so that the tip came out of the back of his neck. It went through him like a bullet. As he staggered back and fell to the ground, his friends were momentarily startled and that gave Cord the opportunity to turn against them.

"*In molles venter it ferrum*," he growled, lifting a big fist as if to punch the men straight in the face. "*Utrumque vestrum!*"

The men screamed as the hands holding the knives came up and plunged the blades into their bellies as if they had a mind of their own. They went down as Ethan, Nash, Archer, Fox, Beck and Colt made haste to back up, away from what was evidently going on. No one knew what was happening and it was best to get clear considering knives were slashing all over the place.

At least, everyone but Cord backed up. He pointed a finger at the men who had just stabbed themselves in the belly.

"*Ferro ad carnem, ferrum ad os,*" he said in a low tone. "*Collum secari debet.*"

The men with knives in their bellies suddenly withdrew those knives and stabbed themselves in the neck, three or four times, until they could stab no more. They simply lay there and bled as Cord turned to his stunned group of friends.

"We need to get out of here," he said quietly. "Before the cops come. *Quickly.*"

No one moved. They stood there, eyes wide at what they'd just seen. Colt, who was the closest to Cord, grabbed him by the arm.

"What in the hell just happened?" he asked in awe. "What did you do?"

Cord looked back at the men bleeding out on the alley floor. "I protected us," he said simply. "We really need to go."

"Protected us *how*?" Fox was at Cord's side, his handsome face seriously. "What did we just see, Cord? Hypnosis of some kind?"

Cord scratched his head. "No," he said reluctantly, looking at the curious group. "Can we just get out of here, please?"

"Not until you explain," Fox said.

He was serious. No one was moving, not really. Exasperated, Cord sighed heavily. "Fine," he said. "I did it to save Colt's life. That guy was going to kill him."

Colt, who had blood running down the right side of his torso, stepped forward. "He probably was," he said. "Nobody is disputing that. But *what* did you do?"

Cord looked at his friend. "It's not something I really talk about," he said hesitantly. "I haven't... I haven't done that stuff since I was younger, but you all know I'm descended from Abigail Williams. When we all talked about our families and stuff, I told you guys that I was descended from one of the chief accusers of the Salem Witch Trials."

"You did," Colt said as his gaze moved to the men on the ground. "But what does that have to do with it? And done *what* stuff?"

Cord was clearly reluctant. "My dad likes to call us Casters," he said. "Abigail Williams was an accomplished witch and that trait is passed down in my family, like red hair or freckles. Only it's some kind of power we can summon. What you saw was a spell. I turned their knives against them."

"You're a witch?" Colt repeated in shock. "Seriously, Cord? Like — magic?"

Cord didn't answer. He just started walking, very quickly, and the others instinctively followed. They came to a walkway that led out onto the street and, nearly running, they headed up towards the main road.

"Yeah, like magic," Cord finally said as they came to the main avenue. "You saw it. I can't explain it more than that, but I wouldn't have done it if I thought we could have gotten out of that without Sheridan missing a kidney. Just... do yourself a favor. Forget you ever saw it."

"Wait," Ethan said as they began to walk, very quickly, towards the area with the car park. "We can't just leave. No matter what happened, or how it happened, we have to call the police."

"And tell them what?" Cord said. "That we got attacked and that I used a spell to turn the weapons against the guys who attacked us? They would think we were nuts."

As Ethan shook his head in disagreement, Archer grabbed him by the arm and pulled him along. "They would want to know who stabbed those guys," he said. "They'd take our fingerprints and find out that none of our fingerprints were on the weapons. How in the hell are we going to explain that?"

Ethan wasn't sure, but he didn't like running from a crime scene. "Guys, we can't leave," he said, trying to drag his feet. "We were witnesses to what happened. We have to..."

Cord suddenly came to a halt and grabbed Ethan by the shirt. "What do you think is going to happen?" he hissed. "Ethan, I don't want to run any more than you do, but I'm the one who killed those guys. That's the bottom line. And I'm not doing time for it and I'm not going to show the York Police how I turned those weapons against them, so forget it. We're not calling anyone. We're getting out of here and you are giving me your word that you'll never repeat what you saw. I need you to swear that to me."

Ethan could see how upset Cord was and he put up his hands in a gesture of surrender. "I swear that I'll never repeat it," he said. "Don't worry about that. But if anyone else saw us..."

"Who is going to see us?" Cord said, letting go of his shirt. "No one saw us. We're going to fly home tomorrow, anyway, and we'll be out of here. Done."

Ethan nodded, but he wasn't happy about it. Even if he wasn't happy, at least he understood. The entire group began walking again, very quickly, with the car park in sight. Beyond that, freedom.

Freedom from something they hoped wouldn't come back to haunt them.

Cord most of all.

"You... you really *did* that?" Beck finally said. He was still astonished by what he'd witnessed. "How in the hell did you learn how to cast spells?"

Cord school his head. "I told you," he said. "It's in my blood. But I don't like talking about it, so let's just drop it... okay?"

"But we saw it."

They had reached the car park by now and Cord came to an abrupt halt, facing the group. He was normally a congenial guy, but the event had him spooked.

"I know you guys saw it," he said. "But you need to swear that you will never repeat it. You will never tell anyone. Because if you do, I'm going to be in a shitload of trouble. How in the hell am I going to explain to anyone that I used witchcraft to kill some criminals?"

"But it was in self-defense," Ethan stressed. "No one is going to convict you, or any of us for that matter."

Cord's frustration bled through. "But we would have to explain *how* it happened," he said. "Don't you get it? One question would lead to another, questions you don't want to answer. Trust me."

Nash, who had been silent for the most part, put a hand on Cord's shoulder. "Cord, where I'm from, voodoo and witchcraft are part of the culture," he said quietly. "I've seen things I can't explain, so I believe what you're saying. I know what I saw. You have a gift, but it's a gift people don't understand. We've all witnessed something tonight that was... well, pretty damn amazing."

Cord registered some relief as he realized he had the support of Nash. The guy wasn't going to hound him. After a moment, he looked at the rest of the group. "You know, we've joked about calling ourselves the Eagle Brotherhood, but I think we really *are* a brotherhood now," he said. "We've experienced something that could have cost us our lives. It was small, but it happened. You saw something you shouldn't have seen because I did something I shouldn't have done. But to protect you guys... I'd do it again. I hope you know that."

"I feel like I owe my life to you," Colt said, reaching out to shake Cord's hand. "You were brave to do what you did, Cord, knowing... well, knowing that it wasn't something for all to see. But you did it and I'm grateful. I'll take an oath of silence on the Eagle Brotherhood if that's what it'll take. To protect you because you saved my life, I'll do anything. And if you ever need me, no matter where I am, I'll come. That's a promise."

More hands began shooting out, covering Colt and Cord's hands. It was a vow, a promise, not to discuss the event that bonded them more than a school or allied nations could. It was a bond that went deeper now because they harbored a secret. More than that, they had crossed into the realm of a brotherhood that would protect or kill for one another.

The true test of a brotherhood.

It was an oath that would take to their graves.

Wherever life would take them.

HISTORICAL NOTE

Louis-Michel Aury was a pirate born in Paris about 1788. He served in the French Navy and on French privateers from 1802 or 1803 until 1810, when an accumulation of prize money enabled him to become master of his own vessels. He sailed from a North Carolina port with a Venezuelan commission in April 1813 and reached Cartagena in May. In August 1813 he was given command over the Grenadine Republic's privateer schooners, a service that ended in January 1816, when he reached Aux Cayes, Haiti, after successfully running the Spanish blockade of Cartagena.

Although he was a compatriot of Jean Lafitte, Aury was very much his own man and one of the great pirates of the Caribbean. What he did in Louisiana and who he spent his time with during his peak of power is cause for speculation. Whether or not he set up roots along the Black Bayou is also pure speculation. Legends of pirates, ghosts, treasure and lost loves are steeped in Louisiana tradition, as thick as the Spanish moss that is so much a part of the region.

This novel reflects those thoughts and much more.

ONE

THE MONTH OF JUNE, PRESENT DAY, ASCENSION PARISH, LOUISIANA

"MOM!" he exclaimed. "It looks like the Haunted House at Disneyland!"

She fought off a grin as her son snorted and giggled, banging on the dashboard of the car as if acknowledging the greatest joke in the world. The eighteen-year-old man-youth was having a great time at her expense.

"I told you it was a historical house, Alec," she said patiently, trying to get a glimpse of it as the gray structure appeared in the distance, intermittently, shrouded by trees and dark Spanish moss that was the heart of Louisiana's mystique. "You knew it was going to be old. I showed you the pictures the real estate agent sent me."

Alec Jentry rolled down the window and stuck his head out, his blond hair plastered back against his skull in the wind.

"Holy crap," he howled again. "That place is scary. I don't want to stay there tonight."

Elliot Jentry bit her lip to keep from laughing. "What?" she hissed in mock outrage. "How can you say that? What in the world are you afraid of?"

Alec pulled his head back into the car and rolled up the window. "Zombies live in places like that," he told her flatly. "I'm going to sleep in the car."

Elliot shook her head reproachfully. "You're pathetic," she told him. "You play too many zombie-killing video games."

He looked at her, dead serious. "I do, right?" he insisted. "So I know what I'm talking about. I'm going to call Penny and tell her not to come."

He began to pull out his smartphone, the one he'd saved his money for from his pizza delivery job back in California, but Elliot put her hand on the phone and sank it back down into his lap.

"Cool it," she told him. "No calling your sister. She's got enough on her mind right now settling into Tulane."

"But I've got to give her some warning."

"No warning. Put the phone away."

He pulled his phone from her seeking fingers and put it back in its case. His blue-eyed gaze moved to the house again, now looming larger as the gravel driveway began to straighten out. In the distance, in the midst of the trees hanging with streamers of green growth, they could see the peeling paint, enormous white columns facing them down like the barred teeth of a snarling beast.

"Wow," he hissed again as the full impact of the old house came into view. "I've changed my mind. I don't want to move to Louisiana."

"Too late."

"But look at that place," he pointed. "It probably doesn't even have bathrooms, just a shed out back with a half-moon carved into the door. We'll have to pee in a hole with, like, alligators waiting to bite our butts off."

Elliot rolled her eyes at him. "Enough, Alec," she said, getting her first good look at the historical home she had purchased based entirely on pictures the real estate agent had sent her. It had always been her dream to own one of these grand old dames in Louisiana bayou country. "It's been a long drive so I'd appreciate it if you kept your whining to a minimum. I know it's a challenge for you to do that, but try."

"I'm going to cry."

"And I'm going to beat your rear if you don't quiet down. I can still put you over my knee, Alec Robert Jentry."

Alec began to roll down the window again as if to escape his mother. "Child abuse!" he howled.

Elliot rolled the window up from her side. "Shush," she scolded softly, noting the real estate agent's car they were following down the driveway was slowing down as they approached the old manse. "The real estate agent is going to hear you and think she's sold this house to a bunch of nuts."

Alec grinned at her. He was an extremely handsome boy in the image of his father, something that both grieved and comforted Elliot. Rob's expressions and mannerisms were genetically ingrained in his only son, and there had been times in her darkest grief that Elliot would look at Alec and weep uncontrollably because he looked so much like his dead father.

Now, one year, eight months, three weeks and six days after Rob's death, the pain from his passing didn't grieve her like it used to and Alec's handsome features now brought her solace, not pain. She didn't know what she would have done without the kid. Her brilliant, cheeky boy had been her saving grace.

"We're from California, so everybody thinks we're nuts already," Alec replied, cutting in to her thoughts. "California is the land of fruits and nuts."

He was giggling as he said it, thinking himself very clever, and Elliot couldn't help but smile at him. But as the cars came to a halt and she put her vehicle into park and turned off the ignition, she put her hand on her son's arm before he could open the door and eject himself onto the gravel driveway.

"Do me a favor," she said softly, seriously. "I know this is a big change for us, but you also know how much we need this. How much *I* need this. No matter what you're feeling about this house or this move, now that we're actually here, I would really appreciate it if you could just keep the commotion down to a minimum. Would you do that for me, please?"

Alec's comic disposition faded as he listened to his mother.

After a moment, he nodded. "Sure," he said, sounding a good deal like his father. "I wasn't trying to be a jerk."

She smiled at him. "You weren't," she said. "You were being your usual goofy self but today, I just need a little peace. This is a really big day for all of us."

He gave her a half-grin. "I know," he said, throwing open the door even though his gaze was still on her. "I love you, Mom."

"I love you, too, bud."

Alec bailed out of the Jeep, stretching his long frame as he gazed up at the creepy monstrosity before him. The day was mildly humid and he could smell the moist leaves and the bayou beyond. It smelled like rot. He almost opened his mouth to point out the legions of zombies that were undoubtedly waiting for them right inside the big, decaying front door, but he kept his mouth shut. His mother had asked him to.

With Alec settled, Elliot exited the car, leaving her purse inside and locking it up just as the real estate agent with the coif of teased blond hair climbed out of her white Mercedes. The entire back window of the car had her name and phone number emblazoned across it in a big, ostentatious font – *Louise Dawn Real Estate*. Ms. Dawn headed back towards them, her expensive high heels crunching against the old, rocky driveway.

"Well?" she said in her sweet Louisiana accent. "What do you think of your new baby?"

Elliot gazed up at the structure that was far bigger than she had imagined it to be. It had six massive columns on the front of the house, once a brilliant white that were now a dark gray with dirt and age. A porch encircled the house on the ground floor and then an enormous balcony encircled the house on the second floor. Instead of windows, there were arch-shaped French doors, peeling and unkempt, but her overall impression of the place was one of decaying magnificence. Still, it was absolutely beautiful.

"It's amazing," she said sincerely. "It looks just like the pictures."

"I hope so," Louise said, looking up at the massive entablature and the disheveled roofline. "I took enough pictures for you. How did you like the ones of the sunset over the bayou?"

"Beautiful," Elliot replied as she looked at the property surrounding the house and noticing what looked like old glass bottles hanging in one of the trees. She pointed at it. "What's that?"

Louise followed the pointing finger. "Oh, those," she said, almost disinterested. "Those are spirit bottles. They're pretty common down here, stemming from superstitious slaves and beliefs in Voodoo. The theory is that the noise that the bottles make when the wind blows will keep the evil spirits away."

Elliot thought it was all very interesting but she was eager to get a look at her acquisition. "Oh," she said, turning to the house. "Shall we go on in?"

"Of course," Louise giggled, holding up the keys and jingling them. They began to walk towards the enormous front porch that wrapped all the way around the house. "Now, if you remember, this house was built in 1818 and is the oldest house in the town of Sorrento. The same family has owned the house since it was built, but the matriarch died about ten years ago and the house has been vacant ever since. But even before she died, the family let it go, so it wouldn't be a stretch to say that the house hasn't been updated since the 1930s."

They had reached the front door and Elliot watched the woman fumble with the enormous, box-shaped iron lock. She peered more closely at it.

"That is the oldest lock I've ever seen," she commented. "Is it original?"

Louise nodded, struggling to turn the tumblers. "This is the original front door and the original lock," she said. "It's two hundred years old."

Elliot hissed. "Good grief," she muttered. "I've never seen anything this old."

The lock gave way and Louise shoved at the door. "Prepare yourself," she said as the door creaked and groaned, opening wide like a yawning mouth. It was dark and musty inside, the bellows of dusty, old breath sighing forth. "Everything in this house is old like you can't possibly imagine."

Elliot took a step inside, the oldness and mold of two centuries hitting her nostrils. Alec, pulling off his sunglasses, pushed past his mother and on into the cavernous, derelict entry hall that was long faded, now the color of dirty mint.

There was an enormous door to the left and one to the right, and then the hallway continued on into the dark depths of the house and they could see the bottom of an enormous staircase back in the shadows. Alec made a gun out of his right hand and began making firing noises into the room immediately to his right.

The sound startled Elliot from her observations of the house. "Alec, what in the heck are you doing?"

Alec blew at his index finger, dissipating imaginary gun smoke. "Killing the zombies."

Elliot shook her head at him reproachfully and he grinned, moving off curiously into the room with the imaginary zombies. The old wooden planks of the floor creaked and popped under his weight, echoing in a house that had been left to the ravages of time.

"So tell me about my investment," Elliot said to Louise. "You described it to me very well but seeing it in the flesh is a different experience. You said that the same family has owned this house since it was built?"

Louise nodded, following Elliot as she pursued her son into the big room on the south side of the house.

"The very same family," she confirmed. "The house went to probate when the owner died and it's been on the market off and on for about six years."

Elliot turned to look at her curiously. "Six years?" she repeated. "Why so long?"

Louise shrugged her shoulders, lifting a hand as if to indicate the very walls.

"Places like this are a rare find but they are also extremely expensive," she said, then lowered her voice as if to disclose a great secret. "Plus, I heard there was a lot of fighting amongst family members because the house had been in the family so long. Some wanted to sell it and some didn't."

Elliot absorbed the information, her gaze moving over walls that had faded, dirty wallpaper with huge blue cabbage roses on it, and the tatters of white chiffon curtains still on the windows. Somewhere, a breeze lifted the shredded curtains, giving them a very ghostlike appearance.

There were various pieces of furniture still in the room, extremely dated, shoved up against the wall and covered with dust. It looked like a tomb, the skeleton of a great home that was now just bones.

As Elliot stood there, digesting the visual aspects of the room, she imagined it as it was when it was first built, with ladies in fine dresses gliding across the floors and gentlemen with cutlasses and flintlock pistols, engaging in a game of cards. She could almost hear the wine glasses clinking and the sound of soft laughter.

Gazing up at the ceiling, she could see that it was dirty, more so over by the fireplace with the ornate hearth. Two centuries of soot blackened the white plaster of the mantel and ceiling.

"What about this furniture?" she pointed to the pieces against the wall. "Is someone coming to get them?"

Louise had been busily checking text messages on her cell phone, shoving it back in her purse when Elliot spoke.

"Yes," she replied. "Actually, he said he'd be stopping by at some point this afternoon. If you see anything you like, I'm sure he'd sell it to you for a fair price."

Having absorbed enough of the room with the blue rose wallpaper, Elliot turned her attention to the room on the other side of the entry hall.

"Who's coming?" she asked.

"The grandson of the woman who last lived here," she replied.

The second room was larger than the first – in fact, Elliot could see that it was attached to another enormous room, separated by giant pocket doors that were half-exposed from their dens.

Even in the dimness of the room, she could see that the doors were of dark wood and very beautifully carved. The hearths in both rooms had detailed marble mantels. In fact, the entire room was ornate, indicative of the former grandeur of the house. Cobwebs covered exquisite moldings and the wide-planked wood floor was dusty but still strong.

"A double parlor," she muttered, more to herself. "Look at the size of these rooms. Those pictures you took didn't do them justice."

Louise was peering at the room over Elliot's shoulder. "I know," she replied. "What you have here are the double parlors that most of these great houses had. They used them for formal entertaining. The room across the hall, the one with the blue rose wallpaper, is the library although when Ms. Jewel lived here, it was her bedroom for the latter part of her life. She was too old to make it up the stairs."

Elliot caught a glimpse of her son as he wandered back in the shadows of the second half of the double parlor. His silhouette was eerie against the covered up windows. She turned to Louise.

"Why on earth did the family sell this house?" she wanted to know. "It's like... like this is their heritage. It's part of the family. I just don't get it."

Louise lifted her shoulders casually. "Who knows? Maybe they just couldn't afford it." She eyed Elliot rather solicitously. "You really got this place for a steal but it's going to take a lot to get it put back together. But I guess all you have to do is write another best-seller and you won't have to worry."

Elliot eyed the woman, thinking it was either a haughty or condescending statement. She couldn't figure out which.

"It's not as easy as you make it sound," she said evenly. "Seven hundred thousand dollars isn't exactly a steal. It's still a heck of a lot of money."

Louise shrugged in agreement. "Fully restored plantation homes go for millions of dollars. If you restored it, you could turn it around for a hefty profit."

Elliot inspected the molding of the doorway, carved into what looked like vines. "I'm not sure I'd sell it," she said. "But I *am* really excited about restoring this house to its former glory."

She left the double parlors and moved back down the dark central hall, inspecting the gracefully curved staircase that lifted to the second story. There were no supports to the staircase as it wove, in a half-circle shape, up to the next level. The banister and railings were carved into the shapes of magnolia blossoms and trees. It was spectacular.

There was a doorway under the stairs leading into a darkened room and she peered into the blackness to see if she could make out any features of the room.

"That's the entrance to the second parlor," Louise came up behind her. "You could actually turn that second room into an office to write your novels. By the way, I purchased one not too long ago after I found out who you were. I loved it."

Elliot turned to her casually. "Which one?"

"It was called *River of Dreams*," Louise replied. "You have a great talent for writing. It must make you millions."

Elliot could sense that all Louise was interested in was money, not that she blamed the woman. Commission from this house would probably support her for an entire year.

"It pays the bills," Elliot replied.

They delved further into the house. All of the floor-to-ceiling windows were covered with cloth or some kind of newspaper, taped to the wood, so the house itself was very dark as they ventured around.

Alec was off on his own trek, in and out of rooms, as Elliot and Louise wandered into a small room off the dining room, then to an enormous room that ran nearly the entire back span of the house that had once been a ballroom, and then the kitchen. When they reached the dark, dirty room cluttered with broken cabinets and a giant iron sink, Elliot came to a halt. For the first time since entering the house, her spirit started to sink.

"Good grief," she breathed. "Would you look at this kitchen?"

Louise had disdain on her face. "Like I said, I think the last time this house was updated was back in the 1930s," she looked around the space. "My great-grandma had an old iron sink like that."

Elliot leaned against the doorjamb, imagining all of the work she had before her to make the house habitable. Even though she had a good idea about the fixer-upper when she purchased the house, still, the reality was something different entirely. She looked up at the peeling ceiling, the faded yellow walls with grease and dirt on them, and the dark and creepy back staircase built against the western wall of the kitchen that led up to the second floor. The whole thing was enough to make her shudder.

"I've already called a contractor to come in and help me evaluate the place," she said, seeing dollar signs flash before her eyes. "He's coming on Monday."

Louise looked at her, an earnest expression on her face. "My husband is a contractor," she said. "He'd love to help y'all out with this place."

So the woman is going to double-team me for money, Elliot thought. Maybe the dollar signs weren't flashing in front of her eyes so much as they were flashing in front of Louise's eyes. She smiled thinly.

"Sure," she replied evenly. "Send him over on Monday. I'll get an estimate from him, too."

That answer didn't particularly please Louise but she smiled in return, weakly, and agreed. Elliot was starting to think that the woman was only in this to see how much she could bilk her for when a voice suddenly sounded from the front of the house.

"Hello?"

It was a male voice, deep and smooth. Louise rushed back into the central hallway, heading for the front door.

"Hello?" she called, coming around a corner and gaining a view of the entry. She lifted her hand in greeting. "Well, hello there! How are you?"

Elliot was still in the kitchen, looking with increasing depression at the state of the room. It was going to cost a fortune to restore it. She could hear Louise and the unidentified man chatting as they drew closer to the kitchen.

Elliot mused that it was probably another of the woman's cronies come to drain her of more dollars, maybe a landscaper or roofer. God knows, the place needed both, but Elliot would have to prioritize what needed to be done. It wasn't like she was made of money but the way things were looking, she was going to be pumping a significant amount of cash into the Sorrento economy.

As she wandered over to the enormous tank-like kitchen sink, she heard Louise's voice in the doorway.

"Ms. Jentry, I'd like for you to meet the former owner," she said. "This is Nash Aury."

Elliot turned around, disinterested, until she saw the man standing next to Louise. The first thing she saw was perfectly combed brown hair and seductive hazel eyes. Then she noticed the rest of him; he was dressed in a sheriff's uniform, a tall, dark and handsome drink of water that threw Elliot completely off guard. He was a few inches over six feet, very well built, with big hands and broad shoulders. His chiseled, handsome face gazed back at her with warmth and curiosity.

Startled and struggling not to make a fool of herself with her gaping-mouth reaction to his presence, Elliot forced herself towards the man with her hand outstretched.

"Hi," she smiled. "I'm Elliot Jentry. It's very nice to meet you."

Nash's striking face broke into an easy smile and Elliot wasn't surprised to note that the man's physical perfection included his teeth. He had a beautiful smile. He took her outstretched hand in his big mitt, shaking it firmly but gently.

"The pleasure is all mine," he said in his rich voice. He just seemed to stare at her for a moment, holding her hand, before realizing he should probably let it go. He indicated Louise. "I told Ms. Dawn I'd be dropping by to pick up the rest of the junk around here. I hope my timing isn't inconvenient."

Elliot could have listened to that voice all day. The man had a smooth, deep Louisiana drawl that was sexy as hell.

"Of course not," she replied, realizing the man made her feel somewhat giddy. "We just got here. Louise was just giving me the grand tour."

Before Nash could reply, Louise interrupted. "Actually, I need to make a couple of calls to my office, so if you don't mind, maybe the sheriff can show y'all around. This is his house, after all. He can give y'all a better tour than I can."

Louise disappeared before either one of them could say a word. They watched her dash off before turning to look at each other, somewhat awkwardly. After a moment, they both broke down into soft laughter.

"I guess you just got appointed my tour guide," Elliot said. "But I completely understand if you don't have time. I'm sure you're very busy."

Nash's hazel-eyed gaze lingered on her a moment before reaching for the radio microphone clipped to his shirt.

"I'm not busy," he told her, engaging the mic and speaking into it. "This is S 1-A. Code four at Purgatory."

The radio crackled back at him in acknowledgement. When he returned his focus to Elliot, she was looking at him with some curiosity.

"Purgatory?" she repeated.

Nash smiled at her, shrugging. "Well, I suppose I can tell you the whole story since you've already bought the house and can't back out." He watched her giggle. "The original name of this house was Sophie, but over the years, it developed another name. The locals call it Purgatory."

Elliot's eyebrows lifted. "Nice," she said sarcastically. "Why didn't anyone tell me this before I bought a piece of Satan's backyard?"

Nash laughed. "Come on," he tilted his head in the general direction of the rest of the house. "Let me give you a tour of hell's half-acre."

With a smirk on her face, Elliot preceded him out of the kitchen.

———

He'd never seen anyone so gorgeous.

That was Nash's first reaction when his gaze beheld Elliot Jentry for the first time. When Louise Dawn had called him the day before and told him to meet her at Purgatory the next day because the new owner was taking possession, Nash really hadn't known what to expect. He didn't particularly care. All he was thinking about was clearing out the last of his mamaw's junk so the trip to Purgatory had been more of a chore than anything else and, like most chores, he was impatient to be done with it.

He was, therefore, genuinely stunned when introduced to the new owner of his ancestral home and when Louise left him in charge as she popped off to make her phone calls, he felt a little like the class nerd being left alone with the homecoming queen. All of that magnificence made him breathless, so he took a deep breath as he followed Elliot out of the kitchen and struggled to regroup.

As she walked in front of him into the dark and creepy room beyond, he stole a moment to inspect her. He couldn't really tell how old she was because she had flawless skin and a spectacular smile, but he guessed she was somewhere in her mid-thirties. She was petite in height, dressed in jeans and a pretty flowing shirt that was both sweet and sexy. Her long hair was pulled away from her face, a brilliant blond shade styled with soft curls. She looked like a little doll.

When she turned to look at him, all Nash could see was the most beautiful blue eyes he had ever had the privilege to witness. It was a little difficult functioning like an intelligent man with all of that beauty gazing back at him. All he wanted to do was stare at her.

"Well," he began, smiling at her because he couldn't seem to help it. "Welcome to Sophie. The home was built by my great-

great-great-great grandfather, Louis-Michel Aury, in 1818 for his mistress, a Scottish woman named Sophie MacGregor. He named the house after her."

Elliot's gaze lingered on him a moment before looking around the cavernous room. "What did your great-great-great-great grandfather do for his money?"

Nash folded his big arms across his broad chest, a twinkle in the hazel eyes. "Do you know anything about Louisiana history?"

Elliot shook her head. "Not much," she admitted. "I know about the River Road and King Cotton, but my family is mostly from Mississippi. I can't tell you how angry they all are that I chose to purchase a home in Louisiana. It's like some weird rivalry."

He laughed softly. "You don't sound like you're from Mississippi."

Her grin was back. "I'm not," she replied. "I'm a first-generation Californian. My mom and dad were born in Mississippi and moved to California before I was born."

"I see," he answered, returning his attention to the conversation at hand. "Louis-Michel Aury was a pirate who sailed the Caribbean. He was pretty famous, like Jean Lafitte. He built this place with his spoils for Sophie and their four children. For decades, it was one of the most visited and popular homes on the river. The Black Bayou backs up to the house and legend has it that many of Louis-Michel's pirates built homes back in the bayou, like a colony that surrounded the house. They would use it as a base when they launched their raids on New Orleans and other towns, and gradually people began to call this place the Devil's Bayou and the main house, Purgatory. Hence, the name."

Elliot was listening with fascination. "That is *so* cool," she gasped softly. "So you descended from a pirate? That's kind of ironic considering...."

She was pointing at his sheriff's badge. He grinned broadly, running a finger over the metal badge.

"I guess I've got a lot to make up for, considering my ancestor was a cutthroat," he replied. "Frankly, I was surprised when I was elected. There are still a lot of people around here that remember Purgatory and the legends surrounding it."

She cocked her head. "Elected?" she repeated, then her eyes widened. "Good grief, I feel like such an idiot. I wasn't making the connection... I thought you were just a deputy. I didn't realize you were *the* sheriff."

His grin was back as he extended his hand to her again. "Nash Aury, Sheriff of Ascension Parish," he pretended to introduce himself all over again. "Welcome to Louisiana. We're glad to have you, Mrs. Jentry."

She felt like a fool as she took his hand again, laughing softly as he shook it. "I'm really not such a dope, you know."

He was still holding on to her hand, the hazel eyes glimmering warmly. "I never thought you were," he replied, reluctantly letting go of her hand. "Is there anything else I can tell you about the place?"

Elliot opened her mouth just as Alec entered the room. The young man wasn't expecting to see his mother standing with a uniformed officer and his concern, his suspicion, was instant. Elliot read her son's expression and hastened to clarify.

"Alec," she said. "This is Sheriff Nash Aury. His family used to own the house. Sheriff Aury, this is my son, Alec Jentry."

Alec's features slackened in understanding as he took the hand extended to him. He shook it politely.

"Hi," he said. "Nice to meet you."

"Nice to meet you, also," Nash replied. "I had no idea your mother was old enough to have grown children."

Alec just rolled his eyes as Elliot grinned. "I have two," she replied. "Alec is eighteen and just graduated from high school, and my daughter Penelope is nineteen and enrolled at Tulane."

Nash's eyebrows lifted in understanding. "Good school," he said. "It's my alma mater so if she has any questions, I'd be happy to answer them."

"Thanks," Elliot said sincerely. "She probably will. This will be her first year."

"I'm sure she'll like it," he replied, looking between Elliot and Alec. "Did you relocate from California to be near Tulane?"

Elliot shrugged. "Sort of," she said. "I've always wanted to live in one of these big, old houses, ever since I was young, and with Penny going to Tulane, it seemed like as good an excuse as any. We're looking forward to living in a completely different culture than California."

"*She* is," Alec clarified. He turned to his mother. "Hey, you need to see the layout upstairs. The rooms are like a maze up there."

Nash was already moving to the main staircase. "Come on up," he said. "Let's continue the tour."

Alec bolted ahead of them, taking the winding staircase two steps at a time with his long legs. Elliot mounted the stairs more slowly with Nash right behind her.

"Did your husband relocate his job, also?" Nash asked.

Elliot's warm expression faded. "No," she said quietly, honestly. "He passed away almost two years ago. It's just me and the kids now."

Nash came to a halt halfway up the stairs and looked at her. "Oh, goodness," he said. "I'm so sorry. I wasn't trying to pry."

A semblance of a smile returned to Elliot's face as she paused, gazing down at his handsome face.

"You weren't," she said, and she meant it. "He was a sheriff's deputy, killed in the line of duty. That's probably something you can relate to."

Nash gazed up at her, feeling a great deal of sorrow. He didn't even know the woman, but he felt an inherent connection to her. He didn't want to convey a bunch of meaningless sympathies, words that she'd probably already heard and wouldn't mean a whole lot. Nothing could replace the loss of a spouse, especially under violent circumstances. He'd witnessed enough of it. Being more of the strong and silent type, he simply nodded his head.

"I can," he said quietly.

With a lingering glance at him, Elliot continued up the stairs until they reached the second floor. An enormously wide hallway opened up that stretched from the front of the house to the rear. There were old French doors on either end, opening up to the balcony. Alec was standing near the front of the hall as sunlight struggled to peek in between tattered pieces of newspaper taped over the French doors.

"There are two bedrooms at the front of the house and both of them have bathrooms attached," he announced. "The bathrooms look like they belong in the Smithsonian. You've never seen such old stuff. Think of all of the years of crap those toilets have flushed!"

Elliot looked at Nash, who wriggled his eyebrows somewhat apologetically at her.

"Did you know this house needed a lot of work when you bought it?" he asked.

She nodded. "I was told that, but the reality of it is something different. I guess I didn't realize how *much* work it needed."

"Do you want your money back?"

She laughed at him. "No way," she said. "This house is mine and I'm keeping it. A few old pipes aren't going to chase me away."

His smile returned as he watched her laugh; she had an incredibly attractive smile. "You haven't seen the pipes yet."

She shrugged, peering into the massive front bedroom. "It doesn't matter," she said. "I have a contractor coming out here on Monday to give me an estimate. My main concern right now is if the house is even habitable. If we have running water and the toilets work, then we can stay. Otherwise, we'll have to go to a hotel until we can get it up to par."

Nash walked into the bedroom and on into the connecting bathroom. Elliot followed, coming to a startled halt when she saw the state of the bathroom.

The toilet had to be eighty years old with a big porcelain overhead reservoir, flushed by the pull of the chain. There was a giant clawfoot bathtub against the wall, badly in need of reglazing, as well as a pedestal basin.

Although it was all incredibly old, she could see that, once, it had been the height of bathroom technology. There was a definite charm to the oldness. As she inspected the bathtub, Nash pulled the chain on the toilet and it flushed with a great groaning sound. It sounded as if the pipes were going to come bursting through the walls until the water circled and drained away. When the commotion died down, they looked at each other and grinned.

"It works," he said with a shrug.

Elliot couldn't help but laugh. It was all pretty comical, all things considered. There wasn't much she could do about it, anyway, having bought the place sight unseen, so she was just going to have to deal with it. Somewhere on the floor, they heard another toilet flush and knew that Alec was inspecting, or quite possibly using, the facilities.

"I'm glad the water is at least working," Elliot said, "because the moving van should be here within the hour and I want to move everything in. This is my house now and I'm staying."

Nash regarded the woman for a moment. She was petite and undeniably beautiful, but he sensed a steely strength below the surface. She was a great curiosity to him and, the more he looked at her, a great interest as well. But he didn't want to act like a wolf and stare at her, so he left the bathroom and wandered out into the giant bedroom.

"This bedroom and the one across the hall are the largest," he said. "There are three more bedrooms that aren't quite as large. They took the dressing rooms attached to the bedrooms, used to store the trunks and stuff back in the old days, and turned them into bathrooms sometime during the 1920s. There are four of them up here. When I was a kid, I used to come here and spend the night with my mamaw, sleeping in one of those smaller back bedrooms. This house was always so damn creepy to me then."

She regarded him. "And now?"

He cast her a long look. "I've gotten over my jitters for the most part."

"Really? The ghosts don't scare you?"

He lifted his eyebrows in surprise. "So Louise told you the stories?"

Elliot opened her mouth to reply but another voice suddenly interrupted. "Dude," Alec was standing in the bedroom doorway, looking rather flustered. "I swear to God that I just heard voices in the bathroom."

Elliot shook her head at the young man. "No more, Alec," she said wearily. "You already had to kill the zombies when we came in here. I don't want to hear about ghosts now."

"But it's true, I swear!"

As Elliot shook her head irritably, Nash spoke up. "He's probably not imagining it."

Elliot looked at him, startled. "What do you mean?"

"I gather from your expression that you *haven't* heard the ghost stories."

Elliot looked at Nash, all of the humor gone from her face.

"I think you'd better tell me what's not on the tour," she said softly.

TWO

"S A-1, DO YOU COPY?" Nash's radio crackled over the air.

Eyes still on Elliot, Nash engaged the microphone. "S A-1 go."

"Sheriff, Mayor Torres has called twice looking for you. He says you're supposed to be at his office right now."

Nash flipped his wrist over, glancing at his watch, and hissed. "Copy that," he muttered in to the mic. "Tell him my ETA is less than ten."

He looked up from his watch, right into Elliot's sky blue eyes. He smiled weakly. "Sorry," he said quietly. "I have to go."

Elliot waved him off. "Of course," she said as she began to lead the way out of the bedroom. "It was really nice to have met you. I'll have Alec put all of the leftover furniture into one room so you can come and pick it up the next time you're around."

Nash politely let her take the lead down the stairs. "I'll get it out by tomorrow, I promise," he said. "I'm sure you don't want my old junk cluttering up the house."

"It's not a problem," Elliot insisted as they descended the stairs. She turned to look at him as they hit the bottom landing. "But you really will have to come back and tell us about the other residents of this house. The ghostly ones, I mean."

He grinned at her as they headed for the front door. "Nothing much to tell, really," he said casually. "All of the old houses around here have stories about them, only this one happens to be a little more vivid than the others. My ancestor, Louis-Michel, is said to have buried a fortune in pirate booty somewhere on the grounds. I'm sure you noticed the big fence and gate around the place when you pulled up."

They were nearing the front door. Elliot slowed down because he was. "I saw it," she confirmed. "It's all covered with vines and moss."

"That fence has been around the property like that since the late 1890s," he said, coming to a halt by the front door, "mostly to keep out people who heard the legend of the pirate's gold and come around trying to dig up the yard. My mamaw kept great big guard dogs to keep people away and during the time that the house was vacant, I had private security patrol it. This place is a magnet for treasure hunters."

Elliot's eyebrows rose. "Are you serious?" Now she was just the least bit perturbed, her gaze finding the big-haired real estate agent still on her phone in the front driveway. "No one ever bothered to tell me that, either."

Nash could see who she was looking at. "She probably should have, although I don't think legends are part of the real estate disclosure law."

Elliot could feel her frustration and anger rise. "And what about the ghost? Do we have to worry about that, too?"

He could see she was riled and he truthfully didn't blame her.

"No," he shook his head, his manner calm, quiet and soothing. "The ghost is said to be that of Miss Sophie herself, looking for Louis-Michel to return from sailing the Caribbean. She wanders the grounds on moonlit nights, looking for her lost love."

"Have you ever seen her?"

"I've seen a lot of unexplained things in my time," he said. "Voodoo and witchcraft. Once, I saw a friend of mine... well, anyway, I've seen things that most people wouldn't believe."

"Like Miss Sophie's ghost?"

He nodded slowly. "Like Miss Sophie's ghost."

"Swear on your badge?"

He snickered. "I swear on my badge," he held up three fingers on his right hand. "Scout's honor. You know, it's really a romantic tale if you stop to think about it."

Elliot didn't have the patience for romance at the moment. She was struggling not to become furious with Louise for not disclosing everything she knew about the property. A rundown, derelict house was one thing, but legends and ghosts were quite another. But she caught a glimpse of Nash smiling at her and she instinctively softened. It was hard to maintain an angry stance with such a handsome face staring her down. She forced a smile at him and extended her hand.

"Well," she said, somewhat resolutely. "It was really a pleasure meeting you, Sheriff Aury. I really enjoyed the tour. Most of it, anyway."

She wriggled her eyebrows ironically and he laughed, taking her hand again, this time just holding it. "You're welcome," he said. "I'll come back and tell you more once you've settled in."

"You're welcome anytime, whether or not we've settled in," she assured him. "This was your house, after all. You're always welcome here."

He just stood there, holding her hand and smiling at her. There were a few moments of silence as they gazed at one another, perhaps sensing more than just common courtesy and amiability. Elliot could feel her cheeks grow warm, sensations from his handsome face and gentle demeanor overwhelming her. It was startling, thrilling and frightening, and she gently pulled her hand away before he could hold it any longer.

"Thank you," he said when the action of removing her hand seemed to startle him from his starry-eyed stance. "I'm glad the house is in good hands."

Elliot just smiled at him and he took it as his cue to leave, something he was finding great difficulty doing. He waved a casual hand to Alec, wandering around the porch and inspecting the broken furniture, and the young man waved back.

Elliot watched Nash climb into his unmarked Dodge Charger sheriff's unit and make his way out of the driveway, spraying gravel as he went. She continued to watch him until he disappeared from view and Louise, off the phone, approached.

"Sorry I took so long," Louise apologized. "Did the sheriff show you the rest of the house?"

Elliot nodded, just the least bit perturbed with the woman for a variety of reasons.

"He did," she held out her hand. "Now, if you will give me my key, I think we'll be okay from this point on. The moving van should be here shortly and we're eager to start unpacking."

Louise had the keys in her jacket pocket, handing them over. There were about fifteen of them, most of them very old.

"Here you go," she was already heading back towards her car. "Those keys unlock the front door, the front gate, and any other locks you'll find around here. I haven't even figured out where all of them go. Sorry to run off like this, but I have something I need to attend to. Y'all have my cell number if you need me."

Elliot simply waved at the woman as she jumped into her white Mercedes and sped off, fishtailing in the gravel as the car gained traction. Elliot watched her go, turning to her son as the young man walked up beside her, his gaze also on the fleeing Mercedes. When the car disappeared from view, he glanced at his mother.

"So," he said, turning to look at the grayish beast behind them. "Are you happy now? I told you this place was creepy. What was the sheriff telling you about pirates?"

She put her hands on her hips and squared off on him. "He told me that there's a horde of pirates that haunt this place and go after whining young men," she pointed to their Jeep. "Go get the stuff out of the car and bring it in. We might as well start doing what we can to make this place livable."

"Can I stay in a hotel tonight?"

"No," she said flatly. "This is home now. You'd better get used to it."

Begrudgingly, Alec headed for the Jeep to grab the items they had packed into it, mostly clothes and some foodstuffs. Elliot watched him unhappily drag himself out to the car before turning back for the house.

With Alec outside unloading the Jeep, Elliot realized that she was alone in the house – no sheriff, no real estate agent, and no son. She made her way to the central portion of the entry hall where the winding staircase rose gracefully to the upper floor.

It truly was a spectacular house, a diamond in the rough waiting to shine again. It was quiet and still at the moment, the only light from the open front door. She stood in the middle of the hall, gazing around at the ancient beast she had purchased.

"Hi," she whispered to the walls. "My name is Elliot Catherine Jentry and I own you now. I promise that I am going to do my very best to restore you to the way you were meant to be and you're going to live again with people and parties and light and music. I... I need you, just like you need me. I think we'll make a good team. I'll take care of you and you take care of me. And if you're really here, Miss Sophie, I promise only to show you the greatest respect if you'll just try not to scare the crap out of my family and me. That's all I ask."

The walls didn't respond. She didn't expect them to, but she felt much better having said her piece. Maybe the wise, old walls were watching her, judging her, hopefully deeming her acceptable as the next mistress of the house. As Alec neared the front door with his arms full of bags, she rushed out to help him.

Together, they brought the first semblance of life and love into an old house that hadn't seen such things for decades.

The old heart began to beat again.

———

"I remember now," Mayor Montgomery Le Blanc Torres pointed a fat finger at Nash. "Louise told me that she finally sold Purgatory. What a relief that must be for you, Nash. So you met the family, did you?"

Nash was standing in the mayor's office, located in a rather nondescript one-story building on Main Street near the maintenance department and the local baseball diamond in the heart of the city of Sorrento.

"I met the owner and her son," Nash replied. "Elliot Jentry and her son, Alec."

Monty sat heavily behind his big desk, his round body squeezing into the big, leather chair. "Louise told me that she's a writer." He lifted his eyebrows knowingly. "You know, smutty novels meant for women. Louise says she's been on the New York Times bestseller list four times. She must be making a fortune."

Nash lifted his shoulders. "I don't know. We didn't discuss that. Mostly, I was making arrangements to pick up the furniture that my family didn't pick over after Mamaw's death. Anything that's left there now isn't worth a dime."

"So...," Monty sat forward on his desk, his dark eyes glittering. "Is she pretty?"

"Who?"

"The famous Ms. Jentry."

Nash was careful in his response. "She's a typical California woman, I suppose, blond and beautiful." He didn't want to discuss her, mostly because Monty was a hound and also because he wasn't quite sure how he would react if Monty showed the normal interest Monty usually did with single women. He shifted the subject. "We've got a city council meeting coming up Tuesday night and we need to make sure we are on the same page about the development measure those hotheads from Baton Rouge have put on the agenda. If they get their way, they're going to tear up everything from John Le Blanc Boulevard all the way down Railroad Street and turn it into a...."

Monty cut him off. "You worry too much," he told him. "Tell

me more about Ms. Jentry. I'd love to see the reaction of the church she tries to join down here when they find out what she does for a living. They'll run her out of town."

Nash sighed faintly. "I don't know anything about that," he said, growing irritated. "She seemed like a very nice woman."

"Is she married?"

Nash didn't want to tell him what he knew knowing that Monty would probably drive to Purgatory right now if he knew the woman was widowed. Nash began to feel either very defensive or very protective of Elliot; he couldn't figure out which. All he knew was that he didn't want Monty getting his hands on the woman.

"She has two kids," he finally said. "Leave her alone, Monty. Don't let the woman's first impression of the town be the mayor who wants to get into her pants."

Monty's eyebrows lifted. "She's a best-selling author and now a local celebrity. It's my duty as the mayor to welcome her."

"You can welcome her, but don't act like you usually do. Don't invite her out for dinner and drinks that don't include your wife."

Nash was taking all of the fun out of Monty's good time. Monty sat back in his chair and began to pout.

"Not all of us can be celibate like you," he countered, meaning it as a dig. "You and Julie divorced six years ago and I don't think I've seen you with a woman since. Have you gone frigid, Nash? Maybe gay?"

Nash and Monty had grown up together; their families both deeply entrenched in the area for generations. Trouble he never really liked Monty a whole lot. The man was a political brown-noser with a penchant for only watching out for himself. He'd been that way even back in high school. Listening to the man, Nash was, once again, reminded of why he didn't like him.

"I've been busy getting an appointment from the governor," he jabbed back at the politically ambitious man. "Some of us actually do our job, Monty."

"What's that supposed to mean?"

Nash stood up, knowing that if he kept going he would say things he shouldn't.

"Nothing," he grumbled. "Look, if you don't want to talk about the city council meeting, then I have things I need to do."

Monty jabbed a fat finger at him. "State Police Commissioner isn't such a big deal," he told him, his manner filled with pure, green jealousy. "You told the entire State Assembly that you were going to rid the state of corrupt police when you took office, but we all know that was just a bunch of bullshit. When I'm governor, I'm going to bust you down to patrolman. You're not so great."

Nash just shook his head at him. "Goodbye, Monty."

Monty started to yell at him but Nash was out the door, shutting the panel to block out the man's bad-humored threats. He was thinking ahead to the paperwork he had waiting for him back at the office and the three o'clock meeting with Human Resources on Sexual Harassment training for parish deputies. But he was thinking more about a luscious blond he left back at what used to be his old, family homestead. He had a mountain of work to do but found he couldn't think of anything other than her.

By the time he hit his car down in the parking lot, his plans for the afternoon had drastically changed.

THREE

"MS. BIFFY, Ms. Tulip and Ms. Leon have sent me to tell you to come and visit them today."

Elliot was standing at her front door, listening to a very old African-American man. He wasn't making much sense but he seemed very sincere in his requests, although demands were more like it.

He was dressed in old black pants, a dirty white shirt, and held his frayed straw hat in his gnarled hands. From the weathered lines on his face, he must have been as old as the hills. He seemed polite enough but Elliot really couldn't figure out who he was or why he had come other than a few politely, and perhaps urgently, uttered sentences.

"Ms. Biffy, Ms. Tulip and Ms. Leon?" she repeated.

"Yes'm."

"Who are they?"

"The *ladies*, ma'am."

"What ladies?"

He pointed off down the gravel road. "The ladies from The Bottoms, ma'am. They want you to come to the house."

Elliot's features screwed up with confusion. "They want me

to...?" She stopped, shaking her head at the man. "Wait a minute; let's start over. You said your name was Mickey?"

"Yes'm."

"And these women sent you to bring me to them?"

Old Mickey clutched his hat. "Yes'm. Ms. Biffy saw you moving in with her looking glass and she sent me to fetch you."

By this time, Alec was standing behind his mother, listening to the old man. His young face showed the same confusion as his mother's. Elliot looked at her equally perplexed son for a moment before turning her attention back to the old man.

"Let me get this straight," she said patiently. "*Mizz* Biffy saw us moving in and she wants me to come over and visit her?"

She said the woman's name just the way he did, with a drawn out "mizz". In fact, she had heard Louise use the same term when referring to the former owner of Purgatory, so it was coming to Elliot's attention that perhaps women were formally addressed that way around here. It would take some getting used to, the legacy of decorum that was evidently used in the South.

Old Mickey nodded fervently to her question. "Yes'm, she does. She says to come before supper."

Elliot glanced up at the sky; it was fast approaching sundown and with the moving truck having come and gone a few hours earlier, she had a ton of unpacking to do. She wasn't going anywhere. With a forced smile, she focused on the old man.

"Mickey, I would love to come and visit Ms. Biffy, Ms. Tulip and Ms. Leon, but I... well, I'm just not presentable right now," she watched the fallen expression on the man's face. "Will you please tell the ladies that I am very honored by their invitation and would be very happy to visit them after I've settled in?"

Old Mickey was working his hat pretty seriously with nervous fingers. "I don't think they'll be none too happy about it."

Elliot shrugged. "I'm sorry, but I just can't visit today. Tell them I will visit next week."

Old Mickey nodded but it was clear that he was unhappy and perhaps even fearful. Alec took the steps from the porch, ending up on the gravel. He focused in on the very old gentleman.

"How old are you, old dude?" he asked.

The old man visibly cowered from the tall, blond young man. "I... I expect I was born when Mr. Wilson was president."

"What?" Elliot came off the porch, fixed on the old man. "He was president back in the 'teens."

"Yes'm."

"Then you're in your nineties."

The old man looked thoughtful a moment. "Yes'm, I am. I'm not sure, but I expect I'm ninety-six or so. I stopped counting when Reagan was president."

Elliot looked at Alec, shocked, before turning back to the old man. Alec was the first one to speak.

"Old dude, you look amazing," he chuckled. "I hope I'm still running around when I'm ninety-six."

The old man sensed that he had somehow met with some approval and smiled timidly.

"I best be getting back," he told them, beginning to shuffle off down the driveway. "Ms. Biffy, she'll be waiting on me. She don't like me being late."

Alec started to follow him, very curious about the extremely old man. "Do you work for her?"

Mickey was still walking as he nodded. "I work for her mama, Ms. Leon. I worked for her husband."

Elliot found herself following Alec as he followed the old man down the drive.

"Is her husband still alive?" Elliot asked.

Mickey shook his head. "No, ma'am. He died quite some time ago. Ms. Leon is one hundred and three years old and she lives with her daughters, Ms. Biffy and Ms. Tulip. We all live at The Bottoms."

"Where is The Bottoms?" Alec wanted to know.

Old Mickey came to a halt, pointing off to the east. "Down there a spell," he said. "I have to go now."

Alec's brow furrowed. "There aren't any houses around here for at least a mile," he said. "Did you walk all the way here?"

Old Mickey nodded. "It ain't far."

Alec furrow deepened. "Don't you have a car?"

The old man shook his head. "Don't need no car. I can walk."

"Dude!" Alec exclaimed, confused that the man didn't see the issue here. "You're ninety-six years old. You shouldn't be walking."

Mickey didn't quite understand the trouble. "It ain't far," he repeated. "Ms. Biffy will be expecting me."

"What do you mean she's expecting you?"

"I have to get on home, young buck. The ladies are waiting."

Alec, the young man born and raised in big-city California and counted several African-Americans as close friends, was genuinely perplexed. The attitude of this old black man in the rural South was foreign to him.

"You realize the Civil War is over, right?" he asked, more out of concern than anything. "Slavery was over one hundred and fifty years ago."

Mickey wasn't sure what he meant. "I know it." He kept walking. "My grandpappy was born a slave but then he was freed. I'm free, too. I got to go now because the ladies are waiting on me."

Alec didn't know what to say. The old man kept walking and he stopped following, turning to look at his mother with a quizzical look. Elliot could see that her son was truly baffled by the man's attitude. The California boy who was raised not to see race or color just got his first taste of class culture in the Old South.

"Come on," she pulled the kid by the arm, back towards the house. "We've got work to do."

Alec wasn't sure what to say. This new place was weird and foreign already and he wasn't sure he liked it. He let his mother drag him back into the house where boxes upon boxes of their possessions waited to be unpacked.

In mostly silence, they continued unpacking until the sun was nearly set and Alec went about trying to turn on some lights. They soon found out that there were only electrical plugs on the lower floor and, even then, they were spotty.

They took a few lamps around with them, trying plugs in different rooms, and came to see that only two plugs in the entire house worked. They put a big lamp with a 100 watt bulb in the first of the double parlors and a second in the kitchen.

But they needed more light so Elliot dug through the boxes in the upstairs bedroom until she came across her collection of candles. Most of them were decorative but a few of them had seen service, so after hunting around for and finding her lighter, she lit up every candle she had. Soon, the entire room was aglow with the haunting and warm illumination of the candles. The scents of *Lemon Sage* or *Golden Myrrh* mixed with the smell of dust.

Alec soon joined her and began taking candles to various rooms on the upper floor so they would at least have light to move around by.

"I feel like I'm in the Dark Ages," he said as he moved into the big bedroom across the hall from his mother that he had claimed. He started singing a bizarre monk-chanting song as he moved around with the candles, sending his mother into laughter.

Elliot followed him to put one in his bathroom, a small box of a room that had a toilet, a small corner sink, and a shower stall that was made out of copper. The poor kid could barely move around in it.

"Remember that this house is used to candlelight," she reminded him. "It's only seen electricity in the last seventy years or so. I think it's pretty cool that we're seeing the house the way it was meant to be seen."

Alec made a face, hauling his mattress up onto his bed frame. "Mom, I know you really like this old house stuff, but I've got to tell you that it sucks." He grunted as he tossed the mattress down. "I want my satellite television and my Xbox Live. I don't like living like the pioneers."

Elliot snorted at him. "You have your smartphone and your

iPad, at least, and satellite internet. At least you're not completely cut off."

"This still sucks."

She shook her head at him. "Don't worry," she assured him. "We'll have the contractor here on Monday and start getting wired in. You're not a total caveman, yet."

Alec tried to make a face at her but ended up laughing, instead. Elliot returned to her bedroom and collected more candles, carefully taking them down the hall to the winding staircase. She put candles intermittently down the stairs and one near the foot of the stairs to light up the dark central hall, then moved to the ballroom that was big and dark with its forbidding shadows.

The floor-to-ceiling windows were still covered with old newspaper, blocking out the moonlight. She stood there a moment, envisioning the room as it must have been two hundred years ago when pirates and beautiful women graced the floors. So little of the house had been touched by modern hands that it was very easy to envision it as it once had been.

The kitchen already had a lamp so she moved to the library in the front of the house, placing two candles on the hearth to give the room some light. Just as she was moving into the dining room, she heard a soft knock on the front door.

Curious, and with candle in hand, she went to the front door and threw the bolt. Jerking open the sticky panel, the first thing that hit her was the smell of barbeque. The rich flavor of molasses and spice hit her like a smack to the nose. In the darkness, she could see two big paper bags and the hands holding them. Lifting the candle, she was met by a friendly, familiar face.

"Hi," Nash said.

Elliot realized that she was extremely pleased to see the man. "Hi yourself," she grinned, nodding her head towards the bags in his hands. "I have to tell you something."

"What?"

"I'm going to rob you of the food you're carrying."

He laughed. "I figured as much," he said. "It occurred to me that you have no stove and probably no way to cook anything, and even if you did, you probably don't know where any of the supermarkets are around here. So I thought I'd save you the trouble and bring you and your son some dinner."

Her smile broadened and she opened up the door wide so he could come in. "Is the state budget so bad that the local sheriff has to moonlight as a delivery boy?"

He laughed again. "It's not that bad, at least not yet," he looked around. "Do you have someplace where you want to sit and eat this?"

"Absolutely," she moved into the double parlors, lit by the screaming-white, bright light, and began to pull boxes off the buried coffee table. "I can't thank you enough for doing this. It's really sweet of you."

He set the bags down as she cleared the table. "No problem at all," he said. "I'm glad to do it."

"Will you stay and eat with us?" she began peering into the bags. "It looks like you have enough food here for an army."

"Sure," he said. "If you're sure there's enough."

Elliot went to her knees beside the coffee table and began pulling out Styrofoam containers.

"There's plenty," she assured him, inhaling deeply. "It smells fantastic."

Nash started to reply but the sound of thunder suddenly stopped him. Something was thumping across the ceiling over their heads, moving for the stairs and making a lot of noise on the creaky old planks. They could hear Alec making his way towards the smell of the food.

"Oh, my God," the young man ended up in the doorway from the entry hall, taking a deep sniff of the air. "I smelled that all the way upstairs. That's the best thing I've ever smelled in my life."

Nash grinned as Elliot held out a container to her son that was loaded with barbecued ribs. "Thank the sheriff," she told him. "He brought the feast."

Alec grabbed the container and snatched a rib, taking a big, juicy bite. He looked like a man who had just fallen in love.

"Thanks, dude," he said to Nash, mouth full. "You're the best. This is awesome."

"That's Sheriff Dude to you," Elliot lifted her eyebrows at her son. "At least pretend you have some manners."

Alec grinned at Nash. "Sorry," he said, taking another bite. "I call everyone 'dude'. Even my mother."

Nash chuckled. "No problem," he said. "I only make people I don't like call me Sheriff. You can call me whatever you want."

"I'll call you My Best Friend for bringing this," Alec said as he slurped up the barbeque sauce. "Where'd you get it?"

Nash threw a thumb in a general southerly directly. "There's a barbeque place out on the highway. They even have barbequed alligator."

Alec stopped mid-chew. "This isn't alligator, is it?"

Elliot started laughing as Nash shook his head. "No, it's beef," he assured him. "But the alligator isn't half-bad."

Alec sat down on the floor next to the table, realizing there were beans and coleslaw and cornbread. As he inspected the dishes, Elliot turned to Nash.

"I'm sorry, but my plates are still packed," she said. "Do you mind eating out of the containers?"

Nash shook his head, looking around for a chair that wasn't piled with boxes. Alec, in the midst of his eating frenzy, saw what the man was doing and immediately went to remove some clutter from an armchair.

"Here," he told him, a rib in his left hand as he pulled the chair towards Nash with his right. "Have a seat."

Nash grinned at him, noticing the kid hadn't missed a beat with his eating. He took the chair gratefully and pulled it up to the coffee table where Elliot was sorting out the food. He smiled and took the Styrofoam container she offered him.

"Thanks," he said, settling down with napkins. "I haven't eaten since breakfast."

Elliot bit into a delicious piece of chicken. "Are your days always so busy?"

Nash took a big bite of a rib, nodding. "Mostly," he said. "It's a big parish and I spend about fifty percent of my time in the field."

"How many deputies do you have?"

"I have one hundred and seventy-two sworn officers to cover two hundred and ninety-two square miles of land and eleven square miles of river," he told her. "It's a big job, especially since we have river jurisdiction, also."

"Don't most of the towns have their own police departments?"

He nodded, wiping the sauce off his lips. "Some do," he said. "But we cover the small towns that don't, plus unincorporated areas, and handle all emergency management for the parish. We also work directly with Homeland Security for the State of Louisiana."

Elliot listened with interest, taking another bite of chicken. "So how did you come into this line of work?"

Nash reached for one of the sodas he had brought. "My dad and granddad were police officers for the City of New Orleans," he said. "Granddad was the chief back in the 1940s and my dad was a captain until he retired about ten years ago. It was always something I knew I would do. I ran for parish Sheriff twelve years ago and won by a landslide. I was one of the youngest sheriffs in the history of Ascension Parish."

"Wow," Elliot exclaimed. "That's quite an accomplishment."

He shrugged modestly. "I enjoy my job." His gaze lingered on her as he chewed. "Speaking of accomplishments, I hear you're a writer."

Elliot grinned, wiping off her mouth. "That's the rumor."

"What do you write?"

She stuck her fork into the coleslaw. "Bodice-ripping romance novels, mostly. Sex, men with swords, damsels in distress, that kind of thing."

She said it so dramatically that he laughed. "How did you get into that line of work?"

She took another bite of coleslaw. "I was always a writer," she told him. "I worked on the school newspaper and, in college, my major was English Literature. After Penelope was born and I was home with the baby, I just started writing full time to mainly stave off the boredom and ended up selling a series of books to a major publishing house. It was really all by luck. Now I write about three novels a year and sell hundreds of thousands of copies. Sometimes I still can't believe how fortunate I am to be doing what I love."

Nash was smiling warmly at her, listening to her story. "It's great to be doing something you're passionate about."

"I think so."

"So you think you'll find inspiration for your books down here in the bayou?"

Her gaze lingered on him a moment, eyes glittering. As she looked at the man, it occurred to her that he would make a great hero in one of her novels. He was damn sexy in every way.

"Maybe," she said ambivalently.

It was another one of those awkwardly warm moments and after a few seconds of silence, they both started chuckling again. Alec, oblivious to the transition from polite conversation to gentle flirting between his mother and the sheriff, closed up his Styrofoam container of stripped rib bones and set them on the table.

"I'm going to get a trash bag," he stood up, wiping his hands off on his jeans. "Did you see which box they were in?"

Elliot shook her head. "No," she replied. "I packed them in with the kitchen cleaning products. It's written on the outside of the box. It should be in there somewhere."

Alec trudged off into the dark house, his big feet echoing against the worn, wooden flooring. Nash and Elliot sat in comfortable silence for a few moments as Elliot continued on with her coleslaw. Nash was watching every move she made, from the graceful sweep of her hands to the way her lashes fanned out against her cheeks. She was an entrancing creature to watch.

"He seems like a nice kid," he said.

She nodded. "He is," she replied, finishing with the coleslaw. "Since his dad's death, he's stuck to me like glue. For the first three months after Rob died, Alec and his friends would sleep at the house just to make sure I was okay. For months, I had four boys living at my house, sleeping in my living room, eating my food, attempting to wash dishes or mop floors. Honestly, I don't know what I would have done without them. It was like living in a frat house sometimes but I really thanked God for them. They kept my mind off what had happened and kept it focused on other things. They were such good kids."

Nash smiled faintly. "Would it be too much to ask what happened to your husband?"

She looked at him, his handsome features and gentle eyes, and shook her head.

"No," she said softly. "Of all people, you would probably understand the most. Rob was a sheriff's captain assigned to the SWAT team. He absolutely loved it. I absolutely hated it. He had been in command of a Los Angeles County Sheriff's SWAT division and even trained SWAT recruits at the Sheriff's Academy. One day, we're at a barbeque at a friend's house and the SWAT team got a call out. He left the barbeque and I never saw him alive again because when the SWAT team deployed at the location, a ricochet bullet took him out as he got out of the van. He never saw it coming."

Nash was no longer smiling by the time she finished. He shook his head and hissed sadly. "Wow," he exclaimed. "That's really rough. I'm so sorry to hear that."

Elliot thought on that very dark day, feeling saddened by the memories that were struggling to heal. They weren't as bad as they used to be, but the sorrow was still there.

"Thanks," she murmured. "When Penelope got accepted to Tulane, I jumped at the chance to move here. I wanted to get away from the memories and start fresh. Not that all of the memories in California were bad, but I really needed a change of scenery. Everywhere I turned I was reminded of my husband and it was just too much to take. I needed to get out of there. Does that make any sense?"

He nodded sympathetically. "Of course it does. I've lost a few friends over the years. Never a spouse, but friends. I get it."

She cocked her head at him, curiously, the focus shifting. "Are you married, Nash?"

He shook his head. "No," he replied. "My ex-wife and I divorced six years ago. She lives in Baton Rouge, as do my two boys."

Elliot nodded in understanding. "I'm sorry to hear that. How old are your boys?"

"Twenty-two and eighteen," he replied. "My oldest is in grad school and my youngest will enter his first year of college in the fall."

"Are either of them going into law enforcement like the three generations of Aury men before them?"

His grin returned. "Maybe Shane," he replied. "He's my youngest. He wants to go through the academy when he graduates, but my oldest, Beck, is in law school and wants to be a prosecutor."

Elliot grinned because he was; he seemed to warm up when speaking of his sons. "They sound like ambitious young men," she said. "Congratulations."

His grin broadened and they entered into yet another of those warm and awkward moments until a shout from the rear of the house brought them both to their feet.

Elliot bolted before Nash could stop her and they raced to the rear of the house, into the kitchen, where Alec was wielding a lamp base like a weapon and unlocking the back door. He yanked the door open, peering into the blackness beyond, and held the lamp up like a club as Nash reached him.

"Hold on," Nash grabbed the lamp. "What happened?"

Alec was tense with adrenalin. "I saw a face in the window looking at me from the outside," he said. "There's somebody out here."

Nash was much cooler than Alec was. He pulled the lamp out of the young man's hands and set it aside.

"Stay with your mother," he told him. "I'll go outside and have a look around."

Alec opened his mouth to protest but Elliot pulled him back, away from the door. Nash pulled his standard police-issue Maglite out of the holster on the left side of his Sam Browne belt and turned on the brilliant beam, shining it out into the overgrown bramble beyond. He stepped outside, taking a good, long look.

"Close the door behind me and lock it," he told the pair. "I'll be back."

Alec closed the door and threw the old bolt. Then he went the windows and began to follow Nash as the man wandered around the exterior of the house.

"What did the face look like?" Elliot wanted to know.

Alec was peering from one of the kitchen windows, peeling back the old newspaper to watch Nash.

"I don't really know," he shrugged. "Just a pair of eyes and a face, like an old man's face. It was really fast and then it was gone."

Elliot thought on that a moment before heading into the central entry hall where three big pillar candles burned on the staircase. They gave off a surprising amount of light and she collected one, carrying it with her into the ballroom. Alec was already there, peeling back layers of newspaper from other windows so he could watch Nash prowl about.

Together, Elliot and Alec watched Nash as he made his way through the vast back gardens, his flashlight the only source of light in an otherwise very dark night. They also noticed a peppering of fireflies, something Alec had never seen before. He watched the glowing speckles float through the darkness, lighting up the bayou with their eerie glow.

"Look at the fireflies," he commented. "Those are pretty cool."

Elliot watched Nash's silhouette against the darkness. "Yes, they are," she said, though she didn't sound like she meant it. She was more concerned with Nash and the prowler. "We're going to have to get some dogs to patrol this house. It's such a large piece of land. I really didn't think about security, but after what Nash told us today and after what you saw tonight, it looks like we're going to have to protect our land."

Alec wasn't distressed about the dogs. "Cool," he said. "We can go to the local pound and get a pack of them."

Elliot wriggled her eyebrows, watching as Nash's flashlight drew nearer to the house. They could also hear his sheriff's radio crackling as he spoke to dispatch.

"I don't know about a pack, but at least two or three," she said. "Maybe tomorrow we'll go and take a look."

"Tomorrow is Sunday," Alec reminded her. "I don't think the dog pound is going to be open on a Sunday."

"Why not?"

"Because everybody is in church down here," he looked at her. "I've been doing some reading about the South and everybody down here belongs to churches. You're nobody if you don't belong to a church. This entire section of the country practically shuts down on Sunday."

Elliot shrugged, noticing that Nash was now up on the porch, talking into his radio and surveying the massive backyard that stretched all the way to the bayou beyond.

"So we'll go on Monday," she said. "Tomorrow, I'd really like to unpack and look around our property anyway. We can see in the daylight what we've gotten ourselves into."

Alec snorted in agreement, watching Nash as the man began to make his way around the house towards the front porch. Elliot and Alec began to follow him when the sound of breaking glass abruptly filled the air. It was coming from the front of the house.

Alec and Elliot took off at a dead run, tearing through the central hall towards the front door. Elliot was behind her son when he turned towards the double parlors, fired off a curse word, and disappeared into the parlor. Elliot came up behind him, shrieking when she saw what had him cursing.

Someone had thrown a Molotov cocktail into the front

window, which had landed smack-dab on a cluster of moving boxes. The liquid in the cocktail had sprayed all over the boxes, igniting them, and a swiftly spreading fire was beginning to consume the cardboard. Dark smoke was already filling the room as Alec grabbed at the flaming boxes.

"Mom, open the front door!" he bellowed.

Elliot ran to the front door, turning the old tumblers and yanking open the warped panel. There was a body standing in the doorway and she yelped until she realized it was Nash. He caught sight of the flames and charged past her, helping Alec pull out the flaming boxes.

Elliot jumped in, pulling out a large box that had one entire side of it on fire. Nash helped her pull it out of the house, pushing her aside as he tossed the box out into the gravel drive. But Elliot would not be moved aside, not when her possessions were burning. She ran at the burning boxes and, fighting the heat and flames, tried to pull them open to get at the contents.

"Alec," she cried. "Help me get the stuff out of these boxes!"

The flames were consuming the cardboard. Alec helped his mother as much as he could as Nash ran to his patrol car and snatched the fire extinguisher. He returned to the blaze, beating it down with the extinguisher, trying not to spray Elliot or Alec in the process. Soon enough, the blaze was out and Nash tossed the extinguisher aside, moving in to help Elliot and Alec.

"Are you okay?" he asked Elliot.

She nodded silently, digging her way into one of the boxes in particular. She seemed extremely determined and Nash didn't understand why until she pulled herself out of the box, pieces of burnt paper in her hand. At least, he thought it was paper until he looked more closely. They were pictures of a man in uniform.

Elliot stood there with the singed and burnt photos in her hand, staring down at Rob's smiling face. Nash began to realize why she was so determined to fight the flames, feeling about as bad as he possibly could, as Alec went to his mother and carefully pulled the photos out of her hand.

"These will be okay," he assured her. "I can scan them with Photoshop and make them look like new again. Don't worry; they'll be fine."

Elliot watched her son as he brushed at the pictures, trying to see just how badly damaged they were. She watched him as he dug into the box again, searching for more photos that might have been damaged. As he wandered back into the house with his hands full of photos, she went to the steps of the front porch, sat heavily, and burst into quiet tears.

Nash watched her, his heart just about breaking. He wasn't sure what to say to the woman. Silently, he went over to her and sat down next to her on the stairs. He watched her gently heaving shoulders, the hands over her face, and did the only thing he could think of. He put his big arm around her shoulders and hugged her gently.

"I'm so sorry," he whispered.

Elliot felt his hand on her shoulder and she reached up, clasping the warm fingers, taking strength from the reassurance.

"It's not your fault," she wept softly. "But what in the hell... why would somebody do that? They don't even know us. Why would they firebomb my house?"

Nash shook his head and gave her another squeeze, holding on to the warm fingers that were clasping his.

"I don't know, darlin'," he said, hearing the distant scream of sirens draw closer. Looking up, he could see at least three squad cars barreling down the quarter-mile long gravel driveway. "I'm sure they weren't after you personally. I told you that this house attracts freaks. Maybe that's all this was, somebody trying to scare you away."

She sobbed into her hand, struggling to compose herself. "I'm sorry," she whispered. "I'm not usually such a cry baby. But I just finished a three-day drive across the country, found out that the house I bought is full of ghosts and pirate treasure, and now somebody tries to burn it down. I guess... I guess it's just been a big day."

Nash didn't say a word. He just sat there with his arm around her shoulders, watching the police units pull into the circular drive in front of the house. There were actually four units, two City of Sorrento police units and two sheriff's units. He gave her a quick squeeze before rising to his feet, facing the officers now bailing out of their cars.

"Someone prowled the place and then threw a Molotov cocktail into the front window," he pointed out the broken parlor window to the arriving officers. "Better see what we can come up with."

The two Sorrento officers called for a watch commander while the two deputies moved closer to Nash. They were both experienced and crisp in their pressed uniforms, looking to their sheriff and awaiting orders.

"Hey, Nash," a big blond man propped his boot on the first step of the porch, looking around. "What do you want us to do?"

Nash pointed to the rear of the house. "Someone was prowling back there," he said. "Dust the kitchen windows and doors and see if we can pull some prints."

The blond deputy nodded. "Anything else?"

Nash nodded his head, glancing over at Elliot, who had since composed herself and now stood up on the porch, struggling to look like she wasn't deeply upset. He motioned his deputies with him.

"Come here," he said quietly.

The men followed him up on the porch. Nash smiled at Elliot when he approached, indicating her to his deputies.

"This is Elliot Jentry," he told them. "She and her son just moved in today. If she calls, you jump. I don't care what time of day it is or what y'all are doing at the time. If she needs you, y'all come running. Understood?"

The men nodded seriously, looking at the beautiful, blond woman with the big, blue eyes. The blond deputy tipped his hat at her.

"Ma'am," he greeted.

Nash indicated his deputies. "Elliot, this is Ken Havereau," he indicated the blond, "and his tall counterpart over there is Steve Pitot. They work out of the substation in Brittany, about four miles up the highway. If you need anything, anything at all, you call over there and ask for them by name."

Elliot forced a smile. "Please call me Ellie," she said. "It's nice to meet you both."

"A pleasure, Ms. Ellie." Steve, the very tall deputy with bright blue eyes, looked at Nash. "We're going to check around back, Nash."

Nash nodded, watching the men disappear around the side of the house. When they were out of his line of sight, he turned to Elliot.

"Can I call you Ellie, too?" he teased.

She broke down into soft laughter. "The only person who ever calls me Elliot is my mother," she said. "To everyone else, I'm Ellie."

"You could have told me that before I introduced you as Elliot."

"You didn't ask."

He was glad to see she was smiling again. "All right, Ms. Ellie," he turned to look at the open front door, smelling the smoke from the fire. "I'm thinking that maybe you and Alec should stay at a hotel tonight. It would be safer than...."

She shook her head strongly, cutting him off. "No way," she said firmly. "This is my house and I'm staying. I'm not going to let some dumbass chase me out of my home."

Nash scratched his head. "I didn't think you would take my advice," he muttered. "Well, I suppose the only thing to do is to post a couple of deputies here tonight. Tomorrow, we can figure out what we need to do to secure the place."

"Wait a minute," Alec was standing in the doorway, his young face serious. He looked at his mother. "Mom, I think the sheriff is right. You need to go to a hotel. I'll stay here and watch our stuff."

Elliot shook her head at her son. "Sweetie, I appreciate what you're saying, but I'm not leaving. I survived Los Angeles and the

Rodney King riots. There's no way a bunch of hillbillies are going to chase me from my new home. I'm staying. But I think you should go to a hotel. You wanted to, anyway."

Alec backed off. "If you're staying here, I'm staying here. I'm not leaving you alone."

"I won't be alone," she assured him. "Nash said he's going to station a couple of deputies here tonight."

Alec shook his head vigorously, much like his mother had a few moments earlier, and backed off into the house.

"I'm not going anywhere," he said as he walked down the central hall towards the staircase. "I'm going to go set your mattress up."

Elliot let him go, turning to Nash once her son disappeared from view. She smiled weakly at him.

"You've run into a couple of stubborn people," she told him. "We're staying."

Nash wasn't particularly pleased but he understood. He tried one last time. "Are you sure I can't talk you into going?"

Her smile broadened. "No. Like I said, we're stubborn. Plus, I spent a hell of a lot for this place and I'm not leaving my investment. But you already know how much I spent for it so I don't have to tell you."

His grin was back. "Are you *sure* you don't want your money back?"

She laughed softly. "Never," she insisted. "The only way someone else will get this place is if I die or if they marry me."

Nash's smile faded. It occurred to him that the latter part of that statement was not such a bad idea.

FOUR

WHEN ELLIOT AWOKE the next morning, bright sunlight was streaming in through the cracks in the taped-on newspaper. The room was fairly bright. Wrapped up in her comforter on her California king mattress, she blinked her eyes several times, orienting herself.

Propping herself up on her elbows, she looked around the enormous bedroom. The bed, as big as it was, was dwarfed by the size of the room. Four massive beds would have fit very comfortably into the chamber.

Sitting up, she yawned and rubbed the sleep from her eyes. It was difficult not waking up in her bedroom in her home in California, the same bedroom that she and her husband had shared for twenty years. As much as she had wanted to get away from it, as she gazed around the dilapidated bedroom of Purgatory, she realized that she equally missed it. It was an odd, somewhat depressing, realization.

But there was no use dwelling on it. She had moved here for a reason and today, she was going to jump into this life that she had sought for herself and for her children.

In spite of the humidity already in the morning air, the floor was cold when she put her feet on it and she hopped around, digging in a couple of boxes until she found a pair of socks. Pulling them on her feet, she went into the bathroom that was part of the master suite.

The clawfoot tub was truly something to behold. It was deep enough to swim in and she stood over it a moment, trying to decide if she wanted to take a bath in the old tub or scrub down in the equally old shower. She settled on the tub, simply because she liked baths, and she really wanted to take a nice, long one. That brought about the issue of no hot water.

Last night in the midst of their unpacking, they had found an old Merker gas-fired water heater positioned under the flight of back stairs that led from the kitchen up to the second floor.

Gas was piped in from a big propane tank on the side of the house, one that appeared as if it hadn't been used in eighty years. The only gas pipes ran to the water heater and the stove, and neither of them apparently worked. It was one more thing for the contractor when the man came on Monday. Until then, as Alec had repeatedly said, they would have to live like pioneers.

Clad in a pair of silky, pink pajamas and her white socks, Elliot used the restroom, brushed her teeth, and made her way from her bedroom through the second door in the bathroom which led to the opposite end of the hall on the other side of the winding staircase.

Her bathroom backed up to the stairwell, making it a long and skinny room. She'd intended to use the back stairs down to the kitchen but ended up wandering around the three additional bedrooms she really hadn't paid much attention to yesterday.

All three of the rooms were twice the size of a normal bedroom even though they were considered "smaller" rooms. Newspaper and old print were taped up on the big floor-to-ceiling windows and she immediately set about tearing down the newspaper. She was sick of seeing it.

As she ripped it away, an entirely new world was revealed. The enormous windows on the northeast side of the house looked out over the gigantic garden that backed up to the Black Bayou, which was glistening golden and green in the early morning sun.

Over to the north, she could see what looked like rows of sheds buried deep in the heavy trees and it took her a minute to realize that they were stables. She paused in her ripping, realizing the view, the landscape, was absolutely heavenly. She felt at peace simply gazing out over the gently flowing waters, a view that stretched out as far as the eye could see.

A smile crossed her lips as she drank in her lush, green lands and the depression she had felt when she had awoken was vanished, replaced by joy and hope. There was a new life down here waiting for her in the bayou and she was ready to embrace it.

Ripping down the rest of the newspaper, Elliot went into the other bedrooms and did the same. Sunlight once again began to pour into the chambers of Purgatory, filling it with light and warmth the old house hadn't seen in years. It was a glorious sight.

Alec's bedroom was empty, the covers all jumbled up on the mattress. Elliot ripped all the newspaper off her son's windows and the early morning sun blasted into the room.

As she pulled off paper, she also inspected the windows themselves, seeing that all of them needed reglazing or replacement. She wasn't surprised. As she passed by the enormous window that faced the front of the house, she happened to glance at the driveway and noticed a sheriff's unit parked there. It didn't take her long to realize it was Nash's car.

Curious, she took the back stairs down into the kitchen. Alec was there, eating granola cereal out of the box. He lifted a granola, dust-covered hand at his mother.

"Hi," he said, mouth full.

She smiled at him. "Good morning," she replied, looking around. "Is Nash here?"

Alec shook his head, tipping the granola box into his mouth. "Not here."

She thought about that a moment and, shrugging off her curiosity, began to peel off the newspaper that covered the big window next to the kitchen door.

"How did you sleep?" she asked.

He shrugged. "Great, I think," he replied. "It's, like, nine o'clock in the morning. You *never* sleep this late."

Elliot pulled off the last of the newspaper and shoved it into the same trash bag that contained last night's barbeque bones. Then she moved to the boxes to hunt around for the coffee pot.

"I'm exhausted," she said. "Yesterday was a pretty crazy day."

"Heck yes, it was," Alec agreed. "The sheriff was parked in the driveway all night."

She looked at him. "All *night?*" she repeated. "How do you know?"

Alec had a mouthful of granola. "Because his car is in the same spot it was in last night when I went to bed," he said. "It hasn't moved. He hasn't been in it, either."

"What do you mean?"

"I mean that I could see his flashlight moving around the yard," Alec pointed to the window. "His deputies were here most of the night, too. All of them were wandering around all night."

Elliot looked at him as if he were crazy. "Are you kidding me?" she set down the coffee she had just found in the box. "They didn't have to do that."

Alec shrugged. "Nash said they would."

She threw up her hands. "I know he did, but I didn't know he meant that *he* would be here all night."

"I think he feels kind of bad about what happened. Maybe he feels guilty."

Elliot shook her head, exasperated. "I don't know why he would. It's not his fault that some crazy person threw a firebomb through my front window." She began to grow agitated. "I need to feed those guys breakfast but I don't have a damn stove. Is there any place around here to get them some breakfast?"

Alec shrugged again, peeling off the newspaper from the window near the sink so he could see outside. "I don't know," he said. "I think there's a McDonald's near the highway."

Elliot made a face. "Not that place," she picked up the coffee again and stuck her arm into the box, pulling forth the percolator.

"Well, maybe I'll just make them all coffee right now and then take them out to breakfast. I feel so bad about them spending all night wandering around my backyard."

As Alec shoved down half of a box of granola, Elliot made coffee in her expensive percolator. Coffee came out smooth and delicious and, as it brewed, she went upstairs and braved a very short, very cold shower in the roomy, copper shower enclosure.

The water came out in sporadic bursts through the mineral-encrusted showerhead and Elliot squealed more than once when cold water suddenly shot into her face. But she washed her hair, soaped her body, and even managed to shave without cutting herself. All in all, it had been a horrific experience in primitive bathing but she was very glad to be clean. Her first shower in her new home, a big milestone as silly as it seemed.

Dressing in yoga pants and a tank-style camisole that clung to her like a second skin, she put her socks back on and proceeded to put on her makeup. The blue eyes got bigger, the cheeks pinker, and the lips became a soft, luscious rose. When she was finished with the war paint, she took a moment to stare at herself in the mirror, wondering if she looked any different now that she was starting her life all over again.

At forty-one years old, people always mistook her for someone ten years younger. She never had looked her age. After yesterday, however, she felt every year of those forty-one. She was still exhausted, struggling to overcome it because she knew she had a heck of a lot to do and she wouldn't back down. She couldn't.

Elliot pulled out her little butane-powered blow dryer and began to dry her long hair. It was cut in long layers and she ran a brush through it as she dried it. Since the house only had two outlets, she didn't want to burn the place down with the wattage from her flat iron so she had to settle for just the blow dryer. Thank the Lord it was butane. Soon enough, her hair was acceptably dried and styled, hanging long down her back, so she packed everything away and headed back down to the kitchen.

As she was coming down the stairs, she could hear voices.

Peering down into the kitchen, she could see at least three bodies, two of them being Alec and Nash. She thought about running back to her room and at least changing her camisole shirt, which really wasn't meant to socialize in, but they spied her and she didn't want to look like an idiot running away. So she descended the stairs and smiled.

Nash was standing closest to her, coffee cup in hand. He just stared at her for a moment as she came down the stairs before breaking into an easy smile.

"Good morning, Ms. Ellie," he said, sounding rather pleased.

She smiled in return. "Good morning," she looked around the room at Ken and Steve, the other two deputies who had big mugs of coffee in their hands. "I heard you guys played watchdog last night."

Nash was having difficulty looking her in the face. In fact, it was so difficult that he was starting to sweat. He could see that she was trying to fold her arms in front of her chest to provide at least a measure of modesty, but no amount of arm-folding could detract from the most amazing body he had ever seen.

In her clingy black pants and equally clingy white camisole, the woman had a figure that put all other women to shame. Looking her in the face and not allowing his eyes to trail to her spectacular cleavage was the hardest thing Nash had ever had to do in his life.

"Uh...," he cleared his throat, struggling. "I told you I was going to leave some deputies here and I just decided to stay along with them."

She fixed on him with those big, blue eyes and he could feel himself slipping. "Alec said your car was in the driveway all night." She looked around to the other deputies. "I can't thank you enough for making sure Alec and I were safe. That just means the world to us. I'd love to make you some breakfast but without a stove, that makes it a little tough. Can I please take you out to breakfast and at least feed you for being so nice?"

Ken was the first to speak. "No need to feed us, ma'am," he told her. "The coffee is good. That's payment enough."

"I'm sorry, but I'm going to have to insist," she countered. "I feel awful that you were up all night patrolling my yard. You have to let me do something for you."

The deputies waved her off. "My wife will kill me if I don't get on home," Steve said as he set the coffee down. "But thank you for the offer. It's very nice of you."

Elliot made a face; she had an animated personality that was beginning to spark up. "I'll let you go this time," she said, wagging a stern finger at them. "But next time, nobody leaves this house until they are full of pancakes and eggs. Agreed?"

The deputies grinned as they set the coffee cups down and headed for the door. "Yes, ma'am," they muttered, one after the other.

She smiled brightly at them, just to let them know the stern routine was a joke. "Okay," she said as they opened the door and headed out into the early morning. "Thanks again for everything. I really appreciate it."

The men waved her off as they headed towards the driveway and their patrol cars. Alec closed the door behind them as Elliot turned to Nash.

"I suppose you have to get out of here, too," she said, putting her hands on her hips. "Are you going to hurt my feelings, too, and not let me buy you breakfast?"

He grinned, scratching casually at his neck. "I wouldn't dream of hurting your feelings."

"Good!" she cheered up, turning quickly to Alec. "Go get dressed. We're going to go eat."

Alec waved his mother off. "I just ate that whole box of granola," he groaned. "I don't want to go anywhere right now. I want to go back to bed."

He wandered off in the direction of the central hall and Elliot shrugged, turning to Nash again.

"Looks like it's just you and me," she said. "Are you okay with that?"

He cocked his head curiously. "Why wouldn't I be?"

She lifted her shoulders. "Well," she said thoughtfully. "You have a reputation to uphold. People might see us together and they might talk."

He couldn't tell if she was serious or not. He decided to go with his gut instinct on his reply and hope it didn't get him into trouble.

"Look here, Ms. Ellie," he said in his best Louisiana drawl. "People will think I'm the luckiest man in the world if they see me with you. Hell, I already think I'm the luckiest man in the world simply to have met you. It has been a true honor and a privilege, ma'am."

Elliot had only been teasing him but his reply was not what she had expected. It was warm, honest and flattering. A genuine smile spread across her lips.

"That's a really sweet thing to say," she said sincerely. "After the craziness of yesterday, I was sure I'd never see you again."

He gave her an expression that suggested she was insane but, not wanting to incriminate himself further with an even more flattering reply, he simply shook his head and pointed to the stairs.

"Go get yourself dressed," he said, sipping at his coffee. "I'll wait here."

With a very sweet smile that had him completely entranced, Elliot slipped up the back stairs. When Nash was sure she couldn't see him, he watched her shapely round butt as it disappeared up the steps.

Thinking sexy, dirty thoughts he hadn't entertained in years, he focused on his coffee, watching the sun rise over the bayou and not at all sorry he had been up all night. The reward, this morning, would be well worth it.

———

It was a dive. Well, not really a dive, but it wasn't what she would have considered a nice restaurant either. Over-dressed in white Capri pants, a beautiful flowery top, silver necklace and sexy little white sandals, Elliot tried not to openly react when Nash opened the door for her and ushered her into a little restaurant that sat right on the water's edge of the Black Bayou. He took her arm and politely escorted her over to a table that overlooked the water.

In the mid-morning sun, the bugs were dancing happily along the green expanse of shoreline and she could feel the humidity rise through the screens. Nash held out the cheap, white chair for her and she sat, smiling at him when he took the chair opposite her.

"I know it doesn't look like much," he said," but, trust me when I tell you they have the best breakfasts in town. They've got a one-eyed old woman back in the kitchen that can out cook anyone on this planet."

Elliot giggled, suppressing her smile when a very old man came to the table, all dressed up like a soda jerk from sixty years ago. It was adorable. He greeted Nash amiably.

"Sheriff," he smiled a toothless grin enthusiastically. "Glad to see ya, glad to see ya. What can I get for ya?"

Nash gave Elliot an impish expression. "Do you trust me?"

She half shrugged, half nodded. "Why not?"

He grinned and turned to the old man. "Eggs with ham and cheese, scrambled, grits, bacon, hash browns and white toast. And keep the coffee coming."

The old man nodded and darted off. Nash returned his focus to Elliot, looking like an angel as the warm morning sun illuminated her lovely features. He'd known the woman less than a day, but in that day, something very odd had happened. He was attracted to her as he'd never been attracted to a woman in his life and already, he couldn't stand the thought of being away from her. He just wanted to be with her, be around her, and never leave that glorious aura she seemed to project. He'd never experienced anything like it.

Elliot smiled and cocked her head. "Why are you looking at me like that?"

He grinned, embarrassed he had been caught daydreaming. "I don't know," he said. "Maybe it's because I rarely get an opportunity to go out to breakfast that doesn't involve work and it's even rarer that I get to share it with a beautiful woman. I guess I'm a little giddy."

Elliot laughed. "There you go, saying sweet things again. You're going to give me a big head."

He laughed. "If anyone was truly entitled to such a thing, it would be you," he said, his smile fading. "But do me a favor and don't change. Stay just the way you are."

She grinned, modestly, not sure how to reply. He had such a gentle, unassuming manner about him, something that she was coming to like a great deal. She could feel herself relaxing in his comforting presence, allowing herself, for the first time in over a year, to think of a man in a non-platonic sense.

In fact, she could get very used to having Nash around but simultaneous thoughts of Rob made her feel torn, almost as if she was betraying the man's memory by even thinking such a thing. But she had to move on, didn't she? As she wrestled with her conflicting thoughts, the old man brought around water and coffee, and the two of them prepared their coffee in warm silence.

"So," Elliot began, just to break the silence. "Did you find anything last night?"

He took a healthy sip of coffee. "No," he said. "Not a thing. No footprints, no car tracks, no fingerprints... nothing. I'm really sorry about that."

She shrugged. "I'm just grateful that you tried. And I'm really grateful that you were there when it all went down."

He sighed faintly, toying with his coffee cup. "We need to get that front window fixed."

She shrugged again, stirring the creamer in her coffee. "I have a contractor coming tomorrow. I supposed I'll just have to cover the window with plastic until I can get it fixed."

He gazed at her a moment and she could literally see the wheels turning behind the smoldering hazel eyes.

"I have a better idea," he said.

He pulled his cell phone out of its case and hit a few buttons on the touch screen. As Elliot listened with increasing curiosity, he contacted someone he apparently knew very well, explained the situation, and then listened to the response. After a few more exchanged words, he hung up the phone and smiled at her.

"My brother will be here in a couple of hours," he said. "He'll take care of the window for you and probably the rest of the house if you want him to."

Elliot's eyebrows lifted in surprise. "What?" she gasped. "Why? Who is...?"

He reached across the table, gathering her hand in his big, warm mitt. "My brother is a general contractor," he told her. "Well, he's actually the CEO of a general contracting business so he doesn't actually do hands-on work, but for you, he'll make an exception. He mostly does the big hotels along the gulf coast and things like that. He's got legions of guys at his disposal."

"Seriously?" she said, awed. "I'm really flattered. And grateful. But how much is this going to cost me?"

He smiled at her, squeezing her hand but not letting it go. He was trying to see how long he could get away with holding her hand before she pulled it away.

"Don't worry about it," he told her. "You'll get the special family discount rate."

She laughed and he squeezed her hand again. Surprisingly, she didn't pull away. "Thanks," she said. "But... well, I have to ask. If your brother is a general contractor, why is the house in such bad shape to begin with?"

Nash's smile faded and he sat back in his chair, very discreetly toying with her fingers. "That's a long and sad story," he admitted, using his other hand to pick up his coffee cup. "The truth of the matter is that my mamaw didn't want anyone touching the house because in her later years, she was completely insane. Well, maybe not completely because she still had her cognitive reasoning skills, but something happened to her when my granddad died. It's like she just gave up caring. Beau and I would go to the house to visit her and she'd sit in her wheelchair on the front porch, blocking the door and shaking her cane at us. She wouldn't let us in."

"Beau?" Elliot was electrified by his touch, his gentle fingers playing with hers. It had been ages since she'd known such pure, wicked pleasure. "Who's that?"

"Beau is my brother," he explained. "My mamaw was born in the year 1900 in New Orleans. She had been a debutant back in the teens and twenties, the belle of New Orleans society, before she met and married my granddad, Case Aury."

"Is this the grandfather who was the police chief?" Elliot interrupted.

He nodded and continued. "Yes, among other things," he said honestly. "He was also one of the biggest bootleggers in New Orleans and made a fortune off his ill-gotten gains. He was as corrupt as they come, kind of like my ancestor, the pirate."

Elliot grinned. "And all of this didn't come out when you were running for sheriff?"

Nash reluctantly returned her grin. "It was a long time ago, so thankfully, people were somewhat forgiving," he said. "They were more interested in my pirate forefather, to tell you the truth. Anyway, Jewel and Case Aury had three children; one boy, my father, and two girls. All of them were born and raised at Purgatory."

Elliot started laughing. "Jewel and Case," she said. "Sounds like they made DVD covers."

He laughed softly. "We all have strange names down here, I guess," he replied. "My father's name is Camp and his two sisters are Lorella and Rudi. Dad had two boys, me and Beau, but my aunts had twelve children between them, all but two of them girls. Anyway, when Granddad died back in the 1960s, Mamaw just seemed to lose her will to live. She let everything run down. When dad would offer to fix something, she would just chase him away.

She did that with all of us until the day she died. What you see of this house is fifty years of utter neglect."

Elliot could see where the story was leading. "So she died and your family figured it would be way too much money to restore the place after she let it go to hell?"

"Sort of," he said, becoming bolder at caressing her fingers. "My brother and I wanted to restore it, but my aunts and their families wanted to sell it. There was basically none of my grand-dad's money left because Mamaw had run through it. Quite honestly, I don't know what she did with it because she certainly didn't spend it on the house or on herself, so we assumed she'd squandered it somehow. We could just never find a paper trail. Anyway, when she died, just the house was left. It was a massive battle for years but in the end, my dad, brother and I just couldn't come up with the money to buy out my aunts. So we took what we could out of the place that had any kind of value, sentimental or otherwise, and put it on the market for two million dollars. It sat there for six years, gradually reducing in price, until you bought it."

By this time, Elliot was looking at him with some horror. "For seven hundred thousand dollars," she breathed. "That's nowhere close to two million."

He shrugged. "Greed does terrible things to people. My aunts got what they deserved, which was very little when all was said and done."

"And you?" she asked. "What did you get?"

He smiled. "I got to meet you."

She gave him such a look, something between disbelief and pleasure, as they were interrupted by the old man bearing two enormous plates of food. Elliot had to remove her hand from his grasp out of necessity as a massive platter of eggs, grits, potatoes, bacon and toast was set down before her. It was enough food for three people.

"I'll get more coffee," the old man said as he scooted away.

Elliot stared at the food, shocked by the amount. "Good grief," she breathed. "Alec is going to be sorry he missed this."

She picked up her knife and fork, unaware that Nash was still staring at her. He wasn't even looking at his food. He was just staring at her. The old man came and went with more coffee before Elliot finally looked up to notice that Nash was just sitting there, looking at her. She cocked her head quizzically.

"What's wrong?" she asked.

He shook his head. Then, he shrugged, sitting there with his knife and fork as if unsure what to do with them.

"I... I've just been thinking," he stumbled over his words.

She smiled curiously. "What about?"

He shrugged again, ending up waving his knife and fork around. He looked really confused and almost frustrated. Elliot's brow furrowed.

"What's wrong?" she asked.

He sighed heavily and finally set the silverware down. "I... well, I really want to do something but I don't want you to think I'm a... a..."

"A *what*?"

He looked at her. "An opportunist. Or that I would do this with anybody. I'm not like that at all."

She had no idea what he was talking about. "Nash, what's the matter with you?"

He grunted again, looked at her with an odd sort of expression, and stood up. Elliot looked up at him as he moved around the table, realizing that his hands were moving for her face. She just sat there like an idiot, knife in one hand and fork in the other, as he cupped her face with exquisite gentleness and planted a warm, soft kiss on her right cheek. She tasted so good that he did it again. Then he dropped his hands, moved back to his chair, and picked up his silverware.

"There," he said, looking at his food because he was absolutely unable to look her in the eye at the moment, fearful of her reaction. "I did it."

Truthfully, Elliot wasn't quite sure how to react. It was the sweetest kiss she'd ever received. But he wouldn't look at her and a smile played on her lips.

"Happy now?" she asked.

"Yes."

"Nash," she leaned forward, whispering. "Look at me."

He did, reluctantly. When their eyes met, she broke out in an enormous dimpled grin. "It's okay," she said. "I'm not mad."

He sighed, dropped his silverware, and was out of his chair in a flash. For the second time, Elliot just sat there like a dummy with a knife and fork clutched in her hands as he kissed her again. But this time, he kissed her on the lips, a deliciously tender kiss that she allowed herself to thoroughly enjoy. It was a little shocking but not at all unwelcome. He suckled her lips gently and she responded in kind, tasting the man just as he was tasting her. In fact, she was disappointed when he pulled away and regained his seat again, collecting his silverware with shaking hands. She could see the tremors.

As he delved into his meal, Elliot was now the one staring. He seemed genuinely confused and despondent of his actions, cutting into his eggs with his quivering fingers. She watched him take a big bite, his eyes looking at everything but her.

"So why won't you look at me?" she asked.

His chewing slowed and he swallowed. "Because I'm afraid to," he whispered. "Sweet Jesus, I'm terrified to look at you. I'm afraid... afraid you're just going to walk on out of here and pretend you never met me. I shouldn't have done that; God knows, I shouldn't have and I am truly, sincerely sorry if I offended you. But you are the most beautiful thing I've ever seen and I have never in my life been so attracted to anyone."

"Do you want me to just forget about it so we can move on?"

"Yes," he said flatly, then looked up at her in horror. "No, I don't. I really don't."

Elliot gazed at the man for a moment before standing up and picking up her plate. As Nash watched, she came around to his side of the table, set her plate down next to his, and pulled up a chair. The table was rather small so she was literally butted up against him, her right thigh against his left one, her torso up against his. When he looked at her with some curiosity and astonishment, she simply smiled.

"I'll sit here until you don't feel so bad," she comforted. "Because, I have to tell you, I don't feel bad about it at all. I enjoyed it."

He was wrought with surprise and hope. "You did?"

"I did."

She pecked him on the cheek and went back to her eggs. Nash could not have been more astonished or more thrilled with her pressed up against him, eating her breakfast. He felt like he was dreaming and thought he should probably poke himself with the fork just to make sure he wasn't. It was the most amazing feeling he had ever experienced.

With his eyes on Elliot, he resumed eating and together, the two of them silently finished breakfast as the sun continued to rise over the bayou.

FIVE

AS NASH'S unmarked car pulled up the driveway and around the front of the house, Elliot noticed a white Nissan parked up near the house in the shadows of a moss-covered oak tree.

"Oh!" she exclaimed softly. "Pen is here!"

She jumped out of the car before it even came to a halt. Nash put the car in park, watching her run into the house.

Reaching over into the back seat and pulling out the take-away bag full of more eggs and potatoes for Alec, he climbed out of the car and entered the house in time to see Elliot nearly strangling a pretty young woman.

As Nash watched, he could see that it wasn't so much strangling as it was enthusiastic hugging. It was a joyful family reunion, the sight of which softened and warmed him. It was very sweet to watch.

In the midst of squeezing, Elliot caught sight of Nash out of the corner of her eye. Still hugging her daughter, she indicated the tall man in uniform standing in the doorway.

"Pen, I'd like you to meet Nash Aury," she said. "His family owned the house for two hundred years before we bought it. Nash, this is my daughter, Penelope."

Nash stepped into the house, a smile on his face. "It's very nice to meet you," he said. "How do you like Tulane so far?"

Penelope Jentry was an absolutely beautiful girl with her mother's big, blue eyes and a big dimple in her chin. She was petite, like her mother, with light brown hair pulled back into a ponytail. She grinned at Nash, taking his outstretched hand and shaking it.

"I've only been there a week," she said. "Moving my stuff in and all that. So far, I like it. It's a really nice campus."

Nash nodded. "I'm sure your mom hasn't had a chance to tell you, but it's my alma mater. If you have any questions, let me know."

Her smile turned sincere. "Wow, thanks," she said. "I'm sure I will. This whole week has kind of been a whirlwind so I'm sure there's a lot I don't know yet."

"I know how that can be," Nash said, suddenly realizing he was still holding a big bag of food. He caught sight of Alec and extended the bag. "For you, son. Compliments of the house."

Alec snatched the bag, peering into it. "Cool, thanks," he took a big sniff. "Hey, that smells good. I'm hungry."

Penelope pulled away from her mother and tried to take the bag from him.

"I haven't eaten yet," she said as it turned into a tug of war. "Let me have some."

They began fighting over it and Elliot took Penelope by the shoulders and directed her away from her brother, towards the kitchen.

"Take it to the kitchen, kids," she instructed firmly. "And quit fighting in front of guests. You're embarrassing me."

Penelope flashed Nash a bright smile as she grabbed her brother's arm and pulled him down the big central hall.

"I get first bite," she told Alec.

He scowled at her. "No way, dude. This is mine." He suddenly came to a stop and turned to his mother. "Hey, before I forget, that old black dude came back this morning wanting to know when you were going to go visit those women. I told him to come back later."

"Really?" Elliot lifted her eyebrows, turning to Nash and seeing his curious expression. "Yesterday, we had a visitor."

Nash's brows drew together. "Who?"

Elliot shrugged. "Some old, black guy by the name of Mickey came to tell us that Ms. Biffy, Ms. Tulip and Ms. Leon wanted me to come over and visit. Do you know them?"

She exaggerated the "mizz" title to be funny, but Nash's face had a stony expression on it. He just stared at her for a moment. Then, he sighed heavily as if something had just occurred to him.

"Now this is starting to make sense," he muttered, more to himself than to her. "You didn't tell me this yesterday."

Elliot wasn't sure why he seemed displeased. "I completely forgot about it," she said. "It was just some old man. He seemed nice enough. Why? Is there a problem?"

Nash scratched his head, almost irritably. "Could be."

"Why?"

Nash glanced up at the young people down the hall, now disappearing into the kitchen and still squabbling over the food. He motioned for Elliot to follow him onto the porch, which she did. He stood there a moment, gazing out over the trees and Spanish moss, trying to collect his thoughts in his sleep-deprived mind. He finally turned to Elliot, who was staring up at him with big, expectant eyes.

"Ms. Biffy, Ms. Tulip and Ms. Leon are from the Loreau family," he said as evenly as he could. "They live in an enormous rundown home called The Bottoms that's about a mile and a half from here, up on a rise overlooking the opposite side of Black Bayou."

Elliot wasn't seeing the problem yet. "The old man said that Ms. Biffy saw me moving in with her 'looking glass'," she giggled. "It was really cute."

He shook his head. "Not so cute," he said, rather sternly. "The Loreaus and the Aurys go back two hundred years to the time when Jean-Pierre Loreau was a sea captain on one of Louis-Michel's privateer vessels. Loreau, by all accounts, was a bitter and greedy man. He wanted everything that Louis-Michel had, including Purgatory and Ms. Sophie. Jean-Pierre built The Bottoms on the opposite side of the bayou so he could keep tabs on Louis-Michel. Old family legends say that when Louis-Michel was away, Jean-Pierre raped Sophie and she became pregnant as a result. Louis-Michel was so enraged that he murdered Jean-Pierre on the spot. Needless to say, there are two hundred years of animosity between the Loreau family and the Aury family."

By the time he was finished, Elliot was staring at him in astonishment. "Good grief," she exclaimed. "That's crazy!"

He nodded in agreement. "Maybe so, but the Loreaus are a bad bunch," he said. "Ms. Leon is the matriarch and she's got to be over one hundred years old. Her two daughters are Tulip and Biffy. Tulip never had any children, but Biffy had a son, who in turn had three sons. They all live at The Bottoms like a bunch of criminals. If there's any trouble in town, there's a good chance that it involves the Loreaus. Now this whole firebomb episode is starting to make some sense."

Elliot was growing a little fearful. "What do you mean?"

Nash shrugged, reaching to take her hand. He began to step off the porch, taking her with him.

"The Loreaus know about the legend of Louis-Michel's buried treasure," he said. "I can't tell you how many times over the years we've had to chase them off the land, or register complaints about them. They even took my granddad to court back in the 1940s, claiming that they were due any gold found on Purgatory's property in repayment for the murder of their ancestor. Whether or not they rightfully believe the gold is theirs or they're just being extraordinarily greedy, I don't know. But now that you live here, I think I'm going to go over there and have a little talk with them."

They reached his car and Elliot came to a halt, tugging on his hand. "Don't do it," she said quietly. "If their family hates the Aurys as much as you've said they do, then they'll think I put you up to it and they'll probably look at me like the enemy, too. I don't need trouble like that right off the bat."

He gazed down into her beautiful face, thinking a lot of things at that moment, some of which had nothing to do with the Loreau family or pirate's gold. He was thinking how much he didn't want to leave her.

"You may have a point," he conceded. "But I plan to talk to them anyway. And under no circumstances are you to go to The Bottoms, ever. You're going to have to trust me on this one."

She nodded seriously. "Sure, if you say so. But I really don't want to come off like a rude neighbor."

"You won't," he assured her, eyeing her as he changed the subject. "Are you going to be all right while I go home and sleep?"

She grinned. "Are you kidding?"

"No."

She laughed. "I've been taking care of myself for a long time," she said. "I'll be fine. We're going to continue unpacking. We've got a lot to do."

He nodded, feeling his fatigue weigh more heavily upon him. He really didn't want to leave, wanting to milk every last moment with her that he could, but he knew he couldn't hold out much longer.

"My brother will be here in a little while," he reminded her. "Introduce yourself and tell him what you need to have done. I'll be back in a while, at least before he leaves."

He began fumbling in his shirt pocket with his free hand, pulling forth a business card. Reluctantly letting go of her hand, he flipped the card over, pulled out a pen, and used the top of his car as a writing desk. When he was finished, he handed the card over to her.

"I've written my home phone number on the back," he told her. "Call me if you need me. Otherwise, I'll see you in a few hours."

Elliot looked at the front and the back of the very officious card. "Nash G. Aury, Sheriff, Ascension Parish," she read his title, grinning up at him. "Do you live far from here?"

He shook his head. "Not far at all," he replied, taking the card back from her and writing down his address. "In fact, I'm only about six miles from here. That's where I live so you can find me if you ever need to."

She took the card from him again, looking at the address. "Where's the city of Gonzales?"

"The town center is about seven or eight miles from here," he told her.

Elliot nodded and finished reading everything on the card before finally turning to look at him. He was leaning against his sheriff's unit, watching her with his smoldering, hazel eyes and a faint smile on his lips. The warmth, the interest, in his expression was unmistakable.

"Well, Sheriff," she held out her hand to shake his. "It's been a true honor coming to know you. Thank you for everything you've done for my family and me. I can't put into words how much it's meant to me."

His smile grew and he took her hand, but not to shake it. He just wanted to hold it.

"As I told you before, I consider myself the luckiest man in the world to have met you, Ms. Ellie," he said. "And I... well, I'd like to call on you if that's okay with you."

So he spelled it out, plain and simple. Elliot gazed into his handsome face, feeling some conflict arise in her chest, once again. Her husband was dead, almost two years now, and he was never coming back. Her life had changed.

She'd moved to Louisiana to further cement that change, to make sure she started a new life with new people and a new outlook. She hadn't come here looking for a new love interest but one had fallen right in her lap in the form of tall, dark and handsome Nash Aury. Part of her still wasn't ready for the attention but the overwhelming majority of her was very interested in coming to know Nash.

"That's quite an offer," she replied after a moment. "You just met me and I just met you. What, exactly, do you mean by 'call on me'?"

He smiled shyly, shrugging his broad shoulders. "That's a term we use down here," he said quietly. "It means spending time with you, taking you out to breakfast, or dinner, or into New Orleans for a good time. It means that there's no one else in the world I'd rather spend time with than you. It means that I think you're beautiful and would very much like the privilege of getting to know you."

It was a very sweet thing to say and she could tell, simply from his manner and body language, that he sincerely meant it. She could feel herself relent.

"I think it would be okay," she murmured. "But I have to tell you, I'm not particularly thrilled with... well, you know, the profession...."

She trailed off and he instinctively looked at his badge. "I know," he said, gently squeezing her hand. "I'm sorry 'bout that. I promise I'll do my best not to let it upset you."

She smiled timidly. "My heart's just a little fragile right now."

"I realize that," he whispered. "I'll take it slow and gentle. We'll just take it one day at a time and see where that takes us."

She simply nodded. "The kids...," she grasped for words. "We need to take it even more slow and gentle with them. They lost their dad, so I'm not sure how they're going to react to their mom starting to live her life again."

He nodded in understanding, looking around to make sure no one was watching before lifting her hand to his lips and kissing her fingers. "You do what you feel is best for them. I'll follow your lead."

She gazed up at him, studying his face seriously. "You know, beneath all of that professional sheriff garb, I think there is an amazing man inside."

"I hope I can show you that."

"I hope you can, too."

They just grinned at each other for a moment before he kissed her hand again and reluctantly let it go.

"I'll see you in a while," he winked at her and climbed into the car.

Elliot stood back as he put the car in gear and took off down the driveway. Somewhat dazed at the turn of events, she realized that she was also very excited about it.

From nearly the moment she had met Nash Aury, there was something completely endearing about the man, something that touched her deeply. Although she didn't know much about him, she was very much looking forward to changing that. He was an unexpected bonus in her life-changing move to Louisiana. In fact, it was probably the very best part.

As she entered the house, she could hear Penelope and Alec arguing in the kitchen and she just shook her head. She had to laugh; some things in her life were changing and some things were not.

SIX

NASH HAD ALWAYS HAD a habit of sleeping with the police scanner on. It was just the way he was, something that had driven his ex-wife into another bedroom during the course of their marriage. He could sleep right through the radio traffic, hearing it in his subconscious, oddly waking up only when something that pertained to him or his deputies came over the air. He'd been doing it for almost twenty years.

In the master suite of his home that sat on the greens of Pelican Point Golf Club in the city of Gonzales, Louisiana, he was dead asleep as the police band crackled quietly in the darkened room. Nash had come home with thoughts of Elliot on his mind, wearily fed his big German Shepherd, Wolfgang, and then dragged himself up to bed in a master suite that was as big as some people's entire house. He barely had time to strip off his clothes before he was falling between the sheets. As the radio traffic peppered the stillness, he slept right through it.

But he didn't sleep through his phone ringing. Slapping at it, he didn't even look at the caller as he put it to his ear.

"Aury," he said groggily.

"Nash?" said a familiar voice on the other end of the line. "What in the hell are you doing sleeping in the middle of the day?"

Nash knew who it was immediately. A sleepy grin spread across his lips as he put a weary hand over his face. "Not usually, but I've been up all night," he said. "Did you call me just to harass me?"

"Not today," the man said. "Any other time, I would, but not today. How's work going?"

Nash rolled onto his back. "The usual," he said. "But things are good. How about you, Colt? Got any national secrets to spill?"

On the other end of the line, Colt Sheridan snorted softly. "You think you're kidding," he said. "But that's kind of why I'm calling you."

"Oh?" Nash said, as interested as he could be given how exhausted he was. "What's up?"

"This is confidential."

"Understood."

"Ever heard of the Norte del Valle Cartel?"

Nash thought for a moment. "I think so," he said. "Nasty outfit out of Sonora, right?"

"Yes," Colt said. "Given your position in law enforcement and the fact that Louisiana has Mexico to the south across the gulf, I thought you might have had some encounters with them."

"Not them specifically," Nash said. "I don't think they've made it to Baton Rouge yet. Why?"

Colt paused. "Just curious," he said. "Before you ask me again, you know I won't tell you anything more, so let's talk about something else. How are the kids?"

Nash rubbed his eyes, not at all put off by Colt changing the subject. "The *kids* are grown men," he reminded him. "They're doing great. You'd have some kids of your own if you ever got married."

"True enough."

"Anything new to report on that front?"

"Maybe," Colt said coyly. "You just never know."

"That's an interesting answer." Nash thought he might have heard something in Colt's voice. He'd known the man a long time and there was something about this call that seemed... odd. As if there was something more Colt had called about but couldn't seem to voice it. "Colt, you're not in trouble, are you?"

"No trouble," Colt assured him. "Since when do I have trouble?"

"Is it with the cartel you asked about?"

"No trouble, Nash. I promise."

"Because if there is... just say the word. I'm here for you. Whatever you need."

Colt sighed faintly. "I appreciate it," he said. "But you know if there is trouble, I'm not going to drag you into it."

"You're not dragging me into anything. We're brothers, remember?"

"Talked to any of the others lately?"

Nash knew he was changing the subject again and he simply rolled with it. "I spoke with Ethan a few weeks ago," he said. "The man loves California and we'll never get him out of there."

"I don't blame him."

Nash paused. "Colt, seriously," he said. "If you need my help, you just have to ask."

He could hear Colt grunt softly. "I don't need your help," he said. "But if I do – personally – I promise I'll ask. Okay?"

Nash had to take him at his word because Colt worked for the Secret Service. More than that, he was the Special Agent in Charge of the President of the United States. The man was trusted with the security of the nation, basically. But Nash had known Colt long enough to know that wasn't all he was mixed up in. Years ago, he'd caught wind of something else Colt was part of and although Colt couldn't tell him, he swore Nash to secrecy on what he suspected. It was a promise Nash had never broken, but he had to admit that he was worried for his friend.

Colt Sheridan seemed to live a more dangerous life than most.

"I'll hold you to it," Nash finally said. "Any chance of you getting down my way sometime soon?"

"Not that I'm aware of," Colt said. "We've got a New Mexico trip coming up, but nothing more than that."

"You can always take a vacation and just come for a visit."

Colt chuckled. "Vacation?" he said sarcastically. "What's that?"

"No kidding."

"It's been great, Nash, but I've got to go. You take care."

"And you," Nash said. "I hope you'll..."

A Medical Aid call suddenly caught his attention as it went out over the radio. He could hear his deputies chattering and then he could hear something about the town of Sorrento. More chatter went on as he focused on signing off with Colt, but one word had him ending that phone call in a hurry.

Purgatory.

Nash set the phone aside and grabbed the radio microphone. "This is S A-1," he said as he keyed the mic. "Detail the medical aid situation at Purgatory."

The dispatcher came on the speaker. "Sheriff, we have a call for an ambulance and police. I don't have any information beyond that. I've got a unit on its way to contact Sorrento P.D."

"Copy that. Update me when you have any information."

"10-4."

Nash threw off the covers, so hard that they flew completely off the bed. In a hurry, he grabbed his cell phone to call Elliot and suddenly realized that he didn't have her number. He'd never gotten it from her.

With a growl of frustration, he took a chance and called his brother, hoping the man was at Purgatory by now. He didn't even know what time it was, looking at the clock as the call went through and realizing he'd been asleep a little over six hours. As he began hunting around for his pants, his brother answered.

"Nash?"

Nash was trying to pull on his uniform pants and talk on the phone at the same time.

"Hey, Beau," he said. "Are you at Purgatory?"

"Yep, I'm here," Beau replied. "We've got a little problem."

"I heard it come over the scanner. What's the problem?"

He could hear Beau sigh heavily. "You'd better get out here."

"Beau, what happened?"

Beau sighed again. "Well, the woman who bought the place – Ms. Ellie...."

Nash cut him off, almost frantically. "I know Elliot. Did something happen to her?"

"No," Beau replied. "Not her. Her son. Honestly, I'm not sure what happened. All I know is that the kid was out back and, suddenly, I hear all of this yelling. I'm sealing up the front window until we can get a glass guy out here, so I run around back and there's the kid with blood all over him and a dead man at his feet. It's a mess, Nash. You'd better get out here."

"Oh, God," Nash hissed. "I'm on my way. Is Alec hurt?"

"Yes. That's who the ambulance is for."

"How bad?"

"He's pretty cut up."

"Call me if the ambulance leaves before I get there."

Nash hung up the phone, realizing that his hands were shaking. Pulling on the slacks he wore earlier, he yanked a clean shirt out of the closet and threw it on his big frame, snatching his badge from the dirty shirt and collecting his keys and wallet. He made a stop by the bathroom on his way out, running a comb through his hair and brushing his teeth in ten seconds. Buttoning his shirt as he raced out to the car, he threw the vehicle into gear and tore off towards the highway.

A six-mile drive had never seemed so long. He turned on his siren and hit his rotators, making people pull out of his way as he sped along Highway 22 that would take him directly to Elliot's driveway. He glanced at the speedometer, once, and saw he was doing about ninety. By the time he hit the long, half-mile, gravel drive to Purgatory, he took the turn so fast that he almost sped off into the trees. Tearing up the driveway, he came to a skidding halt just short of the ambulance.

He jumped out of the car, tucking his shirt in as he headed for the house. There were four Sorrento Police units in the driveway, a watch commander's unit, and one sheriff's unit. He could see activity towards the rear of the house so he decided to head in that direction.

Taking the foliage-shrouded dirt path that led along the south side of the house where the kitchen was located, he emerged into the overgrown backyard and a fairly chaotic scene.

The Sorrento cops setting up the crime scene had to work around the ambulance crew, who were just at the point of helping Alec onto the stretcher. Nash could see Elliot and Penelope hovering near the stretcher, trying to help, but being carefully held back by Deputy Steve Pitot. The big deputy was having trouble restraining Elliot, who was clearly distraught over her son. Nash made his way quickly in her direction.

"Ellie?" he called out as he approached.

Elliot's head came up like a flash, her big, blue eyes fixing on Nash. She looked as if she were ready to erupt but Alec heard Nash also and turned in the man's direction.

"I'm okay," he assured both Nash and his frantic mother. "I don't even need this stretcher. I can walk on my own."

Nash made it to the side of the stretcher, next to Elliot. His instinct was to put his arms around her and comfort her but he restrained himself, not wanting to create a spectacle that could possibly be construed as inappropriate. It was one of the biggest struggles he'd ever had to face. He kept himself cool and professional as he focused on Alec, listening to Elliot's soft sniffles beside him.

"What happened, Alec?" he asked.

"Uh, Sheriff, we got this," a sergeant with a big Smokey the Bear hat spoke from the other side of the stretcher. "We're setting up a crime scene right now. We'll handle it from here."

Nash looked at the sergeant. He knew the man vaguely, a good old boy who tended not to get worked up into a sweat over anything, violent crimes included. This wasn't Nash's jurisdiction so he had to force himself to back off.

"I can see that," he replied. "I'm a friend of the family. My questions aren't in an official capacity."

Sergeant Rollens nodded as if he didn't believe him but, to his credit, he didn't say anything. He turned back to his crime scene as Nash refocused on Alec.

"What happened?" he asked again, more quietly.

Alec tried to shrug but he couldn't; his entire right arm and shoulder were bandaged up tight, including both hands. The medic was hooking the I.V. to the gurney as they prepared to roll it out.

"I was back here trying to figure out if I could get the propane tank to work, you know, pulling away the vines and stuff, and all of a sudden that old dude came rushing out of the trees with a big hatchet in his hand," he pointed to the body lying in the over-growth several feet away. "He caught me in the shoulder so I kicked him away and the hatchet fell. He picked it up and tried to swing it at me again but I blocked it. I finally grabbed the hatchet and he tried to fight me for it, and... well, I stabbed him with it. It was an accident but I swear to you, he was trying to kill me."

Nash didn't react other than to pat the young man consolingly on his good shoulder and move around the gurney that they were starting to roll towards the ambulance.

He went over to the taped off crime scene, gazing down at the bloodied body of an older, white male dressed in a dirty t-shirt, dirty jeans and old shoes. The man was lying in a pile of overgrown weeds with a hatchet buried in his chest. Nash was staring at the body when he felt someone walk up beside him.

He glanced over to see his brother standing there, also looking at the body. Nash snorted ironically.

"Got more than you bargained for today, didn't you?" he said.

Beau Aury grinned up at his younger brother. Shorter than Nash by several inches, he didn't look anything like his studly sibling. He had dark, curly hair, brown eyes, and the round body of a man who used to be muscular in his youth before age and an inactive lifestyle caught up with him. But he was as honest as the day was long and funnier than anyone Nash had ever met.

"You always get me mixed up in the craziest things," Beau muttered.

"Me?" Nash lifted his eyebrows. "All I did was call you over to help out Ms. Ellie. But this...."

He looked over at the dead body, his words trailing off. Beau looked at the body, too, and the scene in general, before sadly shaking his head.

"This is going to be trouble," he muttered.

Nash scratched his cheek. "I know," he mumbled in return. "That's Femmie Loreau."

"I know," Beau glanced around to see if the cops were listening. "Do they know that?"

Nash shrugged. "I'm sure the sergeant does," he said, looking to see where Rollens was. "I'm sure he'll want to talk to me about it."

Beau sighed heavily. "When the Loreau boys hear that their daddy has been killed, they'll be all over this place. Ms. Ellie and her kids need to get out of here."

Nash already knew what Elliot was going to say about that. "Their daddy was trying to murder a young man," he pointed out. "I have no doubt that Femmie was responsible for the firebomb last night, too, only this time, he picked on the wrong person to attack. Alec had every right to defend himself."

Beau nodded, shrugging, thinking that it was going to get real ugly around here. He scratched his head and turned back to the house.

"Well," he said. "I'm going to finish with that front window. I have a glass company coming first thing tomorrow to replace it, at least temporarily. This whole place is falling down, so I told Ms. Ellie that we shouldn't do anything too permanent or expensive until we can figure out what, exactly, needs to be done. First thing I'm going to do is have an electrician and a plumber here in the morning so we can start figuring out the electrical and plumbing of this place. It's a goddamn mess."

Nash turned away from the body, looking up at the tall, imposing house that had once housed pirates and mystery. Even though it belonged to Elliot, still, his blood ran through it. It was a part of him.

"She's not going to leave it," he told his brother. "You'd better do what you can to make this house livable as fast as you can."

Beau looked at him. "That's impossible."

"Then you'd better figure out something. I don't want Ellie living in a derelict, old house."

Beau stared at his brother a moment, his brow beginning to furrow. "Ellie?" he repeated. "What do you mean that *you* don't want her living in a derelict, old house?"

Nash peered down at his brother. "I'm going to assume you've had some conversations with her, at least enough to see what she's like."

Beau shrugged. "Enough, I guess,"

"What do you think?"

Beau gave him a knowing look. "I should have guessed there was something going on when you called me this morning," he said. "And when you ask me a question like that, I'm thinking that *you* think she's something pretty nice."

"She is."

"I know she is. I don't disagree with you at all. But you haven't had a serious relationship since you and Julie divorced. You don't have time. All you do is work."

Nash gave him a half-grin and looked back at the house. "I may have just found a reason not to work too much. God knows, I'd sure like to come home to someone like her every night. Hell, I might never leave the house again if she was in it."

Beau looked surprised. "You?" he shook his head. "What about the commissioner job you're taking at the end of the summer? You're going to be in Baton Rouge."

He shrugged. "Only to work. I don't have to live there. It's only a thirty-mile drive from here."

Beau shook his head, this time in resignation. "I don't believe it."

"Believe it. I'm going to marry that woman."

Beau rolled his eyes. "And I'm going to be sick," he muttered, waving his brother off as he headed towards the house. "I've got to get back to work."

Nash grinned as he watched his brother go. But his grin faded when he thought of Femmie Loreau lying dead behind him and how the Loreau family was going to react.

All of their hostility would be directed at Elliot, and down here in the bayous, the attitude was very much an eye for an eye. People still believed in vengeance. That worried Nash a great deal but he wouldn't let on, at least not now. Elliot had enough to worry about with Alec's injury.

He could hear the ambulance pulling out of the driveway, the siren beginning to wail, and he made a dash for the front of the house in time to see the ambulance driving away with Penelope's white Nissan following it. Elliot wasn't anywhere to be found and he rightly assumed she was in the ambulance with her son. A Sorrento officer was standing a few feet away, writing in his notebook.

"Where is the ambulance going?" Nash asked him.

The man looked up from his paper. "St. Elizabeth's."

Nash thanked him for the information and headed back into the house to find his brother to tell him where he was going. He also corralled Steve and told the man to stick close to the house in case the Loreaus came around looking for their pappy. Steve knew, as Nash did, that there was going to be a heaping load of trouble once word got out about the killing. Sorrento P.D. already had an I.D. on the body and chatter was taking it out over the airways. Now, it was only a matter of time until the knowledge became public.

Nash made a call to the private security company he had used in the past and set up round-the-clock patrols on the property. He wandered through the house, talking to the security company's owner, finally bumping into his brother in the kitchen. He finalized the security arrangements for the property before hanging up the phone.

Beau was inspecting the propane pipes that led into the stove area, which was really the original fireplace that had been converted to fit the stove. Most older homes used the kitchen fire-places as stove receptacles.

Beau was positive that the pipes were bad but made a brilliant suggestion on how to temporarily bring propane from a new unit into the house that would suffice until they were able to do something more permanent. He already had suggestions about bringing more power into the house from a new set of lines he intended to bring down from the overhead powerline that ran adjacent to the structure.

Nash listened to the ideas, liked them, and gave his brother his blessing. It wasn't even his house, but he told his brother to do it anyway.

By the time Nash pulled out of the driveway, Beau had an entire collection of contractors heading for the house in an attempt to make the old beauty at least marginally livable again. Nash figured it was the least they could do considering the trouble Elliot had since setting foot on the property.

But given recent events, he knew the trouble was not going to end there.

———

St. Elizabeth Hospital was the biggest hospital in Ascension Parish, about fifteen miles south of Baton Rouge. Both of Nash's boys had been born here and his ex-wife was a hospital administrator, so he knew the hospital well. He pulled into the parking lot of the emergency room entrance, having arrived less than an hour behind the ambulance.

Entering the emergency room, most of the veteran personnel already knew him on sight. Nash Aury was rather famous around the place, even more famous with the female personnel when he and his wife divorced. He went to the Admissions counter and asked where Alec Jentry was. The Admissions nurse pointed him towards the emergency facilities behind a locked door and he headed in that direction as the woman buzzed the door to unlock it.

"Sheriff Aury!"

He heard his name, turning to see Penelope walking towards him through the crowded waiting room. She was clutching her purse, her mother's purse, and looked pale and frightened. Nash instinctively put an arm around her shoulders to comfort her. She looked badly in need of it.

"Why are you waiting out here all by yourself?" he asked kindly.

Penelope shrugged her slender shoulders. "They would only let my mom in. They told me to wait out here."

Nash turned her for the door that led into the operatories. "Come on, darlin'," he said softly. "You can come in with me."

The Admissions nurse pushed the button to unlock the door again and Nash pulled it open, ushering Penelope through. It opened into a moderately dark hallway with white walls and waxed, tiled floors, smelling strongly of antiseptic. Nash took her arm and escorted her around the corner and into an area that had four big operatories, all in a row. Only a white curtain separated them. All four were full and Nash made his way down the row until he came to the last one where Alec and Elliot were.

A young African-American doctor was with them. Nash recognized the man. He was inspecting the wound on Alec's shoulder blade, looking up when he saw Nash. The young doctor grinned.

"Sheriff Aury," he said, his voice deep and warm. "I haven't seen you in a while."

Nash smiled weakly. "That's a good thing."

His gaze moved to Elliot, sitting in the corner on a rolling stool. Her big, blue eyes gazed back at him and he swore he could see relief and gladness in the deep blue depths. But she also looked very small and scared sitting in the corner, something he didn't like at all. As Penelope left him to go to her mother, Nash stood at the end of the gurney, his gaze moving between Alec and Elliot.

"How's the young man doing?" he asked.

The doctor peered at the wound. "Well," he said, turning to the nurse when she appeared with a suture kit. "He's got a decent wound. It's not deep enough to require surgery but I'm going to stitch him up. He's also got some nicks on his hands that I'm going to suture. We've already given him a tetanus shot and an antibiotic shot, but I think overall, he's in good shape. He'll be out of here in an hour."

"Good." Nash felt a great deal of relief at that, as if it had been one of his own kids. He put his big hand on Alec's leg. "Can you stand it here another hour?"

Alec made a face, as he was so capable of doing quite frequently. "That tetanus shot hurt, dude," he grumbled. "My arm is killing me."

Nash laughed, looking at Elliot as he spoke. "Your mom will take you to get some ice cream when this is all over for being such a good boy."

Alec grinned. "I'd rather have a steak."

"Steak it is." Nash took his hand off Alec's leg and crooked a finger at Elliot. "Can I speak to you a moment?"

Elliot obediently rose from the stool and followed Nash from the small operatory. He took her around the corner into a darkened hall that ran between major corridors. There was another narrow hall off of that and he took her into that one, just to make sure they had complete privacy. The hallway was dimly lit and quiet. Once he was sure there was no one around, he stopped and looked at her.

He tried to speak but at first, nothing would come out except a heavy sigh. He just couldn't get past the pale, sad expression on her face.

"Can I hug you?" he whispered. "Can I at least do that?"

Elliot didn't say a word. She collapsed against his warm, broad chest and burst into deep, painful sobs. Nash wrapped his arms tightly around her, holding her close as she expended her fear. She had held it in admirably but Nash's soft offer had her collapsing. It felt so good to collapse against someone, to stop being strong for just a moment. She had missed this kind of comfort and Nash felt so good, she never wanted to leave his embrace. It was heaven.

"Who...?" she sobbed. "Who would do this? Who did this to Alec?"

Nash leaned back against the wall, holding her tightly against him as she wept. A big hand stroked her head gently.

"The police are working on it," was all he would say. "Alec is going to be fine and that's all that matters."

"But... but...."

He shushed her softly. "It's all right, darlin'," he whispered. "Everything is all right now."

Elliot couldn't pull herself together, not just yet. She'd just spent the past two hours in hell and she wasn't ready to collect herself yet. Nash offered comfort and she was going to take it. They stayed in their tight embrace for several long minutes, at least until she stopped sobbing so painfully. Nash remained silent, stroking her hair gently and hoping that he was, at least, bringing her some reassurance.

"Can you tell me what happened?" he asked gently. "Did you see what went down?"

That set Elliot off again and her sobs renewed with a vengeance as she nodded. Nash rocked her soothingly.

"Okay, okay," he murmured into the top of her head. "You don't have to talk about it now. It can wait."

Elliot's face was completely wet. She suddenly pushed herself off of him, wiping at the rivers on her cheeks.

"I...I don't have a tissue," she sobbed.

Nash had her stay put while he went around the corner and came back with a tissue box a few seconds later. Elliot gratefully pulled out several tissues and wiped at her face, looking up at him with big, watery eyes.

"Will you please still hug me?" she whispered.

Nash immediately wrapped his big arms around her, tucking her head up underneath his chin.

"You don't even have to ask that," he murmured, laying his cheek against the top of her blond head. "I'll hug you as long as you need it. I'll hug you even when you don't need it. I'll hug you until you chase me away and tell me to quit hugging you."

He said it so softly, so comically, that Elliot began to giggle through her tears. "You're crazy," she sniffled.

"Yes, I am," he whispered. "Crazy about you."

She didn't say anything for a moment. Then, she lifted her head, gazing up at him as he held her in an extremely intimate position. She was plastered up against him and he was wrapped around her and, at the moment, they were the only two people in the entire world. Something warm and intimate was settling between them, something deeper than mere attraction.

"You know," she whispered, her hose stuffy from crying, "when I came to Louisiana, I just wanted to start a new life away from bad memories. I really never had any expectations of anything else. I can't even believe how sweet you've been to us. You're like... like my own personal guardian angel. I'm just so thankful in so many ways to have met you."

He smiled at her. "Me, too," he replied. "I have to tell you, however, that when I went to Purgatory yesterday to make arrangements to get the rest of our furniture out of there, I wasn't sure what to expect. I really wanted to meet the person who bought the home that had been in my family for two hundred years just to make sure they were worthy of it. But within the first five minutes of knowing you, I was so glad you had bought the house because you already loved it as much as I did. Soon after that, I realized I didn't give a damn about the house anymore. It was you I was interested in."

She laid her head against his broad chest. "Hug me again."

He did, squeezing her tightly, loving the feel of her against him. It was the best feeling in the world. It was even better when she wrapped her arms around his waist and squeezed back. But eventually, she loosened her grip and looked up at him again.

"I need to get back to my son," she said, wiping at her nose with a tissue. "Thanks for coming all the way up here. You didn't have to do that."

He was reluctant to let her go, holding her hand as they made their way slowly out of the corridor.

"Yes, I did," he replied. "I had to make sure you were all okay. And we need to talk about what happened."

Her smile faded. "I've lived all my life in Los Angeles, practically a hotbed of crime, and nothing ever happened. Now, in two days, I've been firebombed and my son has been attacked. It's almost like... like someone or something doesn't want us here."

"*I* want you here," he countered quietly, entering the corridor where the operatories were. He let go of her hand and faced her. "I don't know what I'd do if you went back to California. It would absolutely break my heart."

Elliot could see Penelope approaching her from the corner of her eye, but she smiled at Nash, anyway. "And mine," she whispered.

Before he could reply, Elliot turned to her daughter and opened her arms to the young woman, giving her a hug. Penelope accepted the comfort, pulling back to look her mother in the eye. She looked suspiciously between her mother and Nash.

"Are you okay?" she asked.

Elliot smiled. "Sure," she said, turning the girl around and heading back to where Alec was. "How's your brother?"

Penelope held her mother's hand as they came to the operatory where Alec was having his back stitched.

"Oh, he's okay," she pretended like it was nothing serious, although she had been scared to death when it happened. "He's just faking."

Alec, having his back dug into, didn't look too happy as he glared at his sister. "Come here so I can smack you."

Penelope giggled. "You can't touch me," she insisted. "The sheriff will arrest you."

Alec frowned at Nash. "Isn't there such thing as Justifiable Smacking if she deserves it?"

Nash shook his head, grinning. "Not even close."

As Alec grumbled and fired off several threatening expressions at his sister, the doctor finished stitching up his back. There were three deep gashes on his hands and by the time the doctor started in on those, a tall brunette with a thick waistline suddenly joined them. Elliot caught a glimpse of the woman from the corner of her eye, turning in time to see the woman focus in on Nash.

"Well," the woman smiled at him. "They told me you were here. What are you doing?"

Nash returned her smile, although it was forced. "Hi," he greeted, gesturing to Alec on the gurney. "I came to see a friend."

The woman tore her brown-eyed gaze off of Nash as if suddenly noticing there were three other people in the room. She seemed particularly interested in Elliot as Nash introduced them.

"This is Elliot Jentry and her children, Penelope and Alec," he said, looking to Elliot. "Ellie, this Julie, my sons' mother."

Somewhat startled, Elliot came up off the stool she had been seated on and extended her hand to the woman.

"It's so nice to meet you," she said sincerely.

Julie smiled, nodding her head faintly as she very obviously inspected Elliot. "Likewise," she said in her soft, Southern drawl. After a few moments of intense scrutiny, she looked at Alec on the gurney. "Did your son have an accident?"

Nash answered before Elliot could. "Something like that," he said vaguely. "Ellie and her kids just moved here from California. They bought Purgatory."

That bit of news brought a strong reaction. "Purgatory?" Julie almost exclaimed, looking back and forth between Nash and Elliot. "Good Lord, Nash, you let her buy that place? What in the world were you thinking?"

Elliot stepped back from the conversation at that point. She could see that Julie wasn't particularly focused on her anyway, other than to dissect her with her eyes. It was that appraising look that one woman gives another when competing for the same man. As Julie scolded Nash about selling Purgatory to a "Californian", Elliot took a moment to inspect her, also.

Julie was tall, made taller by the heels she wore, and had a very pretty face with smooth skin. She was built a little heavy but she wasn't unattractive. At least, Elliot didn't think so. She moved back to her stool, watching Nash and Julie go back and forth about Purgatory. Finally, Nash put up a hand to shut the woman up.

"I appreciate your concern, but it's not your problem to worry about," he told her. "Purgatory is in good hands."

Julie shrugged her shoulders, frustrated with his response. "If you say so," she said, looking to Elliot, sitting in the corner on her stool. "Sorry, Ms. Jentry. I wasn't trying to insult you. It's just that Purgatory is a lot to handle for anyone, much less someone from out of state who doesn't know a thing about it. I'm assuming your husband will be helping you restore it?"

Elliot was all about being polite to the woman until that question. She just didn't like the way she asked it, especially in front of her kids. It was leading, probing and judgmental, and completely rubbed Elliot the wrong way. With the day she'd had already, her patience was gone.

"No, because he's dead," she said flatly, cocking an eyebrow. "Do you have any other personal questions?"

While Julie had been subtle in her interrogation, Elliot fired a shot right over her bow. If the woman was going to start something then she should know who she was starting it with. Nash cleared his throat and looked at his ex-wife.

"It's been a bad day," he told her, gesturing for her turn around and go back the way she came. "Thanks for stopping by."

Julie could see that she had offended the woman and rather than get her dander up, she backed down somewhat. "I'm sorry," she repeated. "I really didn't mean to upset you."

Elliot just looked away as Nash answered. "Go," he said softly but firmly. "Please. I'll talk to you later."

Julie did as she was told. Elliot wouldn't look at anyone; she was embarrassed she had lost her temper, especially in front of Nash. She just sat there and stared at her hands, unaware that Nash and Penelope were watching her with some sympathy. Alec couldn't have cared less; he was more concerned with the doctor being finished. Thankfully, it wasn't too much longer before the doctor put in the final stitch.

"There," he said, taking a look at his handiwork. "Come back in ten days and I'll take them out for you. If you have any problems, like fever or pain and swelling, please give me a call. And try to keep the area dry for the next twenty-four hours if you can. Do you have any questions?"

Alec looked at his hands, holding them up for all to see. "I look like freaking Frankenstein."

"Can you put bolts in his neck, doctor?" Penelope asked innocently.

As Alec snarled at his sister, the doctor laughed and turned to Elliot. "Any questions, ma'am?"

Elliot shook her head. At this point, she was ready to get the hell out of there.

"No," she said, standing up. "Thank you so much for taking good care of him."

The doctor nodded and turned to look at his patient one more time before peeling off his surgical gloves and tossing them into the biohazard receptacle.

"Good to see you again, Sheriff," he said to Nash as he left the room.

Nash watched the man go as a nurse came in to dress the stitches. But something more at the end of the hall caught his attention; he could see a Sorrento police officer heading his way. Not wanting to upset Elliot more than she already was, he met the man halfway down the corridor, well away from Alec and Elliot.

"Hi, Sheriff," the officer identified himself as Officer Bird. "How's the suspect?"

Nash blinked at him. "Suspect?" he repeated. "You mean Alec Jentry?"

The officer nodded, handing Nash the paperwork in his hand. "I've been sent to escort the suspect back to the station for questioning."

Nash read the paperwork. It was all in order. He sighed heavily and handed it back to the man, knowing that Elliot would not take this well.

"The kid was defending himself," he said, his voice low. "Don't cuff him. He's not going to run."

Bird nodded. "I know," he said. "The detectives just want to get his side of the story. We're not arresting him."

"Then make sure you treat him with all due respect."

"I will," Bird agreed, noting the look of extreme displeasure on Nash's face. "Look, Sheriff, if it was up to me, I'd give the kid a medal. He did us a favor by killing Femmie Loreau. But now the man's family has been informed of his death and they're up in arms about it."

It was the bad news Nash had been waiting for. "Do they know who did it?"

Bird shook his head. "No sir," he said. "They just know he was killed on Purgatory property. We had to send more officers over there to keep them out of the crime scene."

Nash put a hand to his face in a weary, frustrated gesture. "Oh, God," he groaned. "Stay here for a minute. Let me inform the family of what's going on and I'll bring Alec to you, okay? But you'd better protect that boy with your life, do you hear me?"

"Yessir."

The officer remained stationery as Nash went back to the small room where Alec was receiving his bandages. Three pairs of blue eyes turned to look at Nash as the man walked into the room. He smiled at all of them but at Elliot in particular.

"Can I have another word with you, please?" he asked.

Elliot came off of the stool and followed him into their customary corridor. When they were quite alone, Nash reached out and took both of her hands. He caressed them tenderly, gazing into her lovely eyes.

"I'm going to tell you something but you're going to have to promise me you won't get upset," he began. "I will preface all of this by telling you that Alec is not in any trouble and he's not under arrest."

She cocked her head at him. "What's going on?"

"He needs to go to the police station," he replied. "It's standard procedure when something like this happens that there is an investigation. You know that, right?"

She nodded and he continued. "Since a man was killed, the police want to make sure they have all their bases covered and get all the information they can to make sure it was self-defense. A Sorrento officer is here to take Alec back to the station so they can question him. It's normal procedure."

Because he had explained it calmly and succinctly, Elliot wasn't hysterical, but she was upset. She gripped his hands tightly.

"But he's been through so much today," she insisted. "Do they have to do it today?"

He nodded before she even finished her sentence. "Yes, while it's fresh in his mind. If you want, I'll go with him to the station and stay with him while they question him. Do you want me to go with him?"

She nodded fervently. "Yes, please," she begged. "Do you mind?"

"Of course not. That's why I offered."

She suddenly threw her arms around his neck and eagerly kissed his cheek.

"Thank you," she said in between kisses. "Thank you so much. You don't know how much that means to me."

Nash held her tightly, thoroughly enjoying her gesture of gratitude. When her lips came close to his, he kissed her mouth lustily. For a few hot, brief moments, they lost themselves in a kiss, the passion of which neither one of them had ever experienced before. Lips suckled, tongues tasted, and eventually Elliot pulled away because they heard footsteps and she was afraid someone would discover them in a heated clinch. But the footsteps faded away without crossing their path and Elliot and Nash just stood there and grinned at each other.

"Ms. Ellie," Nash lifted his eyebrows seriously. "Would it be too much to ask to experience that again sometime?"

She giggled, embarrassed and hot, and fanned her face. "I don't know if I can take that again," she murmured. "But I'd be willing to try."

He laughed and reached out a hand to her. She took it and let him lead her back down the corridor.

"One more thing," he said quietly, trying to fight down the arousal he was feeling over their heated kiss. "Word has gotten out about the incident and the local police have their hands full keeping people off the property now. I would take it as a personal favor if you and Penelope would go to a hotel tonight, just to be safe. There's a Hampton Inn just down the street and I know the manager. We'll get you girls a good room and a bathtub to soak in."

Her mouth opened in outrage. "There are people on my property?" she repeated. "They better get their asses off it or I'll prosecute every one of them. I'll...!"

Nash came to a halt and grasped her firmly by the arms. "I already took care of that," he told her, interrupting her tirade. "I've got private security on the property with twenty-four hour patrol. Plus, my brother's there and he's more than likely going to spend the night because of the contractors coming so early in the morning. There are also police all over the place, so nothing is going to happen to the house or your possessions, I promise. But I am very concerned about you and Penelope going back there tonight. I'd feel so much better if you'd just go to a hotel for the night. Will you please do this for me?"

She stared up at him. "You did all of that?"

"What?"

"Private security?" she seemed to have calmed down dramatically. "Why in the world would you do that for a woman you barely know?"

He smiled and kissed her on the cheek. "Because I like her," he murmured. "And I want to get to know her a whole lot better."

"You're not doing this just to get your house back, are you?"

She was grinning and he started laughing, resuming their walk back to Alec and Penelope.

"No," he assured her. "It's yours and it's going to stay yours. But will you please go to the hotel for the night as a personal favor to me?"

She gave him a reluctant nod. "Okay," she said. "But all of my stuff is back at the house."

"There's a Wal-Mart across the street. You can pick up what you need for the night."

It sounded like a good enough plan and the truth was that she was dying for a hot bath. She could pick up some pajamas for her and Penelope and then retire to a good bed with cable television. It all sounded pretty wonderful.

"But what about Alec?" she wanted to know.

"When he's done at the police station, I'll take him back to my house. I've got four bedrooms and only one of them is used, so he can have his pick of beds and a bathroom that he can actually fit in to. We'll see you and Penelope in the morning."

There didn't seem to be any holes in his plans as far as she was concerned, so she nodded once more, just to seal the deal, as they reached Alec and Penelope.

As Elliot told Alec about his fate for the next few hours, Nash got on the phone and called the manager at the Hampton Inn. When Elliot and Penelope checked in an hour later, two junior suites were waiting for her and Penelope, one next to the other. They both had their own king-sized bed, giant bathtub, and free toiletries. Elliot soaked in the tub until her skin was wrinkled and, still, she stayed in until the water was cold and she was forced to get out.

When she finally slept, she dreamed of a handsome guardian angel with hazel eyes.

SEVEN

WHEN ELLIOT, Penelope and Alec returned to Purgatory the next day, the crime scene was cleaned up and there were a host of contractor's trucks lining the driveway. Penelope had to park her little Nissan far down the driveway and the three of them walked up to the house, seeing that a massive undertaking was already underway.

Truthfully, it was a shock. Elliot stood in front of the house, watching the scaffolding going up on all sides, noting that the front window had already been replaced.

More than a little concerned that work was going on without her consent or knowledge, she walked into the main hall to find strippers and painters in nearly every room. They were stripping off the old paint in the central hallway and carefully repairing the plaster already. Increasingly concerned, Elliot went in search of Beau and found the man in the ballroom, speaking with a dark-haired woman in a suit.

Beau saw her as soon as she entered the room and waved enthusiastically. "Hi," he greeted. "Sorry we started the party without you."

Elliot was a little taken aback. "I can see that," she tried not to sound perturbed. "What's going on?"

Beau grabbed her by the wrist and pulled her over to the dark-haired woman. "This is Hallie Munn," he introduced her. "Hallie is from Tulane University's department of historic preservation. Based on the conversation you and I had yesterday when you told me that you wanted to restore Purgatory's original colors and finishes, I called Hallie and she drove up this morning with a bunch of information on the original plantation, Sophie."

Hallie was a lovely mixed-race woman who extended her hand amiably to Elliot.

"Hi there," she said. "It's so nice to meet you. I'm really thrilled to be called in on this. It's such a great opportunity for me because there aren't many of these great, old houses left that haven't been either restored, remodeled, or torn down."

Elliot forced a smile at the woman. "I'm very happy you're here," she told her. "I really want to be true to the original design of the house, so thank you for coming."

Hallie just grinned and Elliot turned to Beau. "Uh...," she crooked her finger at him. "Can I please talk to you for a moment?"

Beau followed her back out into the central hallway where Elliot drew him out of earshot of her children and of the workers. She turned to him.

"What's going on here?" she whispered. "I thought you were just going to give me estimates today?"

Beau shook his head. "Nash and I talked about this last night," he said. "We need to make this place livable for you and your kids, so we're going to go like gangbusters to restore it. With all of the people I have at my disposal, this place should be looking like it did the day they built it in about four weeks. By tonight, you should have propane for hot water and the stove. I've got a designer coming in later this morning so you can pick out your appliances."

Elliot stared at him in confusion and doubt. "*Nash* and you talked about it?" she repeated. "But this is my house. I don't have all the money in the world to pay for an army of contractors. All of this is going to cost me a fortune, Beau. You really shouldn't have done anything without talking to me first."

He could see why she was upset and he hastened to reassure her. "I wouldn't worry too much about it," he said. "What's your budget for the restoration?"

She blinked thoughtfully. "Well...," she looked around, at the floors, the walls. "My guess is that it's probably going to cost well over a hundred thousand dollars to restore this place but I only have eighty thousand set aside. I have to be really selective about what I pay for now because I don't..."

He cut her off. "We'll get this house fully restored, including furniture, windows, new fixtures and appliances for eighty thousand and not a penny more."

She looked at him as if he were crazy. "How in the world can you do that?" she demanded. "Everything in this house has to be gutted and redone; the floors, the plumbing, the electrical... *everything.*"

He smiled at her. "I know," he patted her on the arm. "Don't worry about it. You're only paying for materials. Nash and I are taking care of the labor."

Her jaw dropped. "You're *what?*"

He laughed at her. "Talk to my brother. It was his idea."

She grabbed him by the arm. "No, I'm talking to you. What do you mean that you and Nash are taking care of the labor? That's got to be at least forty grand!"

Beau waved her off. "You forget who you're talking to," he reminded her, his light demeanor turning serious. "I do this for a living. The State of Louisiana offers grants for the restoration of historic homes and I have feeling I can get enough to cover the labor and then some. Besides, Nash and I always wanted to restore this place but we never had the opportunity. Family fights, crazy grandmothers and all that. Let us at least do something to make Purgatory beautiful and livable again. In a way, it's still our house. Our blood flows through these walls. We want to see it restored just as much as you do."

He winked at her and left her standing in the central hallway, struggling to grasp what he had just told her. Elliot had seen Nash that morning when he dropped Alec off at the hotel on his way to work, but he'd only mentioned the results of Alec's interrogation, which seemed relatively benign.

He told her that the Sorrento detectives, after speaking with Alec, had determined his actions had, indeed, been in self-defense and they intended to file their report and close the case. It seemed that none of them were sorry that Femmie Loreau was dead, a man with a criminal record a mile-long but who had gotten away with much more that wasn't on his record.

Frankly, Elliot was a little surprised with how quickly they were willing to close the case, but she didn't mention it. She was very thankful. Nash had left her with a saucy wink when the kids weren't looking and with no hint of what waited for her at home.

Lost in thought, Elliot began to walk. She ended up on the second floor, where more painters were carefully stripping off eighty-year-old paint. She could hear Alec and Penelope, and she found her way into Alec's enormous bedroom where Penelope was trying to convince her brother that she deserved the bigger bedroom.

Elliot took her daughter back to the bedroom that was positioned over the ballroom, the one with the killer floor-to-ceiling view of the bayou, and Penelope shut her mouth. When Alec attempted to invade, she kicked him out. She'd found her room.

Elliot grinned as she listened to her children bicker; it was like music to her ears. Rob used to throw socks or towels at them to get them to shut up, but it was all in good natured fun. Alec and Penelope were actually very close. It was good to hear them again, in a new house, filling it with their life and youth.

Ending up in her big, master bedroom that overlooked the driveway and the bayou to the north, Elliot hunted for a change of clothes considering she was still in her clothes from yesterday. She'd taken two hot baths and one hot shower at the hotel, cleaning her body and then some, but the clothes were still dirty.

Coming across a box containing carefully folded pants and other items, she changed into clean jeans, a white, long-sleeved t-shirt with a scoop neck that emphasized her sexy figure, and pulled her long hair back into a ponytail. Pushing up her sleeves, she jumped into organizing the boxes. From the craziness of the past two days to the sudden industriousness of today, she was ready to settle in. Thanks to Nash, she was finally thrilled and happy to be there.

She was home.

———

The day flew by and before Elliot realized it, dusk was beginning to fall. The sky over the bayou was turning shades of deep blue and pink as night approached and the fireflies were coming out in droves, creating a galaxy of stars in their own backyard.

Alec and Penelope turned into five year olds when they saw all of the fireflies around the house. They ran outside and tried to catch them, and Elliot watched her grown children act like kindergarteners as they chased bugs around. Standing in the ballroom, she grinned at the sundown entertainment.

Most of the contractors had shut down for the night, leaving Beau and Hallie still perusing the place, discussing what needed to happen. Frankly, Elliot was glad to have the help with the smaller decisions, like fixtures and door knobs, but she had the final word with the colors and finishes. She had picked out her appliances that afternoon, state of the art devices that would work in harmony with the antique surroundings, and she felt like things were finally moving forward. She was happy, carefree, feeling better than she had in almost two years.

As she watched her kids dance around, she could hear Beau and Hallie at the front door. Beau was seeing the woman out. Elliot heard the front door shut softly and Beau's footsteps as he made his way back to the ballroom. He came to stand next to her, watching her California-bred kids have fun with the fireflies. She heard him laugh softly.

"How old are they again?" he asked.

"Eighteen and nineteen," she replied. "Or more like five and six right now."

They chuckled for a moment, their gaze turning to more than the kids as they frolicked. There was an entire world out there being bathed in the colors of sunset. Elliot sighed faintly, her eyes on the sky.

"I have seen a lot of sunsets, but never one like this," she murmured. "There's something so peaceful and timeless about this place. I'm going to have to write a book about it."

Beau glanced at her, trying not to stare. She was so pretty and intelligent, so unlike anyone he had ever met before. Elliot caught him looking at her from the corner of her eye and she turned to him with a smile.

"Are you married?" she asked.

Beau nodded. "Twenty-seven years and counting."

"Kids?"

"Two boys, all grown up."

She wriggled her eyebrows. "Two boys just like your brother," she commented. "Where do you live?"

"Just over the state line in Mississippi, in a town called Bay St. Louis," he told her. "My company is based there."

"Nash told me that you run your own company," she commented. "So you dropped everything to come to Sorrento to help some woman you don't even know because your brother says so?"

"He's bigger than I am. Plus, he carries a gun." He grinned as Elliot laughed. "Besides, once he moves to Baton Rouge and goes to work for the state police commission, I might never see him again. He'll be swallowed up by the state capital when they find out how great he is."

Elliot's smile faded as his words sank in. "State Police Commission?" she repeated, confused.

Beau nodded, obviously proud. "It's a pretty big deal," he said. "Didn't he tell you? He's going to Baton Rouge."

Elliot's smile was gone completely. "No, he didn't," she said, wondering why she suddenly felt sick in the pit of her stomach. "So he's leaving?"

"Just to Baton Rouge," he replied. "It's not far from here, only about thirty miles or so."

Elliot let the subject drop, mostly because she wasn't sure how she felt about it. Nash had made it seem like he wanted something with her long term, but perhaps she had been misreading his signals. He had a government job waiting for him in Baton Rouge, so perhaps all he really wanted was a fling before he took off for the state capital. Perhaps she had been reading too much into everything.

Embarrassed, confused and slightly hurt, she returned her attention to her children, who were now peering into their closed hands, looking at the fireflies at close range.

"Are you staying in town tonight?" she asked Beau.

He shook his head. "I'll be here through the week," he said. "I'll stay with my brother and go home for the weekend."

She looked at him. "Are you sure you have nothing else going on that you can just drop everything to work on this house?"

His grin returned. "Actually, we're working on a five million dollar lobby renovation for one of the casinos in Biloxi," he told her. "I have project managers to handle that. Being here at Purgatory is something I really want to do."

Elliot simply smiled in response, not having much else to say to that. She ended up wandering outside with Beau in tow, avoiding the area that had been covered with crime scene tape earlier in the day, and finding Alec and Penelope as they lingered near the bayou's edge and more fireflies. Both young people were several feet away from Elliot and Beau, trying to catch handfuls of fireflies without falling into the bayou.

"He doesn't seem to have suffered any ill effects from yesterday," Beau commented quietly.

Elliot shook her head. "Not really, except he doesn't want to talk about it anymore," she said. "Who can blame him?"

Beau nodded his head in understanding. "Do you know what's going to happen now?"

Elliot shrugged. "Nash said that the Sorrento Police have concluded it was all in self-defense and are closing the case. But I'd sure like to know who attacked my son."

Beau didn't reply. If she didn't know, he certainly wasn't going to tell her. He wondered if Nash was going to. Given the history between the Aurys and the Loreaus, he was going to have to tell her something if only to prepare her. Oblivious to Beau's thoughts, Elliot wandered closer to her frolicking children.

"We need to figure out what to do for dinner, guys," Elliot called to them. "Obviously, I can't cook, so where do you want to eat?"

Alec was leaping into the air to catch fireflies, his lanky body flailing around. "How about more alligator ribs?"

Penelope immediately vetoed the idea. "Gross!" she exclaimed. "What other restaurants are around here?"

"I saw a restaurant called Mama's on the corner over by the highway," Elliot said. "There's also a McDonald's and a...."

She was cut off by a big splash of water followed by a shout from her son. Alec grabbed his sister and bolted away from the water's edge, howling as if he'd been scared out of his wits. Because he was howling, Penelope was screaming. Elliot watched the pair of them crash into each other and nearly fall to the ground as they tried to move away from the water's edge.

"What in the world are you two doing?" she demanded.

"There was an alligator on the shore!" Alec exclaimed. "It was right by my feet!"

Penelope was laughing hysterically by now, slapping at her panicked brother. Both kids were giggling uncontrollably as Beau cautiously made his way to the water's edge and looked around.

"Y'all need to be more careful," he said, turning to the kids with a grin. "There are alligators in this bayou and they like to come ashore. There used to be a fence to keep them from getting into the yard, but that has long since collapsed. You might want to think about putting up another one."

Elliot looked somewhat horrified. "Really?" she didn't like the sound of alligators in her yard. "Well, that's one more thing I'm going to have to worry about now – alligators skulking around my house."

Beau laughed softly, shoving his hands in his pockets as he took one last look at the water and wandered back in her direction. Just as he turned to say something to her, something caught his attention over her right shoulder, back near the house. The smile vanished from his face.

Elliot saw his expression and naturally turned around to see what had him so serious. She immediately spied three men over by the side yard where all of the police caution tape had been up. They were kicking around the bramble as if looking for something.

"Hey!" Beau called, moving in their direction. "What are y'all doing here?"

Elliot had no idea who the men were other than that they were trespassing. She motioned for her kids to stay where they were as she followed Beau over to the wandering men. Having received no answer to his initial question, Beau snapped again.

"Hey!" he barked. "What are y'all doing?"

The men were still kicking around in the former crime scene but one of them looked up as Beau and Elliot approached. He was a skinny man, in his thirties, with long, stringy hair, a John Deere baseball cap, and dirty clothing. When he spoke, it was with yellowed teeth.

"Looking for anything my pappy left behind," he snapped back. "What are y'all doin' here? You don't own this place no more."

"No, he doesn't," Elliot could sense the hostilities and she was instantly on edge. "I do. What do you want?"

The man's dark gaze lingered on her and Elliot immediately felt dirty just by the way he looked at her. When he smiled, it was gross and lascivious.

"Well," his voice was considerably softer. "You're the new neighbor?"

Elliot nodded. "What do you want?"

The man stopped kicking around the bramble and took a couple of steps towards her. By this time, the other two men, both of them younger with varied degrees of mullets and dirty clothing, also noticed Elliot.

"My pappy was killed here this afternoon," he pointed to the spot where the body had once laid. "Someone killed him but the po-*lice* won't tell us who. He was murdered next to y'all's house."

Elliot immediately went on her guard. She didn't like the look, smell or ambiance of these men and, frankly, she was frightened. She didn't want to provoke a confrontation but she wanted these men off her property.

"Who are you?" she asked.

The man smiled, a nauseating gesture. "I'm Will Loreau," he said, pointing to the other men with him. "These are my brothers, Ed and Nicky. What's y'all's name, sweet thang?"

Elliot avoided the question that made her skin crawl. "Look, I'm not trying to be rude, but I don't like people wandering around on my property. I'd be very happy if you'd leave."

Will's smile faded somewhat. "My grandma said y'all was unfriendly," he said. "She said y'all wouldn't come 'n visit."

Elliot kept her cool. "She asked me to come over the day I moved in. I was very busy. I'm sorry she didn't understand that."

Will simply nodded faintly, dragging his eyes all over her bosom. Elliot resisted the urge to put her hands over her chest to cover herself up. When the man was finished molesting her with his eyes, he pointed to the ground again.

"What happened to my pappy?" he asked.

Elliot glanced at Beau, who was as taut and serious as she had ever seen the man. He met her gaze and she didn't like the apprehension she saw. She endeavored to once again persuade the men to leave before things got ugly.

"You'll have to ask the police," she said. "Will you please leave now? I would appreciate it."

Will turned on her and so did the others. They all seemed to be moving closer and Elliot resisted the urge to back away. She instinctively knew they were trying to intimidate her and she wasn't going to let them. She had to stand up for herself.

"I think I'd like to get to know y'all better," Will said. "What's your name?"

They were coming and coming, closer and closer, and Elliot finally had to back up because Will was almost up against her. She could smell his body odor and foul breath from where she stood. Fear surged in her chest.

"I'm your neighbor and that's all you need to know," she said. "If you and your brothers don't get off my property right now, I'm going to call the police. It's your choice."

Will was still smiling at her, only this time, he reached out a hand to touch her. Elliot jumped back and smacked the hand away as hard as she could.

"Alec!" she yelled. "Go call the cops!"

Will and his brothers just laughed, but now, they were moving to box both her and Beau in. Will reached up another hand.

"Don't be afraid, sweet thang," he crooned. "I won't hurt ya."

Elliot swung hard at the hand coming at her, knocking it away. Another one was coming up and she slapped at that one, too. She shoved Beau away, hoping it would give the man a head start in running for the house, when a shotgun blast suddenly ripped through the air.

It was loud, startling and frightening. The Loreau brothers came to a shocked halt, everyone turning in the direction of the house. Nash stood on the porch with Alec and Penelope standing fearfully behind him, a 12-gauge shotgun in his hand. He looked as deadly serious as Elliot had ever seen him, cocking the gun with one hand and pumping out the spent shell in a very cowboy-like maneuver. It was absolutely surreal.

"If you boys take another step in her direction, this shotgun is aimed at your head," he rumbled. "She asked you to leave. If you want to keep your heads and your health, y'all will do as she says. Get off the property and don't come back."

Ed and Nicky immediately backed away but Will was slower to move. Furious, he pointed to the spot several feet away where his father had been killed.

"My pappy was murdered here," he shouted at Nash. "She knows who done it!"

Nash stepped off the porch, slinging the shotgun in his right hand in such a way that it was aimed at Ed and Nicky. With the pellet radius of the blast, he could take out both of them in one shot if they made a move he didn't like.

"She didn't kill him if that's what you mean," he said. "Your pappy made an unprovoked attack against someone who accidentally killed him in self-defense. What did you think was going to happen when he came over here armed with a hatchet? Are y'all as stupid as he was?"

Will was so angry that he was shaking. He began pointing at the house, at Elliot, and anything else around him as if he couldn't control his movements.

"He was walkin' the woods looking for critters," he fired back. "There's no law against huntin'!"

"There are laws against trespassing, which was exactly what he was doing." Nash had managed to put himself between Elliot and Will. The gun barrel remained trained on the Loreau brothers. "Your father attacked an unarmed man with the intent to kill. What happened to him is just what he deserved. Now, get off this property before they have to take you off in a body bag. If I ever see you here again, I'm going to assume you're hostile and shoot to kill. And if I ever see you near this woman and her children again, in any way, shape or form, you'll wish you were dead because I will make your life a living hell. Do you understand me?"

Will foamed and grumbled, backing away when his brothers began to pull at him. It was a battle they couldn't win and they knew it. Nash Aury was as tough as they came and not even the foolish Loreau brothers were stupid enough to tangle with him. Still, Will couldn't let it go. Even as he was walking away, he was shouting.

"This ain't the end, Sheriff," he yelled. "We'll get our justice. Just y'all wait!"

His brothers were yanking at him and they disappeared back into the heavy, green bramble. They faded off, the sounds of their voices eventually disappearing, before Nash turned to Elliot.

"Are you all right?" he asked.

She looked at him with such anguish in her features that the mere expression impacted him. Rolling her eyes, she couldn't answer, but he could see the tears coming. She bolted towards the house without a word, skipping up onto the porch and into the kitchen door as Alec and Penelope followed. Nash sighed heavily when he heard the door slam, lowering the gun and turning to his brother.

"I figured they'd start prowling around here soon enough," he said, looking at Beau from head to toe. "Good thing I came when I did. They didn't hurt you, did they?"

Beau shook his head. "It didn't come to that," he said. "But they tried to touch Ellie. I was about to make a chivalrous stand when you showed up. Thank God you showed up."

Nash nodded faintly. Then, he shook his head, his gaze moving out over the surroundings.

"Damn," he hissed. "That poor woman. She was hoping to start a new life out here in the bayou and it's all gone from bad to worse."

"What do we do about the Loreaus?" Beau asked. "You know they're not going to give up. They think they've been wronged and that Ellie is responsible."

Nash wriggled his eyebrows and extended the gun to his brother. "Keep this with you for now," he said. "I'm going to go inside and see if I can calm her down."

He turned for the house but a word from his brother stopped him. "Nash?" the man called quietly.

Nash stopped and turned to look at him. "What?"

The warm, humorous glimmer was back in Beau's eyes. "I like her."

"Who?"

"Ellie."

Nash fought off a grin. "So do I."

Nash turned for the house, fighting off the smile that sweet thoughts of Elliot provoked. By the time he entered the house, he found it quiet and still. Uncasing his cell phone, he made a call to the private security company as he wandered from the kitchen into the big central hall. The twenty-four hour security patrols turned into armed security patrols. He also made a call to dispatch for the off-duty deputy list. Hanging up the phone, he headed for the bright lights of the double parlor.

He found Penelope and Alec in the parlor, spread out over the couches that were still huddled in the middle of the room because most of the boxes had yet to be unpacked. It still looked like a war zone. Alec was on his electronic tablet and Penelope was reading a book. They both looked up when Nash entered the room.

"Y'all okay?" Nash asked with some gentleness.

The kids nodded. "We're fine," Alec said. "Mom wouldn't let us get close to those dudes. She took 'em on herself. Hey, did you know there are alligators in the backyard?"

Nash gave him a half-grin. "I sure do," he said. "They used to scare the dog-water out of me when I was a kid."

Alec and Penelope burst out laughing. "What's dog-water?" Penelope wanted to know.

Nash chuckled. "I guess it's kind of like pee," he said, looking around the room. "Where's your mother?"

Penelope pointed to the ceiling. "She went upstairs. She's pretty upset."

"Do you mind if I go up and talk to her?"

Alec was already refocused on his tablet and Penelope shook her head. "Go ahead," she said.

Nash flashed them an appreciative smile and headed back

toward the central staircase. As he mounted the bottom step, he heard someone call his name. Pausing, he saw Penelope approaching in the dim light. He smiled at the girl as she came upon him.

Penelope's big, blue eyes focused intently on him and she cocked her head. "Can I ask you something?"

"Sure."

"Do you have a thing for my mom?"

Nash was a little taken aback at the blunt question. He had told Elliot that he would let her take the lead when it came to her children, but the fact was that her children were intelligent adults. Nash wasn't going to treat them like a couple of third graders that needed to be lied to in order to protect them.

Still, he was careful in his reply because he didn't want to damage the budding relationship he had with the family. It wasn't just Elliot he was worried about; he was worried about all of them.

"Would you have a problem with it if I did?" he countered.

Penelope leaned against the stair banister in thought. "No," she said honestly. "I think it's great. She's been really lonely without my dad and I think you're a really nice guy. You obviously care about her."

He fought off a smile, averting his eyes. "Is it that apparent?"

Penelope smiled faintly. "To me it is, but I notice that kind of thing."

"What about Alec?"

Penelope wriggled her eyebrows. "He doesn't notice stuff like this until it hits him in the face. He's really protective of my mom so I'm not sure how he's going to react if he knows you're in love with her."

Nash's eyebrows lifted in surprise. "In *love* with her?

Penelope grinned. "Yes," she snickered softly. "Don't you even know that yet?"

Nash tried not to look or feel stupid. "I... I guess I haven't really thought about it."

Penelope pushed herself off the banister, heading back towards the front parlor. "You should," she said as she walked away. "It's true."

Nash stood there on the step, stunned with the conversation. He thought about his feelings for Elliot, the utter and complete joy he felt in everything about her, and it began to occur to him that Penelope was right. The young woman had hardly spent any time around Nash and Elliot, but even she could see the feelings that were developing between the pair. They were strong and pure and radiant. Penelope was absolutely right; he was in love with her mother.

Mounting the stairs, he made his way to the master bedroom in the front of the house. The door was cracked open and a soft, golden glow emitted from the room. The second floor was mostly dark without it. He knocked on the door quietly.

"Hello?" he called softly.

"Come on in," came the reply.

He pushed the door open to find Elliot lying on her bed, flat on her back, with her arms up over her face. The room was illuminated by a half-dozen candles, all burning brightly because there was no electricity to the room. It gave it a rather romantic and haunting feel. Nash made his way over to the bed.

"Hey," he said gently. "Are you all right?"

The arms came off her face and she gazed up at him with moist eyes. "I'm trying not to cry again," she admitted.

He smiled sadly and sat carefully on the edge of the bed. His hand found one of hers and he brought it to his lips, kissing it tenderly.

"You are one tough lady," he complimented. "Everything about you is so strong and poised. I'm amazed every time I see you."

She rolled onto her side as he kissed her hand, pushed up against his right thigh. "Were those the guys you warned me about?"

He nodded. "Yes."

"They said it was their dad that was killed. Did you know that?"

He couldn't lie to her. "I did."

"Were you going to tell me?"

He sighed and lowered her hand from his mouth. "Eventually," he said. "I was trying to think of an easy way to break the news to you. I wasn't trying to keep it from you, but you've had enough on your mind. That was one more worry you didn't need, at least not right away."

She thought on that a moment, realizing she believed him. Nash was a man of integrity and she didn't think that lying was in his nature. She squeezed his hand.

"I think I'm going to put an electrified fence around the place, you know, like a prison," she teased. "When those guys come the next time, *zap!*"

He laughed loudly. "It might not be a bad idea," he said. "Knowing that I'm on to them, however, should keep them away, at least for now. They may be idiots but they're not stupid. They won't mess with me."

Her smile faded as she caressed his big finger. "That was pretty impressive discharging that shotgun to scare them off," she said. "If you did that in California, they'd have the media all over you for recklessly threatening innocent people."

He snorted. "That's because the police in California are all afraid of their own shadow," he said. "They're afraid to move because someone might be filming it and put it up on YouTube. Down here, things are a little different."

She shrugged. "I believe it," she said, gazing up into his handsome face as her thoughts turned towards the house, the situation at hand. "So now what?"

He looked around the room. "Now, we finish restoring Purgatory."

She squeezed his hand again. "And that's another thing," she said. "Why didn't you tell me that your brother had already started the restoration? There were a hundred guys here this morning working on the house."

He shrugged. "We need to make this house livable again and

that's going to take a lot of work," he replied. "I told Beau to do what he needed to do to get it done as fast as possible."

She gazed up at him steadily. "Did you stop to think that this isn't your house anymore? What if that's not what I wanted?"

He scratched at his neck. "Did I overstep myself? I wasn't doing it intentionally if I did. I was just trying to help you make this place habitable. You said yourself that you didn't realize how much work it needed and since I sold you the house, I feel somewhat responsible for that."

She softened up. "What's this about you and Beau paying the labor?"

"It's the least we can do. Besides, Beau has some plans about that."

"I know, he told me." She put her hand on his thigh. "Seriously, you're doing way too much. I don't even know what to say."

"Don't say anything. Just let me help."

She knew he meant well. She'd never thought anything else. Since the moment she'd met the man, he'd been kind and thoughtful and considerate. He had treated her as if she were the most important thing in the world. Reaching up, she wound her arms around his neck and slanted her lips softly over his. Nash reacted instantly, wrapping his big arms around her and lowering her back down to the bed.

The soft, gentle kiss turned into something very hot and passionate very quickly. Nash had one arm wrapped tightly around her while the other roamed her torso, feeling the shape of her body and the texture of her hair. It was wildly intoxicating and before he realized it, his hand had snaked under her t-shirt and was now caressed her soft, flat belly. The feel of her tender skin drove him wild.

Somehow, he ended up on the bed next to her, his Sam Browne belt making it very awkward to get close to her, but he really didn't care. The hand on her belly slithered around to her back and he stroked the skin of her naked back, swearing he'd never touched anything so sweet in his entire life.

His mouth left her lips, trailing across her cheek and down her neck. He suckled on the tender flesh of her shoulder, her collarbone, dragging his lips up her neck again and to her jaw line. Then he moved over to her mouth again, suckling her until her lips were red and raw.

"Mom?"

The sound of a voice pierced their haze of desire. Nash bolted up from the mattress before he even realized he had done it. When next he was aware, he was standing at the end of the bed, several feet away from a woman that, seconds before, he had been happily ravaging.

Penelope knocked on the door, shoving it open to see that Nash was a proper distance away and that her mother was lying on the bed, looking rather wide-eyed. Alec was right behind his sister, pushing the door open wide.

"We're hungry," Penelope said. "Can we go get something to eat?"

"Sure," Elliot was trying not to sound breathless as she sat up in bed. "Did you and your brother decide where you wanted to go?"

"Anything but McDonalds," Penelope said with disgust.

"There's a good restaurant down the street called Mama's," Nash offered.

"Or we could go to the market and buy fresh stuff and plug the vegetable steamer into the outlet in the living room," Penelope suggested. "We could eat salads and veggies."

Alec made a face. "I want real food." He pointed at Nash. "So does the Sheriff. We vote for alligator ribs."

Nash grinned and shook his head, getting himself sucked into a family debate. He reached into his pocket and pulled out his wallet, extracting two twenty-dollar bills and extending the money to Alec.

"Go get yourself something to eat and bring back something for your mother, me and Beau," he told them. "Go out of the driveway and take a right and you'll run straight into Mama's, but if you don't want that, keep going and you'll run into several restaurants down by the highway."

"Cool, dude," Alec grinned at the money. "Thanks!"

"Can I go to the market, too?" Penelope wanted to know. "There isn't any food in this house at all."

Before Elliot could answer, Nash pulled out another sixty dollars from his wallet and handed it to Penelope.

"There's a big market right next to Mama's, you can't miss it," he told her. "While you're there, buy a Styrofoam cooler and some ice so you can keep milk in it. Get whatever sixty bucks will buy you."

Penelope grinned broadly. "Thanks!" she said, turning to push Alec out of the door. "Come on, let's go."

"Wait," Alec wouldn't be pushed away from a man giving out money so easily. "I need a car, dude. Can you spare a few thousand dollars from your magic wallet?"

Nash grinned as Penelope shoved her brother out of the door. He could hear them bickering all the way down the hall and down the stairs. When the voices faded away, he turned to Elliot, still sitting on the bed. She was looking at him reproachfully.

"Now you've done it," she shook her head at him. "Now that they know you'll give them money, it's like feeding a cat. You'll never get rid of them."

He laughed softly and unhooked his big police belt with the flashlight and other implements on it, laying it on the nearest box.

"I don't mind," he said. "They're good kids."

She watched him unbutton the top of his uniform shirt. "You really didn't have to do that," she admonished.

He nodded, sitting on the bed beside her. "Yes, I did."

"Why?"

He grinned at her, a very sexy gesture that sent her heart leaping. Then he leaned forward on one big arm, reaching up to push a stray piece of hair from her face.

"Because we now have at least an hour to ourselves with no

interruptions," he confessed. "I wonder what we can do with that time."

She gave him such a knowing look that he started to laugh. Shifting on the bed, Elliot wrapped her arms around his neck and pulled him down on top of her. Nash's mouth was on hers, instantly. Now, they intended to finish what they started.

Nash could feel her all wrapped up around him, her sexy little body clinging to him. His passion, his lust, roared to life and the hand that had only danced around her belly and back now snaked beneath her shirt, moving for her breasts.

Elliot didn't wait for him; she unhooked her bra and her breasts sprang free just as his hand closed in over her left breast. She groaned softly as his hand came into contact with her naked flesh. It had been so long since she'd last felt a man against her that her natural instincts at self-protection completely vanished. She wanted Nash as badly as he wanted her.

The t-shirt came off and so did the bra between heated kisses. Nash bolted up from the bed and slammed shut the door that the kids had left open, returning to Elliot before she barely had time to miss him. As their lips collided in heated passion, Elliot stripped Nash of his uniform shirt, which ended up in a heap on the floor. His undershirt was next, and their naked flesh came together in a rush of excitement.

Nash had a magnificent chest, broad and leanly muscular. Elliot dragged her mouth across his nipples, listening to him hiss with the wild pleasure of it. They couldn't seem to get enough of each other, kissing so ferociously that Elliot came away with a bleeding mouth when Nash drove his teeth into her soft upper lip. She pushed him down on the bed, feasting on his beautiful chest, as her hands moved to unfasten his belt buckle.

"Hello?" came a faint voice. "Nash, where are you?"

Elliot froze, her big eyes coming up to meet his. Nash stared at her, dazed to the point of incoherency, but he managed to collect his wits.

"It's Beau," he whispered huskily.

Elliot climbed off of him and quickly went in search of her bra and shirt while Nash went to the bedroom door and cracked it open.

"Up here," he yelled back. "Stay there. I'll be right down."

He turned around in time to see Elliot pulling her shirt over her head. Their eyes met and, for a moment, no one spoke. What they had experienced went beyond words and they both knew that, somehow, their lives would be forever changed because of it. Finally, Elliot reached down and picked up his shirts.

"Here," she whispered as she went to him, handing him the undershirt first.

Nash took it in silence, pulling it over his head and quickly pulling on his uniform shirt, buttoning it with fast fingers. Elliot smoothed her ponytail, watching him tuck his shirt in, noticing his significant arousal as it strained against his slacks. She was genuinely disappointed that she hadn't had the opportunity to experience it.

When Nash finished tucking his shirt in, he suddenly cupped her face between his two big hands and kissed her deeply. Elliot turned herself over to the kiss completely, a willing victim to his seeking mouth. The kiss was strong and full of emotion, so much so that they were both caught up in the wild maelstrom of hormones and feeling.

"I love you," he whispered.

And then he was gone, disappearing from the bedroom and down the hall. Elliot simply stood there, shocked to the bone, listening to the distant exchange between Nash and Beau downstairs.

Even as she stood there, she couldn't really grasp what he had just said... *I love you*... in the sweetest whisper she could have ever imagined. Could it possibly be true or was it the heat of passion talking?

She wondered. One thing was for certain; she was pretty sure she was falling in love with him, too.

———

Elliot and Nash never had a chance to be alone again that night. Beau was around, and then Penelope and Alec returned with ribs and groceries, so Elliot spent her time packing away perishables into two cheap coolers that the kids had bought. But at least now they had some groceries and the old house was starting to feel more like a home.

After the kids passed out from sheer exhaustion and too much food, Elliot, Nash and Beau sat up until midnight, talking quietly in the big, double parlors about the restoration of the house. Nash wouldn't leave until the armed security patrol arrived, which was just after midnight. One was a K-9 unit.

Elliot stayed on the porch as Nash and Beau talked to the three security guards and explained the situation. Ken Havereau showed up a short time later and Nash posted the man at the driveway with a wide view of the road. Anyone crossing over the road to get on to Elliot's property would be spotted immediately.

As the security guards and the deputy went to their posts, Nash faced Elliot on the porch. The only light was from the bright-white bulb in the front parlor, barely illuminating beyond the house.

Elliot smiled at him as he approached and he returned the gesture. She stood up on the porch while he stood on the driveway, a few steps down, gazing up into her exquisite face.

"You'll be fine tonight," he told her, his voice soft. "I'll swing by first thing in the morning to check on you before I go to work."

Elliot nodded. There was so much emotion roiling in her chest that she was having difficulty focusing. She couldn't seem to form a coherent sentence so she finally broke down in soft laughter.

"I just can't find the words to express what this all means to me," she replied, her eyes glittering. "Or what you mean to me. I'm just speechless with your thoughtfulness and generosity."

He grinned, took the steps up to the porch, and kissed her on the cheek. "If I kiss you anywhere else, I'll never get out of here," he whispered.

She met his gaze, his face so close to hers. "It wouldn't bother me but I'm not going to ask you to stay. Not yet."

He sighed. "I feel like... like I belong here with you, like we belong together. I can't explain it any better than that. I don't want to leave you but propriety says that I have to. I want to pick you up and carry you up the stairs into that torn-up bedroom and finish what we started tonight. I've never felt like this about anyone, Ellie, not ever. You're under my skin and I haven't even known you that long."

She could see how serious he was. "Did you mean what you said earlier when you left me in my bedroom?"

He knew exactly what she meant. The very same thought had been weighing heavily on him since he said it, words that just came out before he could stop them. But he knew that he didn't regret it in the least.

"Every word," he leaned forward and kissed her mouth sweetly. "I'll see you in the morning. You have my phone number if you need me."

He turned and walked down the steps, heading to his car across the dark, gravel driveway. He paused as he got into his car.

"Go inside and lock the door," he told her.

She waved at him and obeyed, going inside and shutting the enormous front door. She threw the old bolt, locking it up tight. Going into the double parlor, she looked out of the new glass window just in time to see Nash driving down the driveway. Truth was, she hadn't wanted him to leave, either. She had wanted him to stay with her, not because she was lustily hot for him, but because she just didn't want him to leave her. She didn't want to be without him, either. The comfort the man gave her, the pure joy, was indescribable.

Lighting a candle, she shut off the lamp and threw the double parlors into utter darkness. It was creepy but she was finding some comfort in the eeriness. This was her house and she was very quickly becoming a part of it and it a part of her. Maybe it was because the house was so entangled in Nash and his family, but whatever the reason, she felt very close to him here.

Making her way down the central hall to the great winding staircase, she could see flashlights through the ballroom windows, patrolling her property, and it made her feel extremely safe.

Sleep came easily that night and when she slept, it was with heated dreams of Nash.

EIGHT

THE NEXT SEVERAL days passed quickly and without incident. The army of contractors would begin every morning, promptly at sunrise, and then end every day around four in the afternoon. The scraping and hammering was Elliot's morning alarm clock and she barely had time to get up and go down to the double parlors to start the coffeemaker in the only working outlet before Nash appeared.

He was always there, bringing her and the kids a box of donuts or bagels or egg sandwiches. He'd already gone twice that week to the little restaurant that overlooked the bayou and come back with scrambled eggs and cheese, enough to make Alec and Penelope very happy people. The kids were starting to get fat and lazy with Nash catering to them.

He would stay with Elliot for about an hour, sipping coffee and speaking about a wide variety of subjects as the sun rose. Then he would collect his gear, kiss her if the kids weren't around, and go off to work. Elliot thought it was just about as heavenly as it could be because the more she got to know him, the more wonderful she thought he was.

More and more, they were settling into an oddly domestic routine as the restoration of Purgatory went on around them. It was the new life that Elliot had hoped for on a level she could have never imagined.

On Wednesday night of that first sweet and blissful week, Nash had taken Elliot to a Rotary Club mixer with him so he could introduce her to the main players in the town. He took great pride in introducing her to people he considered his friends, nice couples who were very sweet and eager to know her and, of course, Monty and his wife were there. Nash begrudgingly introduced her to the lascivious mayor and his ignorant wife.

Monty had done everything but openly drool on her, so very pleased to meet the newest resident of their town. Nash had stood right by her side, stepping in between Elliot and Monty when the eager mayor got too close.

It had been a wonderful evening and Elliot had a wonderful time, but it was very clear to everyone at that mixer that Nash and the new owner of Purgatory were an item. After that night, the gossip began to fly fast and hard.

Nash had heard bits and pieces of it since the mixer and, truth be told, he didn't much care. In fact, he was glad. He felt puffed up like a proud peacock, happier than he had ever been in his life. Even his deputies had started hearing the rumors and jokes and good-natured jibes flew around the office. Someone even found a book-jacket picture of Elliot online and blew it up into a poster, a gorgeous shot of Elliot looking very sweet and very sexy.

At Friday morning's briefing, Nash stepped into the conference room to find the giant poster on the wall with the words "Mrs. Nash Aury" written in black marker across the bottom. He had just stood there and laughed as his commanders roared at the joke. Nash's only comment was that they were all jealous, to which the group heartily agreed.

Nash got off of work early on Friday afternoon, eager to spend the weekend with Elliot. He wanted to take her and the kids down to New Orleans and as he drove Highway 10 south, his mind was on the luscious little blond with the sweet personality. He was so enamored with her that he couldn't put it into words, so in love with the woman that he kept thinking he was dreaming. He never imagined something like this would ever happen to him.

The sun was starting to set as he pulled down the long driveway to Purgatory. He could see where the contractors were beginning to lay the forming for the paved driveway, careful not to drive over the wood forms as he pulled up in front of the house. All of the trucks were gone, including his brother's, as Beau headed back home for the weekend.

Climbing out of the car, Nash's gaze drifted over the enormous structure, noticing that they were already beginning to paint some of the exterior. Plaster had been repaired and the peeling, crumbling entablature was nearly finished being repaired and reinforced.

The army of workers his brother had on the house were doing their jobs in record time and the entire place was really starting to come together. As he slammed his car door and headed for the house, Penelope ran up the driveway behind him and gave him a playful shove.

"Hey," he shouted weakly, pretending to tip over. "Watch where you're going."

Penelope had been out jogging. Sweaty and smiley, she ran backwards as she headed for the house. "You're too slow, old man," she teased. "Did you bring any food?"

He lifted his hands in an offended gesture. "Is that all I'm good for?"

Penelope laughed, slowing down as she reached the steps. "I wouldn't know," she said. "I'd have to ask my mother that question."

It was a rather bawdy comment and Nash lifted an eyebrow at her as she sat down on the big, wide steps of the porch and began untying her running shoes.

"Your mother is too much of a lady to discuss such things," he said quietly. "Besides, it's none of your business."

She looked up at him, still out of breath, and laughed. "I wouldn't want to know, anyway," she said. "What you two do is your business. But I will tell you this; I don't think I've ever seen my mom so happy. I want to thank you for that."

He smiled modestly. "It goes both ways," he said. "She's a wonderful woman."

Penelope untied both shoes and exhaled sharply, trying to catch her breath. "I know," she said. "I think she's kind of great, too."

Nash lowered himself down onto the step beside her, his big leather Sam Browne belt creaking and groaning as he sat.

"I was thinking of taking y'all down to New Orleans this weekend," he said. "Would you like that?"

Penelope looked at him with surprise. "Really?" she said gleefully. "I'd love it!"

He smiled at her. "Good," he replied. "Do you think your mother will...?"

He was cut off when the front door suddenly flew open and Elliot appeared. Dressed in Capri-cut jeans, a pretty white blouse and white sneakers, she ran at Nash before he could stand up from the steps and grabbed him by the hand.

"Come on!" she said excitedly. "I've been waiting for you all day. You have to see them!"

Grinning, he let her yank him up the stairs. "Hi to you, too," he quipped.

She smiled at him as she practically dragged him across the porch. "Hi," she said quickly. "Hurry up. I want you to see them!"

He laughed at her, waiting until Penelope had gone into the house before pulling Elliot to a stop and whipping her into his arms. He kissed her deeply, unable to restrain himself, loving the feel of her hands on his face as he sucked her lips.

"I've missed you," he murmured.

Elliot closed her eyes as he tasted her. "I've missed you, too," she whispered.

He kissed both cheeks and the tip of her nose before quickly letting her go, looking around to make sure no one had seen them. Elliot put her hands on his hips, pursing her lips irritably.

"Why do you do that every time?" she wanted to know.

"Do what?"

"Kiss me like you mean it and then let me go so fast that I nearly fall over," she lifted her eyebrows at him. "Are you ashamed of me?"

He snorted at her. "Are you crazy?" he exclaimed. "I just don't want the kids to see us."

She shook her head at him. "They've already figured it out," she took his hand again and pulled him towards the door. "At least, Penny has. I don't know about Alec."

He pulled her to a halt before she could go through the door. His features were suddenly very serious.

"Come on," he took her hand and tucked it into the crook of his elbow. "Take a walk with me."

"But...," she was pointing inside the house. "I want to show you something."

"It can wait a minute."

With a shrug, she followed him around the porch that encircled the entire house. Carpenters had been repairing the porch and they walked on reinforced board as they circled the north side of the house. Elliot snuggled up to him and he held the hand that was lodged in his elbow.

"I'd like to take you and the kids to New Orleans this weekend," he said quietly. "What do you think about that?"

She looked up at him, surprised. "All of us?"

"Sure. Why not?"

She shrugged. "Oh, I don't know," she looked down at her feet as they walked along the new wood. "Seems like a lot of money for you to spend."

"No, it's not."

"It seems kind of crowded."

"Come again?"

She looked up at him, grinning. "What if I want to be the only one that goes with you?"

The corners of his mouth tugged with a smile. "What are you going to do with your kids?"

She laughed. "It's not like they're little children anymore," she said. "They can spend a day or two alone. They won't burn the house down."

"Are you sure?"

"I am."

He toyed with her fingers. "Well, then we may have a bit of a problem," he said as they rounded the house and ended up over-looking the backyard. "I already asked Penny if she and Alec would like to go. She seemed pretty excited about it."

Elliot shrugged. "She'll get over it. We'll take her another time."

He stopped and faced her, watching the setting sun play off her delicate features. There seemed to be much on his mind.

"It seems to me that you're becoming a little bolder with the courting you and I are doing," he said. "Am I misunderstanding you?"

She met his gaze. "No," she said honestly. "Nash, I just can't explain what I feel for you. It's like... like I've known you all of my life, like you're already a part of me. I was so scared in the beginning to let myself feel something for you but I just can't help myself. I'm crazy about you and I don't care who knows it."

His smile grew. "I am so proud to be by your side," he whispered. "You can't even imagine how proud and humbled I am."

She moved to him, putting her hands on his face as he wrapped her up in his big arms. As the sun dipped down over the bayou, they held each other, drawing strength and life and love from one another.

"You told me you loved me five days ago," she whispered. "I never told you I loved you in return. I do, you know. You're such an amazing man."

He pulled her against him, hugging her tightly, feeling something he'd never felt before in his life. It almost brought tears to his eyes. "God, I've been waiting all my life to hear that from you," he admitted. "I love you so much."

Elliot clung to him. Then, her body began to shake. It took him a moment to realize she was sobbing. Shocked, he pulled back to look at her with great concern.

"What's wrong, darlin'?" he asked with heavy emotion. "Why are you crying?"

She was smiling with tears streaming down her face. "I don't know," she laughed. "I just am. I'm just so happy. Nash, I never thought I'd be happy ever again. You've changed my life."

He kissed her, hard, not caring if the kids were watching them or not. In fact, he was still kissing her when Alec and Penelope suddenly burst from the kitchen door and out to the lawn where the fireflies were now starting to come alive. They didn't even notice the two adults in an amorous embrace as they tried to catch the bugs with a homemade butterfly net.

Nash stopped kissing Elliot long enough to watch Alec trip over his own feet as he chased some bugs around the yard. Nash and Elliot laughed, still locked in a tight embrace, as Alec went down in the thick grass. Penelope leapt over her brother as he struggled up from the ground.

"Stupid bugs," Alec growled until he realized they were also in the grass and he began scooping them up. He sat up with a bunch of fireflies in his hands. "Hey, look at these!"

Elliot shook her head at her boy. Then she looked up at Nash. "You wouldn't have guessed that he graduated as valedictorian from high school," she commented. "He's smarter than all of us combined but you'd never know it sometimes."

"Mom!" Penelope suddenly screamed, pointing at the water's edge. "Alligators!"

Elliot and Nash came off the porch, heading towards the pointing girl. "Just stay back," Nash said calmly. "They won't hurt you if you stay clear of them."

Penelope was jumping up and down, half from fear and half from excitement. She went to hide behind her mother when Elliot approached, but Alec moved up beside Nash so the men could view the fanged creatures. They watched two of the beasts, small ones, as they lay leisurely upon the shore. Nash spoke to Elliot with his gaze still on the alligators.

"You're going to want to think about putting a fence up to keep them from going deeper into the yard," he told her. "There was a time when I was kid that they would get up under the porch. You don't want that happening."

Speaking of the porch reminded Elliot of what she very badly wanted him to see inside the house. Fireflies and passionate kisses had distracted her. She went over to Nash and took his hand one more time.

"Come in the house," she told him. "I really want to show you something."

"Wait a minute," Alec turned to them, his gaze oddly serious. It wasn't often he was serious, but suddenly, he looked quite grown up. "Mom, you go in the house. Penny and I want to talk to Nash for a minute."

Elliot tried not to show her concern or surprise. "What about?"

Alec waved his hand in the direction of the house. "Just... go inside. Please?"

Elliot lifted her eyebrows, her gaze moving between Nash's somewhat amused expression and her son's serious face. After a moment, she shrugged. "Okay," she chuckled, letting go of Nash's hand and walking backwards towards the house. "I'll just... go on inside...."

Penelope was grinning at her mother, which told Elliot that whatever the subject matter, it wasn't all bad. She had a feeling what it was about and she figured that she'd let Nash handle it. This was, after all, between Nash and the kids for the most part. He had to earn their trust and with things picking up between them, perhaps now was a good time. Hopping up onto the porch, she disappeared into the house.

When Elliot was gone, Nash turned to Alec. "What can I do for you?" he asked.

Alec faced the man that was exactly as tall as he was. His expression went from serious to uncertain and then back to serious again.

"Look," he began, as if he didn't know quite where to start. "I know about you and mom and I just want to say that I'm okay with it. I didn't think I would be, but I am. You have to understand that my mom and I are really close. She's always been there for me, no matter what, and I grew up thinking I was pretty lucky to have such a cool mom. When my dad died, it was, like, the worst thing you can imagine. You don't even know what my mom went through. She could barely go to his funeral because she was so devastated. My friends and I spent months spending every single second of the day with her so she was never alone. I couldn't stand to see my mom so upset. It was killing me."

By this time, Nash was listening seriously, hearing the shattered young man who had lost his father, the brave young man who was trying so hard to take care of his mother. His heart ached for Alec, but he was also extremely impressed by the young man's strength of character. That kind of devotion and compassion was rare. But he didn't say anything because he could tell that Alec wasn't finished. As he watched, Alec took a deep breath and ran his hands through his cropped blond hair in a nervous gesture.

"I guess my point is this," he continued. "I should have known that you and my mom were... well, you know, that you guys were hot for each other, but it just never occurred to me until Penny said something. Then I noticed. I watched you two together, the way you look at each other and the way you treat her. You're nice to her and you care about her. My dad treated her really well, too. He said she was the most precious thing in the world to him next to me and Penny. All I have to say is that I hope you're not playing with her, because if you are, I swear to God I'll kill you."

Nash sighed faintly, seeing how deadly serious Alec was. But more than that, it was as if he were begging Nash not to hurt his mother. The threat touched Nash deeply.

"When I look at your mom, I see an angel," Nash explained. "I see the most beautiful woman I have ever seen and I would never, ever, play with her or treat her poorly. She deserves to be put on a pedestal and worshipped and if I could get away with doing it, I would. I don't want to hurt your mom, Alec. I love her very much. I promise I will do everything in my power to make her very happy, always."

Alec seemed to visibly relax, looking at Penelope for the first time and seeing her encouraging expression. But he didn't really have anything more to say so Penelope stepped forward.

"We had to say this, Sheriff," she said. "I hope you understand. We love our mom and she's been through a lot. We just want to see her happy and I think you make her very happy."

Nash smiled. "I'm doing my best."

"It seems to be working."

They stood there a moment in awkward silence, Alec and Penelope fidgeting while Nash just stood and watched them. They were such decent young people and he felt very fortunate to know them.

Finally, Nash walked over to the pair and put his arms around them just because they looked like they needed it. The kids hugged him back, fiercely, before letting him go. Alec looked a little embarrassed about his display of emotion, breaking into a grin when Nash smacked him affectionately on the side of the head.

"Does this mean you're going to be our stepdad?" Alec asked.

Nash was caught off guard by the question. He gave an embarrassed little laugh. "I... I don't know. I haven't asked her yet."

"Take her to New Orleans this weekend and propose. She'd like that."

Nash's eyebrows lifted in surprise until he looked at Penelope and saw that she was giggling. He started laughing just because she was.

"Give me time," he put up is hands as if to slow everything down. "I've only known her a week."

"How long did it take you to know you loved her?"

"Good point."

Alec grinned. "I'll forget we had this conversation if you break out your magic wallet and give us twenty bucks for alligator ribs."

Nash rolled his eyes but dutifully pulled out his wallet, handing over two twenty dollar bills. "That's not because you blackmailed me," he told him. "That's because I want to get you kids out of the house. I need to talk to your mother."

Alec started laughing. "Forty dollars is only good for an hour. Give us sixty and we won't come back for at least three."

Nash snorted, shaking his head at the kid. "Get out of here before I throw you to the alligators over there," he threatened.

Penelope snatched the money from her brother and took off running, screaming when he went in hot pursuit. Nash listened to the distant screaming, grinning all the way back to the house. Entering through the kitchen door, he realized that there were appliances installed. He guessed that was what Elliot had been trying so hard to show him. He took a good look at the new refrigerator and stove, letting out a long whistle of appreciation. They were nice, new and hooked in.

"Ellie?" he called.

"In here," came the response.

He followed the sound of her voice, finding her in the double parlors digging through a box. Without a word, he bent over and scooped her into his arms. Elliot whooped with surprise as he carried her out into the central hall, heading for the sweeping spiral stairs.

"What are you doing?" she asked, arms wrapped around his neck.

Nash didn't look at her as he took the stairs. "Something I have permission to do."

"Permission from whom?" she asked curiously. "And what are we doing?"

He reached the top of the stairs and carried her towards her bedroom.

"Your son and daughter have given me their blessing," he said, finally looking at her as they reached the bedroom. "I gave them forty bucks to get lost for a while. They said that was okay.

Elliot looked at him in shock, then surprise, then giddy pleasure. "Really?"

"Really."

He reached her bed and carefully lowered her onto the mattress. Elliot watched as he pulled off his Sam Browne and laid it across a chair. Then he began to unbutton the top of his shirt.

"Are you doing what I think you're doing?" she asked, a twinkle in her eye.

He looked at her, on the fourth button. "What do you think I'm doing?"

She giggled. "Is that the best you can do to get me into bed?" she wanted to know. "Seriously, Nash? Is this your best come-on?"

He pulled his shirt off, followed by the undershirt. Elliot's humor faded when she gazed at his sexy chest again, feeling her cheeks grow warm. Suddenly, he collapsed on top of her, cuddling her up against him as he gazed down into her lovely face from the dominant position. He was on top of her and loving every minute of it.

"No," he whispered. "My best come-on is to take you to New Orleans for a romantic weekend of fine dining, shopping, and anything else you want to do. I'm going to tell you twenty times a day how beautiful you are and how much I love you, and how much I'm looking forward to the rest of my life because, God willing, I'll be spending it with you. I love you and I don't ever want to be without you, Ellie. I mean it."

Elliot gazed up into his handsome face, feeling more emotion than she could adequately express. Everything seemed to be happening so fast, but in retrospect, nothing had ever seemed so right. Nash was everything she could have hoped for.

She eventually squirmed out from under him and Nash reluctantly rolled off of her, watching her as she stood up and quietly closed the bedroom door. The room was fairly dark as the setting sun dipped below the horizon and she went to the table next to her bed that had several candles on it, lighting only one of them.

Nash watched her curiously because she seemed thoughtful and subdued. He was coming to wonder if his intimation of a marriage proposal hadn't been too much, too soon, as she went into the bathroom and he could hear her banging around. He lay back on the bed, not saying a word, listening to her move around in the bathroom and wondering with increasing concern if he had said too much. He wasn't prepared for what came next.

With the shadows of the room and only the faint glow of a small candle to illuminate her, Elliot emerged from the bathroom completely naked. Her long blond hair was out of its ponytail, draping sensually over her shoulders and back.

Startled, but in a good way, Nash sat up in bed as she approached. He couldn't help but look at her, her perfect breasts, flat belly and deliciously flaring hips. She was absolutely spectacular. As he sat up, she positioned herself between his legs. Cupping his face between her hands, she leaned forward and gently kissed his mouth.

"I'm not on birth control and I don't have any condoms," she whispered. "I don't have any sexually transmitted diseases and I haven't had sex with anyone since Rob died. I'm just letting you know now in case things get out of control."

Nash wrapped his arms around her, flipping her over onto the bed. "They're already out of control," he whispered against her mouth. "I love you, Ellie."

"I love you, too," she murmured.

He closed down over her and it was only a matter of time before his pants came off. In the faint glow of the single golden candle, he lay down next to her, pulling the sheet up over them both and studying her beauty, just for a moment.

Then his hands began to move, touching her everywhere, feeling the texture of her skin before he would smell it and then taste it. Her nipples drew his lust and he suckled her tenderly, listening to her soft pants of pleasure.

Nash took his time with her, at least at first, but as their lust built, so did the power of his touch. Soon enough, he had Elliot panting beneath him, her legs wrapped around his hips and their bodies fused in the primal mating ritual.

He thrust into her tight body repeatedly, feeling more pleasure than he ever imagined possible as her sensual body responded as if she were made for him alone. He took her once on her back, stretched up over her, and then flipped her over and took her a second time as she lay on her belly.

He was able to withdraw in time for his first climax but not in time for his second. When he realized he has spilled himself inside of her, he didn't miss a stroke because there was no use in pulling out after the deed was done. Elliot didn't say a word. In fact, when he came deep inside of her, she had two very powerful orgasms, one after the other, the cries of which were drowned out in the pillow.

Nash lay on top of her, spent, his hands stroking every inch of flesh he could come into contact with and his lips on her neck and shoulders. When he tried to withdraw from her body, she had another series of orgasms that aroused him so much he ended up making love to her a third time, turning her over so he could watch her face as he loved her up. The feelings, the act itself, were pure magic.

Emotionally and physically exhausted, Elliot curled up against him when their passion had cooled and dozed heavily. Nash had his arms and legs wrapped around her, staring off into the dim light of the room and never feeling as close to anyone as he did to her at this moment.

He stroked her back gently as she dozed, his touch conveying more than his words ever could. He had no idea how long they lay there, wrapped in each other's arms in a world of utter contentment, when he heard a car pull up the driveway.

Glancing at his watch, he noticed that the kids had stayed away nearly three hours. Grinning to himself, he kissed Elliot on her cheeks and forehead until she stirred awake.

"What time is it?" she asked sleepily.

He kissed her mouth. "Almost nine. Penny and Alec are back."

She blinked the grogginess from her eyes as Nash sat up and pulled her up with him.

"I should probably get dressed," she yawned.

"So should I," he said, climbing out of bed and collecting his boxer-briefs from the floor.

They could hear the car doors slamming outside. As Nash pulled his briefs on, Elliot stumbled back into her bathroom and found her clothes, pulling them on and emerging into the bedroom just as Nash was pulling on his uniform shirt. She pulled her hair back into a ponytail, fastened the rubber band, and handed Nash his Sam Browne just as he finished tucking in his shirt. He took it from her with a kiss.

"Do you really have to go?" she asked.

He paused as he put his belt around his waist and looked at her. "Do you want me to stay?"

"Only if you want to. I won't force you."

He resumed fastening his belt in a thoughtful manner. "I'd love to stay," he said, finishing with the belt and facing her. "But this is all happening so fast. I'm afraid that one of these days you're going to realize just how fast and put on the breaks."

She cocked her head at him, moving for the bedroom door and opening it to hear her children's voices downstairs.

"Do *you* think this has all happened too fast?" she asked quietly.

He shook his head. "I don't think there's a rulebook for this kind of thing. If it's right, you'll know it's right whether it's in a day or a year or ten years. I knew I loved you the day I met you. That feeling has only grown stronger. It's not me I'm worried about; it's you."

She smiled genuinely at him, hearing her children coming up the stairs and being distracted by the conversation to make sure there were no leftover signs of their sexual activities. Elliot tossed the covers up over the mattress just to be sure as Alec and Penelope neared her bedroom.

"Don't worry about me," she said. "I'm not going to put the brakes on."

"Are you sure?"

"I'm sure."

Someone knocked on the half-open door and Elliot pulled it all the way open to admit her children. Alex handed her a bag.

"We brought you guys some alligator ribs," he said.

"Thanks," Elliot peered into the bag. "Are they really alligator ribs?"

Alec snorted, looking between his mother and Nash. "No," he replied. "Just beef ribs. But they're huge."

Penelope came into the room and went to hug her mother, who handed the bag over to Nash so she could return the hug.

"I'm tired," Penelope announced, rubbing her eyes with a frown. "Alec made me go to some speakeasy and it was full of smoke. I stink like an ashtray now."

Alec was grinning. "It was a cool place," he insisted. "They had these dudes that played customized guitars and sounded like AC/DC."

"Where did you go?" Nash asked.

Alec shrugged. "It was called Mae's."

Nash wriggled his eyebrows. "That can be a rough place. You should probably avoid it in the future. There are lots of fights and stabbings there."

Elliot looked horrified. "You took your sister there?" she scolded Alec. "Get, both of you. Get to bed."

"I'm going to watch a movie," Alec announced.

"Fine," Elliot shooed them out of her room. "Just get to bed at a reasonable hour."

"Are you going to New Orleans tomorrow?" Penelope asked, yawning.

Elliot looked at Nash, who gazed back at her emotionlessly.

"Yes," she finally replied. "Will you guys be okay for a couple of days?"

"Only if the sheriff gives us hush money," Alec muttered as he crossed the hall to his room.

Nash scratched his head. "You've got quite a mercenary streak in you, Alec."

Elliot looked at Nash, arms crossed reprovingly. "I told you not to give him money," she scolded. "Now he's going to bleed you dry."

Nash lifted an eyebrow at the grinning young man across the hall. "Not if I bleed him first."

Alec laughed and disappeared into his room, shutting the door behind him. Penelope went into her own bedroom down the hall and they heard that door shut, also. Elliot turned to Nash, standing there with a bag of ribs in his hand.

"Hungry?" she nodded her head at the bag.

With a grin, Nash followed her down to the kitchen with the new stove and refrigerator. They stood over the stove, the only uncluttered flat surface in the room, ate ribs and drank soda, and had the most wonderful conversation imaginable.

Nash never made it home that night.

NINE

THE KIDS DIDN'T SAY a word when they woke up on Saturday morning and Nash was sitting outside with their mother, drinking coffee in jeans and a casual shirt and watching the sun rise over the bayou. For once, the man wasn't in uniform, especially on a Saturday morning. More than that, it was perfectly normal for him to be at the house when they woke up. They had gotten used to it, like he was one of the fixtures. But what wasn't normal was the massive German Shepherd that Nash had brought with him.

Alec was the first to spy the dog and he raced out onto the porch only to be confronted by a curious, black-masked dog. For all of Wolfgang's tremendous size and breeding, he was really just a big lapdog and he took to Alec immediately. Alec sat down on the scratchy porch board and let the dog lick all over his face.

"He's awesome," Alec said, stroking the furry black back. "What's his name?"

"Wolfgang," Nash replied. "He spends so much time alone that I thought maybe he could come over here and stay for a while. Do you mind?"

"Hell no," Alec exclaimed. "He can hang with me."

Penelope wandered onto the porch, sleepy until she saw the

giant dog. Then she fell to her knees next to him and began stroking his head and face.

"He's so sweet," she crooned as the dog licked her chin. "What's he doing here?"

"Nash brought him over," Elliot watched her kids make a fuss over the very happy dog. "He can hang out with you guys while we're in New Orleans."

"Is he an attack dog?" Alec asked Nash.

Nash nodded. "He's been police trained but he's such a big love bug that he doesn't respond to commands anymore. He just wants to lay in your lap."

Penelope was already in love with the dog. "Can I take him with me when I go running?"

Nash nodded. "I don't see why not, but you need to keep him on a tight leash. He likes to run away and chase things."

As the kids fawned over the dog, Nash looked up at Elliot and winked at her. He had woken up early in the morning and made the six-mile drive home to feed the dog and take a shower. Once he was home, however, he felt guilty leaving the sad doggy face behind so he put Wolfgang into his cruiser and brought him over to Purgatory.

Wolfgang really was an attack dog and would provide protection for the kids while they were in New Orleans. At least, that's what he told Elliot. She loved the idea, grinning over the rim of her coffee mug, watching her children fall in love with the big German Shepherd.

"You'll never get your dog back," she said.

Nash laughed. "Then maybe I'll just have to hang around here more than I already do. Everybody who matters to me is over here, anyway. My house is just a place to lay my head."

Elliot sipped at her coffee. "I've never seen your house."

"Then I'll have to take you over there sometime," he told her. "I bought it about six years ago, right after Julie and I divorced. It sits right on the golf course."

"Do you golf?"

"I do. Do you?"

She nodded. "Rob tried to teach me," she said. "I'm not very good, but I like to play."

He grinned and reached out, taking her warm hand in his. "I'll see if I can pick up where he left off."

She laughed as Alec got up and went inside the house, leaving Penelope to cuddle and stroke the dog. Wolfgang was in doggie heaven, thrilled with the attention. When Alec emerged from the house again, it was with a bright green tennis ball, which he showed to Wolfgang, who perked up and danced all over Penelope sitting on the ground beside him. Alec threw the ball and the dog went nuts.

"Here we go," Nash muttered, watching his dog tear off into the yard. "He'll play fetch all day. You've just made a friend, Alec."

Alec grinned, watching the dog collect the ball and trot back over to him.

"That's okay," he said. "I don't have much to do right now except mess around on the computer and play fetch. Hey, that reminds me; I Googled your name last night just to see if you were really an axe murderer or a drug lord or something. There was an article that said you were a war hero."

Elliot turned to Nash with surprise and curiosity. "War hero?" she repeated.

Nash shrugged casually as he sipped his coffee. "It's not as big as all that," he said. "I was with the First Marine Division during Desert Storm in '91 during the liberation of Kuwait. I was part of the battle for Kuwait City."

Alec wouldn't let him get off so easily. "The article said you led a light infantry battalion into the east side of the city where the Iraqi Republican Guard was in control because of the oil reserves in the area. It said you and your men bombarded the Iraqis for two days before outmaneuvering them when they tried to escape. You captured an entire brigade of Republican Guards with the fewest casualty record of any commander in the liberation of Kuwait City. That makes you a war hero, dude."

By this time, Elliot was looking at Nash in astonishment. "You did all that?" she asked.

He looked at her, smiling. "I had a lot of help."

Elliot grinned and shook her head in amazement, trying to wrap her mind around the information. It was very impressive. "How long were you a Marine?"

"Eight years," he replied. "I graduated from Tulane in '85 and enlisted in the Corps. I was in through '93 and came home to join the Sheriff's Department. Then I ran for Sheriff in '99 and have been Sheriff ever since."

Elliot just shook her head again, impressed with the overall character of the man she had discovered deep in the backwoods of Louisiana. She wrapped her arm around his waist and he encircled her shoulders with his big arm, kissing her temple.

"You're quite accomplished," she said. "I think I'll keep you around a little longer."

He laughed, watching as Alec ran Wolfgang into the ground throwing the ball. But the dog was loving it. "I think I've lost my dog," he sighed.

Elliot giggled, letting go of him and heading into the house. "I'm going to get dressed so we can get on the road," she called to him as she walked in. "How long will it take us to get there?"

"About an hour," he told her. "Don't rush. We've got time."

"That's good," she called back to him, "because your brother is sending a couple of contractors over this morning and I didn't want to leave until they got here."

He turned from the young people playing with the dog and followed Elliot's path back into the house.

"That's fine," he said, sipping the last of his coffee. "While we're waiting, can I impose upon you for a piece of toast?"

"Help yourself."

Just as he put his foot inside the kitchen door, he heard his police radio go off. He had set it in the big front parlor along with his keys and cell phone. In fact, the phone was going off as well and as Elliot took the stairs for the upper floor, he made his way into the parlor in time to catch the phone on the last ring.

"Aury," he answered.

"Sheriff, this is dispatch," a woman with a heavy Louisiana drawl was on the other end. "We've got a situation out on Brown Road near Darrow. There's been a shooting at the Marchant Vocational School. I've got all available units rolling from Brittany substation."

"I'm on my way," Nash hung up the cell phone, picked up the radio, and contacted the watch commander. "Brittany WC-1 this is S A-1, do you copy?"

He was picking up his keys and moving for the door as the radio crackled back at him. "Ellie?" he yelled upstairs to her. "I've got to go, honey."

"What?" Elliot's voice was faint and he could hear her running across the upstairs hall, skittering down the sweeping staircase until she hit the bottom. "Where are you going?"

He went to meet her halfway down the hall, kissing her swiftly before heading towards the front door. He strained to listen to the watch commander through the bad connection they had, but he gathered that at least one of his units was already on scene. There was apparently a mess.

"Copy that," he spoke into the radio as he burst through the front door and flew off the porch. "My ETA is fifteen."

The gravel of the driveway crunched underneath his boots as he made his way to the car. Nash didn't realize that Elliot was right behind him until he opened the door of his car and hit her with it. She bounced backwards with the force of the blow.

"My God," he winced because he had really smacked her in the arm. He shut the door and grasped her gently as she rubbed her elbow. "I'm so sorry, darlin'. I didn't see you."

She grinned at him. "It's okay," she said. "Where are you going?"

He opened the door carefully this time. "The call is a shooting at a vocational school in Darrow," he said, kissing her quickly. "I'll let you know what's going on when I can."

"A shooting?" she repeated.

He nodded, already mentally geared up for the task ahead and oblivious to the tone of her voice. "Yes," he said. "I'm not sure how long I'll be, but I'll call you."

Elliot looked at him with an odd, wide-eyed gaze and the tears started coming. She thought she was being clever by lowering her head and heading back quickly for the house.

"Okay," she said, not looking at him as she climbed up the stairs to the porch. "Call me when you can. Be careful."

Nash finally caught on to the tone in her voice, the tightness of it, and it began to occur to him why. He was halfway into the car but climbed back out again when he saw how swiftly she was moving. It wasn't natural for her to run away from him like that with her head down.

"Ellie," he called after her, his voice soft, deep and gentle.

She came to a halt before she went inside the door but she couldn't look at him. She just stood there, rubbing her elbow, struggling against the tears of fright and grief that were already starting down her cheeks.

"You'd better get going," she said hoarsely. "I'll talk to you later."

She took another step towards the door but one word from him brought her to a halt. "Stop," he commanded gently. "Look at me."

She shook her head and burst into tears, moving for the door but he was on the porch in a flash, slamming the door closed before she could get through it. He captured her in his arms, trapping her against him as she tried to get away. After a couple of seconds of struggling, she collapsed against him in hot, frightened tears.

"The... the last time... it was a shooting and he didn't come back," she wept. "I'm sorry, I'm so sorry. It just brings back very bad memories."

Nash held her tightly, his face on the top of her head. He could feel her fear, her grief, and it broke his heart.

"I'm coming back," he assured her. "I swear, I'm coming back. My vest is in the back of the car and I'll put it on as soon as I get there. I won't leave you, Ellie, not ever. I promise."

She pulled herself together, wiping at her face and trying to pretend she was really okay with all of it. Mostly, she knew he had to go and she didn't want to delay him any more than she had.

"I'm fine, really," she insisted, sniffing and wiping at her nose. "You'd better go. They need you."

Nash wasn't convinced. He gazed down at her, seeing how hard she was struggling, and he cupped her face and kissed her sweetly on the lips, tasting her salty tears.

"I love you," he murmured. "I swear I'm coming back."

She nodded, smiling bravely. "I know you are."

"Don't worry."

"I won't."

He didn't believe her but he didn't voice his thoughts. Kissing her one last time, he gave her a squeeze and made his way to his car, turning on the rotators as he pulled out of the driveway. Elliot could hear the siren sound up as he hit the road at the end of the driveway. She stood there and listened until it faded off into the distance, praying that he was right and that he would return to her.

There was no way she could have stood the grief if he didn't.

―――――

The electrician and plumber showed up about an hour after Nash left. Part of the south side of the house and part of the driveway was torn up with the plumber digging a new septic line and he wanted to finish it. The electrician was working a Saturday shift because Beau had stressed how important it was to get the house fully wired and cabled. He brought three men with him and they got to work sometime before noon.

Meanwhile, Elliot had tried not to think of what Nash was doing but it was difficult not to think of the man every second. She decided that keeping busy was the best thing for her so she focused on unpacking the rest of her bedroom, using Alec to put together the heavy bed frame so she could put her mattress on it. The mattress was still on the floor. Between her and Alec, they managed to get almost everything unpacked from her boxes and into drawers.

Items that were still left in the hanging boxes needed a closet and there were none. Elliot thought they should use the smaller back bedroom where the stairs to the kitchen were for their closet items until they could figure it out what else to do. Alec liked the idea of going to Wal-Mart and getting rolling racks, mostly because he just wanted to get out of the house and do something. Elliot sent her stir-crazy son out to Wal-Mart for the racks while she stayed at the house. She didn't want to leave Penelope alone with the contractors.

With her room at least somewhat unpacked and organized, Elliot did something she hadn't done in almost two weeks – pick up her computer and resume work on a novel that had an October deadline.

This novel had already been purchased purely based on the story outline for nearly a half million dollars, something she was very excited about. It would help pay for the restoration of the house. It was the story of a knight who returned from King Richard's crusade a vampire, having been caught up in a coven in Bavaria on his way home from The Holy Land. Her agent and publisher loved it already and she had to admit it was coming along nicely.

Taking her laptop and a chair out to the newly reinforced balcony, she sat outside of Penelope's bedroom overlooking the bayou and began to work. Her daughter was in the yard below her, still playing with the dog. She could hear Penelope laughing and talking to the dog, which she now had on a leash because of the contractors. As Elliot typed away, Penelope called up to her.

"Mom?" she yelled.

"I'm up here," Elliot called back.

Penelope moved away from the house until she could see her

mother perched up on the balcony. "I want to go for a run," she told her. "Can I take the dog?"

Elliot stopped typing. "I'm not sure that would be a good idea," she said. "He just came here today. We should probably let him get used to his surroundings before we start taking him out and about."

Penelope shrugged. "Okay," she looked around, spying a big chain that was anchored by a spike driven into the ground. It was halfway between the backyard and the driveway, lodged in some trees. She pointed at it. "Did Nash put that chain there for him?"

Elliot looked to see what she was pointing at. "Yes," she said. "He put that there this morning when he brought Wolfgang. Hook the dog up before you go and make sure he has a bowl of water."

Penelope did as she was told, also leaving the dog some of the rib bones that were left over in the new refrigerator. Wolfgang had a delicious meal of barbeque ribs and bones, happy in his shaded and cool spot but missing his new friend when she went into the house to change into her running clothes.

Elliot sat on the balcony where she could see both the dog and the bayou, the perfect relaxing retreat had she not been fighting off thoughts of Nash.

Elliot could hear Penelope banging around in her bedroom behind her. Shortly, her daughter emerged in running shorts, a singlet and her running shoes. Her light brown hair was pulled back in a ponytail as she bent over to quickly kiss her mom goodbye.

"Where are you going?" Elliot wanted to know.

Penelope was stretching out her slender frame. "Down the street, down another street... I don't know. I'm not that familiar with the area yet."

"If you don't tell me where, you don't go."

Penelope frowned. "This isn't California, Mom. There isn't a drug dealer or criminal on every corner."

Elliot looked up from her laptop. "I'm serious, Pen."

Penelope sighed with exaggeration. "I'm going to go down the driveway and to the left for about a mile. Then I'm going to come back and run the other way for about two miles. Then I'm going to come back home."

"So you're just going on the main road?"

"Yes."

"Okay, you can go now."

Penelope skipped off and Elliot returned to her novel. As she wrote about the knight, who by now in the book had turned into a creature of the night, she realized the description of the knight nearly fit Nash perfectly. The knight was older, with brown hair, hazel eyes and a sexy build, only now the knight's eyes were jet black because he had turned into a vampire. She snickered as she thought of changing the character's name from Sloane to Nash. She wondered what he would have to say about that when the book came out and he discovered that there were several very explicit sex scenes in it, one involving a bloody orgy. Much like her not liking what he did for living, he might very well not like what she did, either. She giggled again when she thought of a vampire knight named Nash.

The late morning rolled into noon and the weather remained surprisingly mild for June in Louisiana. Elliot was swept up in a chapter, her cell phone next to her and glancing at it every so often as if willing Nash to call. She heard her car pull up in the driveway, knowing that Alec was home with the rolling racks. Taking the computer inside and putting it down on her bed, she went downstairs to help her son bring in the racks.

By the time she reached the driveway, he was hauling out boxes from the back of the Jeep. Elliot casually noticed the plumbers trenching and the electricians wiring up the porch light as she went out to the car.

"How many did you get?" she asked Alec as he continued to remove boxes.

"Three big ones," he told her. "One for you, one for me and one for Penny."

Elliot scratched her head and suddenly looked around. "Speaking of your sister, did you see her running out on the road?"

Alec shook his head. "No," he replied. "Why?"

Elliot shrugged. "She's been gone a while." She took one of the boxes and began hauling it towards the house. "Go back out there and see if you can find her, okay? She doesn't know this area well and I'm afraid she might have gotten herself lost."

Alec made a face, a normal gesture with him. "She's fine."

"Go. That is not a request."

He looked at her, his handsome face sly. "Nash would have given me twenty bucks by now."

Elliot fought off a smile. "I'm going to give you a kick in the pants if you don't get going."

"Has Nash called yet?"

Elliot's smile faded. "No, but I'm sure he's fine. He'll call."

Alec's gaze lingered on her a moment before nodding. He had seen how upset his mother was earlier when Nash had left on the shooting call and, as always, he was very tuned to that. He didn't like to see her upset. But he dutifully climbed into the car to go find his hopelessly lost sister.

It wasn't fifteen minutes later when Elliot received a panicked call from her son.

TEN

ELLIOT WAS REALLY COMING to hate St. Elizabeth Hospital and she was particularly coming to hate the emergency room. It simply made her ill to be there, fighting off her own anguish in order to comfort her daughter and calm her son. She had both of them emotionally hysterical and it was imperative she keep her cool.

Alec had found Penny crawling out of a ditch about a mile from Purgatory. He had almost missed her, unhappy that his mom had made him go out and look for his sister and thinking the lump by the side of the road was a dog. But then he noticed that the dog had pink shorts on. He almost crashed the Jeep into the ditch pulling it to a screeching halt.

It was evident that Penelope had been hurt. Alec called 911 first and then his mother, describing the condition of his sister and trying not to freak out about it. The ambulance had come quickly and taken Penelope to St. Elizabeth's as Alec followed in his mother's Jeep.

Elliot had taken Penelope's little, white Nissan and ended up following the ambulance also, frantic to get to her daughter because Alec really couldn't tell his mother what was wrong. He didn't know himself. All he knew was that she looked like she had been beaten and thrown away, and she had mentioned something, in a daze, about "those guys from the other day". When Alec told his mother that, she didn't have to guess what her daughter meant. In the deep, nauseating pit of her stomach, she already knew.

A Sorrento police officer also followed the ambulance to the hospital, the same officer who had taken Alec in to the station for questioning. When they took Penelope from the ambulance and wheeled her into the emergency entrance, Officer Bird was right by her side, even when the doctors examined her. He had tried to talk to her to find out what had happened, but Penelope was too shaken up.

So he backed off, standing with Alec and Elliot as the medical staff took great care of Penelope. The young woman had apparently been knocked unconscious for a short amount of time and had no idea if she had been raped. The examination turned into an investigation at that point and a rape kit was ordered.

Alec didn't want to be around when they did that to his sister so he wandered out into the corridor and planted himself on one of the plastic chairs, his head dropping into his hands. He was absolutely distraught. Elliot was deeply concerned for her son's mental state but she was more concerned for her daughter.

She remained in the examination room, on the other side of the white curtain, while the doctor and two nurses did a rape kit. Listening to Penelope cry softly as they poked, prodded and probed, it took every bit of strength she had to keep it together. She couldn't fall apart, not now while her children were so fragile. It wasn't her right.

The afternoon dragged on with painful slowness as Penelope was very carefully examined and Elliot ended up filling out a bunch of paperwork for the insurance. Officer Bird interviewed her and Alec, but they couldn't tell him much other than what Penelope had said when Alec had first found her. It wasn't much to go on.

As Elliot sat against the wall next to her daughter's gurney, exhausted and shattered, she heard a commotion near the emergency entrance. Peering out into the corridor, she saw Ken Havereau and another deputy hauling in an African-American man in his early twenties who was bleeding profusely from a wound to the head. The young man was screaming that the cops beat him and the deputies struggled with him as they dragged him into the operatory area.

Instant chaos was in the air. Coming right on his heels was another young African-American male being escorted by none other than Nash himself and another uniformed deputy. The young man was literally kicking and screaming, blood on his neck and chest as Nash and the deputy held on to him with latex gloves covering their hands.

Elliot heard Nash's voice before she ever saw his face. The man was calmly and succinctly giving orders to his men, his deep voice full of confidence and certainty. Elliot jumped up from her chair and went into the corridor in time to see Nash nearly get toppled on his ass when the youth went wild and kicked off of the wall in an attempt to dislodge the deputies. Nash kept his balance and threw the kid into a choke hold.

"Hobble him," he commanded.

The other deputies that had followed them into the emergency room did as they were told, but not without a big struggle. There were at least eight uniformed deputies, all doing their jobs, and Nash was right in the middle of it. When the suspect was finally hobbled, Nash stepped back, wiping at his forehead with his forearm and pulling off the latex gloves. When he turned to throw the gloves away, he noticed Alec sitting quietly several feet away. His eyes widened with surprise and concern.

"Alec?" he forgot about his fighting prisoners. "What in the hell are you doing here? Where's your mother?"

"Here."

Elliot nearly ran down the hall towards him. Nash instinctively opened up his arms to her, pulling her into both a crushing and comforting embrace. Elliot struggled not to fall apart as he kissed her face repeatedly, holding him tightly and so incredibly glad to see him. The smell of him, the feel of him, told her that things weren't so bad. As long as he was here, everything would be all right.

"What's wrong?" Nash stopped kissing her long enough to focus on her. "What are you doing here?"

So much for trying to be strong. Elliot's big, blue eyes filled with a lake of tears and her lower lip quivered.

"Penny was out running like she usually does," she whispered tightly. "We don't exactly know what happened, but Alec found her in a ditch. She was knocked unconscious and they just did a rape kit on her to...."

That was all Nash needed to hear. He pulled Elliot along with him as he stormed down the corridor, coming to the operatory with Penelope in it. She was dressed in a hospital gown, huddled up on the gurney and looking absolutely terrified. Officer Bird was standing next to the gurney with his notebook in his hand but Nash pushed past the officer on his quest to get to Penelope.

"Penny, darlin'," he put a big hand comfortingly on the side of her head. "What in the world happened?"

Penelope took one look at him and burst into tears. Nash didn't know what else to do but hug the girl and she clung to him, holding him tightly and fearfully. Penelope had always been something of a daddy's girl and the death of her father had left a huge hole in her heart. She had always loved her father's strength and comfort, protecting her. She knew nothing bad could ever happen to her as long as her father was around.

Even though she had only known Nash a week, he had that same strong, protective quality that her father had, and she missed that terribly. She needed it. When he put out a hand to console her, she felt safe again, comforted, and the tears just came bursting out.

Elliot watched Nash hold her daughter, tears streaming down her cheeks. He was so sweet with Penelope, hugging her gently and telling her that everything would be all right. It touched Elliot deeply to see how wonderful he was with her, this man she had only known a short amount of time but who, somehow, had made himself indispensable to them all. They loved him like they had known him forever. As she was watching the tender scene, she heard Officer Bird clear his throat softly.

"Sheriff," he said quietly. "I need to get a statement from the young lady. Do you want to take over, sir?"

Nash was close to tears himself. He shook his head. "No," he looked at Bird. "You go ahead. I've got my own issues right now and, to be honest, I don't think I'd be very good with Penny right now. Too close to home."

Officer Bird nodded. He knew that the sheriff was courting the new owner of Purgatory; once Monty Torres got finished spreading the news after the Rotary Mixer on Wednesday, everybody in Ascension Parish knew. He stood back respectfully while Sheriff Aury comforted the frightened young woman.

Nash rocked Penelope gently for several long moments before letting her go and kissing her gently on the forehead.

"You tell this officer everything you know, all right?" he instructed firmly but gently. "You tell him what happened and don't leave anything out. Don't be afraid; we'll get whoever did this, Penny. I swear to God I'll get them myself."

Penelope wiped at her face. "O... okay," she sniffed.

"Good girl." Nash patted her cheek one last time before turning to Elliot, standing beside him with tears on her face. She looked like a wreck.

"Come on," he said comfortingly, pulling her away from the gurney.

Nash took Elliot back out into the hall outside of the operatory. He held her close for a moment before kissing her and releasing her.

"Are you okay?" he asked.

Elliot nodded, wiping her nose. "I'm okay."

He sighed heavily, fighting off the anger and sorrow he was feeling. "Did she say anything to you about what happened?"

Elliot was struggling not to get too emotional. "Nash, I'm

scared to tell you. I don't want you to go running off like a crazy man."

His brow furrowed. "What do you mean?"

She sighed, grasping at his arms. "Alec said he found her crawling out of a ditch about a mile to the east of the house," she said quietly. "Alec said that all Penny could say was that it was 'those guys from the other day'. She said that they called her 'sweet thing'."

Nash's facial color went from normal to a deep red. "God*dammit*," he exploded with an uncharacteristic hiss. "Loreau."

Elliot grasped him. "We don't know for sure, but it sure sounds like it. Maybe when she calms down, she'll make more sense. Nash, I'm so scared. What if they try something again? I'm terrified for my children."

Nash was beyond furious. His palms were sweating and he was having a very difficult time fighting down his uncharacteristic rage. He could feel Elliot's hands on him, caressing him, and he gazed down into her face to see anxiety written all over it. After that, he labored to calm down because she didn't need to worry about his anger. She had enough on her mind.

"Let me finish what I'm doing here and I'll come back as soon as I can," he assured her.

Elliot could hear the young men Nash had brought in yelling and fighting in another room off the main emergency room floor. It was scary and violent.

"Okay," she accepted his kiss. "Be careful, please."

"I will," he promised. "Right now, I want you to do me a favor, please?"

"What?"

He was serious. "Let Officer Bird interview Penny alone. If she sees you, you'll give her an emotional crutch to lean on and the officer needs all of her focus. She needs to remember every last detail and she'll more than likely not do it if you're there. She'll want to focus on you. Will you do this, please?"

Reluctantly, Elliot nodded. He winked at her, patted her arms, and disappeared around the corner where his deputies were. Elliot stood there a moment, listening to the young men bellow and the soft, firm voices of the deputies. With a deep breath to collect herself, she went to sit next to Alec and wait for the officer to finish with Penelope.

Three very long hours later, Alec and Elliot were still sitting in corridor of the emergency room operatories, waiting for the Sorrento Police to be finished with Penelope. Officer Bird had taken a good solid hour with Penelope, interviewing her, and then he called for the detectives, who had shown up about a half hour later.

Two detectives then interviewed Penelope and Elliot could hear her daughter's stressed voice over those of the detectives. She knew they were trying to help Penelope but Elliot didn't like hearing the stress and pain in her daughter's voice. She just wanted to take her home.

Nash, unfortunately, had his hands full with the situation from Darrow and never made it back to the hospital. The local media from Baton Rouge had gotten wind of the incident, which turned out to be two men on parole that had tried to rob the vocational school of a computer and other valuable equipment. The shooting had resulted when they shot an old janitor who had tried to stop them, and then fired at the deputies who showed up on the scene. None of the deputies had been injured, but both suspects had been injured in the brutal take down that followed.

Men in suits kept coming in and out of the emergency room as a result. As Elliot and Alec sat and waited for Penelope, they could see all of the well-dressed men going in and out of the emergency room annex reserved especially for criminals.

At several points during the afternoon, Nash came out with some of the men, speaking with them, every once in a while looking over to see if Elliot and Alec were still there. He would wink at Elliot when their eyes met, regardless of who he happened to be speaking with at the time.

It made Elliot feel like he was still with her, still comforting all of them even though he was busy with other things. She had no idea how busy he really was until he disappeared, this time for a significant amount of time, and his face suddenly appeared on the television screen on the wall off to their right. Alec jumped up when he saw Nash and turned up the volume.

As Elliot and Alec watched, Nash answered reporters' questions about the incident in Darrow. It was a very short interview as it pertained to the story on the 5 o'clock news, but Elliot was completely entranced watching the smooth manner in which Nash fielded questions. He was calm, collected, and that sexy Louisiana drawl had Elliot's heart racing. At one point, he even smiled while answering a question and his beautiful smile just lit up the screen. Elliot couldn't help but grin as she watched Nash's handsome face fill up the television.

"Where is he?" Alec wondered aloud.

Elliot shook her head, her eyes still on Nash. "I don't know," she said. "But look – the building behind him says Office of the Sheriff. He must be at his office."

Alec looked at her. "Where is it?"

Elliot shrugged. "To tell you the truth, I don't even know. I think it's north, towards Baton Rouge."

Before Alec could reply, the white curtain that had been shielding Penelope and the police from the rest of the emergency room was yanked back and the three officers emerged. Elliot shot to her feet and went over to them.

"Is she finished?" she asked. "Can I take her home?"

Officer Bird nodded. "She can go home," he replied. "We'll be in touch, ma'am."

"Wait a minute," Elliot stopped the three of them before they could get away. "Did she tell you everything?"

One of the detectives, a very large man in a wrinkled beige suit, nodded.

"Yes'm," he replied with a very heavy Louisiana accent. "We're going to go back to the station and work on a few things. You take your girl on home."

Elliot wouldn't let them get away so fast. "Did she tell you it was the Loreau brothers?" she was becoming more agitated. "What in the hell am I supposed to do if they try to come back on to my property?"

The detective in the beige suit tried to calm her. "Ma'am, I doubt that's going to happen," he replied. "We've put a rush on the rape kit and we'll let you know what comes of it. But for now, we can't say for certain who did it. You're going to have to be patient."

Elliot was exhausted, protective and angry, a dangerous combination.

"Patient my ass," she hissed. "Those Loreau creeps have already done a number on my family and I've only lived here for a week. Their crazy father tried to kill my son and now they've gone after my daughter. I swear to God if they come on my property again or come near my children, I'll kill them. I'll blow their fucking heads off!"

The detective put his hands up to quiet her. "Ms. Jentry, y'all need to calm down and let the law do its job. We're heading over to The Bottoms to question them boys, don't worry. We'll make sure justice is served."

Shaken and upset, Elliot struggled to relax. "I'm sorry," she finally said. "I'm not trying to tell you how to do your jobs, but a lot has happened to us over the past week. I'm just a little edgy."

The detective nodded patiently. "I know, ma'am," he said as he turned to walk away. "I'll let Sheriff Aury know what we come up with."

Elliot watched them go, turning to look at Alec after a moment. "Does this whole damn state know I'm dating Nash?" she asked with some bafflement.

Alec shrugged. "I didn't until Penny told me," he said. "But I should have known, I guess. Instead of bringing you flowers, Nash brought you ribs and paid off your kids. Face it, Mom; he bought his way into your heart."

Elliot giggled at him, putting her hand on his head in an affectionate gesture. She gazed at the young man.

"Are you really okay with it?" she asked. "I mean with me and Nash. He's a good man, you know."

Alec nodded. "I'm okay with it. I think Dad would have like him."

Elliot fought off a sudden surge of tears. "Do you really think so?"

Again, Alec nodded. "Yes," he said quietly. "You need to be happy, Mom. Dad would want that the most. Nash seems to make you really happy."

"He does," Elliot confirmed. "I love him very much. He's such a sweetheart."

Alec just nodded, looking uncomfortable with his mother speaking of being in love with another man. Although he liked Nash a great deal, still, he was still trying to adjust.

"He's pretty cool," was all he would say.

Lip quivering, Elliot hugged her son, feeling very emotional on a day that had been packed with emotion. She and Alec watched the rest of the news in silence as the sun set outside and the emergency room grew bright with fluorescent lighting.

Finally, the curtain surrounding Penelope's gurney opened again, this time admitting Penelope dressed in green hospital scrubs. Her hair was all wound up in a green surgical mask to keep it off her face and a round, white nurse was next to her. Penelope smiled wanly at her mother and brother, falling into her mother's soothing embrace.

"She's all set to go home now," the nurse said, handing Elliot three vials of pills. She pointed to each one. "This one is an antibiotic, this one is naproxen if she's sore, and this one is the morning after pill. She's already had a dose and she needs to take another one tomorrow. She'll cramp up and bleed, but that's normal. The doctor wants you to call in on Monday and let us know how she's doing. Any questions?"

Elliot felt rather sick looking at the instructions on the morning after pill. "Is... is this just precautionary?"

The nurse nodded sympathetically. "Yes," she said quietly. "It can't hurt."

"So what now?" Elliot asked. "When will we know the results of her... tests?"

"The police will be in touch with you regarding those, honey," the woman said. "Those will take a little time. For now, take her home and baby her. She needs some of her mama's lovin'."

Elliot thanked the woman and left with her children all huddled around her. It was dark outside in the parking lot, the moist evening air laying heavy across the land. The mercury vapor lamps buzzed furiously overhead as they made their way to the two cars they had left parked in the parking lot, thousands of bugs fluttering madly about the white lights overhead.

Alec made it to the Jeep first, noticing a business card tucked under the windshield wiper. He pulled it free, read the front and the back, and then made a snorting noise. Elliot turned to see him with his lips pursed, making a rude sound. He extended the card to her.

"This is for you," he said.

Elliot took the card. It was Nash's business card and she flipped it over. He had written three words on the back.

Love you much.

She smiled, feeling warm and comforting feelings fill her at the mere thought of the man. He was so very sweet. She grinned at her son, who decided he wanted to drive the white Nissan home while Elliot and Penelope got into the jeep. After driving through McDonald's to get a deliciously unhealthy dinner, they made their way back to the dark and mysterious plantation known as Purgatory.

———

Three Sorrento police units, one Sorrento detective unit, two sheriff units and Nash's plainclothes car made an imposing caravan as they left the Sorrento Police Department and drove east along John Le Blanc Boulevard, passing Purgatory, on their way to the Loreau homestead. They made it up to Fontenot Road and hung a right, traveling about a half-mile down the road until they came to the scrubby, tree-shrouded driveway that led to The Bottoms.

It really couldn't even be called a driveway. It was a road in the literal sense, deeply grooved and unmaintained. Entering it was like emerging into another world, where the creatures chirped in the darkness and fireflies danced through the heavy strains of long Spanish moss. It was eerie and unsettling. The uneven road gave the low-chassis police cars difficulty as they drove up to the house.

The cars came to a halt a distance from the house, not wanting to get too close given the situation. They wanted a clear and wide view of the entire area. The Bottoms had once been a beautiful home two hundred years ago, with a big porch that stretched all the way around the house. The house was of Creole design, which meant the living quarters were all on the second floor while storage and kitchen were on the bottom floor. There was an outside staircase between the porch and the balcony, because back in the day it was built the Spanish Crown would tax the staircases built inside the homes. Therefore, The Bottoms had a big, ungainly staircase right in the front of the house, covered with dogs and debris.

Nash climbed out of his cruiser, his gaze riveted to the house, not entirely sure what he was feeling at the moment. All he knew was that the attack on Penelope was as good as an attack on his own flesh and blood. He couldn't describe it any other way.

The Sorrento police were serving a warrant on William, Nicholas and Edward Loreau based on the testimony of Penelope, and Nash had asked to come along. He wanted to be on hand when the brothers were arrested, if only for his own sense of personal satisfaction. Truthfully, maybe he wanted to get in a lick or two. Sorrento P.D., being that Nash was an elected law official with a good deal of clout in the State of Louisiana, agreed with some reservation to let him come along.

The group of two detectives, three Sorrento police officers, Ken Havereau, Steve Pitot and Nash approached the house. A couple of the dogs barked but that was about the limit of any external activity. They could see people moving inside of the house and hear high-pitched female voices. The two detectives motioned to the Sorrento officers to spread out a bit in case the suspects inside decided to rabbit as one of the detectives approached the front door.

The heavyset detective who was still in the wrinkled beige suit knocked heavily on the door.

"Y'all open up in there," he yelled. "Sorrento Police. We have a warrant."

Nash stood in the driveway in front of the house, watching the entire area, listening to the chatter going on inside. He could hear male voices now, too, and he lost his cool. Marching up onto the porch, he stood next to the detective and banged on the door.

"Will Loreau!" he boomed. "It's Sheriff Aury. Open the door or I'll kick it in!"

The Sorrento detective looked at Nash, shocked, and then shook his head in resignation. Already, this was not going well with the sheriff being personally involved. They could hear more scuffing and whispering inside. The door suddenly shifted as someone threw a bolt and the old, warped panel slowly creaked open.

A very small, old woman with jet black hair stood in the door-way, her black eyes glaring at Nash and the detective, but mostly Nash. She was dressed in a surprisingly clean house coat given the condition of the property she lived in. After digesting all of the law enforcement personnel on her doorstep, her beady eyes focused in on Nash.

"Nash Aury," she spat. "I don't care if ya are the sheriff, y'all is not welcome here."

Nash stayed calm. "Evenin', Ms. Biffy," he said. "We've come for the boys."

Ms. Biffy Loreau scowled. She was a mean woman with a foul streak in her, just like the rest of the family, and even though she had one son, she had never married Femmie's father which was why the man, and his sons, carried the Loreau name. It had been another scandal in a family that was full of them.

"Y'all can't have 'em," she said, waving her hand as if to shoo them away. "Now, get."

"We can't do that, ma'am," the fat detective said. "Now, Ms. Biffy, y'all just stand aside and hand over the boys. We have a warrant."

"Warrant?" Ms. Biffy demanded. "A warrant for what?"

"Their arrest, ma'am," the detective said patiently. "They are identified as having attacked a young girl this afternoon and she's pretty banged up."

Will suddenly emerged from the shadows, materializing in the stench and dirtiness of the interior of the house. In torn up jeans and his John Deere cap, he made sure to stay behind his grandmother.

"We didn't do nothin'," he spat, jabbing a finger at Nash. "You ain't got no proof!"

Nash's jaw ticked. "Please give me a reason to come in there and beat the hell out of you for resisting arrest."

Will took a step back, still pointing a finger at him. "You killed my father and now y'all tryin' to kill me," he said angrily. "This is nothin' more than the Aury family trying to beat down the Loreaus again. Y'all is always trying to put us in a bad way."

"Are you going to come peacefully?"

Will shook his head, his dark stringy hair dusting his shoulders. "I ain't goin' nowhere with you, Aury. We didn't do nothin'!"

"My boys didn't do nothin'," Ms. Biffy took up the cry. "Y'all kilt my son and I haven't stopped weepin' over my boy. Y'all kilt him!"

Nash's expression remained passive. "Ms. Biffy, I am sorry for your loss, I truly am, but Femmie got himself killed. I had nothing to do with it."

"Murderer!" from the dark central hall of the house emerged another figure, this one surreal in an old, stained nightgown and a big cane in her hand. The woman was as wrinkled as an old shoe, her white hair wild about her head. She was gnarled and smelled strongly of urine as she approached with her cane lifted. "Nash Aury, y'all is a murderer!"

Nash watched Ms. Leon Loreau swing her cane at him in slow motion. He easily dodged it but it didn't stop her from bringing it up again and trying to hit him. The two Sorrento detectives stepped into the house to try and regain some control as the entire family seemed to go after Sheriff Aury.

"Ms. Leon, don't be hittin' the sheriff," the fat detective moved in between them. "Y'all can't be doin' that. Now, we need the boys or we're gonna arrest the lot of ya for obstruction of justice. Do you understand?"

Ms. Leon lifted her cane and hit the fat detective in the mouth when he wasn't looking. Nash grabbed the cane, pulled it from her grip, and tossed it.

"Enough," he snarled. "Will, you and your brothers get out here. You're under arrest."

Nash didn't see the flying fist until it was too late as Ed Loreau came out of the dining room and charged him from behind. The fist caught Nash in the jaw and sent him off balance, but Ken and Steve, standing on the porch, saw the attack and burst into the house. In a flash, the situation deteriorated into bedlam.

The women were screaming as the police and sheriff deputies quickly took down Will, Ed and Nicky. Nicky smashed a lamp over Ken's shoulder, tearing him up pretty good until two Sorrento police officers managed to subdue him. Nash had Ed in a headlock as a Sorrento detective cuffed him while Will, underneath a pile of battling cops, howled for his life.

It was a short fight. As quickly as it started, it was over. Nash had Ed by the hair as he and the detective escorted the man out to the police cruisers, followed shortly by Will and Nicky. Will was still kicking and screaming, refusing to cooperate, as Ms. Biffy and Ms. Leon stood in the doorway and cried. All of it was directed at Nash.

"God will punish y'all, Nash Aury!" Ms. Biffy was hollering. "You took my son and now y'all are takin' my grandsons!"

Nash didn't answer as he shoved Ed into the back of the detective unit. He was brittle and edgy, perhaps more than he had ever been in his life. This had nothing to do with the two-hundred-year-old family feud and everything to do with the attack against Penelope. What he did, he did for her and for Elliot and for Alec.

He had always been willing to accept the Loreau hostilities against himself and his family, but now that it was shifting to include Elliot and her children simply because they had purchased Purgatory, there was no way he was going to stand for it. He was going to hit and hit hard. No one would touch any of the Jentrys and get away with it, not while he had breath in his body.

Will was kicking at the detectives who were trying to get him into the car. Finished with Ed, Nash walked up to Will and, in a completely uncharacteristic display, cold-cocked Will in the jaw and knocked the man silly. With Will dazed, the detectives were able to shove him into the back seat of the car and slam the door.

With the suspects subdued for the moment, the fat Sorrento detective turned to Nash. Huffing and puffing, the man pulled out a handkerchief and wiped the sweat off his face.

"Sheriff, I can't say that went too well," he said. "I'm not sure you were much of a help. If anything, your presence around the Loreaus seems to upset 'em."

Nash cocked an eyebrow. "They would have resisted arrest regardless of my presence and you know it," he pointed out, watching the detective reluctantly agree. "Are you going to do a lineup with Penny?"

The detective nodded. "We'll hold the Loreaus a couple of days to cool their heels and then we'll give Ms. Penny a call to come on down and take a look," he said. "We should give the girl a couple of days to recover before we upset her again."

Nash seemed to cool drastically. He realized he'd been agitated and abrupt, something that wasn't like him at all. Usually, he was as cool and amiable as they come. The emotion of the situation had him on edge and he visibly calmed now that the Loreaus were finally in custody.

"Thank you," he said. "Give a call when y'all are ready and we'll bring Penny over."

The detective simply waved him off and climbed into his vehicle. Nash made his way back to his cruiser, his gaze drifting over The Bottoms once more, a place he had been warned about all his life. He still couldn't believe that Ms. Leon tried to whack him with her cane but, then again, he really wasn't surprised with anything the Loreaus did. He knew his brother would get a laugh out of it when he told him that part, at least.

As he pulled down the rutted, overgrown driveway and ended up on the road, he found that all he could think of was returning to Elliot. He just couldn't think of anything else. He knew it was late, but that didn't matter. He had to hold her, be with her, and if he pulled into her driveway and she was asleep, he wouldn't wake her. He'd sleep in his car just to be near her.

ELEVEN

ELLIOT CAME HOME to one deputy's unit parked on the main street next to her driveway entrance and, when she pulled down the gravel drive, there were three private security patrol cars in her driveway. Nash had called off the private security on the weekend because he was around, but he'd apparently changed his mind. They were all over the place.

Elliot took Penelope and Alec into the house, locking up the big front door until Penelope, halfway to the dark staircase, called out to her.

"Mom, the dog," she said. "We can't just leave him outside."

Elliot dutifully unlocked the door. "I'll go get him."

"No," Alec moved past her. "I'll get him. You and Pen go up to bed."

Elliot did as her son told her, going upstairs to get Penelope settled in for bed. Penelope's bedroom had an attached bathroom that was in about the same condition that Elliot's was, but Penelope wanted to take a bath so Elliot filled up the claw foot bathtub with warm water thanks to their new water heater and pipes that the plumbers had carefully laid through the walls and floorboards over the past week. Elliot left her daughter in the tub, going to her room to take off her shoes and get ready for bed.

Passing Alec's room, Elliot could hear her son talking to some-one. Curious, she poked her head inside and saw two pairs of eyes looking back at her, one set of blue and one set of brown. Wolfgang was laying on Alec's bed, his ears happily perking up when Elliot stuck her head in.

"Is he going to sleep with you?" she asked.

Alec nodded happily. "We're buddies, dude."

"Then make sure you take him out to pee first thing in the morning, okay? We don't want him having an accident on these floors."

Alec nodded to his mom, waving at her when she told him goodnight. Going across the hall to her bedroom, she went to the table next to her enormous, four-poster bed and turned on the light, smiling at the electricity she now had in her bedroom. Little by little, the house was starting to come together and feeling more and more like home.

Exhausted, she got into her pink pajamas and prepared for the night.

She was rattled awake some time later by her cell phone going off. Groggy, she slapped at the phone on her nightstand, finally grasping it and glancing at the time before she answered. *1:44 a.m.* She didn't even bother looking at the caller I.D.

"Hello?" she asked sleepily.

"Hey, it's Nash," came the deep, soft voice. "Are you asleep?"

Elliot smiled at the sound of his voice. "I was," she said. "Where are you?"

"In your driveway. I thought I'd come in if you were still awake, but it sounds like I woke you up. Sorry 'bout that."

Elliot sat up and tossed the covers back. "I'm coming right down to unlock the door."

"Are you sure?"

"Meet me at the front door."

She hung up the phone and lit a candle, still next to her bed, to light her way downstairs. The house was incredibly dark and in spite of the electricians working twelve hour days, there was much of the house that was still not wired. Padding down the upstairs hall, she happened to peer in on her daughter just to make sure she was all right. She grinned at what she saw in the room and continued down the stairs.

Nash smiled at her as she opened the front door. Elliot was so glad to see him that she immediately lifted her mouth to him for a kiss, which he responded to gladly. His big arms went around her as she pulled him inside the entry hall and shut the door behind him.

"Did you just get off work?" she asked as he nuzzled her neck.

He nodded, hugging her tightly. "I just finished," he murmured. "I had to come and see how you were. How's Penny?"

Elliot took his hand, leading him down the dark and shadowed hall.

"She's okay," she whispered as they took the stairs. "They sent her home with antibiotics, painkillers and the morning-after pill. Did you talk to the Sorrento detectives?"

Nash was careful in how he answered her. "I have," he replied honestly. "They told me that they've put a rush on the rape kit. We should know the results in the next couple of days. She's also going to have to identify her attackers in a lineup if she can."

Elliot grew depressed. "She doesn't seem to think they touched her but she really doesn't know," she said. "I hope those bastards pay for every little thing they did to my little girl."

Nash kept a straight face, thinking of the arrests earlier that evening. "If I have anything to say about it, they will."

That answer seemed to satisfy her. They reached the top of the stairs and instead of heading down the hall to Elliot's bedroom, Elliot took him to the rear of the house where Penelope's bedroom was. She looked at him and put her fingers to her lips in a silencing gesture as she quietly, carefully opened the door.

"Look for yourself," she whispered with a smile.

Curious, Nash stuck his head in and was immediately greeted by a familiar face. Wolfgang was sleeping next to Penelope on her bed. The dog was all stretched out, as happy as a lark, as Penelope slept with her arm over the dog. They made a companionable pair. Grinning, Nash pulled his head back and quietly shut the door.

"I knew I had lost my dog, I just didn't realize how far gone he already was," he whispered.

Elliot snickered softly as they headed back towards her bedroom. "Alec originally had him in his room, but when Wolfgang saw Penelope, he ran right to her and wouldn't come back no matter what Alec did." She grinned at the memories. "Alec is deeply hurt, just so you are aware. I may have to buy him a dog of his own just so he won't be so upset about it."

They entered Elliot's bedroom and she blew out the candle as Nash quietly shut the door. Elliot went over to the bed and flopped wearily upon it.

"Wow," she sighed. "What a day."

Nash's gaze was on her as he walked towards the bed, shoving his hands into his pockets. "And how is Mom doing after all is said and done?"

"Fine." She sighed again, gazing up at him. "Are you just going to stand there?"

"What do you mean?"

"I mean, aren't you going to take your clothes off and get into bed with me?"

Nash didn't move. He continued to stand there and gaze at her before finally lowering himself onto the edge of the bed. He seemed quiet and subdued, but Elliot attributed it to the busy day he'd had. She crawled over to him, laying her head in his lap and smiling up at him.

"We saw you on the news tonight," she said, reaching up to toy with his shirt. "What was that all about?"

He drew in a thoughtful breath. "The media wanted to know about the shootings in Darrow," he said. "It must have been a slow news day."

"You looked really handsome, my friend."

He grinned modestly, running his hand through her blond hair, feeling the texture against his skin.

"Thank you, ma'am. I'm glad you think so."

He didn't say anything more. In fact, he seemed content just to sit there and run his fingers through her hair. Elliot watched him intently.

"What's wrong?" she asked. "Why are you so quiet?"

He shrugged. "I guess I've just got a lot on my mind."

"Can I help?"

He shrugged faintly. "Maybe," he said. "Maybe not."

"You're starting to scare me, Nash. What's wrong?"

He gazed down into her beautiful face with a thousand things on his mind. He wasn't sure how to approach it other than just come out with it and pray she didn't negatively react. Tonight's episode at The Bottoms had done something to him, something that had him eating his guts out. He had to talk to her about it or explode.

"I've known you for exactly one week," he said.

As he looked down at her, she started tearing up. "You're having second thoughts?"

He scooped her up into his arms, hugging her tightly against his broad chest. "No, no, honey, not at all," he murmured into the side of her head. "In fact, just the opposite."

She sniffled. "What do you mean?"

He loosened his embrace so he could look her in the face. "You know, it's kind of funny," he snorted. "I've only really had one special woman in my life, as long as I can remember. I met Julie when we were both in the eighth grade and we were never apart after that. We got married as soon as we graduated high school and I went to college and did my stint in the Marine Corps while married to her. We had the boys, had our life together, but I can't really say that I was deliriously happy. We were together and that's just the way it was."

Elliot was watching him seriously. "Is that why you divorced her? Because you were bored?"

He shook his head. "No," he said matter-of-factly. "She divorced me but I didn't give her a choice. I found out she'd been having an affair with one of the doctors at her hospital so I told her she could divorce me to save her pride or I would divorce her. The stigma of divorce is still pretty big around here, so I did the gentlemanly thing even though she was the one who cheated."

Elliot looked at him sadly, putting a hand on his cheek. "You didn't deserve that," she murmured. "You're such a wonderful man. I don't understand how she could have done that to you."

He shrugged. "The truth was, I really wasn't all that broken up about it. I can't remember when I stopped loving Julie and, in fact, I can't even remember when I actually *did* love her. We were just always together, like two peas in a pod, but I can't say that either of us were really happy. If I think really hard about it, I don't ever think we were *in* love, if that makes any sense."

Elliot listened seriously. "So why were you with her? You have a right to be happy, you know."

He smiled knowingly. "I know," he said. "I was with her because that's what my mother expected. There is no divorce in my family, or at least there wasn't until Julie divorced me. Anyway, when we divorced six years ago, I wasn't happy or sad. It's just the way it was. I had my career and that was enough, at least until I met you."

She returned his smile, cocking her head as she stroked the left side of his head. "And now look at the trouble you're in."

He laughed again, pulling her more closely against him.

"Ellie, I knew the moment I looked at you that you were what I had been waiting for all my life. Your beauty, your brains, your sense of humor has me hooked. I never knew what it was like to be in love until I met you and now that I know, it's a feeling I don't ever want to lose." He sighed, grasping for words. "I guess what I'm trying to say is that whether I've known you one day, one week, one year or ten, I will always feel this way about you. I don't want to walk out of your door and go back to my house, six miles away, where it's cold and lonely and you're not there. Everything I love is within these walls; you, Penny, Alec, and that big ol' dumb dog. My heart is here, with you. I want to be here, too."

She wrapped her arms around his neck, gazing into his hazel eyes. "So what are you saying?"

His gaze was intense. "I'm saying I want to marry you, more than I've ever wanted anything in my life. I want to marry you and love you and take care of you, and be the best husband and stepdad I can possibly be. I don't expect an answer tonight or even next week, or next month. But I want you to know what I'm feeling and how much you are already a part of me. I want you to know how proud it would make me for people to say 'yep, that's Ellie Aury, Nash's wife'. God, you have no idea how honored I would be."

Elliot stared at him, her big, blue eyes reflecting every emotion she was feeling at the moment. "Oh, Nash," she wound her arms around his neck, holding him tightly. "I... I'm just speechless. I don't know what to say."

He held her tightly, feeling weak and deflated now that he'd spit everything out. "Just say you'll think about it."

She didn't say anything for a moment. Nash wasn't sure if he should be thrilled or devastated from her lack of response, but he didn't say anything. He was holding her and she was holding him and, for the moment, that was enough. But suddenly, she pulled her face from the crook of his neck and placed her soft lips over his.

"I love you," she told him between heated kisses, touching his face, feeling his lips on her fingers. There was such eagerness to their touches. "Of course, I'll marry you. I don't need a day or a week or a month to decide that. I know it now."

He kissed her ferociously, smiling as he was kissing her, eventually laughing with the sheer joy of the moment. Elliot's high-pitched giggles joined his laughter.

Together, they fell back on her bed in a happy bundle, the only break coming when Nash turned off the light. But from that point on, clothes came off and they settled between the sheets, celebrating a moment neither one of them ever believed they would experience.

The start of something truly and wildly beautiful.

———

They awoke the next morning to the sounds of screams.

Nash was out of bed before he even realized he had moved, running to the door until Elliot stopped him. He didn't have a lick of clothing on and as Elliot flew out of bed and pulled on her pink pajamas, Nash yanked on his jeans and threw open the door.

They heard more screaming as they hit the staircase and flew down the stairs, but they realized there was also laughing inter-mixed with the screaming. By the time they hit the kitchen, where the sounds were coming from, they were confronted with chaos.

Wolfgang suddenly zinged by, nearly knocking Nash over. He tripped back, bashing into Elliot and reaching out to grab her so she wouldn't fall down. Penelope and Alec were hot on the heels of the dog.

"Get him!" Alec was yelling. "He stole a whole pound of bacon!"

"No!" Elliot cried when she saw the direction they were heading in. "Not the parlor!"

She raced after them while Nash followed on her heels. Wolf-gang was deep in the double parlors, wedged in between boxes, eating his stolen booty of raw bacon. As Elliot shrieked about bacon grease on her couches, Nash stood in the doorway and grinned. Shaking his head at the antics, he emitted a sharp whistle between his teeth and the dog suddenly appeared.

"Wolfgang, *entlassung*," he said sharply.

The dog trotted right over to him and guiltily dropped what he hadn't already eaten. He lay down contritely next to the bacon, sad doggy eyes looking pleadingly at Nash. He frowned at the dog as Penelope and Alec went to Wolfgang's defense.

"He's just hungry," Penelope put her arms around the dog's neck and hugged him. "We don't have any dog food."

Nash nodded. "Yes, you do," he yawned. "I brought some with me yesterday. It's outside by the kitchen door."

He turned around and headed back to the kitchen with Alec

and the dog following him, Penelope bringing up the rear gingerly carrying the half-eaten bacon.

"We can't eat this bacon now," she pointed out. "We have to cook it for the dog."

"Then why didn't you just let him eat it?" Alec wanted to know. "Why did you scream so we had to chase him down?"

"Because it's raw," she frowned. "He'll get worms."

Alec rolled his eyes. "He's a dog. He's *not* going to get worms."

Elliot was too tired to go back into the kitchen with everyone else. She went upstairs and climbed back into bed, snuggling down under the covers and dozing off. Deep, dreamless sleep settled until big, warm arms wrapped themselves around her and she felt soft breath on her ear.

"Hey, sleeping beauty," Nash whispered. "Breakfast is ready."

She stirred, smiling as she rolled over and wrapped her arms around his neck. "That sounds wonderful," she murmured. "But I just want to sleep. I'm so tired... I think this week has just caught up to me."

"Okay," he kissed her cheek, her lips. "Sorry I woke you up. I'll be downstairs."

"No," she whispered. "Stay with me. Don't leave."

He smiled at her. "If I stay, you won't sleep."

Elliot's answer was to lift her mouth to his, a gentle kiss instantly turning hot and passionate. In the bright sunlight of a leisurely Sunday morning, Nash did things to Elliot than any God-fearing, church-going Christian would have found shocking.

———

"They're not coming down," Penelope told her brother over her plate of eggs. "I told you they wouldn't."

Alec shrugged, throwing pieces of pancake to Wolfgang, who gobbled them up.

"So what?" he chewed. "They're grownups. They can do what they want."

Penelope shrugged, pushing her eggs around the plate. She seemed normal this morning, not a hint of what had happened to her yesterday except for the slightly black eye around her right eye socket. Alec didn't ask her how she was for fear of bringing up bad memories, so he treated her like he normally did – he alternately ignored and harassed her.

"You're usually the one who has a problem when men get around Mom," Penelope said. "Why don't you feel that way about Nash?"

Alec shrugged again, throwing the last of the pancake to the dog. "Because Mom loves him," he said simply.

Penelope grinned, taking one last bite of her eggs and taking the plate over to the big, iron sink. "I'm glad you feel that way," she said. "I will admit I was worried about you."

Alec went to the sink and washed his hands as his sister started to rinse off the dishes. "As long as he loves her, too, and treats her right, I'm okay with the whole thing," he insisted.

"They're upstairs having sex, you know," Penelope teased quietly.

Alec made a face and put his wet hands over his ears. "Shut up."

She made grunting noises. "Sex, sex, sex."

He pushed his hands against his ears harder to block out the sound. "Stop!" he roared.

She laughed as he walked away, turning back to her dishes. "I'm just kidding, you big baby," she called after him. "Come and take the dog out so he can go pee."

Alec was in the dining room, a room that had so far been stripped of the old paint to reveal original wallpaper beneath. The preservationist from Tulane wanted to try and save it, so a small army of art students were coming up from Tulane next week to see what they could do. It was a woodland scene, like a painting, with wispy trees and birds and delicate grass all painted on one hundred and fifty year old linen. The entire room was covered with one continuous scene.

Alec wandered over to the big floor-to-ceiling window, trying not to think of what his mom and Nash were doing upstairs, frustrated because he was bored and not particularly happy here in the wilds of Louisiana. He was a city boy and as the days passed, he was becoming increasingly convinced that he couldn't survive out here.

In just the week he had been here, he'd been forced to kill a man in self-defense and his sister had been attacked. But his mom had found Nash and for the most part, his mom and sister were happy, so he really didn't want to voice his opinion. As Penelope called to him from the kitchen, he wandered around the dining room, teaching her a lesson by not doing her bidding.

He peered at the wallpaper on the wall that bordered the kitchen, the one that had the back stairs built against it on the other side. He could see little dogs and foxes running through the trees. He ran his hand over the wallpaper, although he knew he probably shouldn't, feeling the scratchy linen against his fingers.

The lower half of the walls were wood paneling, untouched by the painters or conservators as of yet. He saw what he thought was a knot on the wood and ran his finger over it, feeling it give way slightly. Curiously, he ran his finger over it again, pushing it all the way down. Suddenly, a huge portion of the wall shifted.

At first, he thought he had broken something, somehow, and he stepped back, looking around to see if anyone had seen him do it. It was a foolish reaction considering there was no one around, and after the initial "oops" moment, he peered more closely at the spot and noticed that the entire section of wall, vertically from floor-to-ceiling, had shifted back about a quarter of an inch, as if there was a seam buried beneath the wallpaper. He gave the seam a push just to see what it would do and the entire section of wall swung back, like a door, and the wallpaper gave way.

Alex muttered a curse, jumping back in surprise and perhaps a little fear. He stared at the gaping hole he was now faced with, with the tattered wallpaper waving in a slight breeze. He could feel damp, cold air drifting from the hole and he swore, in the midst of it, he heard voices. Mouth hanging open, he made a run for the kitchen where his sister was washing dishes.

"Come here!" he grabbed her by the wrist, spraying water. "Quick!"

Penelope was up to her elbows in soapy water, shrieking when her brother grabbed her and pulled her out of the kitchen. She was fighting him angrily, slapping at him, until he pointed out the one-foot gap in the dining room wall that ran from the floor to the ceiling. Penelope's struggles came to a halt and she gasped.

"What happened?" she demanded. "What is this?"

Alec threw up his hands in confusion. "I have no idea," he said. "I just touched the wall and this whole section opened up!"

Penelope's mouth was hanging open in shock as she inched forward, looking at the seam, very cautiously peering into the blackness. She didn't want to get too close, fearful that something might give way. The house was falling apart before their very eyes. But as she peered closer, she suddenly noticed something.

"Steps!" she pointed wildly inside the hole. "I see steps! They lead down!"

Alec moved beside her, also seeing four very narrow, very old, steps disappearing down into the darkness. He bolted from his sister's side and ran into the stairwell hall, taking the sweeping staircase two at a time.

"Mom!" he was yelling. "Nash!"

Behind the closed door of Elliot's bedroom, Elliot was laying flat on her back, naked, while Nash lay on top of her trying to catch his breath. In fact, they were both trying to catch their breath, but Alec's cries roused them. Nash was out of bed in a flash, hunting down his pants.

"Mom!" Alec was banging on her door. "I need to show you something!"

Elliot was sitting up in bed. She and Nash locked gazes, Nash with his pants already on but not zipped. They looked at each other curiously.

"What is it, Alec?" Elliot called.

Alec just banged on the door. "I can't describe it," he told her. "You have to come and see it. Please! It's important!"

Nash finished securing his pants and went for his shirt as Elliot got out of bed and put on her pink pajamas. Nash went to the door, his hand on the knob as he turned to Elliot to make sure she was dressed. When she finished pulling the pajama top over her head, he opened the door.

"What's wrong?" he asked the young man.

Alec's face was taut with surprise and perhaps some fear. "Come on, dude," he grabbed Nash by the wrist and began pulling him down the hall. "You have to see this."

Nash allowed the kid to pull him to the stairwell. He turned around to make sure Elliot was behind him and she was, giving him a puzzled and concerned expression. They took the stairs and entered the dining room, immediately faced with a quarter of one of the walls missing. At least, that's what it looked like on the initial glance. It looked as if someone had pulled out the middle quarter of the east wall. Elliot gasped when she saw it.

"What happened?" she demanded, moving in to inspect her missing wall. "Alec, what did you do?"

Nash was already in the gap, calmly inspecting it, as Alec helplessly lifted his shoulders. "I didn't do anything," he insisted weakly. "I just touched the wall and this... this door opened up."

Mouth agape, Elliot went to stand next to Nash, both of them looking at what was apparently a secret door. The tiny, narrow stairs were built into the wall, incorporating the space from underneath the back stairway in the kitchen into its design. Nash squatted down to get a better look, trying to see what was at the bottom of the secret stairs.

"I'll be damned," he muttered. "A tunnel."

Elliot was leaning over him, looking down into the darkness. "I wonder where it goes."

Nash shrugged. "Under the house, somewhere."

"Could it have been part of some underground railroad?" Elliot wanted to know.

Nash shook his head. "Not down here," he replied. "The Aurys owned slaves and weren't part of any liberation movement, I can promise you. I really have no idea what this is."

Elliot looked up at the open wall, at the tattered old wallpaper. "Whatever it is, they blocked it off when they wallpapered this wall. How old did the conservationist say this wallpaper was? One hundred and fifty years?"

Nash looked thoughtful. "That would put it around the 1860's, right around the time of the Civil War," he said. "That's really strange. Why would they block up something like this?"

"Maybe there's a tomb down there," Alec suggested. "Maybe the undead are down there and they were blocking them in."

Penelope giggled as Elliot rolled her eyes. "More zombies," she muttered. "It's always zombies with you."

Alec held up his hands in a creepy, pseudo-zombie way. "You know how the movies are," he teased. "Four ignorant people go down there and get eaten by zombies who were blocked in by the previous owners. We're going to die, dude."

Penelope laughed and even Nash grinned as Elliot waved her son off. "Enough with the zombies, George Romero," she scolded lightly. Then she looked at Nash. "Do we go down there?"

Nash shrugged. "I don't see why not," he said. "I'll go down and take a look."

Elliot was already leaving the dining room, heading for the stairs. "Let me change my clothes," she called to him. "Don't go without me."

Nash heard her, tearing his gaze away from the old stairs to see that she was already on the move. "Why don't you let me take a look first, darlin'?" he called after her. "Just to make sure it's safe?"

She was already upstairs. "No way!"

Nash pursed his lips in resignation, looking at Penelope and Alec. "I don't suppose she'll forgive me if I go down there alone."

Penelope shook her head seriously. "You'll be in big trouble. You don't even know."

Nash wriggled is eyebrows, the corners of his mouth twitching with a smile. He turned to Alec. "Do you have a flashlight?"

Alec nodded and headed off into the kitchen. Nash sat there, peering down the stairs, his gaze drifting over the door itself, trying to figure out what it must have been. In all his years, he'd never even heard of a secret passage at Purgatory. Maybe it was something that was forgotten with time when the door was sealed off. He seriously wondered why it was sealed off.

He could hear Elliot coming back down the stairs just about the time Alec returned from the kitchen with a flashlight. Dressed in jeans and a blue scoop-necked t-shirt, Elliot was pulling her long hair back into a ponytail as she entered the dining room. Nash took the flashlight from Alec and shined it down the stairwell.

"Well," he said after a moment. "The stairs go down below the house. I can't see much except a wet dirt floor."

Elliot tried to peer over his head. "Can you get down these stairs? They look really narrow."

He nodded. "It'll be a tight squeeze, but I think I can make it."

"Are you sure? It can't be more than a couple of feet wide."

Nash wriggled his eyebrows. "There's only one way to find out."

He stepped into the stairwell, testing his weight on the ancient wooden slats, which groaned and creaked but held. It was so narrow that Nash had to turn himself sideways, taking the stairs extremely slowly and holding out a hand for Elliot as she followed. She held on to him tightly as they descended the narrow steps.

The old walls were tight around them, traditional walls with a mixture of moss, mud and deer or animal hair called *bousillage* slathered in between big cypress posts. Elliot wasn't claustrophobic by nature but she felt squeezed as she followed Nash down the stairs. She felt something bump her from behind, startled until she saw Alec. He wanted to explore, too. Penelope remained in the dining room, gazing anxiously down at them with the big, black head of Wolfgang beside her.

"I remember reading somewhere that cemeteries in Louisiana

are above ground because of the high water table," she whispered, trying not to bump into the walls. "People down here don't really have basements for the same reason. Do you think this is a basement?"

Nash was nearly at the bottom of the steps, all twenty-one of them. He ducked his head to pull it under the floor level of the house, which he would have smacked into had he not been careful enough to squeeze below it.

He set foot on the mud floor that, upon inspection, had about an inch of water. He shined the flashlight around the room, digesting the sights, smells and sounds of the completely dark room. It smelled old and earthy, like mold, and had a horrible damp feeling about it. It was like a tomb.

The bright beam of the flashlight fell on a big structure towards the northwest corner of the room and, for a minute, Nash actually startled when he saw it. He stared at it, hardly able to believe his eyes.

"No, not a basement," he murmured. The flashlight began moving crazily about the room as he hunted around, spying more great blocks of stone and realizing with shocking certainty what they were. "Not a basement at all."

Elliot couldn't see what he was looking at because he was moving the flashlight around so fast. "What is it?" she asked, clinging to the back of his shirt.

He didn't want to tell her. God help him, he really didn't. But he had to; it was her house, after all. She had to know. Shining the flashlight on the original block he had spied when he had first entered the area, he made his way over to it through the blackness. He could feel Elliot behind him, holding on to him tightly.

"Look," he said.

Elliot emerged from behind him, looking at the big block of carved stone. It was long and rectangular, lifted off the ground by a pedestal made from the same grayish stone. Moss grew on the stone and other mold that gave it spots of different color. Elliot gazed at it curiously, not really making the connection.

"What is it?" she asked.

Alec, behind her, had been doing the same inspection, but to him, it was much more obvious what it was because things like this existed more in his world than they did in hers. He saw them in his video games, all of the time, and knew the object on sight. Before Nash could answer her question, he burst forth with a reply.

"Zombies!"

TWELVE

"DUDE, I TOLD YOU!"

Alec was excitedly pacing around the kitchen while his mother, sister and Nash sat at the small breakfast table that they had brought with them from California. The women had cups of tea in their hands, looking rather startled, as Nash sat next to Elliot, his hand on her leg as she sipped at her tea. His concerned gaze moved between the women as Alec wandered about, rather excited.

"Crypts," Alec was excited and smiling. "I told you this house had zombies in it. That room downstairs proves it. It's a burial crypt!"

Nash looked at Alec, who grinned excitedly at him until Nash shook his head and gave him a "kill the enthusiasm" expression. Alec's smile faded as he came to realize that his mother and sister were perhaps not so excited that they had just discovered an underground crypt, long sealed off, beneath the house. In fact, they looked rather frightened and disturbed by it.

"But why would they bury them under the house?" Elliot wanted to know. "I thought everyone was buried above ground in Louisiana."

Nash patted her leg. "Usually, that's true," he said. "But those crypts down there all dated before the Civil War, so who's to say?"

"All your ancestors? Did you look on the crypts?"

"I did," he replied. "Four crypts and four ancestors – Paul-Michel Aury, Joseph Aury, Saturnine Aury and Felicity Aury."

"Who are they?"

"I'll need to check with my dad, but if my memory serves, those are the children of Louis-Michel and Sophie."

Elliot gazed back at him with wide eyes, digesting the information, before turning away and shuddering. "Oh, my God," she breathed. "I don't know if I can live above a cemetery. I love this house and everything about it, but that is sort of a deal-breaker."

"I know why they're there," Alec piped up. "Those people are your pirate ancestors buried down there and maybe they buried the treasure down there, too, so no one could find it. Didn't you say there was a legend about buried treasure around here?"

Nash wasn't really in the mood for Alec's theories, but as he thought on them, they made some sense.

"Sure," he replied. "That might actually make some sense as to why the entrance was sealed up. Maybe my ancestors were trying to keep people from finding whatever was down there."

"But we found it," Elliot said quietly, seriously. "No offense to your ancestors, Nash, but I really don't want to live above them. Can we relocate them to a more appropriate place? Not underneath my house?"

He nodded, trying to keep her calm. "I have no problem with it and I don't think my parents will, either, but you have to remember that those crypts down there are hundreds of years old. The State of Louisiana might have something to say about relocating two-hundred-year-old crypts. They're considered historical treasures indigenous to the history of Louisiana so we need to tread carefully."

They suddenly heard sniffling sounds and turned to see Penelope wiping at her eyes. She was trying not to cry and Elliot stood up and went over to her daughter, wrapping her arms around the girl.

"What's wrong, sweetie?" she asked softly.

Penelope wiped at her eyes. "I... I don't know," she whispered. "I just don't like... Mom, I really like our house but I don't want to live above bodies. It's just gross and disturbing."

Elliot looked at Nash, seeing sympathy reflected in his eyes. "What do you want to do?" she asked Penelope.

The girl shrugged. "I don't know," she said. "Maybe... I don't know, maybe I'm just tired. I don't feel very good and that crypt-thing is just really scary. I don't like it."

"I don't like it either," Elliot agreed. "Nash and I will figure out what to do. I don't want you to worry, okay? Besides, you have your bodyguard, Wolfgang, to take care of you. He'll keep the bad spirits away."

Penelope looked down at the dog, lying at her feet, and felt somewhat better. "That's true," she said. Then she set her tea down and stood up from the table. "I think I'm going to go lay down for a while."

Wolfgang stood up the second Penelope did, looking at her eagerly. She called softly to the dog and Wolfgang bolted after her as she took the kitchen stairs up to the second floor. They could hear the dog's nails clicking on the wooden floors above their head. Elliot sat down where her daughter had been seated, across from Nash.

"I swear to you, this house has been one adventure after another," she said.

Nash smiled at her. "Any regrets?"

She looked at him, returning his smile. "Not all," she winked at him. "Still, I'm with Penny. That whole crypt-thing is disturbing."

Nash sat back in his chair, scratching his head. "Well," he said slowly, "I could make a suggestion, but you're not going to like it."

"What?"

"That y'all move to my house until Purgatory is restored and the crypts relocated. It might make everyone feel a lot better not living in such unsettling circumstances."

To his surprise, she actually considered it. At least, she didn't outright shoot him down. As she opened her mouth to reply, Alec interrupted.

"Mom, can I go back down there and look around?" he asked eagerly. "I'll be careful. Maybe I can see what else is written on those crypts."

Elliot didn't look too keen on the idea, looking to Nash for his opinion. Nash looked at Alec. "I think it'll be okay, but please be extremely careful. Don't touch anything. Stuff down there is centuries old and you just don't know about them, or if something will collapse. And watch where you step; even though there were no obvious exits or windows or holes down there, there could be creatures down there, poisonous or otherwise. I don't want you to get hurt."

Alec nodded seriously. "I'll be careful, dude."

He took the flashlight on the counter and disappeared into the dining room. When Alec was gone, Nash got up out of his seat, went to where Elliot was sitting, pulled her up and took her chair, and then sat her back down on his lap. He hugged her close, his head against her cleavage.

"Honey, I think the first thing we need to do is call the State of Louisiana and have them send archaeologists or anthropologists down here," he said. "That hidden room down there is an intact treasure trove and they're going to want to study it before we do anything to it. I've never heard of anything like it, not in all my years."

Elliot had her arms wrapped around his neck. "If you think so," she agreed. "And I'll think on your offer of letting us stay at your house. That's very generous."

He smiled up at her. "You're my family now," he murmured. "My house is your house."

She laughed. "Does that mean I can redecorate your house and spend all of your money?"

He snickered. "Somebody should," he teased. "I sure don't have the time."

Elliot's laughter grew. "Oh, sweetie, I can *make* the time." She hugged him, sobering. "You realize when we get married that Purgatory will belong to the Aury family again, right?"

He lifted his eyebrows. "That's *not* why I proposed to you."

"I know that, but it's kind of ironic, isn't it?"

"It's like it was meant to be."

She liked the sound of that. As she and Nash hugged each other and spoke of things related to their future together, down below, Alec was standing at the base of the hidden stairs with the flashlight in his hand, carefully inspecting every aspect of the room.

He shined the flashlight on the ceiling, realizing that there was a layer of planks and more mud or earth between the ceiling and the floor above. The crypt was well insulated. He stepped into the room, listening to the mud and water making sucking noises around his shoes, shining his flashlight on the first crypt far off to his right.

Two of them were tucked off against the walls of the hollowed-out hole and as he made his way towards them, he noticed that the walls of the room seemed to have been reinforced with planks of wood that had long since rotted away. He could still see their imprint in the walls.

The room itself wasn't the length or width of the house – in fact, it only seemed to encompass the area of half of the central hall and a small portion of the ballroom. The room had no windows, no vents, and no other connection with the outside world than that cobwebby, narrow staircase. The whole thing looked a lot like the vivid graphics in his zombie-killing games.

Alec wandered to the two crypts that very nearly blended in with the wet and moldy surroundings. He peered at the heavy stone, wondering how in the world they moved the thing down the stairs. There was no way they could have moved the crypt down that narrow passage, which led him to think the obvious, that there had to be another way in to the room.

Alec was extremely intelligent in spite of his rather juvenile social skills and he did what he promised Nash he wouldn't do; he began to drag his hands over the crypt, wiping away the mold so he could read the names and epitaphs on them.

It was very fascinating stuff for a young kid from California who had never seen such old and decrepit things. He moved to all of the crypts, wiping away at the epitaphs and reading the names on the stone and the dates of birth and death.

On the largest crypt of stone, it read:

Paul-Michel Aury
1813 – 1830
à tous qui sait

Alec's brow furrowed as he read the epitaph in French. Having taken four years of French in high school, he was surprised to realize it would actually come in handy. French was like Algebra, learning something he would never use, but today, his French classes had actually served a purpose. He could read what was written.

"'To all who know'," he mumbled the translation.

With a shrug, he moved to the second crypt purely out of curiosity and wiped away the moss that covered up the lettering on the stone. More words came into view.

Joseph Aury
1820 – 1830
La question d'avidité est décidée

Alec read the epitaph four times. It was an odd one just like the one on his brother's crypt. He shook his head.

"'The matter of greed is decided'," he muttered, then shook his head again. "Dude, what a weird family."

He moved to the third crypt, wiping of the moss and growth because now he was curious what this epitaph would say. This one was the woman's crypt.

Felicity Lydia Aury
1816 – 1830
Avec le sang et maudit nous avons trouvé

Alec's eyebrows lifted as he read this particular epitaph. "'With blood and curses we found'?" he translated verbatim, suddenly looking between the three crypts, repeating what all three epitaphs had scribed.

"'To all who know the matter of greed is decided, with blood and curses we know'...."

Realization slammed him. Electrified, Alec ran to the fourth crypt, a smaller one off from the rest. This one was nearer the floor, sinking deep in the stinking mud of the room as if set apart from the others. It looked pathetic, beat-up, and untended. Alec scraped of the mud and moss of the smallest crypt, straining to read the words.

Saturnine Aury
1822 – 1830
L'enfer que nous avons condamnés à dans les intestins de
Purgatoire

Alec didn't remember running from the crypt until he was already upstairs in the great central hall.

He had to find Nash.

———

"Well," Nash said slowly as he read the epitaph on Saturnine Aury's crypt. "You were right. That's exactly what it says – *To all who know the matter of greed is decided, with blood and curses we know the hell we have condemned ourselves to in the bowels of Purgatory.* Good job with your French translation, son."

Alec was standing behind Nash with the flashlight, feeling anxious and a jumpy. "I wasn't sure if you could read French or not. I figured you could, living in Louisiana and all. It's kind of like knowing Spanish in Southern California just by association."

Nash glanced around at the other crypts. "En effet je peux," he said fluently, pointing to the other crypts. "Each one of these has a part of a message that, when put together, reads *a tous qui sait la question d'avidité est décidée, avec le sang et maudit nous avons l'enfer que nous avons condamnés à dans les intestins de Purgatoire.* It's really quite fascinating."

"Fascinating?" Alec repeated, wondering why the man was so calm. "But look at the year of death on all the crypts. They all died the *same year.* They were just kids, dude. What in the hell does that mean?"

Nash made a career out of remaining cool in a crisis, no matter what it was. It was. perhaps. one of his greatest attributes. He stood up from where he was crouched over Saturnine's crypt and brushed his hands off on his jeans, outwardly much calmer than he felt inside. Secretly, he was just as baffled and disturbed as Alex was, only he wasn't going to show it. At least, not at the moment.

"I don't have a clue," he said honestly, turning to Alec. "But I do know one thing; you're not going to tell your mother or sister about this. They're already upset about living on top of a crypt and this will send them from this house and we'll never get them back. Okay?"

Alec pursed his lips, unhappy but understanding. "Okay," he agreed. "But what are we going to do about it?"

Nash shrugged. "What can we do about it?" he asked the obvious. "I'll be the first to admit that this is bizarre, but the fact of the matter is that we can't do anything about it today. I've already put in a call to the State of Louisiana Department of Culture and it's my intention to get them out here to check all of this out. Maybe they can help piece it together. Meanwhile, I'm going to call my dad and see what he knows about Louis-Michel's children. Maybe there's some explanation to all of this, like they all died of Yellow Fever at the same time. I'm sure there's a logical explanation."

Alec wasn't convinced but Nash made sense. "Doesn't this epitaph make you wonder at all?" the young man pushed.

Nash grinned. "Of course it does," he said. "As you would say, that's some crazy shit. But it's also really, really intriguing. I'd like to find out what happened as much as you."

Alec didn't have anymore to say. He still thought it was all creepy and mysterious and weird, but he followed Nash out of the crypt chamber and up to the dining room above. Nash pulled the panel closed as much as he could, leaving it cracked about an inch. He and Alec went into the kitchen where Alec put the flashlight back on the counter.

"Now," Nash said in a quiet tone. "Your mother is upstairs doing something on her computer and your sister is taking a nap with the dog. Not a word of this to them, Alec. I'm serious."

Alec's features hardened. "I heard you the first time," he said. "I've been taking care of them a long time. I don't need you to tell me not to upset them."

Nash could see he had offended the young man and immediately backed off.

"I'm sorry," he said sincerely. "I know you've been taking care of them and you've done an excellent job. I didn't mean to insult you. I guess... I guess I just want to take care of them, too, like a natural instinct. I don't mean to step on your toes, Alec. I would never knowingly do that. It's just that I love your mom and sister, too."

Alec's anger cooled somewhat, knowing that what Nash said was true.

"Well," he said after a moment, kicking at the floor as if embarrassed he had become snappish. "If you want to know the truth, I would have punched anyone else who talked to me the way you just did. But you... I know you mean well. Just don't treat me like I'm an idiot. I know I sound like one sometimes, but I'm not."

Nash threw up his hands. "God, no," he insisted. "I'm truly sorry if it came across like that, Alec. I didn't mean it."

Alec gave him a quirky grin. "No worries, dude."

Nash returned the grin, thankful that he hadn't irrevocably upset the young man. "Good," he replied. Then he threw his thumb in the direction of the front door. "I've got to run some errands. Dog food and all that. Are you going to hang around here?"

Alec shrugged. "Yes," he said, sitting heavily at the breakfast table. "Where am I going to go? I don't have any friends, no one to hang out with. I'll be here."

Nash regarded him a moment. "It's pretty boring for you, I would guess."

Alec shrugged again, fidgeting with the marks on the tabletop. "I'm so used to having my friends around all of the time. This has been an adjustment, not being able to pick up the phone and call ten people to come hang out."

Nash scratched his chin and began to head out of the kitchen. "I'll see what I can do about that," he told him. "I'm going to say goodbye to your mom. I'll see you later."

Alec watched him go, his thoughts inevitably turning to the creepy crypt down below. He just couldn't stay away. When Elliot ended up going with Nash to run his errands, Alec slipped back down to the crypt for a second round of inspections.

THIRTEEN

THE SUN WASN'T EVEN UP YET on Monday morning when a team from the State of Louisiana Division of Archaeology and Office of Cultural Development were in Purgatory's driveway.

Nash heard the cars roll in and saw the headlights reflecting in the windows of the upstairs bedroom. He lifted his head and looked at the clock, seeing that it was a little before five in the morning. Then he looked down at Elliot, curled up against him and sound asleep. He kissed her gently, twice, before carefully disengaging himself and going in search of his clothes.

In jeans, a long sleeved pullover t-shirt and shoes, he closed Elliot's door behind him quietly and peered across the hall into Alec's room to see if the young man was awake. He had to grin to see the kid all spread out over the bed, covers on the floor, sleeping the sleep of the dead. His boys slept much the same way. He called out quietly, three times, before Alec finally stirred.

The blond head came up from the bed, eyes still closed. "What's up?" he mumbled.

"The people from the State of Louisiana are here," Nash whispered loudly. "Do you want to come down and meet them?"

Alec nodded, eyes only partially opened as he climbed out of bed. "Yeah, dude," he stumbled as he got out of bed. "Thanks. Is Mom awake?"

"No," Nash said. "Let's you and me handle this for now, if you're okay with that. I'm afraid it'll just upset your mother, especially if we get into the subject of the epitaphs and all."

"Good idea," Alec staggered towards the bathroom. "I'll be right down."

Nash closed the door softly behind him, moving down the hallway and checking on Penelope and Wolfgang before he went downstairs. Cracking the door open, he saw Penelope sleeping on her side and the dog stretched out at the bottom of her bed. He whistled softly to the dog. Wolfgang leapt off the bed to come with him. Closing the door softly, he took the dog downstairs to let him do his doggy business, letting him back inside before he went to open the front door.

By the time he walked out onto the front porch, he could see his brother pulling up, as well as three or four other contractors, ready to continue the restoration of Purgatory. Nash watched the people from the State climb out of their cars and he went out to meet them. He approached a silver-haired, heavyset man with a pair of glasses perched on the end of his nose.

"Hi," Nash extended his hand. "I'm Nash Aury."

The man quickly shifted his books and paper pads to the opposite hand and shook Nash's hand amiably.

"Sheriff Aury, it's a pleasure to meet you, sir," he said in a booming Louisiana drawl. "I'm Bob Whitney, Senior Field Archaeologist for the State. I can't tell y'all how excited I am to finally be at Purgatory. This place has quite a history."

Nash nodded. "Yes, it does," he agreed. "When I called yesterday, I spoke with Dr. Mann about the situation here. Did he explain everything to you?"

Dr. Rob Mann was the Regional Director for Archaeology for the State. He had happily taken Sheriff Aury's call, even on a Sunday. Dr. Whitney nodded firmly.

"Gladly and thoroughly," Dr. Whitney confirmed. "He said

you found an old family crypt underneath the house. I have to tell you, I'm dying to see it. I've never heard of one built underneath a house, so this will be a first."

Nash smiled at the man's enthusiasm. "It's something else, that's for sure," he agreed. "We only found it yesterday and called y'all right away."

"Well, sir, we're delighted." Dr. Whitney turned to the two other people with him. One was a silver-haired African-American woman and the other was a very young Caucasian girl with dark hair and big, blue eyes. Dr. Whitney indicated the silver-haired woman first. "This is Dr. Myla Clarke, a cultural historian, and this young lady is Lucy Hennig, an intern."

Dr. Clarke extended a slender hand to Nash. "Sheriff Aury, it's an absolute pleasure to meet you," she said in a deep, lovely voice. "One of my areas of expertise is of the pirates who used to infiltrate these lands, and I'm extremely familiar with Louis-Michel Aury. It's such a thrill meeting one of his descendants."

Nash greeted the woman kindly. "I'm flattered, thank you."

Dr. Whitney had apparently had enough of the introductions. He was eager to get started. "We'd love to take look at your crypt, Sheriff," he said, indicating the house. "Shall we?"

Nash nodded, turning to the house just as Alec emerged. In his faded jeans, wrinkled t-shirt and flip-flops, he looked like he just walked off the pages of an Abercrombie and Fitch ad. He was slovenly stylish, not unnoticed by the young intern. Nash introduced everyone when Alec drew close.

"This is Alec Jentry, the owner's son," he said. "Alec is responsible for this find, in fact. He's the one who found the secret door."

Alec shook everyone's hands as Dr. Whitney looked rather curiously at Nash. "I thought you were the owner, Sheriff?"

As Nash thought on the complicated reply, Alec spoke up. "He and my mom are getting married," he explained, yawning. "He's practically the owner. He sold her the house and when he marries her, he'll get it back, so what he says goes."

Nash tried not to react to Alec's hurtful statement as he led everyone inside the house. Immediately, Dr. Whitney and Dr. Clarke were entranced with the place and Nash turned on a few of the working lights so they could see everything. Dr. Whitney was a man in love as his gaze moved over the entry.

"Look at this place," he sighed. "That's the beauty of having it in the same family for so long. There are so few changes."

"Dr. Whitney," Dr. Clarke was in the central hall, pointing to the staircase. "Look at the self-supported staircase. A truly amazing architectural feat."

As Dr. Whitney and Dr. Clarke inspected the main staircase with awe, Nash began to smell coffee. He noticed the kitchen light was on and he peered inside. Elliot was standing in front of the coffeemaker dressed in a sparkly gray, velour, designer jogging suit, her hair pulled into a stylish ponytail. She looked radiant and lovely, even at five-thirty in the morning, and Nash slipped up behind her and wrapped his big arms around her torso, nuzzling her neck.

"Good morning, sunshine," he murmured, kissing her head. "I was trying to let you sleep in a little."

Elliot grinned, snuggling against him. "That's okay," she said. "I heard the cars drive up, too, so it's not like I'll be able to sleep much longer with the contractors here."

He nodded, conceding the point. "True," he kissed her lips. "The people from the State are here. I was just getting ready to take them downstairs."

Elliot opened her mouth to reply when Alec walked in. "Hey, mom," he greeted, going to the refrigerator and yanking it open. "Did Nash tell you the people from the State are here?"

"He did," she replied. "I'm ready when they are."

Nash glanced at Alec, who immediately shook his head. "Not right now," Alec told her. "Let the men handle this for now. Can you please make me some cheesy scrambled eggs with ham? I'm really hungry."

Elliot was going to argue with her son but the request for food naturally made her give in to his demands. "Sure, I guess," she appeared a little hurt that she was being left out. She looked at Nash. "Are you hungry?"

Nash nodded. "Sure," he said. "We shouldn't be too long. Besides, it's nasty and wet down there. You don't need to be down in that mess. We'll tell you everything they said."

She thought on that and eventually shrugged. "Okay." She turned for the refrigerator. "I'll make some breakfast for everyone. Is Beau here?"

"Yes, he's here."

"He'll smell the food and come running."

"You know my brother well."

She grinned at him and began busying herself with the food as Nash slipped out after Alec. He caught the kid as they made their way back to the people from the State, still inspecting the self-supporting staircase.

"How did you do that?" he asked.

Alec looked at him curiously. "Do what?"

"Make her stay out of it? I thought we were going to have a fight on our hands."

Alec grinned. "You just have to know how to handle the Jentry women," he said confidently. "Requests for food will always be promptly obeyed. Stick with me, Sheriff. I'll teach you a thing or two."

Nash laughed but as he did so, he was reminded of the comment that Alec had made outside about marrying Elliot and getting the house back. He felt the need to clarify things, for his own sake.

"Hey, Alec?" he said.

Alec looked at him. "What?"

"I'm not marrying your mom just to get the house back. I'm marrying your mom because I love her. I don't give a damn about getting the house back."

Alec looked confused for a moment before realization dawned. "I know, dude," he said sincerely. "I didn't mean it the way it sounded. I just meant that you're the boss and can make decisions about the house."

"You're sure?"

"Yeah, dude. If I thought you were marrying my mom just for the house, I would have buried your body in the backyard long before now."

"You're starting to scare me."

Alec burst out laughing and Nash grinned, shaking his head at the kid. He was truly coming to appreciate the relationship they were establishing, like the relationship he had with his own boys. He treasured it. By that time, they were back over at the staircase, collecting the people from the State and showing them the secret door. The inspection of the door alone took the next two hours.

———

Nash eventually had to go to work, leaving Alec with the State historians and Elliot with Hallie, the preservationist from Tulane. Elliot spent several hours with the woman, going over the original paint colors for the interior of the house, which they discovered had originally been a plain whitewash. Not wanting the entire house to be Institutional White, Elliot and Hallie spent hours going over white pallets that would complement the rooms.

They eventually chose a series of soft whites that would work magnificently with the original exterior color, which was a peach color with big, white pillars and white trim. With the paint colors selected for all of the rooms and the exterior, Elliot felt as if a weight had been lifted off her shoulders. Finally, progress everyone would be able to see. Purgatory was beginning her transformation.

Hallie eventually left to go and talk to the painters, leaving Elliot with some time on her hands. Alec was still down in the crypt with Dr. Whitney and his intern, while Dr. Clarke was outside, sitting in the car with her laptop computer and chatting on a cell phone.

Elliot went upstairs to find her daughter lying on her bed with the dog, messaging on her computer, so she left the pair alone and went to her bedroom to envision how it would be laid out once it was painted. Still, everything was bunched up in the middle of the room, away from the walls. She would be glad to get it set to normal.

Flopping on to her bed, she picked up her cell phone and dialed Nash. On the fourth ring, he picked up.

"Hey, darlin'," he greeted. "I'm so glad you called. How are you?"

Elliot smiled simply at the sound of his voice. He made her feel all warm and cozy inside. "Good," she cooed. "How are you?"

"I'm always good when I'm talking to you," he said sweetly. "What are you doing?"

"Well," she rolled over onto her back, staring up at the ceiling. "Hallie and I just picked out all of the colors for the house. Did you know the walls were originally whitewashed? I can't stand stark white walls. I'll need a straightjacket to go along with them."

He laughed. "What are you going to do?"

"Well, since I really wanted to stay true to the original colors, we selected harmonious white shades that are softer and more muted," she assured him. "Hallie's talking to the painters now. Hopefully we can start getting the place painted by tomorrow."

"Good," he said. "I think you should... wait, hold on a second...."

He covered the receiver but she could hear him talking to someone else. Eventually, he came back on the line.

"Honey, I've got to run," he told her. "I'll see you tonight. I love you."

"I love you, too. See you later."

He made a kissing noise into the phone and hung up. Elliot set the cell phone back on the nightstand and looked around for her laptop, realizing she had left it in the kitchen. Heading downstairs, she ran into Dr. Clarke as the woman was coming in from the driveway. She smiled at the handsome, black woman.

"Dr. Clarke," she greeted. "How do you like my house so far?"

Dr. Clarke sighed happily. "It's a truly remarkable example of an untouched Spanish Colonial home," she said. "I'm just in awe of it."

"Good," Elliot said. "What a fascinating job you must have, studying these places."

Dr. Clarke held up a finger. "Ah, it's not studying the home," she clarified. "It's studying the people who lived here, their life and culture. Purgatory is truly in a class by itself because of its relationship to the pirates that sailed the river."

"How is that?"

"Well," Dr. Clarke began thoughtfully. "Before I came here, I knew generally of the place and its history, just like I knew of most of the houses along the River Road and beyond. I knew that Louis-Michel Aury had an entire colony going on around here, as the men that sailed with him also had homes in the area. That's why they used to call this place the Devil's Bayou."

Elliot nodded. "Nash told me that. It's an amazing story."

Dr. Clarke nodded. "Yes, it really is. Essentially, Purgatory was the center of a vivid and prosperous city, one that used profits from privateers and pirate raids to thrive. Whereas most cultures during that time were dependent upon trade or agriculture, Purgatory was almost entirely dependent upon the spoils from the pirates. This house was built on theft, death and destruction."

Elliot lifted an eyebrow. "That's a pleasant thought."

Dr. Clarke grinned. "It's just the way it was back then," she insisted. "This entire area was very lawless, so it wasn't unusual at all. Murder, rape, all of those things that we today consider uncivilized were considered common occurrences back then. People struggled to survive any way they could."

Elliot shrugged. "I guess that makes sense," she said. "So what do we know about the family of Louis-Michel Aury and Sophie? Nash says that their children are buried down in that crypt."

Dr. Clarke nodded. "Here's where it gets interesting," she said. "I had a friend of mine at the University of New Orleans Department of Regional Studies do some research on the life of Louis-

Michel and Sophie and she came up with some interesting things based on documents from that time, and from other plantations, such as Destrehan and Mary. These were plantations also known to have association with pirates, particularly Destrehan. Destrehan was owned by the same family for generations, but the second owner, a man by the name of Nicholas Destrehan, married a woman by the name of Louise de Navarre. Mrs. Destrehan kept a meticulous journal, which today is a huge help in our understanding of the plantation way of life. Anyway, it would seem that one of her journal entries included information about Sophie MacGregor, Louis-Michel's mistress."

Elliot was completely hooked on the story. "What did she say about her?"

Dr. Clarke continued, her manner serious. "Apparently, the rumor was that Ms. Sophie, despondent over the evident death of Louis-Michel because the man had not returned to Purgatory in years, went mad and poisoned her children. At least, that was the rumor that Ms. Louise heard. She wrote about how she could not understand why Sophie would do such a thing because she clearly adored her children, but because Purgatory and the area surrounding it were so lawless and wild, Mr. Destrehan would not allow his wife to travel north to see her friend. Louise writes that she later heard that Ms. Sophie killed herself after the death of her children and since we have never found Sophie's crypt, we don't know for certain if that rumor is true."

Elliot was staring at the woman in increasing horror. "But...," she swallowed hard and continued. "They were just babies. The oldest is seventeen and the youngest one is only eight years old."

Dr. Clarke nodded sadly. "I know," she said quietly. "But mental illness was unknown and untreatable back then. Who's to say what happened? Perhaps when we excavate the crypts below, we'll know for sure."

Elliot nodded, still caught up in the shockingly tragic story of Sophie and her children. "Then if all of the children were murdered by their mother, who does Nash descend from?"

"The eldest boy, Paul-Michel," Dr. Clarke told her. "He was married the year before to a local girl by the name of Julia Loreau. They had one son, the only child that carried on the Aury blood lines."

Stunned by the deep and tragic tale, Elliot couldn't think of anything else to say. She thanked Dr. Clarke and, forgetting why she had come downstairs in the first place, wandered back upstairs feeling increasingly despondent. She simply couldn't understand how a mother, any mother, could kill her own children.

It was the worst thing she had ever heard.

FOURTEEN

IT WAS after seven in the evening by the time Nash was headed back to Purgatory. An impromptu Ascension Parish Council meeting had held him up and even though he had called Elliot to let her know, still, he felt the disappointment of not seeing her right away. He was anxious to get home to her.

As he drove the Airline Highway south, his cell phone rang. His father's number came up on caller I.D. and he answered.

"Hey, Dad," he greeted. "How are you doing?"

Camp Aury sounded gruff and irritated. "My prostate is too big, my bunions are killing me, and the doctor wants to remove a few big moles from my back," he grumped. "Other than that, I'm living, son. I'm living."

Nash tried not to laugh, mostly because he knew his father was serious. The man was as tough as nails but a notorious hypochondriac. It was an odd combination.

"Sorry to hear about your troubles," he said. "Other than that, how's everything? I haven't talked to you in a while."

Camp grunted. "That's because you've been busy, from what I've been told," he said. "I saw your brother this weekend. What's this I hear, you have a girlfriend?"

Nash laughed. "Well," he began, wondering how and where to

start. "It happened kind of fast, so don't be upset that you didn't know. Nobody knows, except Beau, and that's because he's been working on Purgatory."

"That's another thing he told me," Camp grumbled. "You're in love with the woman who bought Purgatory."

Nash's smile faded. "Dad, don't jump to any conclusions," he said. "There's no ulterior motive or whatever you might be thinking. I met her when I went to go collect the remains of Mamaw's junk and fell in love with her, pure and simple. She's a wonderful woman and I know you and Mom are going to love her."

On the other end of the phone, Camp just shook his head. "Nash, you were always my level-headed kid," he said. "You can do no wrong. I'm not sure I'm comfortable with you falling in love with a woman in a whirlwind romance. Love takes time, son, you know that."

Nash thought of the petite blond he was so crazy about. "You may not be comfortable with it but I'm asking that you respect it," he said quietly. "You know I'm not given to whims. But what happened... it was right from the beginning, Dad. I've never felt this way about anyone, ever, and I've never been so happy in my entire life. Can you at least support me even if you don't agree?"

The phone was silent for a few seconds. "I'll always support you, son, you know that," he said, less gruff and more understanding. "I just don't want to see you hurt, that's all."

Nash's smile was returning. "I'm a big boy," he said. "I can take care of myself. What did Beau say about her?"

Camp was back to grunting. "That's she's the most beautiful woman he's ever seen and if you weren't already with her, he was going to leave his wife for her," he teased, then turned serious. "He says you have his blessing. I guess that should be good enough for me."

Nash's smile broadened. "Good," he said. "Anyway, that's not why I called earlier. I called because I wanted to pick your brain about something."

"What?"

Nash was entering the city limits of Sorrento as he spoke. "What do you know about Louis-Michel and Sophie's children?"

"What do you mean?"

"Like, do you know the history on them? When and how they lived, and how they died?"

Camp stretched out in his armchair and kicked up his feet, getting comfortable for the conversation. "Well," he said thoughtfully. "The oldest boy, Paul-Michel, was my grandfather several times over. Yours, too. He died very young, from what I recall."

"How?"

Camp scratched his chin. "From what I remember, his mother killed him. Him and his siblings. The story passed down through Mamaw was that Sophie thought she was poisoning Louis-Michel and ended up feeding the kids whatever she intended to feed him. At least, that's what Mamaw told me. I don't know if it's true or not. Didn't I tell you that before?"

In those few, brief sentences from his father, Nash was feeling sick and apprehensive. "If you did, I didn't remember," he said. "So she killed the kids?"

"That's what I was told. Killed them and threw them in the bayou, because no bodies or graves were ever found. Why do you ask?"

Nash debated about telling him because Camp could get very worked up over things. Still, he decided to do it. His father knew everything about the family history and needed to hear it.

"Because we found a crypt underneath the house yesterday," he said. "It had four coffins in it, those of all four of Louis-Michel and Sophie's children. The date of death was the same for all of them, Dad – the year 1830. They all died so young and I couldn't recall hearing anything about why they all died at once. I thought it might have been Yellow Fever."

"What?" Camp burst. "You found a crypt under the *house*?"

Nash nodded. "We sure did," he replied. "The access was hidden by a secret door in the wall of the dining room."

"My God!" Camp hissed. "I… I don't even know what to say.

I'd never heard anything like that about the house, not ever. How in the hell did you find it?"

"It was by accident, trust me. But the State of Louisiana is out there examining the crypt. Do you want to come over and see it?"

"Hell, yes!" Camp shouted. "Your mom and I will be out there tomorrow!"

Nash grinned. "You'll get to meet Ellie."

"Ellie?" he repeated, initially puzzled. "Oh, yes. Your girlfriend. Well, at least she's got a good Southern name."

Nash laughed. "Her name is Elliot, but everyone calls her Ellie. She's from California."

"Elliot?" Camp didn't like it. "What kind of Yankee name is that? Well, we'll see about her. We'll just see."

Nash was laughing. "She's a little bundle of fire, Dad. I wouldn't test her if I was you. You might come away missing an eye."

Camp started to grump at him but ended up laughing. "Then you deserve her," he said. "Maybe she can keep you in line."

Snorting, Nash said goodbye to his father and hung up just as he neared the turnoff for Purgatory. Shortly, he was in the crunchy gravel driveway, pulling up the long, tree-lined avenue until he reached the massive house at the end. His brother's truck was still there, as were the cars from the State of Louisiana people. He got out of the car and went to the house.

The front door was unlocked and he entered. It was relatively quiet as he walked back towards the central hall and the winding staircase, but he could see light coming from the dining room, kitchen and ballroom.

Entering the kitchen with its mix of new appliances and old counters, he caught sight of Elliot sitting at the breakfast table with Beau. His heart warmed as his gaze fell on her as she talked quietly with his brother. It was what he had wanted from the beginning with her – coming home to her sweet face every night.

When Elliot caught movement from the corner of her eye and saw Nash, she smiled brightly and stood up.

"Hi," she said. "How was your day?"

What sweet words, he thought. He'd been waiting to hear words like that his entire life. He smiled at her and wrapped his arms around her, kissing her sweetly.

"Long," he said truthfully. "How was yours?"

Elliot's smile faded somewhat. "Interesting," she said. "Are you hungry?"

"Don't go to any trouble."

"That's not an answer. I already have dinner for you if you want it."

He smiled. "Then I'm hungry."

She had him sit down with Beau, who had apparently waited to eat with his brother. Elliot pulled a bunch of asparagus out from the refrigerator and put them under the broiler along with the plates of chicken and rice she had heating in the oven. As she busied herself with preparing dinner, Nash pulled off his sport coat and slung it across the back of one of the chairs.

"Where are the kids?" he asked her, looking around. "It seems kind of quiet around here."

Elliot began mixing something in a saucepan. "Alec found movie theaters about twenty miles from here, so he and Penny went to see a movie."

"Good for them," he commented as he sat down and rubbed his eyes. "Man, what a day."

Beau had a half-empty beer in his hand. "No rest for the wicked, eh?"

Nash shook his head. "My office has been investigating corruption charges against one of the parish councilmen and now the FBI is involved."

Beau took a drink of his beer as Elliot brought one over to Nash and popped off the top. He stroked her fingers when she handed it to him, smiling gratefully.

"Thanks, honey," he said to her.

She winked at him and returned to the stove. Beau watched

the exchange between the two, how absolutely enamored they were with each other, as he took another drink.

"Have you been directly involved in the investigation?" he asked his brother.

Nash took a long drink of beer and shook his head. "No," he smacked his lips. "I've been informed at every step, but my detectives have it pretty well in hand. It's going to take a while because this guy is so buried in corruption; it's all over the place."

Beau shook his head. "Must be a mess," he said. "Well, at least you won't have to worry about it when you take the job at the state capital."

Nash froze, his eyes widened as he looked at his brother. Beau had no idea why until Nash's eyes flicked at Elliot and he shook his head faintly. But Elliot had heard the comment as she made sauce for the asparagus on the stovetop.

"I heard about that," she said, not looking at Nash. "Your brother told me you were going to work for the state police commission."

Nash looked over, feeling incredibly guilty for not having told her all of this before. The truth was that it hadn't crossed his mind and it had never come up in conversation. It had been the proudest moment in his life before he had met her, now paling in comparison to what he felt for Elliot. She had trumped everything.

"The police commissioner is leaving office next month," he said. "I'm sorry I didn't mention it before. It just never came up."

She looked over at him as she whisked something in a saucepan. "That's okay," she smiled. "You can't tell me your whole life story in a week. When do you take the new job?"

"September first."

"What will you be doing for the police commission?"

Beau spoke up before Nash could because he knew Nash was too modest to point out the truth. They'd be here all night beating around the bush.

"He *is* the Police Commissioner, Ellie," he said. "He was

appointed by the Governor back in March. Nash will be the new State Police Commissioner when he takes office."

She stopped whisking and looked at Nash with shock. "Are you serious?"

Nash nodded humbly. "Yes."

Her eyes opened wider. "Oh, my God!" she exclaimed. "That's.... that's amazing!"

He smiled faintly. "Does that change your mind about me?"

She laughed. "I don't know," she said. "Should it?"

"I won't take it if it means losing you."

Her smile vanished. "Why would you lose me?" she asked seriously. "Unless one of your job perks is a harem of women, I'm not sure what one has to do with the other."

Beau thought that now might be a good time for him to leave but Elliot barked at him to sit back down and he did, like an obedient kid. He pretended to drink his beer as Elliot approached Nash with the whisk in her hand.

"I'm going to be spending a lot of time in Baton Rouge, honey," Nash pointed out. "I won't be seeing you as much and...."

"Are we getting married before or after you take office?"

He looked surprised. "I... I don't know," he said. "I haven't really thought about it. But I'll tell you this – I'd sure like you by my side when they swear me in. That would mean the world to me."

"Then we'll do it before," she said decisively, turning back to the stove. "That way, you'll be coming home to me every night so it really won't matter if I don't see you during the day. We'll sleep in the same bed every night and that's what matters. Are you going to sell your house over in Gonzales?"

Nash blinked, looking at his brother, who was amused by the way Elliot had taken charge of the situation. Beau just grinned.

"I wasn't planning on it," Nash replied, looking back at Elliot. "I was planning on commuting. It's only about thirty miles away."

Elliot whisked the saucepan furiously and turned off the stove.

"But I want to live here at Purgatory," she said. "What are we going to do with two houses?"

"Then I'll sell it."

She reached into the oven and began pulling out the plates. "So why did you ask if I had changed my mind about you?"

He sighed, toying with his beer bottle. "Because I'm stupid and insecure, I guess," he said, shrugging when she looked at him. "I don't know why I asked. I'm sorry I did. I should have given you more credit."

Elliot smiled as she brought the plates over to the table and set them down. She poured Hollandaise sauce over the asparagus before sitting down next to Nash. Once she sat down, she and Nash gazed at each other a moment before exchanging tender kisses right in front of Beau. Beau kept his head down, eating the delicious meal and trying not to pay attention to the lovebirds.

Not another word was spoken about the State Police Commission job. It was the first time Elliot had actually cooked for Nash and he discovered, with delight, that she had a talent for good cooking. He chowed down on the herbed chicken and rice dish, finishing it off with a pineapple upside-down cake that was heavenly. When all was said and done, he'd stuffed himself silly and had four beers. Beau wasn't much better. Together, the brothers wallowed in gluttonous misery.

As they all sat around the table and enjoyed the after-feast of light conversation, they heard faint knocking at the front door. Elliot moved to get up but Nash stopped her, crossing through the dim central hall and going to the door himself. Unlatching the bolt, he pulled open the panel.

Two familiar faces were gazing back at him. Nash grinned, pulling each young man towards him in turn, planting a fatherly kiss on the head.

"Well, it took y'all long enough," he said.

Beck Aury and Shane Aury smiled back at their father. Beck was nearly the spitting image of his dad, handsome and well-built, while Shane resembled their mother, a bigger-boned lad with dark-brown eyes and hair. They were very handsome young men and were very glad to see their father.

"We came as soon as we could get here," Beck said. "Shane had to work."

Shane was much like Alec in his demeanor, kind of the big, easy-going type. "Yeah, but I'm off for the next three days," he said, looking around the porch of the enormous house. "Are you going to invite us in or do we have to stand here all night?"

Nash stood back, ushering the boys in. Since Purgatory had been inhabited by a crazy old woman and had spent years in probate during their lifetime, they had never really seen the interior. Both of them looked around with awe.

"So this is it," Beck said, peering into the front double parlor. "This place is a monster."

Nash watched his boys look around. "I'll give you a tour."

While Shane agreed, Beck put his hand on his father's arm. "In a minute," he said, his voice quiet. "So what's going on, Dad? Why are you here? Why are *we* here?"

Nash had planned this moment in his mind for days, what he was going to tell his sons about him and Elliot. He had been very close to his sons, especially since the divorce when both boys had elected to live with him. Julie had fought him on it and a nasty custody battle had ensued until a judge in Baton Rouge decided that a sixteen-year-old and a thirteen-year-old were capable of deciding where they wanted to live.

Therefore, the boys had stayed with Nash during the week, seeing their mother on the weekends. Now, they had their lives up in Baton Rouge where they were going to school, young men growing up and finding their places in the world. Still, Nash desperately wanted them to be okay with him and Elliot.

"Well," Nash scratched his head. "It would seem that your dad has fallen in love. She's the most amazing woman I've ever met and she happens to own Purgatory."

Beck didn't react at first but Shane looked shocked. Both boys waited for more of an explanation to be forthcoming but when Nash didn't continue, Beck lifted his eyebrows expectantly.

"And?" he said. "What else? How did you meet her? Were you going to tell us this at some point or just mention it in passing some time down the road?"

Nash put his hand on the young man's shoulder. "Look," he said. "I haven't had a chance to tell you because she and I have really only been together a matter of a week. I don't know how else to tell you that I love the woman and we're going to get married. She's intelligent, beautiful and amazing in every way and I really hope you'll give her the chance to come to know you. It would mean a lot to me."

Beck looked at his dad, shaking his head with the shock of the situation, before turning to look at his brother to see how the younger brother was reacting. Shane merely shrugged. Beck turned back to his father.

"Isn't this happening kind of fast?" he scratched his head.

Nash lifted his shoulders. "If it had happened to you, I would have said the same thing," he replied. "All I can say is yes, it happened really fast, but in my whole life, other than you boys, nothing has ever felt so right. I don't make swift decisions and I don't act on whim, so all I can tell you is that Ellie is a wonderful woman and I adore her. Give her a chance, okay? And don't think she roped me into anything because I promise you, it was the other way around. I pursued her until she had no choice."

By this time, Shane was grinning. "Right on, Dad." He fist-bumped his old man. "Is she hot?"

Nash snorted. "Smoking."

Shane laughed. "Then if you're happy, I'm happy."

"I'm happy," Nash assured him, looking at Beck. His oldest seemed to be the only hold-out. "And you? What are you thinking?"

Beck wriggled his eyebrows much in the same way Nash did. "I'm thinking that I'm smelling something really good in this house."

Nash grinned at him and clapped him on the neck, pulling him into an embrace. The three of them headed back towards the kitchen.

"The reason why I called you was to not only introduce you to Ellie, but to introduce you to her kids," Nash said. "She's got two kids your age and they don't know anybody around here. I was hoping you could take a couple of days to show them around. I know they'd really appreciate it."

Shane shrugged easily while Beck, as always, was more resistant. "Great," he grumbled. "Now we're tour guides?"

"No, you're being friendly to two people who really don't know anyone in the State of Louisiana," Nash said pointedly. "Ellie's oldest is Penelope, a very lovely girl who just enrolled at Tulane, and her youngest is her son, Alec. I think you'll like them."

Beck seemed to perk up at the mention of a girl. "Penelope?" he repeated. "And she's cute?"

Nash cast him a long look. "You're a gentleman, remember? I raised you better than that."

Beck shrugged. "I know," he said defensively. "But if I have to drive people around, then at least one of them can be nice to look at."

Nash grinned at him as they entered the kitchen. Beau, seeing his nephews, jumped up from the table where he had been in quiet conversation with Elliot.

"The troublemakers have arrived!" he said happily, embracing Shane and then Beck. "Y'all have grown up right before my eyes."

Beck smiled at his Uncle Beau but his gaze was drawn to Elliot, who had risen from her chair and was smiling at the strange young men in her kitchen. Nash held out a hand to her and she came to him.

"Honey, these are my boys, Beck and Shane," he indicated each young man in sequence. "Boys, this is Ellie Jentry."

Shane was the first one to extend his hand. "Nice to meet you, Ms. Ellie."

Elliot shook the young man's very large hand. "It's so nice to meet you as well," she looked at Nash, a little flustered. "I had no idea you were coming."

Nash had his hand resting on her shoulder, an affectionate and possessive gesture. "I wanted to surprise Alec with some young men his own age," he said, "but Alec and Penny had plans of their own."

Elliot waved him off. "They'll be back soon," she extended her hand to Beck, who looked a good deal like his father. "I'm so happy to know you. Have you guys eaten dinner yet? I'd be happy to make you something."

"No, thank you, ma'am," Shane said. "We ate on our way over."

Elliot was ushering them all to the table, the only table in all of Purgatory at the moment. "Please, sit," she insisted. "Would you like some cake and coffee, then? I just got this stove and it's the very first thing I've ever baked in it."

Beck started to decline but Shane wouldn't let him. "Thank you, ma'am," he said. "We'd like some."

Beck kept his mouth shut and sat next to his Uncle Beau. He watched the petite, beautiful woman as she happily cut cake and doled it out. He watched his dad as the man stood next to her, helping her, and he saw the smiles that passed between them. He'd never seen his father smile like that before. All surprise at the situation aside, he couldn't decide how he felt about the whole thing.

So they sat with cake and coffee, getting to know each other in the brightly lit kitchen of Purgatory. Shane did most of the talking between the two boys and Nash couldn't help but notice that Beck was unusually silent.

Beck was usually the more mature and understanding of the pair but it was evident he wasn't happy. He wondered if Beck was going to give him any trouble about it. As he sat in increasingly brooding silence over Beck's behavior, Elliot turned her attention to the oldest Aury son.

"Your dad tells me you're in law school, Beck," she said politely. "Where did you get your undergrad?"

Beck's attention turned to the woman. She was really very

lovely and in observing her for the past several minutes, he could see that she was sweet and intelligent. She had already managed to tease Shane about something and had her brother nearly as enamored with her as their father was. Sure, he wanted to see his father happy and if pressed to admit it, Elliot Jentry was a worthy candidate. She seemed okay. But he was still struggling with the speed of things.

"I went to LSU, ma'am," he answered. "My undergrad is in American History."

Elliot smiled at him. "Did you always know you wanted to go to law school?"

"Yes'm, as far back as I can remember."

"What form of law are you going to pursue?"

"Criminal law."

Elliot was listening intently, as if he were the only other person in the room. "So your dad will throw them in jail and then you'll get them out? Don't be surprised if he leaves you out of his will."

Everyone laughed at the tease and Beck actually smiled. "With any luck, I'll be richer than my dad and won't need his money."

Elliot laughed softly and Nash, who had so far only sat next to her but did not try to touch her in any way, put his hand affectionately on her shoulder. He just couldn't help himself. Beck watched the interplay, realizing that he was coming to like the woman. There wasn't one thing about her not to like. But still, he didn't want to accept her, not yet. His acceptance was going to have to be earned.

"Well," he glanced at his watch. "How about if Shane and I come back over in the morning to meet Alec and Penny? It's getting late."

Nash sat back in his chair. "You can stay here," he said. "There are several bedrooms upstairs to sleep in."

Elliot began to get up from the table. "I'd better go see if I can find those blow-up mattresses I have. I think they're packed in Alec's room somewhere."

Beck gave his father an odd look. "We're not heading back home?"

Nash shook his head. "No," he replied. "There's been a lot going on around here, namely with the Loreaus, so I've been staying here just to make sure everything stays peaceful."

Elliot was already heading up the back stairs from the kitchen, disappearing into the upper story. Beck waited until she was gone before answering his father.

"So you've been sleeping here?" he asked. "I'm assuming with her."

Nash cooled when he saw the look on Beck's face. "Yes," he said honestly. "I told you, we're getting married. I don't see...."

Beck cut his father off, outrage in his voice. "Are you nuts?" he hissed. "Dad, if Shane or I did something like this, you'd hog-tie us until we came to our senses. You just met this woman a week ago and already you've moved in with her? What in the hell are you thinking?"

Nash remained calm. "I'm thinking that I didn't raise my son to speak to me like that," he replied evenly. "Beck, I understand where you're coming from. I really do. But I'm an adult and I can think for myself. It's not like I've shacked up with some woman that I'm going to be tired of next week. I don't operate like that and you know it. I'm with the woman I love and we're getting married...."

Beck threw up his hands, getting up from the table. "You keep saying that, but do you hear yourself? You're making excuses because you met a beautiful woman and you wanted to have sex with her, so you're making excuses by saying 'we're getting married anyway' so that makes it all okay. Well, it *doesn't* make it okay. It makes it cheap."

Nash bolted to his feet, as did Beau and Shane. As Shane went to his brother, Beau went to Nash.

"Cool off," he said quietly. "He's just upset. He doesn't mean it."

Truthfully, Nash wasn't sure what to say. He was afraid that he was actually going to strike his son so he turned away and disappeared into the darkened ballroom just to get some breathing space. Beau followed Nash as far as the door, pausing as he watched his brother wander over near the floor-to-ceiling windows. With a heavy heart, he turned to Beck.

"That was really uncalled for," he told the young man. "Your dad has finally found the love of his life and all you can do is berate him for it? What's wrong with you? I've spent a lot of time with Ms. Ellie and I can tell you from experience that you wouldn't find a finer woman anywhere, ever. She's so good for your dad, you don't even know. Now, if I were you, I'd think hard on what I just said to him and figure out how to apologize."

Beck was furious, being held in check by Shane as Beau left the kitchen. Realizing that his brother would probably be better off if he was away from their dad and out of the house, Shane started pulling Beck towards the front door just to get him outside and get some fresh air. Just as they walked past the graceful main staircase, Elliot descended the stairs and ran right into them.

"Hi," she said, holding a deflated air mattress. "Do either of you happen to have a bicycle pump in your trunk?"

It was a perfectly innocent question but Beck flared. "Look, lady," he spat. "I don't know what spell you cast over my dad, but I don't have to stay here and watch. Why don't you leave him the hell alone and go back where you came from?"

Shane was yanking his brother towards the front door. "Shut up," he hissed at him, looking at Elliot and smiling wanly. "Thank you very much for the cake, ma'am. It was nice to meet you."

Shocked, Elliot stood at the bottom of the stairs as Shane practically threw his brother out of the house. She had no idea what had just happened as Nash appeared beside her.

"I'm sorry, honey," he murmured, putting his arm around her shoulders. "He's not very happy with me right now. I'm sorry he took it out on you."

She looked up at him, baffled. "What happened?"

Nash sighed heavily. "He... oh, hell, I don't know. He's just upset because of what's happened between you and me."

Elliot faced him, deeply concerned. "Go after him and resolve it. Don't let him leave like this."

Nash shook his head. "No," he said quietly. "He's too fired up and he's going to get me fired up. We both need to cool down."

"Nash," she grabbed his arm firmly. "He's your son. Don't you dare let him leave in anger. Hash it out, punch each other out or whatever you have to do, but for Heaven's sake, don't let him leave angry. Don't ever let someone walk away from you in anger."

He gazed down at her, realizing she was probably right. He cupped her face and kissed her, and bolted out after his boys. Elliot stood there a moment, shocked and hurt by the direction the evening had taken. As she stood there wondering what had Beck Aury so angry, she felt someone standing beside her. Looking over, she saw Beau. He smiled weakly.

"Beck isn't usually so hot-headed," he said. "He's a good boy. He's just very protective of his father."

"I understand," she said. "I think Alec and Nash have had their run-ins, too, although neither one of them will talk about it. It's all about growing up and accepting change. Sometimes that's hard, especially with a parent involved."

Beau smiled at her as he followed his brother's path out of the front door, thinking that perhaps he should be a part of the discussion in case Beck and Nash's argument went from bad to worse. Nash was very emotional about Elliot and Beck was very emotional about the situation in general, which could mean disaster if things went wrong. Beau thought he should hang around, if for nothing else than to support his brother.

Elliot sighed as all of the Aury men walked from the house. She was feeling very bad about the whole thing, not at all offended by Beck's harsh words. She understood about children being protective over their parents.

As she turned to take the inflatable mattress upstairs, she heard commotion in the dining room and stuck her head in. Dr. Whitney and Dr. Clarke were emerging from the crypt passage, their arms laden with notepads and books. Elliot set the mattress on the ground and went to help them.

"Let me have that," she said and took a laptop from Dr. Clarke. "Are you getting internet access down there?"

She sounded so incredulous and Dr. Clarke laughed. "Not at all," she replied. "I have a flash drive with research data on it we were using."

Elliot watched Dr. Whitney barely squeeze through the narrow passage. "Are you finished for the night?"

As Dr. Clarke nodded, Dr. Whitney spoke. "For the night," he confirmed. "We'll be back tomorrow morning. Ms. Jentry, I have to tell you that I've never seen anything like it down there. It's the most amazing room I've ever seen."

Elliot smiled at his enthusiasm. "Forgive me for my uneducated observations, but I read that no one builds anything underground in Louisiana because of the high water table. Why on earth would the Aurys build a crypt beneath the house?"

Dr. Whitney wiped his handkerchief over his sweaty face. "Oh, that's not the original purpose of the room," he told her seriously. "It's my belief that it was the house's original kitchen. That means there's a secondary access somewhere, perhaps long filled in or overgrown. There is no way they could have moved those coffins down into that room with this passage being the only access. There had to be another way."

"Really?" Elliot was fascinated. "Is an underground kitchen uncommon?"

He shook his head. "Not at all, but they're more common on the east coast where the water table is lower and the climate is colder," he replied. "For the house's owners to turn the kitchen into a burial crypt... well, I've just never heard of anything like that before. I need to go back to the office and do some research."

Elliot thought about the room below her feet with four children buried in it. "What are you going to do from this point?"

The intern pulled herself from the narrow passage, looking

disheveled, and Dr. Whitney began to move to the front door. Everyone followed.

"We're going to clean up and study every one of those crypts," he said. "We're also going to study the house and possibly do some ground radar scans to see if we can come up with the secondary access. I'd really like to publish all of this work in Archaeology Review Magazine because I think it's a very important piece of information on regional history. It really gives us unusual insight into a forgotten way of life here in the bayou."

Elliot nodded. "I think it's a great idea," she said. "After the crypts are studied, what then?"

Dr. Whitney had reached the front door. "Well, then we may want to talk to Sheriff Aury and see if he wants to relocate his ancestors."

Elliot nodded in agreement, thanking everyone for their time. As the people from the state wandered out to their cars, Elliot looked over to the south side of the driveway where she could see Nash and Beau facing off against Beck and Shane.

If body language said anything, there was still a lot of tension there. Dr. Whitney and Dr. Clarke were pulling out of the driveway and she was thinking seriously about retreating upstairs and making herself scarce when she heard movement behind her.

Casually turning, she heard something bang softly in the dining room. Thinking it was the secret door that was hanging loose, she went to go secure it for the night. But no sooner had she taken a few steps than she looked up and saw something passing from the dining room, into the central stair hall, and disappearing into the ballroom. It was wispy and shadowy, like a fog blowing through, but the fog was in the unmistakable shape of a child. It undulated and rolled back into the darkness.

It took Elliot a moment to realize she had just seen a ghost, something she hadn't even thought about since her arrival. In fact, she had pretty much forgotten about the stories with everything that had gone on.

As quickly as it appeared, it vanished, and Elliot let out such a whoop of surprise that it resonated throughout the entire house. She shot out of the front door just as Nash and Beau were running for the house. Nash caught her when she was out in the driveway, heading for her car.

Elliot was startled and terrified, but not particularly in a bad way. She was laughing uncontrollably by the time Nash grabbed her.

"Ellie," he had his big arms around her. "What happened, honey?"

She was gasping, shrieking, pointing and laughing all at once. She sounded as if she were going crazy.

"In there," she jumped up and down as he tried to contain her. "I saw... Nash, it was a ghost! I saw it coming from the dining room and disappear into the ballroom!"

He had his hands full with her squirming. "A ghost?" he repeated. "Are you sure?"

She held on to him for support, laughing. "Yes," she gasped. "It looked like... like a fog of some kind that drifted from the dining room into the ballroom and disappeared. I saw it plain as day. It looked like a child."

Nash wasn't sure if he should be concerned or laugh with her. "Are you okay?"

She giggled, trying to catch her breath. "I'm fine," she sighed. "It just startled the hell out of me. Wow... that was really something!"

By this time, Beau, Beck and Shane were listening. Beau looked fearfully at the house but the two boys actually looked intrigued. "A ghost?" Shane repeated. Then he grabbed his brother. "Come on; let's go see if we can see it."

Beck still wasn't over the whole Dad and Elliot situation, but he had to admit, the lure of a ghost was intriguing and almost enough to distract him. He'd grown up loving Ghostbusters and scary movies, so he was definitely interested. While he stood indecisively, Shane grew frustrated and turned to his uncle.

"Uncle Beau!" he motioned to the house. "Come on!"

Beau shook his head. "No way," he said. "I don't go in for ghosts. Y'all go get the crap scared out of you. I ain't going to do it."

Over her hysterical laughing, Elliot could see the four of them standing around looking uncertain and curious. She took a deep breath to steady herself.

"Come on," she said. "I'll show you."

She went towards the house with Nash and Shane right behind her. Suddenly, they could hear Wolfgang barking wildly and they all ran into the house to find the dog in the dining room. No one could help but notice he was barking at the secret door, which was open by about a foot. Nash called the dog off but the animal was reluctant to back off. Nash finally pulled the dog back by the collar and made him sit.

"What's this?" Shane wanted to know, pointing at the secret door.

Nash put his hands on his hips, looking at the gaping hole. "That," he said, "is a hidden passage that leads down to a room underneath the house. That's why we had people from the State of Louisiana out here today. No one has ever seen anything like this before."

Shane was deeply curious. He went to the door, looking closely at it without touching it. In fact, he didn't want to touch anything in this dilapidated old house that was in the furious process of restoration.

"Wow," he said after several moments. "That's so cool. Can I go down there?"

Nash shook his head. "We're going to string some lights down there tomorrow, but right now, it's pitch black. I'd prefer you wait until tomorrow."

Shane stuck his head into the stairwell just to see what he could see, realizing that his father was right. It was as black as tar down there. He wrinkled up his nose.

"It stinks down there," he said.

As Nash, Shane and Beau went back and forth about the crypt below the house, Elliot stood back and watched Beck. The young man seemed to want to participate with the rest of his family but he was still upset. He wasn't yet ready to be one of the gang again, still disoriented over the entire situation. As Elliot debated whether or not to try and speak to him, the front door opened again and she could hear her children's voices. She went into the central hall, peering towards the entry.

"Hey, guys," she greeted. "How was the movie?"

Penelope was all dressed up for her outing, even if it had been with her brother. She reckoned that all she ever wore were running shorts or hoodies, so she jumped at the chance to dress up. She was in tight jeans, a sexy shirt that showed off her slender torso, and platform sandals. Her hair was curled and she had taken the time to put on makeup.

"It was blood, guts and aliens," she declared. "But it was fun."

Elliot grinned as the pair made their way back towards her. "Glad you had a good time," she said. "We have visitors."

Penelope lifted her eyebrows. "Who?"

"Nash's sons."

Neither Penelope nor Alec seemed particularly overjoyed, but they responded politely. They followed Elliot into the dining room where everyone was gathered. Immediately, Beck and Shane looked in the direction of the incoming group and, in an instant, an odd and curious ambiance filled the air. Elliot smiled at Nash's boys as she introduced her children.

"Alec and Penny, this is Beck and Shane Aury," she went through the pleasantries. "They came down for a visit. We were just showing them the secret door."

Penelope and Beck fixed on each other right away. Penelope smiled at the handsome oldest Aury boy and extended her hand. "Hi," she said, smiling prettily. "It's nice to meet you."

Beck was somewhat speechless as he took her hand. "Nice to meet you, too," he said, suddenly looking uncomfortable yet strangely interested. He shook Alec's hand but his gaze inevitably moved back to Penelope. "Uh... how y'all like it here?"

Penelope turned on the charm. "I love it," she said. "I didn't think I would, but this place kind of grows on you. What do you think of it?"

Beck actually smiled as he glanced around the dining room. "It's kind of creepy," he admitted with a chuckle.

Penelope giggled. "I wasn't going to say it first, but as long as you did, I agree with you."

They laughed, Beck laughing mostly because she was and he couldn't help it. Looking at her smile made him want to smile, too. Wolfgang, hearing Penelope's voice, trotted over to her and she went to her knees beside the dog and hugged him.

"Here's my beautiful boy," she crooned, kissing the dog's snout. She looked up happily at Beck. "So how long are you and your brother going to stay? Are you going to show us a good time?"

Beck half-shrugged, half-nodded, completely upswept in Penelope's charms. "Uh... yes," he said. "Dad said y'all didn't know anyone so we thought we'd come down and show y'all around. Have you been to New Orleans yet?"

Penelope's face lit up. "Not yet," she said. "Nash said something about taking us there but, to tell you the truth, I'd rather go with people my own age and not the old fogies."

As Beck and Penelope shared a laugh, Nash heard the comment and he looked at Elliot. "She means us," he pointed out.

Elliot grinned. "She means *you*, Methuselah," she teased. "I'm not that old yet."

His eyes narrowed at her. "Let me see," he cocked his head. "If my math is correct, you had to at least be in your early twenties when you had Penelope."

"I was twenty-one."

His eyebrows lifted. "She's nineteen, which makes you forty."

"Forty-one, this past April."

He seemed dramatically sad. "You're right," he sighed. "You're not an old fogy yet. *I* am."

She laughed at him. "You're only forty-something, right?"

"Forty-eight," he said glumly. "Forty-nine in November."

She patted his cheek to comfort him. "How's that Geritol working out for you, Grandpa?"

"You're a mean, mean woman."

She laughed again as they returned their attention to the young people, now increasingly interested in one another. Shane and Alec were talking the nitty-gritty details of their gaming interest while Penelope had Beck laughing at nearly everything she said. Elliot sighed gratefully as she watched the pair.

"Thank God for Penny," Elliot muttered. "She's saved the day."

Nash watched his oldest son warming to Elliot's lovely daughter. "How could he possibly resist her?" He gave Elliot a quick squeeze and kissed the top of her head. "She's just like her mother."

The conversation eventually moved out of the dining room, where no one made mention of the ghost that Elliot had seen mostly because Elliot would kill any subject that seemed to drift in that direction. Alec would take the news calmly but she doubted Penelope would. For tonight, they had enough on their minds with the addition of Beck and Shane Aury without the added thought of the supernatural.

Gradually, they all moved into the double parlors where Penelope talked Beck and Shane into playing a trivia board game. Beau, not wanting to make the drive back to Nash's house, ended up blowing up the two air mattresses and passing out on one of them in the small bedroom above the kitchen.

The young people played games in the parlor long into the night as Nash and Elliot sat in the parlor with them, cuddled up on one of Elliot's couches, until Elliot fell asleep on him and Nash made her get up and go to bed.

Beck ended up staying at Purgatory that night. When he woke up in the morning, his father was lying right next to him, sound asleep on a makeshift bed of couch cushions.

FIFTEEN

SORRENTO POLICE CALLED Nash early Tuesday morning and asked if Penelope could come to the station to identify her attackers in a lineup. After the blissful and surreal past couple of days Nash and Elliot had experienced with each other, the house and with the kids, Nash wasn't any too excited about again bringing up the horrors that had plagued them. But the Loreau boys needed to either be charged with a crime or released, so Nash broke the news to Elliot, who in turn broke the news to her daughter.

Penelope was shaken but brave. As Elliot made a huge breakfast of egg casserole, pancakes and potatoes, Beck and Shane caught on to Penelope's distress and she told them what had happened.

Nash stood in the doorway between the ballroom and the kitchen, coffee in hand as he listened to Penelope's story, casting a glance at Elliot now and again as the woman busied herself over the stove. He could tell she was shaken, too. He stepped into the ballroom for some privacy as he called his office to let them know he'd be out for the morning.

Elsewhere at Purgatory, Beau had already been up for hours, supervising the installation of the new windows on the front of the house. The electrician was finishing with the wiring upstairs while the plumber was plumbing a new downstairs half-bath that they were building into a corner of the massive library to make it a sort of entry-cloak room. Hallie was supervising the interior work because, as a preservationist, it was her job to make sure no original walls were removed or overtly disturbed during the restoration. She would follow the plumber around like a watchdog as the man carefully lifted floorboards to lay pipes.

Upstairs, the plumber had more men pulling out the pipes in the old bathrooms. The goal was to keep as much of the old fixtures, like the bathtubs, as they could, while replacing the old, copper shower enclosures with beautiful new tile.

They had started on Elliot's and Alec's bathrooms this morning. The sounds upstairs were loud enough to wake the dead. And speaking of the dead, Dr. Whitney and Dr. Clarke had returned at dawn to resume their study of the crypt below. The old house, from a very early hour, had been rocking with activity.

As the restoration of Purgatory went on around them, the Aurys and the Jentrys crowded into the kitchen to finish up breakfast before Penelope went down to the police station. In watching the interaction between Beck and Penelope, Nash wasn't surprised when Beck asked Penelope if she would like for him to go with her to the police station. In fact, he had expected it. Penelope smiled sweetly at the offer.

"That's so nice of you to ask, but you really don't need to," she said. "It's not going to be... well, very pleasant, I guess. I really don't know. I've never done anything like this before."

Beck wouldn't be put off. "I don't mind," he insisted. "I can come along and then when you're finished, maybe you'd like to take a drive along the River Road. There are some really nice houses and some of them do tours."

She perked up. "Really? That sounds great."

Nash, listening to their conversation, pushed himself off the doorjamb and went to put his coffee cup on the sink.

"Honey, are you going to go with us to the station?" he asked Elliot.

She was spooning out the rest of the egg casserole for Shane and Alec. "It's up to Penny," she said, looking at her daughter. "Do you want me to go with you?"

Penelope nodded. "Yes," she said her features uncertain. "I'm kind of scared."

Elliot smiled at her daughter and went to set the dish down. "Give me twenty minutes and I'll be ready."

Nash watched her disappear up the back stairs before pouring himself another cup of coffee. The kids started bringing their plates to the sink and Nash had Shane rinse everything off in the big, old, iron sink. The fixtures were still old and more than once, water sprayed up in Shane's face.

"Dad," he said after being hit in the eye for the third time, causing him to leave the sink entirely. "I'm going to take Alec up to Denham Springs. There's a gaming place up there and we're going to play Xbox Live."

Before Nash could reply, Alec spoke up. "Dude, that would be awesome," he said sincerely. "I hate living like a pioneer. I need my electronics."

Nash wiped his hands off on a paper towel. "Go ahead," he said. "Drive carefully."

Shane and Alec waved him off, talking as they went. "Are there any hot chicks wherever you're taking me?" Alec wanted to know.

Shane gave him a queer look. "At a gaming store?"

Alec shrugged. "Yeah, that's what I thought. Not only am I living like a pioneer, I'm living like a priest, too." He called back to Nash as they passed into the central hall. "Don't tell my mom I said that!"

Nash grinned, tossing a paper towel away as Penelope got up from the table. "I'm going to get my stuff," she said, pausing when she came near Nash. "They won't be able to see me, right?"

"Who?" he asked.

"The guys in the lineup."

Nash shook his head. "No, honey, they won't."

She thought on that a moment. "Good," she said. "I've been thinking about what happened and it occurred to me that when I was running down the road and then pushed down from behind, I thought I heard a woman's voice, too."

Nash's eyebrows lifted. "A woman's voice?"

Penelope nodded. "It was weird," she said. "I remember someone hitting me from behind and I fell down into the ditch. Then I remember people following me down into the ditch and calling me 'sweet thang' and all that, and as these guys are trying to touch me, I kept hearing this woman's voice screaming at them. It was, like, high-pitched, screeching-like."

Nash listened to her seriously. "Did you hear what she said?"

Penelope thought hard. "Something like 'eat her' or 'beat her'. I couldn't really tell. But I know for sure it was those hillbilly guys that came around after Alec was attacked. I definitely know it was them."

Nash remained cool and patient with her as his mind raced with the possibilities. He suspected who the woman was simply by the way Penelope described her voice. Biffy Loreau had a voice much like that and wasn't beyond egging her grandsons on during an attack.

"We're going to determine that for sure this morning," he told her. "Did you tell the Sorrento detectives about the woman?"

She shook her head. "That only really came to me yesterday. I guess I was so out of it I didn't realize it."

Nash patted her arm in a comforting gesture. "That's okay," he told her. "Go get your purse so we can go."

Penelope grinned. "We're still waiting for my mom. It's going to take her longer than twenty minutes."

Nash gave her a half-grin. "So... in the future, I need to multiply her estimate by a factor of two?"

Penelope laughed as she mounted the kitchen stairs. "Exactly," she said. "For example, if you want to leave by five o'clock, tell her she needs to be ready by four o'clock. It's the only safe thing to do."

She skipped upstairs, leaving Nash and Beck alone. Nash's thoughts were lingering on the woman Penelope had mentioned when he realized it was just him and Beck in the kitchen. He hadn't really spoken to his son since their blow up yesterday. He had even gone to sleep next to him the night before simply because he felt so bad about what had happened, but when he woke up, Beck had already been up and getting coffee.

He and his kids never fought, so he was rightfully disturbed but he figured Beck would talk to him when he was ready. He glanced at his son's lowered head as he turned back to the sink, wiping out his coffee cup simply to give himself something to do.

"Dad," Beck's quiet voice filled the silence.

Nash glanced over at him. "Yes, son?"

Beck was fidgeting with a napkin on the table. "Hey," he groped for words, having difficulty expressing what he was thinking. "Well... um, I'm sorry I got mad at you yesterday. I shouldn't have done that. I didn't mean to call you cheap."

Nash leaned back against the sink. "There's nothing to forgive," he said. "I'm just sorry that this whole thing with Elliot has upset you so much."

Beck shrugged. "It's not that," he said. "I've been thinking about it and I guess ... dad, for six years, it's just been you and me and Shane. It was our own tight family. We always talked about things, you know, like a family should. We made decisions together. I guess... I guess I was just upset because you didn't talk to me and Shane about Ms. Ellie before you did anything. I guess I looked at it as a decision that we all should have made together, but it's not like that at all. I'm sorry I got mad at you."

Nash sat down at the table across from his son. "I can understand where you're coming from," he said. "And you're right; it was just you and me and Shane for six years. I love you guys more than anything on earth. But just like I wouldn't expect to have the final word in any relationship you or your brother would have with a woman, I expect the same courtesy. Even if you don't agree with it, all I ask is that you support my choice just like I would support yours."

Beck nodded. "I *do* support you, Dad," he insisted. "I guess if you really want to know the truth, I was a little jealous. Now, it's not just the three of us anymore."

Nash nodded faintly, understanding his boy's point of view. "Ellie's a very special lady," he told his son. "But what I feel for her doesn't diminish my love for you and Shane. Y'all are my flesh and blood. All I ask is that you give Ellie a chance, okay? It would mean everything to me if you would just do that for me."

Beck was already nodding before Nash finished his sentence. "I can already see that she's a good person. She's funny."

"Yes, she is."

"And her kids are okay. I like Penny."

Nash smiled faintly. "I know you do," he said. "So... do you think that we can all get along as one big, happy family?"

Beck was still tearing up the napkin in his hands. When he looked up and saw his father grinning at him, he broke down into snorts of laughter.

"Don't marry her, Dad," he said as he laughed.

Nash's eyebrows lifted. "Why not?"

"Because it would be too weird if I was dating my stepsister."

Nash just rolled his eyes. "You'd better back off of that talk, son," he said, standing up and stretching his big frame. "If Penny catches wind of that, she's going to think we're a bunch of kissin' cousins down here."

Beck snorted and stood up from the table, captured by his father in a bear hug before he could get away. Beck hugged him for a moment before forcing Nash to let go.

"Geez, Dad," he pushed the man away. "Stop getting so clingy. You're embarrassing me."

Nash chuckled at him. "It wouldn't be the first time," he said. "While we're waiting for the women, do you want to take a look around the place? It's your heritage, after all."

"Can we go down into the crypt?"

"Sure."

"Do you really think there are ghosts down there?"

"Hard to say. But if you believe in that kind of thing, maybe."

Beck was fired up about going into the underground room. He and Nash disappeared down the narrow, secret staircase just as Elliot and Penelope came down the main staircase. Elliot had changed into tight jeans, a pretty, white blouse that, even though it covered her up, was jaw-droppingly sexy, and a pair of strappy, white sandals with a four inch heel. With her hair pulled back into a ponytail, she looked fresh and lovely. Penelope was a bit more demure in jeans and pink t-shirt.

Penelope began to look around for Nash and Beck as her mother stuck her hand in her purse and dug around.

"Where's Nash?" Penelope wanted to know.

Elliot was looking for her sunglass case that held a pair of two hundred dollar designer sunglasses. "I don't know," she said, looking around. Then she called out. "Nash?"

She heard a faint response, so she and Penelope headed towards the front door, expecting to be joined by the men. But Elliot began to smell paint and she gasped with delight as she realized the painter already started in the double parlors, a gorgeous, ivory color that would go perfect with the ivory curtains and gold tones she was planning on using in the parlors.

The old walls had been stripped and very carefully buffed because they were of *bousillage* and plaster. When the paint went on, it showed the imperfections underneath but Elliot loved the imperfect look. As she stood there and beamed at the ivory paint going up on the walls, she felt a body behind her.

Nash was looking up at the walls, too. "Hey, that's nice," he commented. "I like it."

Elliot grinned excitedly. "The double parlors and the library are all this same *Ivory Tulle* color," she told him, as if he really cared. "The central hall and the staircase will be a color called *Ivory Snow*." The further back you walk in the house, however, the rooms will all graduate from this ivory color to almost an ecru. The ballroom and kitchen will be a color called *Ivory Sands*."

"But not the dining room."

She shook her head, so excited to talk about paint colors. All of the ancient bathrooms, secret rooms and ghosts, aside, this was the fun part of home restoration and she was thrilled.

"The dining room has that hand-painted wallpaper, which we're going to restore. I'm thinking about turning the ballroom into a big family and game room. What do you think?"

He nodded. "I think it's a great idea. It's a big room."

Pleased that he liked her idea, she turned around to watch the painters very carefully stroke ivory paint on the molding above the fireplace. "I'm going to turn that little back bedroom upstairs into my office and I was thinking that the library could be yours," she turned to look at him again. "We can turn it into a man-cave, but not too tacky."

He grinned at her. "You mean I can't have a big ol' buffalo head above the fireplace?"

"Not on my watch, buddy."

He laughed and put his arm around her shoulders, pulling her out of the house. Beck and Penelope followed, waving at Beau as he perched on a second-story scaffold looking down at them. Outside, it was mild and a bit muggy, but not too bad. The sun was shining brightly in the brilliant, blue sky.

"Where are y'all going?" Beau called.

Nash waved at him. "We'll be back."

It wasn't the answer Beau was looking for so he just shrugged his shoulders and pointed at his nephew.

"Bring me back some lunch," he told him.

Beck just waved his uncle off, not wanting to shout to the world that he wasn't going to be back for lunch because he was going to take Penelope on a drive along the River Road. He went to his truck just as his dad, Elliot and Penelope went to Nash's sheriff's cruiser. The four of them stared at each other in confusion as to why they needed two cars until Penelope went towards Beck's truck.

"I'll ride with Beck," she said.

Nash and Elliot looked at each other, shrugged, and climbed into his car. The two vehicles then carefully maneuvered out of the driveway, dodging state cars and contractor trucks.

As they headed towards the Sorrento Police Department, which was less than a mile away, Nash kept glancing over at Elliot, looking beautiful and stylish sitting next to him. He finally put his hand on her thigh and she smiled at him, gripping the hand that rested on her leg.

"You are so beautiful," he said almost wistfully. "Do you have any idea what I feel every time I look at you?"

She shook her head. "No, what?"

He sighed, watching the road ahead. "Like I'm the luckiest man in the world. I told you that once, Ellie; I meant it. Every day I spend with you is the best day of my life."

She caressed his big hand. "Have you always been this sweet or is it just with me?"

He laughed softly. "I guess you bring it out in me."

She watched him, the handsome lines of his face. "Have you dated much since your divorce?"

He shook his head. "No," he said honestly. "Call it a lack of worthy candidates, but I just haven't gone out much in the past few years."

"No girlfriends at all?"

He thought about the question. "There was one gal from Baton Rouge I dated for about three months," he said. "She worked in the governor's office."

"What happened?"

He shrugged. "She was nice enough, but there just wasn't much of a connection once we got down to it," he said. "Besides, she was only interested in being with someone who could further her political agenda. She was one of those socially progressive Southern women your mama warned you about."

Elliot giggled. "Where I come from, those aren't the people my mama warned me about," she said. "Out where I come from in Southern California, you generally avoid three groups: anyone in the entertainment industry, professional athletes, and Persians from Beverly Hills."

Nash wriggled his eyebrows. "I think that covers almost everyone in California, right?"

"Pretty much."

The conversation died into warm silence and they held hands as Nash pulled into the Sorrento Police Department's parking lot. He pulled up to a parking spot in front of the squat, brick building with the white-trim windows, getting out of the car and going around to open Elliot's door.

Just as he unlatched her door, Beck's truck came barreling into the parking lot, spinning out on the loose gravel at the entrance. He could hear Penelope laughing as Beck pulled the truck in beside his dad's cruiser. Nash, however, hadn't let Elliot out of the car yet because he didn't want her to see his son driving so recklessly with her daughter in the truck.

Elliot finally opened her door. "Can I come out now?"

Nash opened the door and helped her out, all the while eyeing his son as the young man climbed out of the truck, laughing along with Penelope. Nash took Elliot's elbow politely, directing her and Penelope towards the front door of the police station. As they were mounting the steps, he leaned over to Beck.

"Son," he muttered. "This is one of those times when I'm going to tell you you're not too old to spank. If I ever see you driving like that again with Penny in the car, you're going to get it."

Beck looked at his father, surprised. "What did I do?"

"You spun out when you pulled into the parking lot," Nash hissed. "Do I really have to talk to you about that?"

Beck was genuinely surprised. "I didn't do it on purpose."

"Let's hope not. I'll beat you within an inch of your life if I catch you doing that again."

Beck just shrugged and Nash went to open the door for the

women, hit by the smell of cheap carpet and cigarette smoke. Ushering Beck into the cool lobby of the small police station, Nash was moving toward the desk sergeant when a shrill voice caught his attention.

"Nash Aury!"

Nash turned quickly towards the sound of the voice. He knew it all too well and was immediately on his guard. Biffy Loreau had apparently been seated back against the wall of the lobby, by the front door, so he hadn't seen her when he had walked in. Dressed in a clean, if not ugly, housecoat and white, orthopedic shoes, her black hair was pulled tight against her head as she marched up on Nash as if he were the only one in the room.

"I've come for my boys," she snapped. "Y'all can't keep 'em here any longer. I've done got me a lawyer now and he says y'all can't hold them any longer without charging 'em."

Nash tried to get between Biffy and Elliot, Penelope and Beck. He didn't want the old bird focusing her venom on the others.

"Ms. Biffy, I'm sure one way or another, things will get resolved today," he said evenly.

She thrust a finger into his face. "Have y'all come to set my boys free?"

He shook his head. "That's not my job," he told her. "The police will do what they feel they need to do."

Unfortunately, Biffy caught sight of Penelope cowering behind Nash and her focus immediately shifted. She pointed a finger at her.

"Y'all can't do nothing!" she told her. "Y'all come here and... and mess things up! We don't want your kind here!"

Nash watched the woman carefully. "What do you mean 'she can't do nothing'?" he asked, calculated. "How would you know why she's here?"

For the first time, Biffy lost her venom, looking at Nash with a startled expression. "I...," she began pointing in Penelope's general direction but she was backing off. "She don't need to be here. My lawyer will be here and he'll fix y'all good!"

As the old woman swiftly backed away, Penelope grabbed Nash's arm.

"That's the voice I heard," she whispered urgently. "Remember I told you I heard a woman's voice when I was attacked? That's it!"

He turned to look at her, seeing she was already in tears. Putting a protective arm around her shoulders, he turned her around and headed for the back offices where the detectives were located, away from the lobby. Penelope was wiping tears by the time he took her to one of the detective's desks and set her down in a worn, vinyl chair.

The police department had an open floor plan so most of the desks crunched up against each other. The only offices in the place were those for the chief and the conference room that doubled as a briefing room. The fat detective who usually wore the beige suit was wearing cheap gray today; he saw Nash come in with Penelope Jentry and waddled over to him from where he had been standing against the briefing room door.

"Sheriff Aury," he greeted. "I'm glad y'all are here. It seems we've got a...."

"Hello, Nash."

A voice cut the detective off. Nash looked over at the briefing room and noticed a familiar face smiling back at him. A man about Nash's age stood in the doorway dressed in jeans, cowboy boots and an expensive camel hair sport coat. When he smiled, it was impish and bright. Nash looked at him and just shook his head.

"Oh, no," he grunted. "Don't tell me...."

"That's right, old friend," the man came out of the briefing room with his hand outstretched. "I'm afraid so. It's good to see you."

Nash took the man's hand reluctantly and shook it. It was apparent he was displeased. "The only way you'd be here is if someone was in need of a shark, so I can only assume you're here for the Loreaus."

"Why would you say that?"

"Call it a wild guess."

The man put up his hands as if cheering. "Then you would be right." He could see that Nash was thoroughly displeased. "It's been a long time, Nash. The first time I'd heard your name in a couple of years was when Ms. Biffy contacted me. Now tell me how in the hell you fit into this mess with the Loreau boys?"

Nash shook his head. "You tell me what you've been told and I'll tell you what the truth is."

The man lifted his eyebrows, considered the proposal, and started to talk. "It's long and complicated, but it starts out with a complaint of assault against you and the Sorrento Police Department," he reached into his jacket pocket and pulled out a pair of reading glasses and a piece of paper. He read the paper as he spoke. "I'm filing a civil suit for wrongful death against Alec Jentry in the death of Femmie Loreau in addition to defending Will, Ed and Nicky Loreau against potential assault charges. Know anything about those?"

Nash just stared at him, digesting the ridiculous information. He could hardly believe his ears, yet, on the other hand, he wasn't particularly surprised.

"Buck, you know the Loreaus," he hissed. "You know who and what they are; you grew up around here, for God's sake. You know those charges are bullshit and you further know that they don't have any money to pay your legal fees."

Buck Thompson, a criminal defense attorney born in Sorrento but based in Baton Rouge, folded up the paper in his hand and pulled off his glasses.

"They will once they win the civil suit against the owner of Purgatory where Femmie was killed," he said frankly. "A best-selling author by the name of Jentry. I spoke with Louise Dawn earlier today and she gave me all of the information I need on the new owner since she handled the transaction. Since Purgatory used to be your property, I'm assuming you at least know of the family."

Nash felt sick to his stomach. He closed his eyes briefly, as it to ward off the impact of Buck's words, thinking of how he should respond. He didn't dare look at Elliot, fearful he would lose control of the situation and his composure if he did. If she was upset, and she would be, it was a foregone conclusion that he would be upset right along with her.

He went to Buck and grabbed the man by the arm, pushing him towards the briefing room.

"Let's go and talk about this someplace private," he said quietly.

Buck did as he was asked, entering the briefing room with Nash. Elliot and Penelope were still standing with the Sorrento detective, wide-eyed with shock at the revelations being put forth. Just when they thought things were getting better, something like this brought them right back down again. It was just too much to take; Penelope finally buried her face in her hands and started weeping. Stunned, Elliot put her hand on her daughter's head, comfortingly, as she turned to the detective.

"Can... can we just please get this lineup over with, please?" she asked hoarsely.

The detective wasn't unsympathetic. He'd hoped to warn Sheriff Aury off of Buck Thompson but he hadn't been fast enough. Thompson had been around the station all morning, causing problems as Ms. Biffy wandered the lobby calling for justice.

"Yes'm," he said quietly. "If you and Ms. Penny will come with me, we'll get this going just as quick as we can."

Penelope wiped her face and stood up just about the time Nash came shooting out of the briefing room, slamming the door behind him. He pointed out in the direction of the lobby.

"You're going to arrest Ms. Biffy Loreau on accessory to assault charges," he told the detective. "Miss Jentry has identified Biffy as one of the accomplices to her assault and I want that woman charged along with her grandsons."

The detective was caught off guard but he didn't argue. What Sheriff Aury wanted, Sheriff Aury got. Now, the harried morning had just gotten worse. He motioned to one of the uniforms seated at the report-writing desk to his left.

"Go get the chief," he told the man quietly. "We got a wildfire on our hands here."

Only when things were in motion did Nash dare look at Elliot. She was standing with her arm around Penelope, gazing at him with a mixture of horror and trust. It was a strange combination, one that inflamed Nash. He was already bent on murder as it was. Anyone who came after Elliot and her family was going to pay a fair price, indeed.

Not surprisingly, Biffy Loreau did not go quietly.

SIXTEEN

"HOW DID they find out it was Alec?" Elliot was seated at her breakfast room table, a box of Kleenex in her lap. "I just don't understand."

Nash sat beside her, his arm around her shoulders, trying to give her what comfort he could. He felt worse than she did about the turn of events, like he should have prevented it and didn't. It was unnecessary guilt he carried around.

"Buck subpoenaed the police report and Alec's name was on it," he said softly. "It's a civil suit, Ellie. It doesn't mean that Alec is being charged with murder or even that he's going to jail. He's not. It simply means that the Loreaus are suing him for the death of Femmie. All they want is money. When and if it goes to trial, it's not going to go anywhere, trust me. No sane person is going to believe any of the Loreaus."

Elliot sniffled, wiping at her nose with a tissue. It was early afternoon and they were alone in the house for the most part. After the lineup at the police department in which Penelope correctly identified all three Loreau brothers, everything erupted into bedlam between Will professing their innocence and Biffy's screamed threats.

Beck took Penelope out of there in a hurry and on a drive to get her mind off of everything, leaving Elliot and Nash to determine their next move. Now, not only did the charges involve Alec and Elliot, but Nash was named as well in the separate charge of assault. It seemed that they were all interwoven into the situation now, like the fine threads of a cobweb. It was growing sticky and uncomfortable.

"Poor Alec," Elliot began sobbing again. "What was he supposed to do? Not defend himself?"

"Of course not," Nash pulled her close, his lips against her forehead. "He did what he was supposed to do. Femmie was a worthless excuse of a human being long before he attacked Alec. He got what he deserved."

"And you," she was so upset she could barely speak. "They've charged you with assault. And you're supposed to take that new job next month. How is this going to affect you?"

He shushed her softly. "Assault charges against cops are a dime a dozen," he told her. "This isn't the first one I've had and I'm sure it won't be the last, but it's certainly the most ridiculous. Please don't worry about it."

Elliot collapsed against him, sobbing softly. Nash just held her, giving her time to work out her fear, thinking of all of the lawyers he knew and which one he would hire to represent Alec. He could think of a brilliant defense attorney in New Orleans, an African-American woman that was abnormally sharp and cunning. She had done some work for defendants against his office and he'd seen her in action.

Nash decided to give Elpheda Benson a call at some point, once Elliot calmed down and he had a few moments to spare. Meanwhile, he was thinking about taking Elliot to a nice dinner that evening just to soothe her. He was coming to think that the entire family might need to be soothed.

"Knock, knock," Beau was standing in the dining room doorway, timidly banging on the doorjamb. When Nash and Elliot looked up at him, he smiled weakly. "Sorry to interrupt, but an interior decorator from New Orleans is here. She says that Hallie told her to come."

Nash didn't know anything about it, but Elliot did. She wiped at her eyes, laboring to compose herself.

"I'd forgotten about her," she looked at Nash, wiping quickly at her cheeks. "Hallie said this woman specializes in furnishing old homes like this. She's going to help me pick out furniture."

"Perfect," Nash pulled her out of her chair, eager to get her off the subject of the lawsuit. "Go spend some time talking furniture. We'll deal with the rest of this later."

Elliot was heading for the kitchen steps so she could go upstairs and pull herself together before meeting the woman.

"Beau, you said we could get this whole place put together, including furniture, for eighty thousand dollars," she looked at Nash's brother still in the doorway. "How much of that do I have to spend on furniture?"

Beau suddenly looked doubtful. "Well," he began slowly. "We just added that new bathroom downstairs, Ellie, and the floor boards in the library had a lot of rot on them. We're having to replace them and...."

Elliot put her hand to cut him off as she mounted the steps. "I get it," she said. "Not a lot. Well, I guess I'll just have to figure something out."

"Spend what you want," Nash told her. "Don't worry about the cost."

She paused halfway up the stairs. "Really?" she said, showing some delight for the first time all day. "Whatever I want?"

Nash snickered when he saw her happy expression. "Whatever you want, honey. If you want it, buy it."

She eyed him, trying to determine if he was serious. "We could be talking tens of thousands of dollars to do this right, Nash," she pointed out, wanting to make sure he understood what he was stepping into. "I have an advance on a book contract, so I can spend a little outside of the eighty thousand your brother promised me."

Nash shook his head. "Save it," he said. "If this is going to be my house, too, then I should contribute to it. You have no limit on what you can spend, darlin'. Do your worst."

Elliot threw her hands up. "Hallelujah," she said as she began to swiftly take the steps. "I've been waiting to hear those words my whole life!"

Nash grinned as he watched her disappear upstairs, finally turning to look at his brother. His smile faded.

"God, what a mess," he grunted.

Beau looked at his brother, looking weary and edgy, which was unusual for the man who was perpetually easy-going. He shook his head.

"I only heard part of what you were saying," he said quietly. "I gather it didn't go well this morning with the Loreaus?"

Nash half-shrugged. "That depends on what you consider 'going well'," he said. "Penny identified Will, Ed and Nicky as the men who attacked her and Ms. Biffy as having been an accomplice so, in a sense, that portion of it went very well. But when we arrived at the police station, Buck Thompson was there."

Beau's eyebrows flew up. "Buck Thompson? What was he doing there?"

Nash sighed heavily. "He was hired by Ms. Biffy to defend her grandsons. But we also found out that she hired him to file a civil suit against Alec in the wrongful death of Femmie. This whole situation is just going from bad to worse."

Beau was genuinely upset. "Civil suit?" he repeated, aghast. "That just means they want money, Nash. That's all they ever want. Go pay them a few thousand dollars and they'll go away."

Nash shrugged. "Maybe," he said. "I'm going to call a defense lawyer who's done some work at my office and see what she says. I guess we need to lawyer up just like the Loreaus have, with a bigger law shark than Buck Thompson."

"Good luck finding someone who's more ruthless than he is."

Nash cast his brother a knowing look. "You forget who y'all are talking to," he said. "I've got connections."

"I have no doubt that you do," Beau agreed sincerely. He

watched his brother as he tried to take a few deep breaths to calm himself. "So what now?"

Nash drew in a last, long, deep breath and stared at the ceiling as he composed his thoughts. "I'm heading into the office for a while," he said. "As long as Ellie is occupied and calm, I can focus on work for a while."

"You're a busy man."

Nash snorted at the irony of that statement, pulling his cell phone from its case and taking a look at the display. "Busy, hell," he shook his head as he put the phone away. "Seventeen missed calls, eleven text messages from the office. I think I'd better get over there."

"I'll hold down the fort here."

Nash grinned at his brother as he moved past him, out of the kitchen and into the dining room. There were two conservators from Tulane working on the fragile hand-painted wallpaper and half of the dining room looked like a laboratory with all of the white coats and white gloves.

The secret door was propped open and Beau had run lights down into the crypt to give the historians some illumination. Nash poked his head into the opening, seeing the wet, moldy room down below now lit up with one hundred watt bulbs.

As he moved from the dining room into the central hall, Elliot was just coming down the stairs. She had freshened up and composed herself, and he waited for her at the bottom of the stairs as she descended.

With her long, blond hair pulled into a ponytail that draped over one shoulder, she looked delicious. Nash smiled at her as she came close and he reached out, lifting her off the stairs and giving her a fairly juicy kiss.

"I've got to go into the office for a while," he told her, setting her carefully on her feet. "Beau is here if you need anything. I'll see you before dinner."

"Okay," Elliot wrapped an arm around his waist as he walked her towards the entry. "I'm not sure I'll be cooking dinner, though. I may be too wrapped up in spending your money."

He laughed softly. "Then we'll go out."

"You may not be able to afford it by tonight."

He laughed at her. "We may be starving, but at least we'll have a great place to do it in."

She smiled brightly at him, the first time he'd seen her smile like that all day, and he bent down to kiss her again as they reached the front door. No sooner had his lips left hers than he heard a familiar voice.

"Nash, I take it this is your Ms. Ellie," a deep male voice filled the air. "Because if it's not, Ms. Ellie might have something to say about the way you just kissed that woman."

Nash turned around to see his mother and father standing in the doorway. He grinned at the pair.

"Yes, this is Ms. Ellie," he looked at Elliot, who was looking slightly embarrassed and unsure with the introduction of two strangers. "I'm sure she didn't want to be introduced to you in a compromising position, but that can't be helped now. Ellie, these are my parents, Camp and Elizabeth Aury."

Elliot was startled. She had no idea that Nash had invited his parents over and she made a mental note to kill him later. She gazed at the older couple, noting immediately that Beau resembled their father a great deal while Nash favored his elegant mother. They looked at Elliot with friendly interest and she did the only thing she could do; she smiled brightly and extended her hand to Camp.

"It's such a pleasure to finally meet you," she said, shaking Camp's hand before turning to Elizabeth. "Welcome to Purgatory. I'm so glad you could come."

Elizabeth shook her hand, holding it a moment as she inspected Elliot. Her hazel-eyed gaze was curious, yet pleasant. When she finally smiled, Elliot could see where Nash got his good looks. He looked exactly like his mother.

"It's so nice to meet you," Elizabeth said, her voice soft and rich. "Nash hasn't told us much about you except to say he's marrying you."

Elliot giggled nervously, looking to Nash for help. Nash grinned at his mother.

"As always, Mama, you go right to the point," he said, taking Elliot's hand back from his mother and holding it tightly. "Elliot purchased Purgatory last week. We met when I came to pick up Mamaw's remaining possessions."

Elizabeth did the same thing Beck had done when his father told him of Elliot; she lifted her eyebrows, expecting more of an explanation, but her son seemed to think he'd told her plenty.

"Where are you from, Ms. Ellie?" she asked politely.

"From California," Elliot answered. "I was born and raised in Southern California."

"What made you decide to move to Louisiana?" Elizabeth asked. She seemed genuinely interested to know about the beautiful young woman who had stolen her son's heart. "It's quite a change from California."

"My daughter is enrolled at Tulane," Elliot explained. "I've always wanted to live in one of these big plantation homes, so we got lucky and found Purgatory. We just thought it was such a great opportunity to come and live in a new place and experience a new culture."

Elizabeth was still smiling at her. "And have you enjoyed it so far?"

Elliot carefully worded her reply. "Nash and Purgatory have been the very best things about it," she said. "I love this house so much and your son...well, you raised him well. He's a keeper."

Elizabeth studied Elliot's face for a moment, feature by feature, before reaching out and taking her hand back from Nash.

"Will you show me the house?" she asked. "I would love to see it. I haven't been here in twenty years, you know. The last time I was here, it smelled like a toilet and a crazy old woman was screaming at me."

Elliot was very happy to take Elizabeth into the house. Nash and Camp followed them in as far as the entry, standing in the cavernous central hall while the women went into the double parlors. Camp's gaze lingered on Elliot, trying not to stare at her lovely backside.

"Well," he finally said, turning to look at other things. "Your mother likes her. She's a beautiful girl, Nash. She seems very nice."

Nash was still looking at Elliot as she held Elizabeth's hand and showed her the new ivory paint that was going up. It brought a smile to his lips, warming him, feeling love for her more than he ever had. He watched the two women he loved best get acquainted.

"She is," he said quietly, turning to his father. "Before you and Mama probe her too much, you should know that her husband was killed two years ago. He was a Sheriff's Deputy in L.A., shot in the line of duty, so please don't bring it up if you can help it. She moved here to start a new life and that's exactly what we're going to do."

Camp hissed sadly as his son spoke, shaking his head with sorrow. "Bless her heart," he muttered. "Nash, you're not latching on to her because you feel sorry for her, are you? That's no way to start a relationship, son."

Nash's brow furrowed. "That has nothing to do with it," he said. "I fell in love with her wit and beauty and charm. She's like no one I've ever met before. Dad, I just went through this with Beck and I'll tell you what I told him; even if you don't agree with my decision, at least support me because I feel it's the right thing to do. I love Ellie and I'm going to marry her."

His dad put his hands up in a calming gesture. "Son, I'll support you in whatever you do, you know that," he promised, eyeing him. "Since when did you become such a whiner?"

Nash cocked an eyebrow at his father, who was snorting at his rough sense of humor. Nash fought off a grin, turning to see that Elliot and his mother were now speaking to a woman he didn't recognize. He assumed it was the interior designer. The day, having started out so bad, was, at least, getting better.

As he started to give his father a tour of Purgatory, now that it was being restored, Beau joined the group. Nash took the opportunity to slip off to work, with his dad and Beau occupied. Last he saw, Elliot and his mother were engrossed in inspecting the piles of fabric that the interior designer had brought. Knowing she'd be occupied for at least the next few hours, he bounded off to his office.

Nash returned that night to a full house of his kids, her kids, his parents, and one the most emotionally and spiritually fulfilling moments of satisfaction he could ever remember. In spite of the lawsuits, the sadness, the ghosts, volatile neighbors and the like, Nash had never been happier.

As he sat with Elliot, her kids and his family all crowded around the breakfast table, he knew that every day he spent with her, days like these, were the best days of his life.

SEVENTEEN
AUGUST

IT WAS dusk over the bayou on a particularly steamy evening. The humidity had been unbearable since late June, something that Elliot and her children were unaccustomed to. Therefore, when the humidity index rose, so did Elliot's need to install central air conditioning in the big house.

As the plumbers carefully re-plumbed the entire house and re-plumbed and remodeled the upstairs bathrooms, the HVAC contractors carefully laid out their vents next to the new plumbing. Elliot and Hallie were concerned that the least amount of flooring and walls be disturbed as they made the house twenty-first century habitable and, with Beau's assurance, that seemed to be the way to go.

As of July, the HVAC system was running full bore, fed by the new electrical system, and Elliot had the system running day and night. Nash would come home at night and turn it up slightly and, like some weird sensor, Elliot would somehow know that it was no longer set at 70 degrees and she would turn it down again.

Nash finally got to the point where he would just let her do what she wanted, even when the electricity bill for the month of July turned out to be almost four hundred dollars. If Elliot was happy, he was happy. It was a small price to pay.

The rest of the house was coming along as well, now almost ninety percent complete. All of the painting was done, the new windows were in as well as the brand new bathrooms, and as of mid-July, all of the window treatments were up. Gauzy, soft white chiffon curtains graced the elaborate double parlors with their soft gold and green tones, while the library had been turned into the ultimate man-cave of brown leather couches, a fifty-two inch plasma screen, and a big antique desk.

Nash was in love with the room and he couldn't get his brother out of it. Beau, who was still acting as the job superintendent in spite of his own work waiting for him back in Bay St. Louis, would park himself on Nash's new couch for a good portion of the day and pretend to work.

The dining room and the ballroom had been transformed as well. The dining room now had fully-restored, hand-painted walls while the ballroom had become the ultimate family room with two giant plasma screen televisions and a full-sized pool table.

The kitchen was the one room that wasn't fully transformed yet because of the rot and mold that had been found in the walls and floor. That room was still being worked on but was functional. The creepy back staircase had been restored into a gorgeous wood structure.

The bedrooms were also fully restored and functional. Everyone got to choose their own paint color, with Elliot going for a golden ivory tone to go with her new bedroom furniture, while Alec chose a chocolate brown and Penelope chose a sage green.

The smaller back bedroom above the kitchen had been made into Elliot's writing room and the middle bedroom next to Alec's room had become a guest room with two big queen beds and its own bathroom, regularly used by Beck and Shane when they came down on weekends from Baton Rouge.

The crypt beneath the house was also still a work in progress. Dr. Whitney and Dr. Clarke had been fixtures in the room and Dr. Whitney had found what he believed to be the secondary access into the room.

Ground penetrating radar sponsored by the University of New Orleans had shown an anomaly running north from the house towards the derelict stables and Dr. Whitney had engaged a group of grad students to do some summer digging. As the house itself came together, the garden, at about one hundred yards between the house and the old stables, had become an archaeological dig. The landscape architect revamping the grounds had to work around it.

On this Thursday evening in mid-August, Nash was trying to get Elliot moving for an invitation they had to Monty Torres' birthday party. It was a fancy affair at the Pelican Point Golf Club, but Elliot wasn't moving as fast as Nash would have liked. She had been in the bathroom a very long time and Nash was growing impatient.

"Ellie!" Nash was putting on his Kenneth Cole watch with the black alligator skin band. "Honey, we're going to be late. Are you almost ready?"

No sooner did the words come out of his mouth than the bathroom door opened and Elliot appeared. In a gray metallic minidress and sky-high pumps, she looked fantastic. Nash took a moment to watch her appreciatively as she went to her dresser for her jewelry.

"Honey, you look amazing," his eyes moved up the curve of her buttocks. "But I'm not sure you can wear that dress."

She looked at him, putting her earrings on without an ounce of humor on her face. "Why not?"

He smiled at her. "Because Monty won't be able to look at anything other than you and I might have to deck him."

A wan smile crossed her lips as she turned back to her jewelry and put the other earring in. Nash could see that she was putting her lipstick into her purse, usually a precursor to them heading out the door, so he went to the dresser and kissed her on the side of the head as he picked up his keys.

"Ready?" he asked.

She half-nodded and he turned for the bedroom door. But a

word from her stopped him. "Nash," she said softly. "Wait a minute."

He paused halfway across the room and looked at her. "What?"

Elliot straightened her necklace as she gazed into his eyes, finally looking rather miserable as the hand on her necklace went to her belly. She approached him with her sexy dress and sexy shoes, putting a hand on his arm.

"I... I need to talk to you," she said quietly. "Can you please sit down a minute?"

He tried not to act impatient. "Can we talk in the car?" he asked. "We really need to get over to the club, darlin'."

She didn't like that suggestion at all. "You can't give me five minutes for something really important? When do I ever tell you that I need to talk to you?"

She was starting to get upset so he nodded his head quickly, with thinly veiled impatience, and sat down in one of the two beautiful high-back wing chairs in their bedroom. They were spectacular pieces that fit perfectly into the gold, brown and white scheme of their bedroom.

"Okay," he folded his hands and faced her seriously. "I'm all yours. What's so important?"

Dander down at his surrender, Elliot moved quietly to the other chair, sitting down very ladylike and crossing her beautiful legs.

"I've been trying to figure out how to... hey, buddy, my face is up here," she pointed at her head. "Stop looking at my legs for a moment, please."

Nash fought off a grin as he looked her in the eye. "Do I have to?"

"*Nash.*"

"Your legs are like a magnet for my eyes, baby. I just can't help it."

"*Nash!*"

He started giggling, suppressing it when he saw that she wasn't laughing with him. "I'm sorry, darlin'," he sobered up. "I'll be serious. What do you want to talk about?"

She sighed heavily, irritated. "I want to talk to you about something very important but you just want to goof around."

"So talk, honey. I'm listening."

She just looked at him and he could see the thoughts rolling through those big, blue eyes. She was irritated, true, but she also seemed kind of edgy. His humor started to fade, wondering what could be so serious, when she suddenly stood up and disappeared into the bathroom. Nash called after her.

"Honey, I'm sorry," he said. "I didn't mean to intimate that I wasn't taking you seriously. I am. Don't go away mad."

Elliot came out of the bathroom with something in her hand. Nash found himself watching her great legs as she approached and the way the skimpy mini-dress swung seductively around her thighs. He was caught off-guard when she stuck whatever was in her hand into his face.

"Do you know what this is?" she asked.

He had to blink and tilt his head back in order to focus on what she was indicating. He grasped her wrist and moved the object away from his face so he could see it. It was a long white stick with writing on it and his brow wrinkled as he looked at it.

"I'm not sure," he said. "What is it?"

She pointed a red fingernail at one end of it. "See that?"

"It's a plus sign."

"It's pregnancy test."

It took a couple of seconds for her words to sink in. Then, his eyes widened and he looked up at her, shock on his face. "A *pregnancy* test?" he repeated.

Elliot nodded. "A plus sign is positive. It says I'm pregnant."

Nash's jaw dropped. He looked back at the plastic pregnancy test with the plus sign on it and he just stared at it. Elliot waited for him to say something but he didn't. He remained silent, staring at it. Then, he gently took it out of her grasp, stood up and, while still looking at it, wandered away from the chair.

Elliot watched him as he came to a stop near the front window, feeling increasingly distressed. He hadn't said a word, nor had he even looked at her. He just stared at that pregnancy test, the weight of his silence weighing heavily between them.

"Please tell me what you're feeling," she pleaded.

Nash was still staring at the test. "I... I really don't know."

Elliot burst into quiet tears. Nash turned swiftly to her, throwing his arms around her and holding her tight. The plastic pregnancy test clattered to the floor.

"Honey, don't cry," he begged. "I didn't mean to make you cry. I'm just.... Ellie, if you want me to say I'm sorry about this, I'm not going to say it. I'm not sorry at all that you're pregnant."

She wept pitifully against his chest. "I told you I wasn't on birth control," she sobbed. "More than once we haven't used a condom. We tried to be careful, but...."

He abruptly held her out at arm's length, looking into her wet face. "Are you saying that you're sorry about this?"

She shook her head. "No," she sniffed, wiping at her eyes. "I'm really not. But I am scared."

"Scared?" he repeated, sounding distressed. "Why?"

She wiped at her nose, trying to compose herself. "Because... Nash, I'm forty-one years old," she said. "I'm too old to be having a baby but on the other hand, I want this baby so badly that I can't even verbalize it. I want this baby because it's part of you and part of me, someone that belongs just to us. I'm so scared that you won't feel the same way."

His eyebrows flew up. "Are you crazy?" he exclaimed. "Ellie, I said I didn't know how I felt because there was so much joy and excitement spinning around in my head that it momentarily over-whelmed me. This baby... this will be the most loved and antici-pated and welcome child ever born. It's going to be loved beyond belief and spoiled like crazy because every time I look at it, I'll see you. I'm thrilled, honey, truly."

She gazed up at him with her big, watery eyes. "I need a tissue."

He darted into the bathroom and came back with a wad. She took it and wiped at her eyes as he stood there, watching her anxiously. She went to sit back down on the chair and he followed, standing over her as she composed herself.

"You know," she said softly, "if one of my kids had come to me and told me they were pregnant, I would have gone through the roof – especially if I found out they hadn't used condoms and relied instead on the all-powerful withdrawal method like we've been doing. I knew better but I guess I really didn't care all that much. Maybe deep down, I wanted to have your baby. How do I explain this pregnancy to Penny and Alec? I'm supposed to be the grown-up here. Things like this aren't supposed to happen."

He crouched down in front of the chair, one hand on her knee and the other on her shoulder. "I love you, Ellie," he murmured. "You know I love you more than anything and your kids know I love you more than anything. There's no shame in this; we love each other and we're going to get married."

She fixed on him. "When?"

"Tonight. Tomorrow. As soon as we possibly can."

She gazed at him a moment, seeing the light of happiness in his eyes coupled with a good deal of anxiety due to the way she was reacting. He was afraid things had somehow changed between them. After a moment, she wrapped her arms around his neck and he pulled her close, holding her tightly with his face buried in her neck. She took a moment just to feel him against her, to experience the joy of the love they had for one another and this unexpected yet not unhappy news. The more she thought on it, the better she was coming to feel.

"I don't need a church wedding," she told him. "We can just go to the Justice of the Peace or County Clerk."

He pulled his face from her neck and looked at her, smiling. "I know a few of those," he said. "In fact, Monty has the authority to marry us. He can do it tonight."

She returned his smile, although it was dubious. "But I want the kids there, all of them."

He nodded. "Me, too," he said, backing down. "Sorry, I was just excited. I'm getting ahead of myself."

Her smile grew and she touched his face, smooth since he had shaved. "I love you so much."

He leaned forward, kissing her sweetly. "I can't tell you how happy I am right now," he murmured as he kissed her again. "This is all like a dream, Ellie, a dream that I don't want to wake up from. I feel like I'm getting a chance at a whole new life with you, and now the baby... it's all like a dream. That's the best I can do to describe it."

She stroked his cheeks, his hair, her blue eyes twinkling at him. "Still eager to get to that party?"

He laughed. "Not now, not really," he admitted. "But I suppose we should. They're expecting us. Besides, if I want Monty to marry us, then I don't want to tick him off. Do you feel well enough to go?"

"I feel okay."

"Are you sure?"

"I'm sure."

He stood up, pulling her to her feet. He looked her up and down, the sexy dress, her stunning figure. "God, darlin'," he hissed. "You look so good. I'm the luckiest man in the world."

She smiled, flattered, and went to the dresser to pick up her purse and touch up her lipstick. "There's a lot to think about right now," she said, snapping her clutch closed and heading for the bedroom door. "We're going to need to turn my writing room into a nursery."

"That's fine."

"I'll need to take over your man cave. I need a place to write."

He pretended to frown. "Wait a minute," he followed her out the door. "That's *my* room. I may have something to say about that."

"You have nothing to say about that. I'm confiscating it in the name of the Queen."

He laughed at her as they took the stairs, watching her take the steps on those enormously high shoes. "Be careful there," he admonished, gently gripping her arm. "I think in the future, you need to ditch those high-heels altogether."

She rolled her eyes at him as they reached the bottom. "Nash, don't start that already," she said quietly, noticing Penelope, Alec and Shane in the ballroom watching a movie. "I'm fine."

Nash just raised his eyebrows at her as he stuck his head into the ballroom. "We're heading out now. Don't burn the place down while we're gone."

Penelope and Alec waved at him while Shane threw a piece of popcorn in his direction. Wolfgang, lying contentedly next to the couch, jumped up to eat it.

"Go, Dad," Shane ordered.

Nash waved at his son, lying on one of the couches with his legs draped up over the sides, and took Elliot's hand as they headed for the entry. When he opened the front door for, he paused to kiss her hand.

"Thank you," he said.

She cocked her head at him. "For what?"

"For letting a good ol' boy from Louisiana court you. Thank you for making his life such a wonderful thing."

She grinned. "You're the sweetest man in the world, you know that?"

He smiled and shut the door behind them, taking the steps down to the driveway. His cruiser sat right in front on the new concrete and paver stone drive, so gorgeous and harmonious with the restored house.

Great concrete and plaster urns with huge sprays of live plants lined what was now a circular driveway, an enormous plaster fountain in the shape of an angel right in the center of the circle. Purgatory didn't look like Purgatory any longer, and Elliot had a beautiful bronze plaque made that had been mounted to the big new front gates. It read: *Sophie, Est. 1818.*

Nash opened up the passenger door for Elliot. "I have to tell you that my stomach isn't so great these days," she said, climbing in. "Isn't Monty's wife having a big sit-down dinner?"

Nash nodded. "We're going to catch it for being late."

Elliot frowned. "Don't you dare tell them why."

He laughed as he shut the door and went around to his side, getting into the car and turning it on. "When I was pregnant with Alec and Penny, I was sick the whole time with her but not with him," she said. "I'm guessing I'm about five or six weeks along right now and already my stomach is in knots, so if that's any indication, we're going to have a girl."

He looked at her, surprised. "Do you really think so?"

She grinned. "Maybe," she said. "Would you be okay with a girl?"

He turned the car down the driveway, lit at dusk by hidden solar-paneled lights and lined with great plaster urns and trimmed oak trees. "Are you kidding? I'd be ecstatic to have a daughter. In case you haven't noticed, I don't have one."

Elliot's smile grew and she gripped his hand, holding it tightly as they pulled from the driveway and out onto the main road.

———

Will Loreau sat in a blacked-out pickup truck across from Purgatory. He'd been sitting there with his brothers for the better part of two hours, hovering just off the road in the darkness, waiting for Nash Aury to leave. Not that he had expected him to, but he'd spent the past three nights sitting here, waiting for Aury to leave and being disappointed until tonight. They saw the sheriff pull out and head on down the road towards Gonzales.

"Is that him?" Nicky asked.

Will was sucking on a bottle of Jack Daniels. "Yep," he said, taking another hit. "Looks like he's got that woman with him."

"What woman?"

"The woman, you know. The one that owns the house. He's screwin' her, ya know. Ed 'n me were sneaking around the house about a week ago and they were out back on the porch. Them kids must not have been around because they were goin' at it right on the chairs in the back."

Ed snorted lewdly and Will smiled as he thought on that night, getting hot and bothered when he thought of that pretty blond woman, straddling the sheriff's lap as she rode him with her skirt hiked up around her waist, swinging that long hair around. The sheriff had his hands up her shirt, playing with her breasts. Will blew out his cheeks at the memory.

"She's somethin' else," he said. "Her daughter is, too."

Nicky was sitting in the back of the pickup, leaning in between the front seats where Will and Ed sat. "So what are we gonna do?"

Will had the neck of the whisky bottle up to his lips. "I'm not sure yet," he said. "Maybe nothin'. Or maybe we'll just scare the daughter. She's probably home."

"Her and her brother," Nicky said. "That's one big kid."

Will gave his brother a look of disgust. "He's the one who killed Daddy."

"So he may kill us."

"There's three of us and only one of him. We'll get him before he gets us."

Nicky, the youngest of the three and normally the more reserved, shook his head and sat back in the old, torn seat.

"Didn't Mr. Thompson say that we had to stay away from them on the 'count of our probation?" he asked. "I don't wanna get in more trouble, Will. We're supposed to stay out of trouble while we're on probation."

Will sighed heavily before taking another long drink of whisky. "This is Louisiana," he said, smacking his lips. "Sometimes there be law here, sometimes there ain't. Our family's been taking care of itself for two hundred years. We don't need no lawyer or sheriff or lawman to tell us how to get justice. We take care of our own."

Nicky just shook his head, picking at the torn cloth seatback. "I don't wanna go back to jail," he said. "The lawyer has already filed papers to sue them. If we do something now, we'll just mess that up."

"It's takin' too long," Will smacked the steering wheel angrily. "The courts don't care 'bout us. So we sue them. So what? They just give us money and that's the end of it. No sir, we need to do something about it. Daddy would want us to. Now it's revenge."

Nicky just shook his head, infuriating his older brothers. "If you're so scared, you can walk home," silent Ed spoke up to his younger brother. "Get out of the truck before I kick you out."

Nicky climbed out of the back window, onto the bed of the truck, and jumped off. When his brothers had been drinking, they were mean and combative and he didn't want to get caught up in whatever they were doing. In fact, he had never wanted to get caught up in what they were doing but, being the youngest, they had naturally pulled him along.

Will spun out of his hidden parking space, spraying dirt and rocks onto Nicky. He tore off in the same direction the sheriff had gone, the older-model pickup with the rifle rack on the floor weaving crazily as he sped down the road. Nicky watched the truck until it disappeared, not at all comfortable with what his brothers were up to. He didn't want to go back to jail. That thought alone was stronger, at the moment, than family ties.

He was still standing in the trees across the road from Purgatory. His brown-eyed gaze moved to the driveway across the road, now set up with big security gates and a new fence that encompassed the entire three-acre property. They had found out about the fence three days ago when they had tried to get onto the property again, which is why Will had camped out across the road to watch it. Nicky knew, instinctively, that his brother was planning something nasty.

Nicky wandered across the road, hoping no one would see him. The road for the most part was quiet. Going to the big security gates, he noticed that there was an intercom button on one of the big, brick pillars next to a massive, bronze plaque that said *Sophie, Est. 1818*. He hung around the gates for a few moments, contemplating his next course of action and the possible repercussions. He sincerely did not want to go back to jail.

His hand hovered above the intercom button. Then he lowered it and ran.

EIGHTEEN

"NASH!"

Nash had barely taken a step inside the posh clubhouse at the Pelican Point Golf Club that smelled heavily of air freshener when someone was calling his name. His arm possessively around Elliot, he looked over the sea of finely-dressed people to see an Indian-American man in an expensive suit waving furiously at him. Elliot saw the man, too, but had no idea who he was until Nash bent down and whispered in her ear.

"That's the governor of the State of Louisiana," he murmured. "Jimmy Singh."

Elliot's face lit with recognition as Nash escorted her over to the gesturing governor. Rajhal "Jimmy" Singh was a native of Baton Rouge, a Rhodes Scholar, and much beloved by his constituents. He was also very young; Elliot guessed he was probably her age or younger. His wife, a lovely Indian woman, was younger still. Jimmy shook Nash's hand happily.

"I was hoping y'all would be here," Jimmy said, looking at Elliot for the first time. He extended his hand before Nash could introduce them. "Hi, I'm Jimmy Singh."

He's definitely a politician, Elliot thought as she shook his hand. The man was all teeth and personality. "It's a pleasure, Mr. Governor," she said. "Elliot Jentry."

Jimmy's eyebrows lifted. "Elliot Jentry?" he repeated. "The writer?"

She smiled. "Guilty as charged."

He laughed at her, putting his arm around his wife and introducing her. "This is my wife, Jenny," he said. "She loves your books. We have them in our home."

Elliot smiled at Mrs. Singh. "I'm flattered," she said. "That's so nice of you to say so."

Jimmy was fast. He moved from Elliot swiftly back to Nash. "How in the world did you get a hold of this one?" he wanted to know. "She's too good for you."

Nash laughed, his hand on Elliot's back as she spoke quietly to Jenny Singh. "I know she is," he said. "But I've been blessed all the same. It's good to see you, Jimmy. I didn't know you'd be here."

Jimmy nodded. "Monty's wife and my sister are best friends," he reminded Nash of what he'd already told him, once. "I have to come to Monty's functions to keep peace in my family."

Nash wriggled his eyebrows. "Now that you're here, I may be able to stand this a little longer."

Jimmy laughed, pulling Nash towards the lavish bar by giant floor-to-ceiling windows overlooking the golf course. "Come on over here," he said. "Let's talk."

Nash went with the governor, turning to Elliot as he walked. "Honey, you comin'?"

Elliot started to nod but Jimmy cut her off. "Let the women get acquainted," he told him. "I need to talk to you."

Elliot passed Nash a somewhat wistful look, one that almost had him contradicting the governor's edict, but Jenny quickly engaged her in conversation and her focus was shifted off of Nash. Jimmy dragged Nash over to the bar and ordered him a bourbon.

"So," Jimmy sipped at his own bourbon. "How did you meet the famous Elliot Jentry? I didn't know you traveled in those circles."

Nash accepted the bourbon from the bartender. "I don't," he sipped his drink. "I met her when I sold her Purgatory. She lives there now, as do I, and we're getting married."

Jimmy's eyebrows shot up. "Is that so?" he was genuinely surprised and pleased. He held up his glass to Nash, who clinked his own against it. "Congratulations, my friend. It couldn't happen to a nicer guy."

Nash smiled. "I thank my lucky stars every day. We're truly, truly happy. In fact," he eyed the governor, "I was going to ask Monty to officiate our wedding but I'd be honored if you'd do it, instead."

"Me?" Jimmy's dark eyes widened with pleasure. "I'd be thrilled to do it, Nash. We'll do it at the governor's mansion. When were y'all planning on getting married?"

"This weekend," Nash replied. "We've been planning it for a while. We were just going to keep it low-key."

"Forget about that," Jimmy said. "You're going to have it at the mansion and I'm going to host it. We can do it in October when the weather is better."

Nash scratched at his neck. "We really want to do it sooner," he said. "We were really thinking this weekend. We don't need a big celebration."

"Nash," Jimmy put his hand on Nash's big arm in order to emphasize his position. "You're my next police commissioner. You're marrying a best-selling author. Let the rest of us share in the celebration, boy."

Nash grinned. "I *am* letting you share in it, which is why I'd like you to officiate."

"Then we'll do it in October. We'll have a big ball and...."

"Jimmy, listen," Nash cut him off, lowering his voice. "If Ellie knew I was telling you this, she'd murder me, but we *can't* wait until October, if you get my drift."

The governor had no idea what he was talking about until realization dawned. His eyes bugged. "She's in a family way?"

"I couldn't keep my hands off her."

"No!"

"Yes."

Jimmy started to laugh but he slapped a hand over his mouth to keep from booming out loud. "Congratulations," he ended up shaking Nash's hand furiously. "That's great news."

"Yes, it is, but we'd really like to get married as soon as possible for obvious reasons."

Jimmy understood. "Say no more," he said. "We'll do it Saturday at the mansion. I'll have my social secretary give you a call and arrange it."

Nash smiled. "Thanks," he said. "Now, not a word to anyone, okay? Especially not to Monty. I'll never hear the end of it."

Jimmy started to reply but they were cut off by the birthday boy himself. Monty strolled up on them, well into his fourth Seven and Seven. His suit was already stained and his tie was already half-undone. He slapped Nash on the back.

"Well, well," he slurred. "You finally showed up with my date. I've been waiting to see her all day. Nash, I consider her my birthday present from you."

Nash's humor fled. "You'd better look elsewhere for that," he told Monty. "She's my present and I don't share."

Monty looked disappointed. "Can she at least sit next to me during dinner?"

"No."

Monty went from disappointed to clearly unhappy. "You keep her all to yourself up at that... that house y'all are living in and you never let her out," he was swinging his arm around. "You need to let the woman be friendly, Nash. Y'all keep her bottled up and it's not fair."

"Sorry. You'll just have to learn to deal with it."

Monty made a face of distaste and turned towards the bar, leaning awkwardly on it. Then it was if he suddenly noticed Jimmy standing next to Nash. He eyed the governor.

"Y'all are gettin' a good man, Jimbo," he said. "Nash will do something for y'all up at the capital. He's got goals and integrity. We'll miss him around here."

Jimmy watched Monty make an ass of himself. "I know we're getting a good man," he said. "That's why I appointed him. Oh, speaking of that, Nash, I wanted to let you know that Commissioner McCready is having some health issues and he's opting out early. I know we discussed a September 1st turnover, but I need to make it sooner."

Nash looked at him seriously. "How much sooner."

"Next week?"

Nash lifted his eyebrows. "Hmmm," he leaned on the bar thoughtfully. "I've been winding up everything to pass over to my captains until the new sheriff takes office, but I thought I had at least two more weeks. I don't expect I'd be able to take the new position next week but probably the week after."

Jimmy nodded. "We'll talk more about it this weekend when you... uh, I'll call you."

Nash and Jimmy exchanged knowing expressions, Nash fighting off a grin as he sipped his bourbon and Jimmy downed his. Monty was still standing next to Nash, drunk and fairly oblivious to what they were talking about.

"Nash," Monty demanded his attention. "What are y'all going to do about the Loreau charges? What's going on with all that?"

Nash drew in a long breath. "Well," he said thoughtfully. "The boys are out on bond, as is Ms. Biffy. They are scheduled to appear on all charges the first week of September. As far as the assault charges against me go, that's pending. It's their word against mine and the Sorrento Police, and we have dashboard cameras that recorded the entire arrest and show the Loreaus resisting. The case should easily be dismissed."

At least it didn't catch me clocking Will Loreau in the jaw, he thought to himself as Monty mulled over the information.

"But what about the assault on Penny and the wrongful death case against Alec?" the mayor wanted to know. "Those poor kids have been through enough."

Nash nodded, sipping at his drink. "Yes, they have, but they're doing fine," he replied evenly. "The Loreau boys pleaded out on Penny's assault case and they've got three years on probation. The rape kit came back negative, so we agreed to the terms of probation. As for Alec, we've hired him a good lawyer and she'll take care of him. I'm guessing the case gets thrown out before it ever makes it to a courtroom."

"Who did you hire?"

"Elpheda Benson."

Monty looked as surprised as his drunken state would allow. "She's good," he agreed. "Very, very good. Nash, you've got your whole life all planned out, don't you? Nothing can touch you."

Nash glanced at Jimmy, who rolled his eyes and ordered another bourbon and water. "I'm just lucky, I guess," Nash said.

Monty shook his head and nearly fell over. "It's more than luck," he insisted. "You're a good man. You've done a lot for the parish, Nash. We'll never forget it. We'll...."

He was cut off when Elliot suddenly appeared next to Nash. Mrs. Singh was with her. As Elliot smiled at Nash and he gladly put his arm around her, Monty was undressing her with his eyes.

"Ms. Jentry," he greeted, his gaze dragging up and down her body. "You look absolutely stunning. Yessir, you do. You look like a Hollywood actress."

Wrapped up in Nash's big arm, Elliot turned to the drunken mayor. "Thank you," she said. "Happy birthday."

The mayor smiled lasciviously. "Care to share a birthday dance with me?"

"There's no music."

"We don't need any music."

Elliot smiled coolly. "No, thank you."

"But it's my birthday," Monty insisted. "I'm the birthday boy which means you have to do what I want."

By this time, Nash was focused in on him. "*No*, Monty," he told him firmly, quietly. "I think they're about to serve dinner. Why don't you go find Margie?"

Monty was quickly verging on a tantrum. "Nash, you can't spoil my fun, not today."

He reached out and grabbed Elliot by the wrist, jerking her away from Nash's embrace. The action caught Elliot off guard and, in her enormous high heels, she stumbled and would have fallen had Nash not grabbed her. With Elliot righted, Nash was in Monty's face.

"If you weren't an old friend, I'd make sure they had to carry you out of this place on a stretcher," he rumbled threateningly. "Keep your hands to yourself and your mind off Elliot or you're not going to like my reaction. Have I made myself clear?"

Monty gazed up at Nash, who was taller than him by at least a foot. Suddenly, he didn't look quite so drunk anymore.

"I'm sorry," he insisted. "I didn't mean to make her fall. I'm sorry if I hurt her."

Nash was so angry that his cheeks were red. He could feel Elliot's soft hand on his arm, pulling him away. He started to go with her, but not before he had final words with Monty.

"Next time, I'll break every bone in the hand that touches her. Got it?"

Monty blanched, nodding his head to acknowledge that he understood the seriousness of Nash's threat. Fact was that he believed him. He was glad when his wife came to his rescue, pulling him over towards the dining area.

"Come on," Elliot had Nash by the arm, pulling him away from Monty and away from the bar. "It's okay, sweetie. I'm fine."

Nash looked at her and she caught a flash of the deadly intensity the man was capable of. She'd never seen it before. His features were tight and his jaw was ticking. She wrapped both hands around his elbow.

"Hey," she said softly, smiling when their eyes met. "Don't be so upset. No harm done."

Nash wasn't willing to be so easily cooled. He forced a smile at her but she could tell that he was still upset.

"Let's get out of here," he told her. "Let's get dinner some-where else."

Elliot looked surprised but she went along with him. "Sure," she said. "Whatever you want to do, sweetie."

Nash said his goodbye to Jimmy and Jenny, and to a few other people, as he and Elliot headed for the exit. He was frankly too angry to stick around. If Monty made another move towards Elliot he was afraid of what he would do, so it was best just to get out of there.

The moon was full and they could see the river in the distance, the ghostly glow from the moon lighting up the water-way. Elliot kept silent as they wound their way through a residen-tial neighborhood out of the golf club, unsure what to say and knowing that Nash needed to cool down. When he finally reached over and took her hand, kissing her fingers, she smiled at him.

"So where are you taking me?" she asked. "Someplace secluded where you can take advantage of me? Oops, forget I said that. You already did that and now we're in trouble."

He laughed. Somehow, she always knew the right thing to say to him to loosen him up and make him smile. His anger drained away as thoughts of killing Monty shifted to thoughts of Elliot.

"You say trouble and I say heaven," he said, sighing as his normal demeanor gradually returned. "At least something good came out of this evening."

"What?"

He squeezed her hand. "I get to have you all to myself for dinner," he said, winking at her when she grinned. "But something else good came out of it, too."

"What else?"

"Jimmy is going to marry us on Saturday at the Governor's Mansion in Baton Rouge," he told her.

"Really?" she was excited. "That's great!"

He loved her enthusiasm. "I'm glad you think so," he said. "I need to let Beck and Shane know as soon as possible so they'll have something decent to wear. Beck has suits but I doubt Shane even knows what one is. I may have to take him shopping tomorrow."

"Maybe we should just go home and share the news with the kids right now."

Nash kissed her hand again. "We will," he said. "Give me a couple of hours to share it with you first before we spread it around the family. That reminds me that I have to call my parents, too. And Beau. They'll want to come."

Elliot thought of her family back in California. "I'll call my dad," she said. "I don't even know where my mom is. Remember I told you that my parents divorced when I was little?"

"I do."

"What I didn't tell you is that my mom is kind of a free spirit," she said. "She's spent the past several years riding around on her motorcycle, painting landscapes and writing poetry. Did I tell you that she named me after T.S. Eliot, the poet? He's her favorite."

He grinned. "I was wondering where you got your name."

Elliot laughed softly. "'The Hollow Men' is one of her favorite pieces of literature. Do you know much about him?"

He cocked his head. "Isn't that the poem that ends with 'this is the way the world ends, not with a bang but a whimper'?"

She was impressed. "Very good, Sheriff. You're a man of some refinement."

"Or a man who was forced to read it in an English Literature class."

Elliot laughed at his words, gazing out of the window and watching the landscape pass. "Anyway, my mom sells enough of her art so that she can support herself. She just never was the settling-down type. She's always got to be on the move."

Nash smiled, seeing their destination up ahead, illuminated by the full moon. "What about your dad?"

"All he ever wanted was a family," she replied. "What he got was me. He never remarried."

"Do you think he'll be able to make it out by Saturday?"

She nodded. "I don't see why not. I need to call him right away, though. He can jump on a Southwest flight to New Orleans tomorrow."

Nash slowed the car down and pulled into the parking lot of what looked like a few cabins all huddled together with foliage and patios surrounding them. Elliot looked at the area curiously.

"What is this place?" she asked.

Nash turned off the car and opened his door. "A good restaurant."

Elliot sat in the car until he came around and opened her door. He was very chivalrous and would get agitated if she tried to open her own door. She climbed out, her sexy legs drawing Nash's attention again until she caught him looking at her butt. She pointed at her face.

"My eyes are up here, Aury," she pretended to be angry. "Remember?"

He laughed and pulled her into a tight embrace. "And they're beautiful," he murmured, kissing her sweetly. "But so is your butt. And your legs."

She giggled as he kissed her once more and let her go, taking her hand as he led her towards the restaurant. It was a small place, an old slave cabin that had been matched with other old slave cabins to form a restaurant that was appropriately called "The Cabin Restaurant".

Elliot loved the rustic atmosphere immediately, trying to be careful and not twist an ankle on the gravel walkway as she looked around. There were several cabins, one of them being a general store, and she was very curious about everything.

The main part of the restaurant was an authentic slave cabin, big and open. The hostess on duty knew Nash on sight. She showed Nash and Elliot to a very nice table by a window that overlooked the garden. She gave them a menu and left them to look over the goods.

"Do you come here often?" Elliot asked, looking around the very rustic interior with the original brick fireplace.

Nash shrugged. "I eat most of my meals out," he said. "This

place is close to my house, plus it's good, so I've come here a fair amount."

Elliot looked over the menu. Nash already knew what he wanted so he watched Elliot as she perused the offerings. He just sat there, watching her, before abruptly standing up.

"I'll be right back," he said.

Elliot just smiled at him, thinking he was going to the restroom but he went outside, back to the parking lot. Elliot returned her attention to the menu and had nearly decided on her order by the time he returned to their table.

She smiled at him as she lay the menu down. "What did you do?"

He began to unroll his silverware from the napkin, pausing when she asked the question. "I, uh, forgot something," he said, changing the subject. "What are you going to have?"

Elliot turned back to the menu. "I think I'm going to have the French Onion soup."

"Is that all? Get something substantial, honey."

She made a face at him. "My belly is kind of funny right now."

He smiled. "Well," he said after a moment. "Maybe I have something that can help."

She looked up from the menu. "What?"

He couldn't seem to take his eyes off her and Elliot sensed that there was something more on his mind. She set the menu down as he reached across the table and took her hand. He didn't say anything for a few moments; he simply stared at her.

"We seem to be doing this all backwards," he finally chuckled, suddenly looking nervous. "I proposed to you within a week of knowing you. Now there's a baby on the way and we're getting married on Saturday. I think my dad would say I'm closing the barn door after the horse has escaped."

Elliot giggled and he continued. "I just can't express how much I love my life right now," he said softly, his hazel eyes glimmering warmly at her. "I've told you so many times how much I love you and how lucky I feel that you're going to get sick of hearing it."

"No," Elliot shook her head firmly. "I'll never get tired of hearing it."

He smiled at her, learning forward on the table and pulling her forward as well. They huddled over the tabletop, holding hands sweetly in the dim light of the restaurant. Finally, he dug into his coat pocket, pulled out small box and set it on the table between them. Elliot looked at the object, recognizing it as a ring box, and her pulse began to race. Nash saw her features soften with realization.

"My mother has an old heirloom ring that has been in her family for over one hundred years," he told her. "She wanted me to give it to you but I wanted to give you something more, something that no one else has worn. So I took the heirloom ring to a jeweler in Baton Rouge and he helped me design something around it. I really hope you like it because it's something I put my heart in to, making sure this ring was designed by me just for you. Ellie, I love you so much and I'm so happy you're going to be my wife. I hope this ring is a small token of that."

He handed her the box and she accepted it gratefully, her eyes already starting to well up. Nash watched her face as she flipped open the top and the ring came into view. Elliot gasped when she saw the ring, tears of joy coming as she pulled it out to inspect it.

The original heirloom ring had been a simple round solitaire, easily four carats, probably more, mined and cut back in the days of no income tax and industrial billionaires like Astor and Morgan. Nash had the jeweler design a jacket to wrap around the platinum setting with dozens of pavè diamonds encircling it. It was the most glorious ring Elliot had ever seen.

"Oh, my God," she gasped, handing him back the ring as she wiped the tears off her cheeks. "Put it on me."

Nash grinned as he took her left hand, slipping the ring on her third finger. It was a little loose but not too terribly. He looked at the ring on her finger and had never felt so content or complete in his entire life.

"Do you like it?" he asked.

She was trying not to sob. "I love it. It's spectacular."

His grin broadened. "Good," he kissed the ring and her hand, "because this is where it belongs."

Elliot laughed through her tears, trying not to make a scene but not doing a very good job. She jumped up from her chair and ran to him, throwing her arms around his neck and nearly toppling him off his chair. He joined in her laughter, kissing her sweetly, and Elliot ended up sitting on his lap. As they cuddled and kissed, the waitress came over.

"Are y'all celebrating?" she asked. "Can I get you something to help?"

Nash looked at Elliot, thinking of the baby she carried. He doubted she would go in for a bottle of champagne, which the place probably didn't have, anyway. He grinned at her as he spoke to the waitress.

"Yes," he told her. "Two diet colas, one French Onion soup, and one flatiron steak, medium well."

The waitress took the order and headed off. Elliot remained on Nash's lap until the soup came and she finally had to return to her seat. Nash chewed on a roll as she gingerly sipped her soup and talked about her free-spirited mother who had been on a bicycle trip when both of her grandchildren had been born. When she was halfway through the soup, her cell phone rang.

Elliot pulled it out of her purse and answered it on the fifth ring. "Penny?" she had seen the caller I.D. "What are you doing, sweetie?"

There was a lot of screaming and laughing going on in the background as Penelope spoke. "Mom, you'll never believe it!" she gasped. "We saw your ghost!"

Elliot grinned and put the phone on speaker so Nash could hear it. "What did you see?" Elliot asked.

Penelope was laughing hysterically and they could hear Alec and Shane yelling and whooping in the distance. "We were watching a movie with the lights off in the ballroom and the dog started going nuts," she said. "I looked up to see what he was barking at and I saw this weird fog coming out of the dining room. Alec and Shane saw it, too. It moved from the dining room and then disappeared once it came into the ballroom."

Nash grinned broadly, listening to all of the hollering going on in the background. He took the phone off speaker and put it to his ear. "Tell those ladies in the background to keep it down," he told her. "Your mom and I will be home in a little while."

Penelope was reduced to giggles. "I'll try to keep the boys quiet," she said. "But I wanted to tell my mom that we saw her ghost. It was little, like a child."

The waitress brought Nash's steak. "Weird," he said. "Well, try to tough it out. We'll be home in a little bit."

"Alec and Shane are afraid to go to sleep now. They said they're going to sleep with you and mom."

"They're *not* sleeping with me and your mother. They're just going to have to man up."

He hung up the phone, handing it back to Elliot with a grin. "What a couple of goofballs," he shook his head, picking up his knife and fork.

Elliot took her fork and speared one of the roast potatoes, chewing with relish. "I'm really glad that Alec and Shane are getting along so well," she said. "Alec really likes him."

Nash took a bite of steak. "They're both essentially the same personality," he said. "They're both easygoing and a little immature. It works for them."

She shrugged. "I guess," she said. "Beck still can't seem to decide how he feels about Penny, though."

Nash snorted. "Don't get him wrong; he knows how he feels. But with you and me getting married, he's not sure he wants to date his stepsister. What does Penny say about it?"

She took another potato. "She thinks he's nice and cute, but I don't think she wants to date him. He's just somebody fun to hang out with."

Nash just lifted his eyebrows and cut another piece of steak. "It's going to break his heart, but that's probably for the best."

Elliot nodded, returning to her soup for the moment. "So they saw my ghost?"

Nash nodded. "So they say. I might have to check the house for the crack they were smoking."

Elliot shrieked softly in outrage. "You said that you believe in ghosts," she pointed out. "You said you believed me when I told you about the ghost in the dining room."

He nodded. "I did," he said. "But the way those two were screaming in the background...."

Elliot giggled as he shook his head and rolled his eyes. She continued to pick at his plate, eventually deciding she liked his potatoes better than her soup, so Nash ordered her a side. The waitress brought the potatoes and she dug into them as she and Nash spoke of what they needed to accomplish before Saturday. He was in the process of trying to convince her to take a bite of steak when his phone rang. He set his fork down and answered his phone.

"Aury."

It was Sheriff Dispatch and before a word was even said, Nash could hear a lot of traffic on the radio in the background.

"Sheriff," a woman with a heavy drawl was on the line. "We've got an officer needs assistance call at the Dutchtown Mobile Home park off Highway 10 and Cornerview Road."

Nash swallowed the bite in his mouth. "What happened?"

Dispatch came back. "It's kind of sketchy, but it sounds like an ambush," she said. "Now it looks like we've got a barricaded suspect and he's shooting at anything that moves."

"Were any of my deputies hit?"

"No, sir. But I've got a watch commander and a Special Weapons team rolling."

"I'm on my way," Nash said. "Have the watch commander call me as soon as he arrives."

"Yessir."

When he hung up the phone, Elliot was watching him with big

eyes. He smiled weakly. "We need to go, honey. I've got a situation...."

She cut him off, already standing up. "I know," she said softly. "Do you want to take your steak home?"

He could see that she was trying to act normally about it and he let her. He would let her handle it however she felt she could, knowing what a tough time she had the last time he had a call out. His heart ached for her as he hoped she didn't ask him the details. *He's shooting at anything that moves....*

"Take it for the dog," he said, spying the waitress across the room and waving her over. He dug into his wallet and pulled out a fifty dollar bill. "Do you want to take the potatoes?"

Elliot shook her head. "No," she told him, watching him hand the money over to the waitress and get a takeout box. "This is a nice restaurant. Thank you for dinner."

He smiled at her as he took her by the hand and led her from the restaurant. Elliot didn't say a word as they made their way back to the car, nor did she say a word as he drove eighty miles an hour back to Purgatory. The only sign of her anxiety was the fact that she held Nash's hand so tightly that she nearly broke his knuckles.

The full moon loomed high in the sky as they drove the six or seven miles back to Sorrento. The big, new gates opened automatically with his remote and he pulled in, parking the car in front of the house to let her out.

Elliot was trying very hard to be brave. She turned to him, their eyes meeting, and she put her arms around his neck, kissing him tenderly.

"Be safe," she whispered against his lips.

He returned her kiss. "I'll call you when I can. I love you."

"I love you, too."

Elliot climbed out of the car, waving at him as he pulled around and headed back out the driveway. Turning for the front door, she made her way up on to the porch, congratulating herself for not bursting into tears in front of him. At least she waited this time until he pulled back down the driveway.

NINETEEN

IT WAS WELL after midnight when Elliot heard the intercom for the front gates buzz. She had been in her writing room, working away on the *Knight of the Vampire* novel, when she heard the buzz go off. There were three points of contact for the intercom – one in the kitchen, one in the man cave/library, and one in the master bedroom. Setting aside the vampire blood orgy scene she had been working on, she went down the back stairs and into the kitchen about the time the intercom buzzed again. She hit the reply button.

"Who is it?"

The intercom crackled back at her. "Ms. Ellie, it's Ken Havereau. Can you please open the gate?"

As Elliot pushed the button to activate the gates, she began to wonder why Deputy Havereau had come. Nash had called about an hour before to say that everything was fine and he would probably be home very late, so she wasn't really thinking doom and gloom when Havereau's unit pulled up in front of the house.

Dressed in one of her favored velour jogging suits, she crossed the dark and silent central hall on her way to the front door. She opened the big panel about the time Ken was mounting the stairs to the porch.

"Hi," she said. "You're up late."

Ken smiled wanly at her and it was then that Elliot noticed Steve Pitot pulling up behind Ken's car in another unit. Ken didn't wait until Steve got out of the car before he started speaking.

"Ma'am, we've been sent to bring you to Nash," he said.

Oddly, and given her history with men in uniform, Elliot still wasn't anxious. She cocked her head curiously. "Why in the world did he send you?" she was genuinely baffled. "Did his car break down? Do I need to drive over and get him?"

Ken sighed, glancing at Steve as the man joined him on the porch. Nash had warned them that Elliot would not take the news well so he tried to couch it carefully.

"No, ma'am," he said. "Nash is at St. Elizabeth Hospital. He got in a little scrape tonight and he wanted us to bring you over to the hospital."

Now, the real reason for their appearance was starting to sink in. Elliot had no idea why she hadn't figured it out before, but given that Nash had called her not long ago, she just didn't think anything was wrong.

Now, it was evident that something was wrong, wrong enough that Nash was at the hospital and he had sent deputies to escort her there.

"Oh, my God," she breathed. "What happened to Nash?"

Ken was sincerely trying to be gentle. "He got shot, ma'am, but...."

That was all Elliot needed to hear. She stumbled backwards, hands over her ears, sobs bubbling up from her throat. There was nothing she could feel, see or hear at the moment other than blind horror.

It's happening again, she thought, *oh, God, not again, not Nash!* The room started spinning and she tried to look for something to hold on to. She took about three steps into the entry hall before collapsing in a heap on the new rug that had just been shipped from New Orleans.

The world had gone black.

————

Nash was lying in a private operatory room just off of the main emergency room floor. He had two I.V.s dripping fluids and meds into his right arm while a tube drained fluid from a hole in his chest into a bag secured to the gurney.

He could breathe much better now than he could less than an hour before, the moment a bullet from the barricaded suspect happened to pierce him precisely in the left shoulder in a spot where his vest didn't cover, sending the bullet tearing down into his chest and lodging by his left shoulder blade. It had nicked his left lung, collapsing it, and they'd had to put a tube in his chest to equalize the pressure until they could repair it.

All in all, it wasn't as bad as it could have been. The doctor didn't seem to think he'd be in the hospital more than a couple of days once the bullet was removed. No bones were broken, no vital veins or arteries nicked.

The doctor had called him extremely lucky and Nash was forced to agree, but he wondered how Elliot was going to view his stroke of luck. He'd sent Ken and Steve for her almost the moment he'd been hit, knowing it was bad enough that they were going to evacuate him to St. Elizabeth's.

Nash told his deputies to be gentle with her given what had happened to her first husband, but he knew that no matter how gentle they were, it wouldn't be gentle enough.

So he lay on the gurney and worried about her, staring up at the ceiling as a nurse prepped his shoulder wound for surgery. By his time estimation, Elliot should be walking through the E.R. doors any minute and he very much wanted to see her before he went into surgery to assure her that he was fine. This wasn't a repeat of Rob Jentry; even so, he was deeply concerned for her, much more than he was for himself.

As he counted the dots on the ceiling tiles while the nurse carefully shaved his shoulder, he caught movement out of the corner of his eye and looked over to see Penelope, Alec and Shane in the doorway. The kids looked terrified and he smiled, waving them over.

"Come on in," he told them. "It's okay. I'm going to be fine."

Shane and Alec entered. Shane went right to his father and held his hand, looking sick and worried. Alec just stood next to the bed, looking at all of the medical paraphernalia and not quite sure how he felt about anything. The last time he saw someone like this, it was his father on life support.

Penelope, however, was slower than the boys. It took her a few seconds to make her way into the room. She paused by the head of the bed.

"Are you sure you're going to be all right?" she whispered tightly.

Nash looked up at the young lady who had lost her father in not dissimilar circumstances a couple of years ago. He reached up with his good arm and gently cupped her cheek.

"I'm going to be fine, honey," he assured her. "Please don't worry. It just passed through my chest without really hitting anything vital so they just need to go in and remove the bullet."

Penelope nodded, tears of fear and relief streaming down her cheeks. Nash wiped away the tears. "Don't cry, darlin'," he begged. "I promise I'll be fine. Where's your mother?"

Penelope wiped at the tears that wouldn't stop falling. "The ambulance brought her in," she told him. "She passed out when the deputies told her what happened."

"What?" Nash was seized with concern. "Where is she?"

Penelope sniffled, pointing out of the door to the general emergency room beyond. "Out there."

Nash was trying to get out of bed and the nurse who had been carefully shaving his shoulder threw her arm across him to prevent him from moving.

"Sheriff Aury," she snapped. "You're not going anywhere."

He was livid, like a madman. "Get me out to see my fiancée or bring her in here to see me," he ordered in a tone that left no room for doubt. "One way or the other, I'm going to see her so you'd better figure it out."

The nurse was aghast, already buzzing the nurse's station for help. Several nurses rushed in, followed by a couple of doctors, and Alec, Shane and Penelope were pushed aside as they all tried to calm Nash down. He had already pulled his chest tube out and was starting to have trouble breathing again, and when the surgical nurse explained what had happened, the on-call doctor could see they were going to have trouble unless they did something.

As the group was trying to figure out what to do and Nash was arguing strongly, Ken and Steve entered the room. They had followed the ambulance in, bringing Alec and Shane with them as Penelope rode with her mother. What they were met with was chaos, looking with shock to Alec, Shane and Penelope huddled against the wall. Ken went to the young people.

"What's going on?" he asked.

Penelope was weeping again. "Nash wants to see my mom but they won't let him."

Ken could see the struggle going on. He made his way over towards the gurney, trying to position himself so Nash could see him.

"Sheriff?" he called above the noise. "Nash?"

Nash heard the voice, looking up to see Ken standing back behind the herd of doctors and nurses. He waved him over.

"Ken," he sounded very glad to see him. "What happened? Where's Ellie?"

"Sheriff, she's fine," Ken assured him. "She just got a little upset, that's all. She passed out when we told her what happened so we called the ambulance just to make sure she was taken care of. We thought it was what you would want. The doctor gave her a tranquilizer and she's lying right outside your door. I promise, she's fine."

Nash seemed to calm dramatically and the nurses started reattaching tubes and I.V.s. He motioned to Ken, who came close enough for Nash to grab him. He pulled the man down to his level so he wouldn't have to shout.

"You go tell her doctor that he has to be careful what medications he gives her," he whispered. "She's pregnant. The kids don't know yet, so keep it to yourself, okay?"

Ken nodded and fled the room. Nash lay there as the nurses and doctors finished with him, weakened after his outburst. He looked up at the doctor by his right arm.

"Please," he asked softly, "I just want to see her before you take me into surgery. Please?"

The doctor lifted an eyebrow at him. "Only if you promise to stay calm."

"I will, I promise."

The doctor sent a nurse out to where Elliot was as Nash turned to look at the kids, still huddled over by the wall. He held out a hand to them.

"Come over here, y'all," he said. "I'm sorry I got upset."

The kids came away from the wall, gravitating back in his direction. Shane went back to holding his father's hand, still very frightened for the man.

"Dad, what happened?" he asked.

Nash took a deep breath as they re-secured the chest tube. "I'm not exactly sure," he said. "We had a barricaded suspect and I was in a vest, back behind the Special Weapons van. All I did was step out a bit to get a look at what our lookouts were talking about, you know, how well the suspect was embedded, and suddenly I felt this blow to my shoulder. It hit me so hard that it knocked me to the ground and as I lay there with this searing pain in my shoulder, it occurred to me that I'd been shot. It further occurred to me that Ellie was going to kill me when she found out."

The boys grinned but Penelope remained deeply distressed. Nash let go of Shane's hand to grasp hers.

"Can you go outside and tell your mama that I love her?" he asked. "Tell her I'll be fine."

Penelope shook her head, wiping at her nose. "She's still unconscious."

Nash's smile vanished and he started to get worked up again, but Penelope put her hands on his chest to still him.

"If you don't stop freaking out every time I tell you something, I'm just not going to tell you anything at all," she threatened. "We're already worried about you, Nash. You need to stay calm so the doctors can help you. My mother is fine; she's just sleeping now. They gave her a sedative."

Nash forced himself to calm, seeing how upset she was becoming. "I'm sorry," he told her sincerely. "I'm not trying to upset you. I just want to see your mom."

Before Penelope could reply, they heard a noise at the door and saw that two orderlies were bringing in a second gurney. The kids could see that it was Elliot, curled up in a drug-induced sleep on her left side. They cleared the room as the orderlies positioned the gurney next to Nash's bed. They bumped it right up against him and lowered the sides so Nash could touch her.

As the orderlies vacated the room, Nash took a good, long look at Elliot. It was like medicine to him, the calming effect unfathomable. She was sleeping peacefully, dressed in the comfy pink jogging suit he'd seen her in so many times. She looked so fragile and sweet. He couldn't help the tears coming to his eyes as he reached out and gently grasped the hand that was near her head, clutching her fingers.

"Ellie?" he said softly. "Honey, can you hear me?"

She remained dead asleep. A young male nurse had followed her in and now stood at the base of her gurney. As Nash held her hand and struggled not to cry, the young man spoke.

"Sheriff, your deputy told me about her pregnancy," he said quietly. "But the doctor had already given her a shot of Valium by the time we were told."

Nash nodded, blinking back tears. "Will...," he swallowed away the lump in his throat. "Will the medication hurt the baby?"

The nurse looked uncomfortable. "Had we known before, we

would have given her something else," he said. "It wasn't a full dose, so that's good news. She should be all right."

Nash just nodded his head, gazing at Elliot's sleeping face and toying with her fingers. The nurse backed out of the room but Nash caught sight of someone else standing in the doorway. His gaze locked with Penelope's as she stood there, watching. He could tell just by her expression that she had heard every word.

"Your mom and I were going to tell you before all of this happened," he whispered. "We've got a date with the governor to get married this Saturday, but it doesn't look like that's going to happen."

Penelope stepped into the room, her young face serious. "Mom is pregnant?"

Nash nodded. "Yes," he said. "We just found out about it, Pen. We weren't trying to keep it from y'all."

Penelope was gazing at her sleeping mother. "I didn't think that," she said, looking rather shocked. "So she's really pregnant?"

"Yes."

Penelope kept looking at her mother as if seeing the woman through new eyes somehow. "Wow," she finally said. "A new baby."

Nash couldn't tell if she was happy or sad about it. "We're very happy about it," he said. "I hope you'll be happy as well."

Penelope was gazing at her sleeping mother. "Sure, I guess," she replied. "It's just a lot to absorb."

"Believe me, I know. I'm still trying to wrap my mind around it."

Penelope tore her gaze away from her mother and looked at Nash. No longer weeping, she looked drawn and intense.

"Nash, I just have to say this," she said quietly. "Alec and I already told you what she went through when my dad died. I will admit that when we first came here and you and mom got together, I thought it wouldn't last. I figured if she was happy, I was happy, and maybe you would just help her get on her feet emotionally again. But my mom... she loves you so much, Nash. She loved my dad, but I never saw her show the same love and affection for him that she shows for you. It's like you've become a part of her somehow. Anyway, what I wanted to say is that we all love you, Nash. You took a family that had been broken by grief and you healed all of us, not just my mom. If something happened to you, I don't think we could take it. So I hope this job that you're taking in the capital takes you away from guns and violence, because we don't need to go through that hell again."

Nash was gazing up at her as the nurses began to come back into the room to take him into surgery. He ignored the people who were beginning to unlock his wheels.

"I understand," he said. "On the day your mom and I get married, there's a little church about a half mile from Purgatory and I was planning to go there and have a talk with your dad. I'm going to tell him how much I love his family and how I promise I'll take the best possible care I can of them. I'm going to ask him if it's okay with him that I love you and your brother as if you were my own flesh and blood. I would never try to replace your father, Penny, but I'm hoping you'll let me love you and take care of you in his place. And this new baby... well, she'll just bind us all together. She'll be something that belongs to all of us and she'll be life renewed, maybe a piece of that new life y'all were looking to start. I'm pretty sure your dad would be okay with that. If it was my family, I'd sure be okay with it."

Penelope was back to crying again at Nash's sweet words. She wiped the tears from her face and went around to the other side of Nash's bed, kissing him on the cheek and trying to hug him without messing with the I.V. lines.

"I'll sit with mom while you go in surgery," she whispered. "Don't worry about her. She'll be fine."

Nash smiled at her, his attention moving back to Elliot, still sleeping like the dead on the gurney next to him. He couldn't kiss her because he was too far away, so he gripped her hand tightly.

"Love you, honey," he whispered to her. "I'll see you in a while."

Penelope, Shane and Alec walked with Nash to the operating room door. When they wheeled him inside, the kids stood there, looking lost, for about a half-hour until Penelope finally made them all go back downstairs to where Elliot was.

Exhausted, upset, they settled down into chairs and couches for a good, long wait.

TWENTY

NASH WOKE up to Elliot standing next to his bed.

He was groggy and his mouth felt like paste, but surprisingly, he didn't feel as bad as he thought he would. There seemed to be a moderate amount of sunlight in the room, and as he blinked his foggy vision, he could see bunches upon bunches of flower arrangements. They were everywhere. Nash smiled weakly at the woman standing next to him.

"Hi, honey," he murmured. "How are you feeling?"

Elliot stood there with her arms crossed, gazing down at him. She looked stiff and uneasy. "I should be asking you that question. How are *you* feeling?"

He licked his dry lips. "Not too bad, I guess," he muttered. "Thirsty. Can a guy get a drink of water around here?"

Elliot buzzed the nurse, who came in and checked Nash's tubes and monitors. Then she poured him some water and held the straw to his lips. Nash took a few sips and she took it away, setting it down on the table near the bed.

Elliot stood back, watching the nurse check out Nash. The woman smiled at her as she left the room, leading Elliot to believe that Nash was doing just fine. Perhaps he was fine, but Elliot wasn't. It was around eleven in the morning following the night of hell, and she wasn't recovered yet, not by a long shot. She watched Nash as he groggily licked his lips and struggled to shake off the effects of the anesthesia.

"Why are you standing over there?" he asked, his voice weak. "Come over here and give me a kiss."

Elliot just stood there, her arms folded. Then she took a step towards him but came to a halt. Before Nash could say another word, she broke down into deep, painful weeping.

"No," she sobbed, turning away from him. "I can't... Nash, I can't do this. I'm going home, back where I belong. I can't go through this again."

Nash struggled to clear his vision and his mind. "Can't do what?" he asked. "What's wrong, honey?"

She pointed at him, an exaggerated gesture. "This!" she wept. "You! You almost got yourself killed and I can't go through this again."

He was trying to sit up, trying to go to her so he could comfort her, but it was fairly impossible for him to move at the moment.

"Honey, slow down," he said calmly, trying to sound firm. "I'm not dead, not even close. I'm going to be fine. I'm sorry this upset you so much, I really am. I just feel sick about it. But...."

Elliot was quickly approaching hysterics. "I'm going home," she repeated. "I'm going back to California and I'm going to forget about this new life I tried to start. It was stupid. I shouldn't have tried. I shouldn't have fallen in love with another cop because I knew what could happen, and it almost did. *Again.* I just... I can't take it...."

She was sobbing deeply. Nash could hardly move but he could certainly feel; he could feel every emotion of fear and terror radiating from her. He struggled to keep a level head.

"Ellie," he said gently. "Come here."

"No," she almost shouted at him.

He tried again. "Ellie," he said, very gingerly. "Please, baby. Please come here. Don't make me get up and get you. You know I will if I have to."

She was sobbing into her hands, turning to look at him. "Why did you have to go on that call last night?" she demanded. "You're the sheriff, for God's sake – you shouldn't have to go on calls. You need to stay in the office where it's nice and safe. You don't need to risk your life."

"You're right," he said evenly, hoping if he let her vent she would calm sufficiently. "I don't want you to worry about this anymore because it's never going to happen again. I'll be sworn in as Police Commissioner in a couple of weeks and spend all of my time in an office after that. I'll never go on a call-out again."

"No," she snapped. "No more police work. No more cops. I don't want to have anything to do with cops ever again."

Nash was becoming more lucid along with feeling a distinct sense of foreboding. "Ellie, don't say that. What do you want me to do, honey?"

She looked at him, then, and he could see the turmoil in the big, blue eyes. She became less angry and more grieved.

"I don't want you to carry a gun," she sobbed. "I don't want you to get shot at. I don't want to have to worry about that anymore."

"All right," he said agreeably. "Then I won't accept the commissioner appointment. I told you I wouldn't take it if it meant losing you."

She looked at him, guilt in her expression. "But... but what else will you do?"

He sighed. "My mother's family is wealthy," he said quietly. "They own a sugar company in New Orleans. They have for almost two hundred years. I'll go work for them."

"Sugar?" she repeated. "What sugar? You never mentioned that."

"If you come over here, I'll tell you."

Arms still folded stiffly in front of her, Elliot went over to him. Nash reached out and grasped her right hand, pulling it to his lips and kissing it reverently. He kissed her fingers, her wrist, and he could see that he was softening her. He could tell simply by her expression. Then he gave a little tug and pulled her towards him.

"Come here and give me a kiss," he whispered. "Don't make me beg."

Elliot's angry stance snapped and she fell against him, her lips on his. She began to cry again and he shushed her softly, his good hand on her back, pulling her to him. She ended up climbing on the bed and curling up against him, sobbing her heart out. Nash finally had her where he wanted her, holding her tightly with one arm as she wept.

"My mother's family owns Gammon Sugar," he told her, stroking her back and comforting her as her sobs lessened. "Since 1823, Gammon has owned two major refineries along the Mississippi River and controls a vested interest in the world's sugar trade. My mother is one of the heiresses to the Gammon fortune."

Elliot lay with her head tucked against his right shoulder, wiping at the tears that were falling on his hospital gown. "She's rich?"

"Wildly."

"So why couldn't she give you the money to buy Purgatory when it was sold during probate?"

He smiled faintly. "Well, now, that's a good question," he said. "I guess the short answer is that my brother and I were the only ones that really wanted to buy the place that badly. I suppose she would have given us the money had I asked her, but I didn't ask her. I haven't asked my mama for money since I was eleven years old. Or maybe I just didn't want Purgatory badly enough; I really don't know. I had my career, my own home, and I was too busy to take over a derelict, old house even if it was my legacy. Or, it's just possible that maybe I'd heard of an interested buyer through Ms. Dawn, a best-selling author by the name of Elliot Jentry, and it's further possible that I looked her up online and saw just how beautiful and talented she was. Maybe I wanted her to buy the house just so I could meet her."

Elliot didn't say anything for a moment. Then, her head came up. When she looked at him, she was grinning.

"That is *so* not true," she accused.

He smiled at her. "How do you know?"

"Because you wouldn't do something like that."

"I'll ask you again; how do you know?"

She wiped at her nose, still grinning. "I guess I don't," she said. "So you're saying you sold me Purgatory just so you could meet me?"

He just grinned at her, a sleepy grin that had her both giggling and frustrated.

"I don't believe you," she said flatly, lying her head back down again on his good shoulder, listening to his heart beating strong and steady. "Let's get back to Gammon Sugar. Would they let you go work for them just like that?"

His right arm went around her again, his hand on her shoulder, stroking it. "When my granddad, Nash Gammon, died, the company went to my mother and her brother," he said. "My uncle runs the company but he's forever trying to lure me into the business. I guess I'm just an independent cuss because working for the family business isn't something that's ever appealed to me. I've always made my own way."

Elliot fell silent a moment, digesting everything he had told her, her mind shooting off in many different directions but one in particular.

"Nash, if I ask you a question, will you tell me the truth?"

"Always."

"When I was furnishing Purgatory, you told me I could spend whatever I wanted. We ended up spending almost one hundred and fifty thousand dollars on furniture, antiques, televisions, rugs, driveways, gates, you name it. That amount was more than it cost me to restore the entire house. My budget was only eighty thousand dollars, but I know for a fact that it cost much more than that. You and Beau said you would pick up the rest, and you did. You never even batted an eyelash."

"What's your question?"

"How much did it cost you total for the restoration of the house, including the construction labor?"

He grunted. "I'm so tired," he mumbled. "I think I need to go back to sleep."

She sat up and looked at him. "Go back to sleep, my foot," she countered firmly, struggling not to smile at him. "You said you would answer the question."

His eyes were closed but he peeped one open to look at her. "Why do you want to know?"

She softened up, putting her face the crook of his neck, her lips on his flesh. "Because I do. Please tell me."

When she kissed his neck and snuggled up to him, he would do or say whatever she wanted. It was a secret little hold she had over him and he sighed heavily.

"Three hundred and thirty-four thousand, two-hundred fifty dollars and sixty-three cents," he muttered.

Elliot stopped kissing his neck and her head shot up, her eyes wide with astonishment. "You spent *how much?*"

"You asked."

She was growing agitated again. "What kind of dummy are you?" she demanded. "You spent that kind of money on a house that doesn't even belong to you?"

He grinned at her, casually, and put his hand on the back of her head. "*You* belong to me," he pulled her down and kissed her lips. "I told you I wanted to see you happy. If you're happy, I'm happy."

She let him kiss her a couple of times. "Where did you get the money from?"

"You said one question."

"Please, Nash. I feel like I need to pay you back."

He sobered quickly. "You'll do no such thing," he said firmly. "I wanted to do it."

"Then please tell me where you got the money."

He gazed into her serious eyes. "I have a trust fund that my mother's father set up for me when I was born," he explained. "Both of my boys have trust funds also, as will our baby. I think I'll set up one for Alec and Penny, also. Anyway, as a grandson of the founding family, I'm also a partial owner. Since Gammon Sugar is the largest producer of refined sugar products in the United States as well as a publicly traded company, I earn yearly dividends on the profits. Depending on the year, the weather conditions, the price of fuel, and on and on, I can earn anywhere from a hundred thousand dollars to upwards of a million. It just depends. Julie took a chunk of it when we divorced and I also give my boys a portion of that money, held in a trust fund until they're twenty-five."

Elliot stared at him to see if he was teasing her but when she realized he wasn't, her jaw dropped. "Nash," she scolded. "You never told me any of this. You really should have."

"Why?" he wanted to know. "Does it change your mind about me?"

She shook her head. "Of course not," she said. "But it's only fair. I would feel like an idiot not knowing everything about the man I'm going to marry."

He nodded. "Point taken," he said. "So I guess to answer that question you asked several minutes ago, my uncle has always wanted to hire me on as the Chief Administrative Officer for Gammon. It's a legal position and since that's my background, I would fit into it easily."

"You're a cop, not a lawyer."

"My graduate degree is in law."

She stared at him a moment before lying back down against him. "Wow," she said simply. "This is a lot to take in."

His hand ended up on her head, gently caressing her scalp. "Do you want me to call my uncle?" he asked. "I will if you want me to. Nothing is more important than your happiness, Ellie. I don't want to make you miserable working at a job that terrifies you every time I walk out the door."

Her hand was on his chest, hearing his strong heartbeat. She closed her eyes, savoring the sound.

"It would be so easy to say yes," she admitted, "but I just can't. I'm sorry I got angry with you, Nash. It's just... well, you know why. I won't go into it again. I guess I had to take my frustrations out on somebody but the truth is that I know why you went on the call-out. You're the sheriff and those are your men out there, laying their lives on the line, and you're responsible. I get that. As far as the police commissioner appointment, that's such an honorable and prestigious thing for you. I would never dream of taking it away from you because you've earned it. But the fact that you're willing to give it all up for me says so much."

He kissed the top of her head, his fingers caressing the blond strands. "So what do you want me to do?"

"When you're sworn in as Police Commissioner Aury, I'll be right next to you."

"Are you sure?"

"I am."

When the nurse came back in a half hour later, both Nash and Elliot were sound asleep together on his narrow hospital bed.

TWENTY-ONE
LATE SEPTEMBER

ELLIOT SAT in her writing room, typing out the last chapter of *Knight of the Vampire*. There was slashing and sword fighting going on her mind as she patiently tapped it all out on the keyboard. The floor-to-ceiling windows were open and a soft breeze blew in off the bayou.

It was a surprisingly mild September day and she kept getting distracted by Wolfgang down in the dog run they had penned in for him, barking eagerly at the bayou. Elliot suspected there was a gator down there she couldn't see but the dog was so agitated, she eventually put aside her writing and went downstairs to let him out of the dog run.

She took the back stairs with some lethargy, stretching out the kinks in her back as she went. At around three months pregnant, she just wasn't moving as well as she usually did. The baby was growing, stretching her out and giving her a nice little baby bump. She still fit into her beloved velour jogging suits, but the fit was getting tight. At fourteen weeks pregnant, she was feeling her daughter grow every day.

Due to the fact that she was termed a geriatric pregnancy, a label she detested, her doctor in Baton Rouge had already done two ultrasounds on her to make sure everything was progressing well with the pregnancy. On the first ultrasound, all she, Nash and Penelope could see was a kidney-bean shaped dot, but on the last one, they could actually see the baby and the doctor informed them that it was a girl. Courtesy of her father, Baby Sophie already had a name. It only seemed fitting. Nash would come home every night, lay his head on her stomach, and talk to the baby. It was the sweetest thing Elliot had ever seen.

Hand on her growing belly, she came down the stairs into the kitchen where the kitchen contractor was still working, even after all these months. Elliot had new countertops, a new island, new sinks and new cabinets, but a portion of the wall between the stove and the dining room door was still opened up as more rotted boards had been found when they were plumbing the new vegetable sink. They'd been working on that for nearly a week.

The contractor noticed her when she came off the stairs. "Hey, Ms. Aury," he said. "You got a minute? I want to show you something."

Elliot nodded. "Sure," she said. "But I've got to get the dog out of his run before he worries himself to death."

The contractor grinned. "He sure misses the kids, don't he?"

She grinned as she opened the kitchen door. "He misses Penny," she clarified. "Alec is home every night from community college, but ever since Penny started at Tulane, the dog is having separation anxiety."

The contractor laughed as she went out onto the porch and headed towards the dog run. The yard was beautifully landscaped now except for the digging that was still going on between the house and the old stables. Because of the historical significance of the access tunnel, Dr. Whitney had convinced Nash and Elliot to let them continue to dig for a while to see if they came up with any artifacts or any further information on the house and the reason behind the crypt.

So far, Dr. Whitney and Dr. Clarke had come up with something of a sprawling time capsule of history. Along with the secondary access tunnel that ended in the collapsed stables, they had also uncovered the foundations of three slave quarters about a quarter of a mile to the north, which they were excavating.

Dr. Whitney was starting to think they weren't slave quarters as much as they were maybe pirate or sailor quarters due to the nautical items they had so far uncovered. Each day, he and his team of students would find more and more, prompting Elliot to suggest they open some kind of museum. Nash was onboard with the idea, as was Dr. Clarke, who very much wanted to curate it. The artifacts they were daily coming across were very rich, indeed.

As she moved across the yard, Elliot could see a group of students working on the secondary access trench. These days, there were people all over Purgatory so she never felt lonely or isolated when Nash was away at the office.

Sometimes, he'd be gone fourteen hours a day with his new position and she missed him a great deal, but she was very proud of what he was accomplishing. Already, there was anti-corruption legislation afoot that he had authored and bits and pieces of it were all over the news every night. Commissioner Aury, barely in office for a month, was already making waves.

Releasing Wolfgang from his pen, the dog immediately raced over to the digging students. As Elliot tried to get him to come back to her, he happily climbed all over the college students, who laughed and hugged him. He was looking for food and until someone gave him something, like a peanut or piece of a granola bar, he wouldn't leave. A young grad student ended up giving him a piece of beef jerky and Wolfgang ran back to Elliot, happy and satisfied.

Shaking her head at the naughty dog, she went back into the house and he followed. The dog ran straight for the ballroom and his favorite chair while Elliot went to the contractor.

"I swear that dog is worse than a toddler," she muttered.

The contractor grinned. "Well, you'll be finding that out soon enough," he said. "By the way, my wife saw the pictures of your wedding in the Baton Rouge Advocate and wanted to know where y'all got the dress for your daughter."

Elliot cocked her head. "We got married over a month ago and you're just asking me now?"

His grin spread. "I keep forgetting. She'll kill me if I don't find out."

Elliot laughed. "At the Mall of Louisiana in Baton Rouge," she told him. "We got it at Macy's."

"I'll let her know."

"Now, what did you want to show me?"

"Oh, right," the contractor refocused on the open wall before him. "I'm going to pull this out so you can see it because I've got to re-plaster this wall anyway, but it looks like you've got a dumbwaiter in this wall that was sealed up."

"A dumbwaiter?" she repeated, surprised. "Where does it lead to?"

The contractor had his head in the old wall, trying to see in the dark. "To the bedroom directly above us."

Elliot thought about that. "It's the smallest bedroom in the house," she said. "Nash said it used to be where the servants slept, so that makes sense. They would put food in the dumbwaiter, send it up to the servants, who would then take it to the people of the house."

The contractor pulled his head out of the hole and began to pull back the section of the wall that was built over the dumbwaiter. "Let's take a look," he said.

Elliot stood back as he pulled away the plaster, which was very fragile with age. It wasn't the original *bousillage*, but something more recent. Someone had taken the time to cover up the dumbwaiter for whatever reason. The contractor pulled off a good deal of old plaster, revealing the treasure beneath.

It looked like an old iron box attached to a series of pulleys and extremely old rope. In fact, the rope was so old, it looked as if it were made from horse-tail hair. Cobwebs, rot and age had deteriorated the rope and pulley system but the iron box looked relatively intact.

It was literally a square-shaped box with a sliding front door that was closed. The contractor got his fingers on the door and tried to work it open, but his cell phone rang and he had to take the call.

Elliot moved in where the man left off. She was very curious about the dumbwaiter, something that was so old it wasn't even made out of wood. It was constructed purely of iron, like some crazy treasure chest lodged in her wall. Elliot got her hands into the wall and began to work the sliding door on the dumbwaiter, trying to work it free as she listened to the contractor on the phone out in the hall.

As his voice grew more agitated, her fingers grew stronger, working the sliding door like a stuck bolt. It seemed to be jammed so she went into her cabinets and found the spray olive oil, spraying a small amount on what looked to be the moving parts of the box. Setting the can aside, she was able to work the door enough to lift it halfway.

Elliot didn't really expect to find anything inside. Maybe there would be a tray or utensils left behind by a forgetful servant, something to add to the growing collection for their museum. Her first look inside showed a black box with black walls, smelling of something old and timeless. But as her eyes adjusted to the darkness, she realized there was something on the bottom of the box.

Elliot reached in and grasped what looked like sheets of paper. She really couldn't tell. Very carefully, she pulled them out of the box and quickly realized that it was a book of some kind, leather bound. She thought that it might be an old household ledger or family records.

Excited, she inspected the binder, noting the dried out leather cover and hand-stitched binding. She was sure Dr. Whitney could tell her exactly what it was stitched with.

The contractor was still on the phone and she waited impatiently for him to get off the phone so she could show him what had been inside. Taking the binder over to the kitchen table, she set it down, pulled up a chair, and carefully opened it.

The pages inside were very old and very fragile. She couldn't tell if it was parchment or actual paper. Being a writer, she was somewhat familiar with the history of paper and she knew that milled wood pulp had been used as paper as early as the Middle Ages.

As she inspected the paper, she glanced up at the careful script written in faded ink at the top of the page.

Le journal de Madame Sophie MacGregor Aury

A bolt of shock ran through Elliot as she stared at the title. Although she didn't really know much French, the words staring back at her didn't need any translation. Her heart began to race, quickly understanding what she was looking at. There could be no doubt.

Shocked, she looked up at the dumbwaiter, wondering why in the hell the journal had been sealed up inside. Perhaps by a frightened servant, perhaps by Sophie herself... she simply didn't know. Closing the cover of the journal with shaking hands, she collected it against her chest as she quickly made her way up the back stairs.

The contractor, off his call, entered just as she disappeared upstairs. He called after her.

"Ms. Aury?" he said. "What do you want me to do about this? Can I seal it up?"

Elliot paused at the top of the stairs, journal clasped to her breast. "Uh... no," she called down to him. "I want the archaeologists to take a look at it before we do anything. Can you just leave it until tomorrow?"

"Yes'm," he said.

Leaving the contractor to finish up, she quickly made her way to the master bedroom, locating her cell phone on the nightstand. Still holding the journal, she called Nash.

He picked up on the third ring. "Hi, honey," he said pleasantly. "How's my beautiful girl?"

"I'm good," she said, trying not to sound too anxious. "Are you busy?"

He smiled. "Never too busy to talk to you, you know that," he said. "How are things at the house? Did the contractor finish that wall in the kitchen yet?"

"That's what I wanted to talk to you about," she lowered her voice, although she didn't know why. It wasn't as if anyone was listening to her. "He was working on the wall between the kitchen and the ballroom, and he came across an old dumbwaiter sealed up into the wall."

In his plush, big, new office at the State Capitol building, Nash leaned back in his leather chair, taking a break from the paperwork on his desk to talk to his wife. She was never far from his thoughts and hearing from her, no matter what he was doing, always made his day. Her latest statement had his interest.

"Really?" he said. "That's very cool. What does it look like?"

"Like an old iron box."

"Text me a picture of it."

"Okay," she said, somewhat hesitantly. Then the truth started coming out. "Sweetie, there was something in it. The contractor doesn't know because I took it out before he could see it. When are you coming home?"

He shifted in his chair, noticing one of his aides standing in his office door, politely waiting for his attention. "Not soon enough," he muttered. "I'll try to get home a little early. Why? What did you find?"

Elliot glanced at the journal she had laid on the bed beside her. "You're not going to believe it," she said. "I think it's Sophie MacGregor's journal."

That brought Nash to attention. "Really?" he was startled. "Are you sure?"

Elliot nodded. "It's all in French, but I can clearly read her name. I don't read French but I know you do. Can you come home now?"

Nash could see two aides standing in his doorway now, both waiting politely to speak with him.

"Baby, I'm not sure I can," he ran a weary hand over his face. "But I promise I'll come as soon as I can. I'm dying to take a look at it."

"Me, too," she said. "I'm not going to show it to anyone until you and I go through it. Given the woman's reputation for having killed her kids...."

Nash nodded as she trailed off. "Say no more," he said. "I'm with you. I'll be home as soon as I can."

"I'm making a roast chicken for dinner."

He grinned. "Now you're not being fair. You're trying to lure me home with food."

"That, and the fact that Alec went to stay with Shane for the weekend. We have the house to ourselves."

He laughed knowingly. "Okay, you win," he folded easily, eyeing the aides. "Give me a half hour and I'll get out of here."

Elliot smiled happily. "Good. Love you, sweetie."

"I love you, too. I'll see you in a bit."

———

Nash was home much earlier than normal. At seven in the evening, right on the nose, he pulled in front of the house and parked his new Lexus, courtesy of the State of Louisiana. It was a high performance car and he liked it much better than the Crown Victoria he had been driving. Climbing wearily out of the car, he made his way into the dimly lit house.

Everything was quiet at this hour. The contractors had gone home, as had the archaeologists. He headed for the kitchen, smelling chicken in the air. When he passed through the dining room and didn't see his wife in the bright kitchen, he peered into the darkened ballroom.

"Ellie?" he called.

Wolfgang's head popped up from where he had been laying on his favorite chair and the dog bolted in his direction. He petted the dog, heading to the staircase as the dog trotted behind him. Taking the stairs to the second floor, he went to the softly-lit master bedroom. It was the only room on the second floor that had a light on. Everything else was dusk and shadow.

Elliot was lying on the bed, curled up on her side. Nash pulled off his sport coat as he went to the massive four-poster bed.

"Ellie?" he said softly, watching her eyes open as he bent down to kiss her. "What's wrong, honey? Why are you in bed?"

She looked up at him, miserable. "I thought I was strong enough to make chicken," she said. "The smell just makes me gag. I can't be downstairs right now."

He fought off a smile, sitting on the bed beside her. "I'm sorry, baby," he stroked her head. "I thought you were feeling better these days."

She sighed. "I did, too, but apparently not," she said. "Can you go open up all the windows downstairs so the chicken smell goes out of the house?"

He nodded. "Sure," he replied, taking off his tie. "Where's the chicken?"

"In the oven."

"Is it done?"

She nodded, closing her eyes again. He stroked her blond head, bending down to kiss it. "What can I bring you?" he asked.

"The usual."

"Green Jell-O?"

"Yes," she said. "But if you're going to eat the chicken, do it downstairs. I'll throw up if you get it anywhere near me."

"Do you want the Jell-O now or later?"

"Go eat your dinner and I may be strong enough by then."

He grinned, kissing her head again as he tossed the tie aside and went downstairs. He and Wolfgang went to every window in the house, opening up the great floor-to-ceiling panels and letting the soft bayou evening breeze infiltrate the house.

When they went into the kitchen, Nash inspected the big hole in the wall and the iron dumbwaiter with the ancient rope and pulley system. He ran his hands over it, studying the detail, truly amazed at the discovery. Purgatory continued to reveal her secrets.

Opening up the oven, he pulled out the beautifully roasted chicken that had sent his wife running for cover. There was rice and broccoli on the stove. He sat down to eat at the breakfast table with Wolfgang sitting expectantly beside him. For every two or three bites he took, he tossed the dog a scrap or some skin.

"This is really good," he told the dog. "Too bad Ellie can't eat it."

Wolfgang licked his chops and waited for the next morsel. Between Nash and the dog, they finished off the entire chicken and Nash took the garbage out, including the chicken carcass, so Elliot couldn't smell it. He paused as he came back from the dumpster, his gaze moving out over the moonlit bayou. It was peaceful and beautiful, and he couldn't remember ever being so happy in his entire life. Every morning when he woke up, he thanked God for what he had. He thanked Him every day for Elliot.

When he came back into the house, he found Elliot standing in the open refrigerator with a can of whipped cream in her hand. As he stood there and watched, she sprayed whipped cream into her mouth directly from the can. After two or three squirts and choking down the contents, she turned to him and noticed the odd expression on his face. She licked her lips.

"Why are you looking at me like that?" she asked.

The truth was that Nash was trying very hard not to burst into laughter. He fought off the grin that threatened.

"I'm not looking at you like anything," he said innocently. "So we're back to Jell-O and whipped cream again?"

Her lip stuck out in a pout. "I can't help it," she said miserably. "They're the only things that don't make me gag."

He went to her as she made miserable sounds, feigning tears, when the truth was that she really did feel awful. He wrapped his arms around her and rocked her gently.

"The doctor gave you a diet to follow," he suggested carefully. "Maybe you should give it another try?"

She sounded like a petulant child. "I don't want to," she frowned. "I don't want to eat bananas and rice. They make me gag."

"I know, but they're better for you than Jell-O and whipped cream all the time."

Her frown was deepening. "I haven't gained any weight, if that's what you mean."

"That's not what I mean and you know it," he said, softly but sternly. "You've lost eleven pounds in the past three months and the doctor wants you to gain weight, not lose it. It's not good for the baby."

She started crying, this time for real. Nash hugged her tightly, relenting as he reached down into the refrigerator and pulled forth a cup of green Jell-O. He put it in her hand and pulled a spoon from a drawer.

"Come on," he directed her towards the stairs. "Let's go eat your Jell-O and you can show me the journal you found."

She was angry, miserable and teary. "You have no idea what it's like to be pregnant," she told him with a pouty face. "I feel nauseous all of the time. Even looking at dog kibble makes me nauseous. If I feel like eating Jell-O, I'm going to eat it because it's better than eating nothing."

He was patient with her as they went up the stairs. "I know, baby. I'm not criticizing. I'm just trying to help."

"Then don't tell me to eat bananas."

"I won't anymore, I promise."

She was already halfway into the green Jell-O by the time they entered their bedroom. Nash directed her over to the bed but she went to her nightstand first, opening the first drawer and pulling out something that looked like a brown leather album. She extended it to Nash.

"This is it," she said, setting the Jell-O cup down as they both sat on the bed. "Did you get a look at the dumbwaiter?"

Nash was entranced as he gazed at the book, running his hands carefully over the leather, inspecting the stitching on it as Elliot had done.

"Yes," he said. "It made me think that this house has a lot of secrets and they just keep coming."

Elliot wriggled her eyebrows in agreement as Nash carefully opened up the journal. The writing on the first page stared up at him.

"*Le journal de Madame Sophie MacGregor Aury,*" he read aloud in perfect French. "You were right; it says the Journal of Madam Sophie MacGregor Aury."

Nausea all but forgotten, Elliot could feel her excitement growing. "Open it up and read it. I want to hear what she has to say."

Nash gazed at the cover for a moment longer before opening up to the second page and beginning to read. The journal was written in very carefully scripted long hand, the ink so faded in spots that it was difficult to read, but the first thing that came to mind was how lovingly it was done.

He started to read. As he read the first few paragraphs out loud so Elliot could share the experience, already, he got the overwhelming sense of resignation and duty through the eyes of a woman who was not only the daughter of a pirate, but also the mistress of one.

He read on, page by slow page. The journal seemed to be written as more of a series of separate entries, some dated and some not. There wasn't much organization to it. As the hours ticked away and Elliot lay down on the bed next to him as he read, Nash relayed stories of the harsh conditions, the "vicious beasts" who ate man and animal alike, which Nash took to mean alligators, the savages and the sickness that seemed to plague all of them. It was all very fascinating and very, very real.

But there was something more he noticed as he read. Sophie also, strangely enough, referred to herself in the third person as she wrote, as if she was on the outside looking in at everything that was happening. It was an odd perspective.

He continued on and as he got deeper into the journal, he began to better understand the manner in which it was written. From what Nash could tell, the journal only seemed to encompass time spent at Purgatory because it started well after the house was built.

There was no mention of the particulars of the house, like who designed it, or how it was built because Nash had always wondered if it had been slave labor or shipwrights who built the very sturdy home. Obviously, Louis-Michel had shipwrights as well as slaves at his disposal, so that was a genuine curiosity.

As Nash read, he was hoping to find a mention of the room beneath the house and its original purpose, but she made no mention of anything to that regard. She did, however, speak on goods and the prices of things, in true housewife fashion.

He continued reading deep into the night. The journal wasn't particularly long but it was difficult to read, making each passage slow going. It gave Nash and Elliot insight into the world of Sophie, and of Purgatory, that they could have never imagined. Sophie would speak of her and the house as if they were one, using an odd sentence structure and word tense that had Nash re-reading passages several times to figure out what she meant.

Then, the journal started speaking of the children. It was close to midnight by the time Nash got around to passages about the kids and Elliot had been struggling to stay awake, but at the first mention of Sophie's firstborn son, she perked up and listened. Sophie spoke of all four children together, which was odd because she had not mentioned or documented their births. She spoke of Paul-Michel when he killed his first deer and of Saturnine who liked to eat mud. Elliot, snuggled up against Nash, thought it was all rather strange.

"She's not writing like a diary," she yawned. "It's like she's just writing about whatever she feels like writing when the mood strikes her."

Nash nodded, peering at the pages through his reading glasses.

"That's strange," he agreed. "You would think she would have kept a daily record of things, not just events or thoughts. I think the one thing I've come to see is that she's not particularly organized in thought or in her life."

Elliot had to agree. "She writes about the cost of flour and then in the next sentence, she's talking about a neighbor's cow."

"Like she can't keep a train of thought."

"Do you think she really was crazy like Dr. Clarke suggested?"

"Maybe," he said. "But the way she writes... it's not that she's uneducated, because she clearly is, which is unusual in itself for a woman of that time period. There's just no rhyme or reason to what she writes about."

Elliot yawned again, her head on his chest. "Keep going," she told him. "She's talking about the kids. Maybe she'll say what happened to them."

Nash continued to read, slow going. Sophie was writing mostly about the children now, how they had hired a woman from the east to come and educate them and how she smacked the children with a stick if they didn't get their lessons correct. Then she rambled on about Louis-Michel, only the second time in the journal she had ever mentioned his name.

Nash was coming to think that she wasn't his mistress by choice because her words regarding the man implied bitterness. She wrote of how the man was grooming Paul-Michel to succeed him, and how their son had the same "dark hatred" in his eyes that his father had. Now the journal was starting to get interesting.

Nash was starting on the last few pages when he heard soft snoring. Glancing down, he saw that Elliot had fallen asleep against his chest. He carefully pulled the covers up over her but continued reading, no longer out loud.

Sophie's writings were growing more bitter and negative as she spoke of "dark days" and "hellish nights" with Louis-Michel. Then he seemed to be gone because she only wrote of the children and of a pet pig, and then it was of Paul-Michel's marriage to Julia

Loreau. Somehow, the subject of wealth came up and he began to pay close attention.

She wrote of "golden wagons" from the Mississippi River, which he wasn't sure about until she spoke of giving equal portions to each child. Nash was coming to think that she meant the wagons that must have transported the wealth from the pirate ships docked at the river to Purgatory, because to her, they surely must have looked like wagons laden with gold, hence, golden wagons.

The more he read, the more it began to look as if Louis-Michel had, indeed, brought treasure of immense proportions to Purgatory and Sophie began to speak of the wealth being "in the very walls" of Purgatory.

Again, Nash wasn't sure if she meant they had paid a good deal for the house, or spent money on a lavish lifestyle and furnishings, or if she meant the literal walls. His pulse was beginning to race with excitement and he found that he had to wake Elliot up. She would never forgive him if he didn't.

She didn't wake up easily. He had to shake her, very gently, four times before she finally roused. As soon as she became lucid, she groaned.

"Oh, God," she breathed. "I feel so nauseous."

He kissed her forehead. "I'm sorry I woke you, but I think you're going to want to hear this."

Her eyes weren't quite open. "Hear what?"

"Sophie writing about treasure."

As he suspected, she very quickly perked up. "Treasure?" she repeated. "What does she say?"

Nash went back a page to the part where Sophie spoke of the golden wagons and of the treasure being in the very walls of Purgatory. Elliot sat up, rubbing her eyes, as he read the passage.

"That's completely plausible," she said, both sleepy and excited. "When we restored it, we really didn't touch the walls because of the *bousillage*. The only walls we had to tear up were in the kitchen because of the rot, and even that was on a minimal scale. It's absolutely plausible for some kind of pirate treasure to be sealed up in the walls of Purgatory. We just haven't found it yet!"

He looked at her, thinking on the possibility. Being the less excitable of the two, he wasn't ready to start tearing up the walls yet. He looked back to the journal.

"Listen to this part," he said. "Let me see if I can make sense of it. She speaks of greed, tremendous greed... but I don't see who she... wait a minute. She's speaking of Paul-Michel."

Elliot was hanging on every word. "What does she say?"

Nash's brow furrowed as he continued to read. "Wow," he finally said. "She says that Paul-Michel was wrought with greed and wanted everything for himself. The kid was only seventeen, right?"

Elliot shrugged. "He was seventeen when he died. Did she date that passage so we know when she wrote it?"

He looked over the page, shaking his head. "No," he replied. "But by this time, he was already married, so he had to be at least sixteen or seventeen."

"What does she say about his greed?"

Nash read carefully, translating Sophie's own words. "*'My first son, my angel, has turned dark and against us all. He wants for himself what his brothers have. As this day turned dark, my heart wept at the sight of Joseph and Saturnine as they joined our holy God in heaven. Their souls are consigned to God as their brother's greed destroyed them. My dearest angel, Felicity, fought against the darkness with others who sought to take rewards for themselves, but Paul-Michel rose up to smite them all. Now my Felicity lays at my feet with her army of dead souls, and all I see is my first son as he lays claim to what his brothers were given.'*"

Nash paused when he came to the end of the passage, looking up at Elliot. She was staring back at him with shock.

"My God," she breathed, a hand to her mouth. "It sounds like some kind of battle, doesn't it? Paul-Michel against Felicity after he apparently killed his brothers."

Nash puffed out his cheeks, struggling to digest what he had read.

"It sure sounds like it," he agreed. "That's the craziest thing I've ever heard of, but on the other hand, I guess it makes sense. All of these people were pirates, including the kids. In their world, battles and greed were perfectly natural."

Elliot was thinking of the children, doing battle against each other.

"So Paul-Michel decides he wants everything and kills his brothers to get it," she said thoughtfully. "Only his sister, who wasn't more than fourteen or so, decides to rise up against him. Maybe she did it out of self-protection because if Paul-Michel went after their brothers, then it was only a matter of time before he went after the sister. Sophie said that Felicity fought with people who wanted to take the wealth for themselves but ended up dying along with them. Oh, God, Nash; imagine being the mother of these children and watching this go on. Why didn't she do something to stop it?"

Nash shook his head. "I don't know," he said. "Women back then were chattel, especially the mistress of a legendary pirate. She wouldn't dare resist her son who was going to take over the empire. But Felicity fought back, so I'm not sure why the daughter fought her brother but the mother didn't."

Elliot thought of the children buried in the crypt below as the horrific tale came to light. Her gaze moved around the walls of the room, wondering what horrors they must have seen two hundred years ago. She couldn't even fathom it. As she thought of the battling children with a heavy heart, Nash continued reading.

"Sophie goes on to say this – '*in the darkness of the morning, my first son, my angel, came for me as well. He would take me also for his dark deeds but God spoke to me and told me to seek vengeance for my littlest angels. Justice would be in blood, in my hands*'," Nash paused, staring at the words. When he continued, it was a whisper. "*Comme je lui ai donné la vie, donc faire je le prends. Comme sa vie draine loin, donc extraira.*'"

Elliot stared at him. "What does that mean?"

Nash sighed heavily. "Roughly translated, it means 'as I gave life, so shall I take it. As his life drains away, so shall mine'."

Pregnant and emotional, Elliot's eyes filled with tears. "That's so sad," she whispered. "She must have killed him. She killed him because he killed the others."

Nash looked up at her, reaching out to hold her hand to comfort her. He looked back at the journal.

"There's more," he said quietly. "She says that their greed is buried with them for eternity. Then there's this last passage here that says...."

He trailed off and she looked up at his face, noticing his strange expression. "What is it?" she asked.

Nash blinked as if not quite believing what he was reading. When he spoke, it was with awe. "'*To all who know the matter of greed is decided, with blood and curses we know the hell we have condemned ourselves to in the bowels of Purgatory*'."

Elliot's eyes nearly popped from her skull. "That's what those crypts say!"

He nodded, having a hard time comprehending everything. He stared at the writing, reading it over and over, word for word.

"So the matter of greed was decided because Paul-Michel, greedy for everyone's inheritance, killed his siblings and tried to take it for himself," he looked up at Elliot. "But Sophie sought vengeance for her children that he killed and killed him herself. She knew she would go to hell for it, but she did it anyway."

Elliot thought hard on the passage, on the meanings, and gradually shook her head.

"No, I don't think that's what it means at all," she said earnestly. "I don't think she meant condemning them all to hell, literally. I think she just meant in the house itself. Nash, the house itself is a symbol of greed and if what she alludes to is true, there's pirate treasure buried in the very walls. *That's* your greed. But that wouldn't have accounted for her saying that their greed is buried with them for eternity. She's not poetic enough to use metaphors like that. What if... what if she means it *literally*?"

He cocked his head. "You mean... you mean that she buried the wealth, what Paul-Michel wanted so badly, with her children?"

"Yes," she was electrified at the thought, hopping off the bed. "What if the treasure rumored to be buried at Purgatory isn't only within the walls, but in the crypts themselves?"

Nash was following her train of thought. "It makes a hell of a lot of sense," he agreed. "But two things don't add up."

"What?"

He pointed a finger at her. "Namely, what happened to Sophie? She killed her eldest son, buried all of her kids with their inheritance so no one else would be cursed by such greed, and then she presumably killed herself. Where's her body?"

Elliot shook her head. "I don't know," she thought hard, trying to get up a head of steam in the logic train. "If I'm Sophie MacGregor and all my kids are dead, I'm going to want to be with them. I'm not going to be far from them at all."

"Unless," Nash held up a finger, "your body is found by people who think you killed all of your kids before committing suicide, they're going to either toss you in the bayou or bury you in unconsecrated ground."

Elliot agreed with him. "So she's either alligator food or she's buried on unholy ground. Is there any unholy ground around here?"

Nash shook his head. "I've never heard of any, other than.... Oh, my God...."

Elliot couldn't stand it. "What?"

Nash tried to be rational. "Because of the nasty dealings and the dark character of the family, The Bottoms used to be considered cursed ground. It still is to some of the old people around here. It's quite possible that even back then, with the bad blood between the Loreaus and the Aurys, that people associated with Purgatory considered The Bottoms cursed ground."

Elliot's jaw went agape. "So maybe she was buried there?"

Nash shook his head and climbed out of bed. "Maybe," he said. "It's pure conjecture, but it's possible. If she was, I'm sure it was unmarked and long lost by now."

Elliot thought on that. The revelations from the journal were staggering and she was still trying to absorb it all. "You said that there were two things that didn't add up. What's the second?"

He was still thinking on Sophie MacGregor and The Bottoms but shifted gears. "The second question is who wrote the passage from the end of her journal on the kids' crypts and then sealed the journal up. Who in the hell would do that?"

Elliot shook her head. "I don't know," she replied. "But I think we need to go downstairs and visit those crypts."

Nash was already leading the way.

TWENTY-TWO

IT WAS WELL after midnight as Nash and Elliot made their way down into the crypt. Even though Nash had flipped on the string of lights that Beau had installed, the crypt was still a dark and eerie place. Elliot held on to Nash tightly as they made their way down the narrow secret stairs.

A sump pump had been installed to drain the water away from the floor of the crypt and they stepped on dark Louisiana dirt as they came off the stairs instead of two inches of standing water. It still smelled swampy and moldy, however, and Elliot sneezed twice.

Dr. Whitney and Dr. Clarke had spent two months studying the four individual coffins, gently clearing away the centuries of mold and dirt, bringing to light the fact that all four crypts were carved from white-veined marble. Dr. Whitney consulted with experts that concluded the marble was Italian, based on the quality and vein characteristics, leading him to the conclusion that the crypts must have been shipped by Louis-Michel's privateer fleet. Only someone of immense wealth and means could have brought them to America.

"Sweetie," Elliot ventured, clinging to Nash's shirt as he made his way over to Paul-Michel's coffin. "Didn't Dr. Whitney say that these marble coffins couldn't have been the vessels that the children were originally buried in?"

Nash reached the cleaned and nearly pristine white marble crypt. "That's what he said," he replied. "He said that they must have been buried in wooden coffins which are probably set within these marble ones."

Elliot stepped out from behind him and was looking at Paul-Michel's crypt. She ran her fingers over the French lettering. "This reminds me of what we were talking about upstairs."

"What in particular?"

She cocked her head thoughtfully, looking at the words. "When these kids were all killed, we've got to assume it was quickly, like, maybe in a matter of just a few days."

He looked at her. "And?"

She met his gaze. "And, they had to bury them right away, which means they had to put them in whatever they had – a wood casket."

He crossed his arms. "Go on."

She pointed at the marble. "Dr. Whitney said that this was Italian marble, which means it had to be cut and shipped from Italy. Back in the early nineteenth century, that kind of trip would have taken months, if not years, by the time it reached here. These marble crypts weren't put here until a year or more after the kids, and after Sophie, were dead."

"What's your point?"

She jabbed a finger at the writing on the crypt. "So who put the passage from Sophie's journal on these crypts? It had to be the same person who took the love and care to have these crypts made. Maybe someone who came home to find his mistress and children dead, and the only record of it being a disjointed journal."

Nash lifted an eyebrow. "It makes sense," he agreed, looking at the marble. "Someone put a lot of money and effort into these crypts, and the only person who had those means was Louis-Michel."

"He came home, or maybe he was called home, to find his entire family dead."

Nash could see the pieces of the puzzle fitting together. He put his arm around Elliot's shoulder as they gazed at Paul-Michel's crypt. There was a distinct sense of sadness, of regret, thinking of the battling children and of his grandfather many times over who had suffered such a great loss.

"If all of that's true, and I have no reason to think otherwise, then Louis-Michel allowed all of that treasure to be buried with his kids," he said quietly. "Think about it – if what Sophie wrote was true, then she buried the reason for their greed with them. Then Louis-Michel comes home, finds everybody dead, commissions crypts for his children, waits for those crypts to come all the way from Italy, and then reburies his kids with the treasure... I think that says a lot about the man's mental state. He was willing to let all of that wealth be buried with his children and not take it all back for himself."

"Because it was blood money," Elliot added. "It had the blood of his children on it. Why on earth would he want it back? As superstitious as people were back then, I'm sure he thought it was cursed and it was better off buried."

He kissed her forehead. "That makes the most sense of almost anything I've heard today."

They just stood there, staring at the crypt. "So," Elliot wondered. "Are we going to open it?"

"Do you want to?"

Elliot thought on that a moment. "I think if we do and if there's treasure there, then we know that everything Sophie said was true. It exonerates her and I think that's important. She doesn't deserve to be remembered as a woman who killed all of her kids if that's not what really happened."

Nash paused a moment longer before letting her go and heading back up the steps. She could hear him opening kitchen drawers upstairs, banging around. Strangely, Elliot wasn't creeped out being alone in the crypt. She could only feel an overwhelming sense of sadness as she turned to her right to see Felicity's sad-looking crypt. She went over to it and put her hand on it.

"I'm so sorry," she whispered. "I read what happened. It sounds like you tried to fight back but ended up losing the battle. At least you tried and that's very brave."

"Ellie!"

She jumped at the sound of her name, running to the hidden stairs to see Nash at the top, motioning furiously to her.

"Quick," he hissed. "Come here."

Elliot flew up the stairs and Nash put a finger to his lips, indicating silence, as he took her hand and pulled her into the dark ballroom. Quickly and quietly, he pulled her over to one of the floor-to-ceiling windows that faced the north side of the yard, where the big trench was located that ran from the house to the stables.

It was dark and quiet outside, a massive full moon hung in the sky, bathing the landscape in a brilliant silver glow. Everything was colored in gray as a peppering of fireflies swarmed over the yard and through the trees. Spanish moss made for a dark and creepy contrast to the silver-lit ground. Elliot turned to look at Nash curiously, but he just shook his head and pointed outside.

"Just watch," he whispered. "Let's see if it happens again."

Elliot had no idea what he was talking about but she dutifully waited for something to happen. As she stood there and gazed into the moonlight over the bayou, she leaned back against Nash and he wrapped his arms around her. Her mind began to wander to green Jell-O and whipped cream, and she began to wonder if she was strong enough to eat some cereal. Milk sounded really good right now. So did ice cream. As she dreamed of dairy products, it took her a moment to notice that something was happening outside.

At first, she thought it was moonlight streaming in through the tree branches but, soon enough, she began to realize that the moonbeam was moving. She must have gasped because she felt Nash's arms tighten around her as they both watched a silvery, flowing figure float from an area back towards the old stables in the direction of the house.

Elliot could see the figure plainly, the details of a vintage flowing dress, long silver hair and a face that was fairly indistinct. She watched it move towards the house, ripple through the shadows of the trees, and then disappear entirely about the time it reached the trench. Almost as quickly as it had appeared, it had vanished.

Mouth hanging open, she began to point to the yard. "Oh, my God!" she gasped. "It... it looked like a woman!"

Nash nodded. "Remember I told you I had seen the ghost of Sophie as a child?" he said softly. "That was her. I was in the kitchen looking for something to pry open the top of the crypt when I happened to look into the ballroom and saw that through the window. I remember as a kid when I would see her, she'd do it three or four times a night, the same path, just repeating her steps, so I knew she'd do it again. She'll probably do it a couple of more times before the night is out."

Elliot put a hand over her gaping mouth, shocked as she turned her gaze out to the yard again.

"That was crazy," she breathed, turning to glance over her shoulder at the kitchen door but instead, her gaze fell on the door from the central hall into the ballroom. She grabbed Nash in a panic. "Nash, look! In the doorway!"

He spun around, seeing a small mist undulating in the ballroom doorway. Shocked, he could clearly make out two little arms and a little leg, with jacket sleeves and short pants. He thought he could see lace or some kind of frilly material on the end of the jacket sleeve. It was the weirdest thing he had ever seen. But as he and Elliot continued to gaze at it, the mist dissipated into thin air. It just vanished.

Elliot just stood there, clinging to Nash. He could feel her trembling. In truth, he wasn't exactly sure how to feel at the moment. They were being bombarded from all sides by otherworldly visitors and if he allowed himself to feel scared, he could very well have been. With Elliot so shaken, however, he labored to keep a level head.

"It looked like a kid," Elliot finally breathed, turning to look up at Nash. "Didn't it? Didn't it look like a child? I could see little hands and, like, a frilly little jacket. Did you see it?"

He nodded. "I saw it," he replied. Then he sighed heavily. "I've never heard of a child ghost in this house, but since you moved in, that's the third time he's shown up. Always in the central hall by the dining room and then...."

Elliot suddenly grabbed him, her eyes wide. "Ever since we found the crypt!" she hissed. "We started seeing him right after we found it. Nash, it's got to be one of the children. Maybe he's looking...."

She suddenly trailed off, looking outside the big ballroom windows again to the spot where the silver wraith had disappeared. A thought occurred to her, one so terrible that tears popped to her eyes.

"Looking for what, honey?" he asked.

She whispered in response. "You told me that Sophie wanders the grounds looking for her lost love."

Nash could hear her sniffling and he looked down at her, concerned. "That's the tale," he said. "She wanders the grounds looking for her lost love. You saw her yourself."

Elliot shook her head, looking up at him with big, watery eyes. "You read her journal," she insisted. "It doesn't sound like she was particularly fond of Louis-Michel at all. But her children... Nash, what if she's not wandering the grounds looking for Louis-Michel, but looking for her children? What if she's trying to get to them? She vanished near the trench; you saw that yourself. That used to be an access tunnel back in her day. What if she's trying to get to her kids underneath the house?"

Nash was beginning to understand her logic and his gaze inevitably turned towards the ballroom door where they had seen the child's apparition.

"And what if her kids are looking for her?" he murmured. "We opened the crypt and now they're coming out and looking for her."

Elliot broke into sobs. "That's so terrible," she wept. "Sophie can't come in and they can't go out. She disappears before she reaches the house and the child disappears when he reaches the ballroom. They're within feet of each other but they can't make it. That's the most horrible thing I've ever heard."

He comforted her as she wiped her eyes, thinking that maybe this entire night was just too much for her to take all at once. It was almost too much for him to take in all at once, as bizarre and fascinating as it had been.

"Come on," he finally said. "Let's go to bed. We'll finish it up in the morning."

Elliot balked. "No," she insisted. "I'm fine, really. It's just that this is all so sad. But I'm fine to continue, I promise. I really want to see if Sophie's right about everything. Please?"

He was clearly reluctant but relented like a gentleman. He really wanted to see if Sophie was right, too, but not at the expense of Elliot's emotional state. Still, she insisted she was fine. He suspected that even if he forced her to bed, she wouldn't sleep. So he gave her a resigned kiss and took her hand.

"Come on, then," he said. "Let's see what we can see."

Elliot followed him into the kitchen where he collected a hammer, an ice pick and a mallet from a kitchen drawer. He wasn't sure how effective kitchen tools would be against marble but it was all they had.

They proceeded down to the crypt but Elliot kept looking around for the little ghost child in the dark shadows of the house, still spooked. The crypt somehow seemed danker and more eerie than she remembered as she followed Nash over to Paul-Michel's crypt.

He handed her the hammer as he inspected the crypt closely. The archaeologists had cleaned off most of the dirt and mold, presenting him with fairly defined lines and grooves. He pointed to the flat-slab top.

"Look at this," he said. "This thing is in two distinct pieces. See the seam for the lid?"

Elliot peered at it. "Yes," she said. "How heavy do you think it is?"

He wriggled his eyebrows. "Hard to say. Less than a ton, I would think, but I guess I'm going to find out."

"Can you move it by yourself?"

He turned to give her a threatening look. "If I can't, it'll have to wait until someone else can help me. You're not touching a thing."

She shook her head innocently but his eyes narrowed at her as if he didn't believe her. Then she smiled brightly and he couldn't help but smile in return. She always knew how to play him, to soften him up. He turned back to the crypt.

"I'm serious, Ellie," he told her, holding the mallet in his right hand and positioning the ice pick against the lid seam with the other. "Stand back, honey. I don't want anything flying off and hitting you."

Elliot moved several feet away, clutching the hammer to her chest and watching as he took the first few hard whacks at the seam. He began to work all along the seam itself, chipping away at it, loosening the seal of dirt and mold that had filled up the seam like caulk. Elliot watched him work his way around three quarters of the lid before stopping and wiping the sweat off his brow. He grinned at her.

"It's a lot of work," he said. "My brother is the hands-on guy, not me."

She grinned. "Maybe we should call Beau."

Nash took a deep breath and repositioned his hands. "He'll be here tomorrow," he said. "If I can't get this moving, then he'll have to come help his weakling brother."

"You're not a weakling, sweetie," she winked at him when he looked at her. "I ought to know."

He laughed as he went back to work, hammering along the work he had already done, every once in a while giving the lid a shove to see if he had managed to loosen it. Because of the way the crypt was up against the wall, he couldn't get to the fourth side of it very easily. He would have to loosen what he could and then hope it would be enough to weaken the fourth side.

As Elliot stood by with increasing anxiety, Nash methodically worked the seam with his ice pick and mallet. Finally, he motioned her over and handed her the pick and mallet.

"Now, stand back," he told her. "I'm going to try and move this thing."

Elliot moved far away, almost as far as the secret stairs. Clutching the hammer, pick and mallet, she held her breath while Nash threw his weight into his arms and gave the big marble slab a big shove. The lid didn't move. Repositioning his hands, he grunted as he pushed and this time, the lid moved slightly.

Encouraged, he gave another big shove. Sounds of grating, stone against stone, filled the air. This time, the lid moved about two inches, sliding along the length of the crypt. Elliot gave a little yelp of fear and excitement, as Nash gave another shove and the lid slid another few inches. A big corner of it suddenly chipped off and Nash had to move quickly or risk having it fall on his foot.

Now, there was about a six inch gap in the top of the crypt so he could look down and see into it. The smell of rot and putrid stench filled his nostrils and he had to take a step back, away from the foul air. Elliot came running over, trying to see inside of it but it was just above her eye level. She tried climbing up but he stopped her.

Nash was peering into the crypt, his hazel eyes full of curiosity. Elliot was practically jumping up and down beside him.

"What do you see?" she demanded.

He didn't say anything for a moment. Then, he cocked his head slightly. All the while, his eyes were riveted to the dank and moldy depths of the crypt.

"It looks as if one time, there was a wooden coffin in here," he began, "but it's deteriorated into big piles of mold. The moisture of this room must have gotten into the crypt somehow and it just all fell apart. But I can see a body; at least, I can see a skull, but it's so decrepit that the wood of the coffin and the body have basically become one entity. It's one big moldering pile."

Elliot gazed up at him, distaste on her face. She wasn't sure she wanted to see it now. The foul smell of the dead had reached her nostrils and she pinched her nose shut with her fingers.

"Is that all you see?" she asked. "No pirate booty?"

Nash stared at the scene before him for the longest time. It was clear that he was digesting everything, analyzing it, wondering what kind of teenager would kill his own siblings out of greed. Lying before him was Paul-Michel Aury, his great-grandfather many times over, a young man who thought he could take everything and then some.

It was an iconic moment in Nash's life, more than he had expected. All he could feel at the moment was sadness coupled with disgust at Paul-Michel's actions. At the base of what would have been the corpse's feet, something caught his eye. He reached into the crypt and pulled out an object.

But it wasn't any object. It looked like string, or rope, but Elliot quickly realized it was neither. It was sparkling weakly in the dim light of the crypt, reflecting precious metal that hadn't seen the light of day in over one hundred and fifty years, and as Nash wiped away the dark rot and tarnish on the metal, an exquisite gold necklace started to come to light.

As Elliot gasped in awe and realization, Nash used his shirt to polish the mold off of a walnut-sized emerald. He extended the emerald for Elliot to see.

"My God," Elliot breathed as she gingerly touched the murky green stone. "It... it's a necklace. *That's* an emerald."

Nash nodded, looking at the piece in his hands, understandingly seeing the blood money Elliot had talked about. It was a magnificent piece, no doubt worth millions, and as he peered closer into the crypt, he could see other pieces intermingled with the rot and mold of the coffin and body. The entire bottom of the crypt was covered with it. The more he recognized what he was seeing, the more he came to understand just how rich the trove was.

"It's everywhere," he said quietly. "The entire bottom of this crypt is covered with it and if Sophie says she buried the greed with all of her children, that means the other three are like this, too. There's literally millions of dollars covering the bottom of this crypt, Ellie."

Elliot stopped inspecting the emerald and looked up at him. There was sadness to his tone and she, too, was coming to feel the weightiness of the blood money. It was tragic on so many levels.

"At least what Sophie said was true," she pointed out. "She didn't murder her children, Nash."

Nash nodded, still looking at all of the booty, his gaze finally coming to rest on the skull of his long-dead ancestor. There was bitterness in his voice when he spoke.

"I hope it was worth it," he said to Paul-Michel. "I sincerely hope killing your brothers and sister was worth the price you paid."

Elliot was watching him closely because now, it seemed to be affecting him emotionally. He seemed almost angry and resentful. She pressed up against him, her hand stroking his back comfortingly as she gazed into his handsome face.

"So what do you want to do?" she asked. "Now that we know the truth, what do you want to do? Do you want to seal this all back up and leave it alone or do you want to let the world know that Sophie MacGregor did not murder her younger children, and that the death of her oldest son was because he was a greedy bastard and she had to stop him?"

Nash sighed heavily as he gazed at the body. He was glad that Elliot couldn't see it because it was truly ghastly to behold. After a moment, he simply shook his head and reached out to take the tools back from her.

"I don't know," he murmured. "I need to sleep on it."

She watched him carefully. "Nash, I realize this is your family's legacy, but can I please say something?"

"Of course."

She worded her comment carefully. "If we take the treasure out of these crypts and donate it, display it, or whatever we decide to do with it, think of it this way – at least Paul-Michel doesn't get to have it for eternity. Right now, he has what he wants – his treasure, buried with him, forever. I doubt Sophie thought about it that way before she buried the symbol of greed. But if we take it away from him... Paul-Michel doesn't win. Sophie does, because she's exonerated."

He looked at her, nodding as he saw her train of logic. Still, his mind was too muddled to think clearly at the moment.

"Let's talk about it in the morning," he said.

"We don't have to if you don't want to. It's your decision, Nash. I'll support whatever you want to do."

Nash appreciated her understanding. He put the necklace back into Paul-Michel's crypt and pushed the great marble lid back into place. In silence, he and Elliot made their way back upstairs and closed the secret door.

Shutting off the kitchen light, they went up the back stairs, making their way to the master bedroom as Nash was drawn to Penelope's bedroom by the sounds of snoring. He peeked in to see Wolfgang sound asleep on Penelope's bed. Through all of the ghosts and treasure hunting, the dog had slept right through it. He had to grin at the irony of it.

It was after three in the morning by the time Nash and Elliot finally went to bed. Elliot fell asleep almost immediately but Nash remained awake, his arms wrapped around his sleeping wife as his mind wandered to the days of pirates, treasure, and sugar cane empires.

TWENTY-THREE

PAUL-MICHEL AURY WOULD NOT WIN.

After two hours of sleep, that was what Nash had ultimately decided and even though it was Saturday, he called Dr. Whitney and told the man what had happened. Dr. Whitney had shown up a little over two hours later with three other archaeologists from the State of Louisiana, the museum curator from the University of New Orleans Cultural Museum, and Dr. Clarke.

Following behind Dr. Whitney in four or five more cars were several archaeology students from LSU, an anthropology professor, and two journalism students. Dr. Whitney wanted everything well documented because if the discovery was anything close to what Commissioner Aury had told him, they had an amazing historic find on their hands.

It was late morning by the time Nash opened the front door to admit everyone. Wolfgang danced excitedly next to him because he knew that these people meant food in his belly, so Nash held on to the happy dog as he told everyone to keep the noise level down if possible. His pregnant wife wasn't feeling well and she'd only been asleep a few hours. With as much silence as possible, Dr. Whitney led his brigade down into the crypt and the process of historic discovery began.

Nash produced Sophie's journal for Dr. Clarke, explaining to the woman where it was found, and Dr. Clarke immediately retreated to the kitchen to not only inspect the dumbwaiter, but to also began examining and photographing the journal.

As a cultural anthropologist, having an unstudied and pristine journal from early Louisiana history was a rare honor, especially from a woman who was the mistress to a famous pirate. Knowing what she did of Sophie MacGregor, Dr. Clarke was deeply grateful to be able to examine the woman and the truth behind the mystery for herself. For a research scientist, it was a dream come true.

Nash spent his time between Dr. Clarke and Dr. Whitney, explaining the conjecture that Elliot and he had come up with as it pertained to the fate of the Aury children. Dr. Clarke agreed that the idea was quite reasonable as she delved into Sophie's journal.

Dr. Whitney was more interested in the archaeological aspects of the find and sat down with Nash for about an hour to write out a contract for excavation between the State of Louisiana and Nash and Elliot Aury, owners of Sophie Plantation. Nash basically gave his permission to excavate all four Aury crypts but reserved the right to make any and all decisions over content. Before anything truly got started, Dr. Whitney called his boss, Dr. Mann, and everything was set in stone.

Noon rolled into early afternoon. The crypt was packed with students and professors while Dr. Clarke and one of the journalism students were in the kitchen deciphering the journal. Nash had the dog penned up in his run but he was very unhappy with all of the activity going on around him, barking everytime he would see someone near, in or around the house.

Nash was sure his barking had awakened Elliot, but he had checked on her several times during the morning and she seemed to be sleeping through it all. However, when he went to check on her around two-thirty, he found the bed empty.

Nash looked around the room and, not seeing anyone, was about to call Elliot's name when he heard her in the bathroom vomiting. Concerned, he went into their newly-remodeled bathroom to find her bent over the toilet.

"Honey?" he stuck his head in the door. "Are you all right? Can I get you something?"

Elliot wasn't finished retching yet. With nothing in her stomach, it was all reduced to dry heaves and she ended up collapsing onto the bathroom floor, miserable and exhausted. Nash bent down to pick her up but she resisted.

"No," she breathed, the right side of her face against the cold, tile floor. "Just leave me here. The cold feels good."

Poor Nash was feeling the nausea right along with her, distressed that there was nothing he could do for her. He sat down on the floor next to her.

"Honey, I can't just leave you here," he said, stroking her arm gently. "Let me get you a cold cloth and put you back to bed."

"No," Elliot whispered. "I'll start throwing up again. Just leave me here for a minute. Please."

Worried, he ran a washcloth under cold water anyway and knelt down beside her, wiping the cool water on her face and neck. Then he left the bathroom and went downstairs, heading for the kitchen and green Jell-O just as Penelope, Shane, Alec and Beck came in through the front door.

The door popped open and the four young adults made their presence known, in Alec's case, loudly when he stubbed his toe on the doorjamb. Nash forgot about the green Jell-O, surprised and pleased.

"Well," he put his hands on his hips, inspecting the motley crew. "The gang's all here. What are y'all doing?"

Penelope, with bags and backpacks in her arms, marched right up to him.

"We've been talking, Nash," she said resolutely. "We're here because you're going to take Mom to New Orleans this weekend on your honeymoon. You guys got married and came right back here without even going anywhere. We're going to watch the house while you go because we know you don't want to leave it alone."

Nash raised his eyebrows. "Y'all didn't have to come home just to force us to leave," he said. "We've been talking about going for a while now, but your mom's been feeling so bad that she hasn't felt like traveling."

Alec and Shane pushed past him, heading for the kitchen. "We just came home to eat," Alec said, nursing the toe. "Shane doesn't keep anything but energy drinks in his refrigerator."

Nash shook his head reproachfully at his youngest son as the kid moved past him, but Shane ignored the look from his father.

"I hope you've got food in this place," Shane said. "Hey, why are all those cars outside?"

Nash turned to answer him but Beck caught his attention. "Dad, just get out of here because if you don't, then all four of us are going to New Orleans instead, and you know what that means."

Nash rolled his eyes. "It means that I'll be bailing one or more of you out of jail for public intoxication," he followed Shane and Alec into the kitchen, where they were already raiding the refrigerator. "You remember Dr. Clarke, boys? Show some manners and say hello."

Alec waved at the woman as Shane pulled lunch meat out of the refrigerator. Dr. Clarke waved back.

"Hey, why is there so much green Jell-O in here?" Shane wanted to know.

Nash had to move out of the way as the hungry boys began moving from the refrigerator to the counter, preparing to make some lunch.

"Because Ellie's still not feeling well," he replied. "That's all she feels like eating these days."

"Then maybe you shouldn't have knocked her up," Shane suggested helpfully as he stuck a pickle in his mouth.

Nash lifted an unhappy eyebrow at his son, preparing to scold him, but then he just started chuckling. It was such joyful and, sometimes, irreverent chaos when the boys were around. He put up his hands in surrender and headed out of the kitchen.

"I'm leaving," he announced. "Keep it down out here. Ellie's trying to rest."

"You didn't tell us who all these people were," Alec reminded him.

Nash stopped and turned around. "You're right, I didn't," he said, then he tilted his head so he could see into the ballroom where Penelope and Beck were greeting Wolfgang. "Hey, y'all come in here. You're going to want to hear this."

Beck and Penelope came into the kitchen with Wolfgang following Penelope. Nash realized he was very excited to tell them the story of the discovery of Sophie's journal, watching their faces as he spoke of murderous siblings and pirate's treasure.

For that afternoon, the four young people lost themselves in history two hundred years in the making. For that afternoon, it wasn't the Jentry children and the Aury children. It was three boys and one girl, just as there had been three boys and one girl, all children of Sophie MacGregor.

Listening to the story of tragedy and triumph as told by Nash, that afternoon, all of them became irrevocably part of the history of Purgatory.

———

Between Penelope and Nash, they were able to convince Elliot that a few days in New Orleans might make her feel better. It took them most of Sunday to do it, but by Sunday evening, Elliot was looking forward to her honeymoon.

Nash had reserved a Club Executive Suite at the Ritz-Carlton in New Orleans and already had a Marie Laveau Lovespell couples massage booked in their exclusive spa. He was eager to get his wife away from ghosts and plantations and murdered children, into an environment that would be sweet and pampering to them both. They both needed the break.

Penelope, Beck and Shane had to go back to school on Monday but the agreement was that they would return on Thursday and stay with Alec through the weekend so he wouldn't be by himself. As the only one of the four children living at home and going to the local community college, neither Nash nor Elliot wanted to leave him alone with all of the activity going on around the house. It was activity that was only going to get worse.

Sunday and Monday had been bad days for Elliot physically. She had been nauseous day and night. But she woke up Tuesday feeling much better, so much so that she got up with Nash and made him breakfast before he went to work. She was even able to eat breakfast with him, chatting over morning coffee as the sun rose.

It had been a rare and unexpected treat to share breakfast with her. Nash kissed her and hugged her, perhaps a little longer than usual, before heading out of the door just as the Clarke and Whitney brigade drove up. He waved at the doctors as he pulled out of the driveway and blew his wife a kiss.

Elliot proceeded to shower and do laundry in preparation for their honeymoon to New Orleans. She was feeling amazingly well as she went about picking out the clothes she would take, finally pulling out a pair of her favorite designer jeans just to try them on to make sure they fit. She expected them to be snug, but she didn't expect to not be able to button them. Her baby bump had become so big that it was time for the transition to maternity clothes.

Picking up her cell phone, she dialed Nash. As usual, he picked up by the third ring, which he usually did when she called him. It never mattered what the man was doing or who he was with, when he saw Elliot's name on the caller I.D., he answered as fast as he could.

"Hi, darlin'," he said sweetly. "How are feeling?"

Elliot sat on the edge of the bed. "Surprisingly good," she said. "It looks like I won't have to kill you after all for getting me pregnant."

He laughed. "Is that where it was headed? I wondered."

"Well, now you know," she giggled. "In fact, I feel so good that I have a proposition for you."

"A proposition?" he lowered his voice, grinning. "Tell me more. I'm intrigued."

"You should be," she said. "How often do you get propositioned by a beautiful blond?"

"Not often enough since she found out she was pregnant. I'm all ears, honey."

Elliot grinned as she flipped on the television to watch the morning news, cradling the phone against her ear as she began to go through the pile of clothes on the bed again.

"Here's the deal, Mr. Commissioner," she said. "I was doing some laundry and packing this morning for our trip, but I came across an unfortunate discovery."

"What's that?"

"I can no longer fit into my pants. The baby has taken over my body completely, so I need to do some shopping. I was thinking about going to the mall in Baton Rouge and was further hoping you could buy me lunch because you feel so sorry for me for outgrowing my clothes."

On the other end of the line, Nash grinned broadly. "That," he answered, "would be my pleasure. Plus, I can introduce you to some of the people I work with around here. They're dying to meet you."

"Where should I meet you?"

"Come to my office first. Call me when you're in the parking lot and I'll come and get you."

"Okay," she said. "I'll see you in a couple of hours."

"I love you. Drive safely, please."

"I will. Love you, too."

Excited at her first outing in quite some time, Elliot went about the difficult task of trying to find something to wear. The best she could come up with was a beautiful, flowing caftan top and leggings with strappy high heels that Nash was going to kill her for wearing when he saw them. As she tried on shoes to see which pair went best with the outfit, she happened to glance up at the television and saw a big graphic next to the news anchor that said "Pirate Treasure". Curious, she turned up the volume.

Almost immediately, she could see that the story was about Purgatory. There was video of her front gates and the news reporter was standing across the street as she delivered her story. In fact, there was more than one news van that she could see and she instinctively went to the window to see if she could spy anything down the long driveway. She didn't see any news vans but she saw people milling about in the driveway down below. Her concern and confusion grew.

Elliot went downstairs, wanting to speak with Dr. Whitney to find out who had leaked word of the discovery to the press. She and Nash hadn't talked about announcing the find, so she hoped that Dr. Whitney hadn't jumped the gun. She wasn't sure they were ready to announce everything to the world yet, for a myriad of reasons.

As she approached the dining room, she spied Dr. Clarke at her kitchen table with a young girl. Both were buried in papers and laptop computers. Elliot stuck her head into the kitchen.

"Dr. Clarke?" she said. "I just saw something on the news about Purgatory. You didn't tell anyone about what's going on here, did you?"

Dr. Clarke looked up from Sophie's journal, removing her reading glasses as she did. "Not at all," she looked concerned. "You saw it on the news?"

Elliot nodded. "Right now," she said. "There was a reporter outside the gates doing a story."

Dr. Clarke immediately got up from the table and went to find Dr. Whitney. Elliot stood at the top of the secret steps as Dr. Clarke descended into the crypt and she could hear her exchanging words with Dr. Whitney. Suddenly, Dr. Whitney seemed very agitated and she could clearly hear him when he demanded to know from the group gathered in the crypt who had notified the press.

Elliot descended the narrow stairs, peering into the crypt about the time Dr. Whitney was having a stern conversation with one of the grad students, a young girl who looked terrified.

As Elliot stayed on the steps and watched, the story seemed to come out; apparently, the girl had mentioned the find to her roommate, who happened to work for the local news station up in Baton Rouge. Even though the girl insisted she had told her friend not to tell anyone, it appeared as if her friend hadn't kept her part of the bargain.

Dr. Whitney yelled at the girl, reducing her to tears, as Elliot went back up the steps and headed for her bedroom. She needed to tell Nash.

He picked up on the second ring this time. "Don't tell me that you're cancelling our lunch date," he said as he answered. "I've been looking forward to this all day."

She grinned. "I only called you a half-hour ago."

"Don't spoil my fun."

She giggled. "Actually, I'm calling you about something that's going to spoil your fun a whole lot more. It seems that one of Dr. Whitney's grad students leaked our find to the press. I saw a story on it about five minutes ago and there are news vans in front of the house. I really don't feel comfortable leaving right now. If the media starts banging down the door for a story, one of us should be here."

"What?" he sounded genuinely shocked, hinting at anger. "Hold on... let me turn my television on and see if there's anything on about it."

She waited patiently while he turned on the television. She could hear chatter in the background as he flipped channels.

"Hold on, honey," he told her. "Don't go anywhere."

"I won't."

She could hear him talking to someone else in his office, telling them to find out what they could about news on Purgatory. Elliot stayed on the phone with him, going to the great front window of the bedroom that overlooked the driveway to see if she could see any more news activity. So far, it was still quiet in her driveway, another mild September day outside. She stood there for several minutes, listening to Nash on the other end of the phone as he spoke with people in his office.

Suddenly, he was back.

"I'm coming home," he told her. "It seems that the major news stations have picked this up and one of my aides just saw a story with my name attached. I'll be home as quick as I can."

Elliot's brow furrowed. "Why? It's not like they're storming the gates, sweetie. I can hold down the fort for a while."

Nash sighed. "It's not that easy, honey. The news outlets that my people have seen so far are mentioning millions of dollars in discovered pirate treasure, which means we're going to have all sorts of people trying to overrun the property trying to catch a glimpse of it. Maybe even thieves. Anyway, I'll be home shortly but I'm calling the police in the meanwhile to keep the peace."

Elliot didn't like the sound of that. "Now you're scaring me."

"I'm sorry, I don't mean to," Nash said. He was already up from his desk and gathering his keys. "Just stay in the house and keep Wolfgang with you."

"Okay," she said, sounding uneasy. "Don't break your neck driving home. I'll be fine until you get here."

"I'm on my way. Love you."

"Love you, too."

The phone went dead and Elliot set it back down on the nightstand. She could hear Wolfgang barking outside so she changed from the flowing top and leggings and into stretchy black Capri pants and a white top that showed off her growing belly. With white tennis shoes on her feet, she went back downstairs and out the kitchen door, heading towards the dog run where Wolfgang was making a racket.

He was a happy dog when he saw Elliot, sitting patiently as she opened the run and put his leash on. Oddly, for as excited as the dog could get, he never pulled on the leash, so Elliot was able to walk him around without getting her arms pulled from their sockets.

Elliot walked him across the yard, skirting the trenching area that had a few students working on it today. The students waved to her and to Wolfgang, and she allowed the dog to go over and receive some love. Then she continued around to the front of the house, walking the dog around the big fountain and peering down the long driveway to see if she could see the news vans parked outside.

The driveway was easily a quarter of a mile long so she began to walk the dog down the tree-shrouded driveway, Spanish moss hanging heavy and moist in the branches. Wolfgang walked happily by her side, his big tongue hanging out as they made their way towards the gates.

As they drew close, she could see a portion of a van parked across the street with its aerial up. She could also see some people congregating near the gates, who turned suddenly when one of them pointed at Elliot. Immediately, the media and spectators were clamoring at the gates and Wolfgang started to go crazy, savagely barking at the people who seemed to back off at the sight of the vicious dog.

"Ms. Jentry!" they were calling to her. "Comments on the pirate's treasure, Ms. Jentry?"

Elliot had never seen such a circus. It was a little shocking, to tell the truth. There were at least twenty people congregated around her front gates and she shook her head.

"No comment," she told them. "I'm sure Commissioner Aury will make a statement when he returns. He'll be here shortly."

"Ms. Jentry!" they were still calling to her. "Can you tell us about the bodies beneath the house?"

Elliot listened to the shouted questions, wondering just how much the media already knew. She began to silently curse the girl with the loose lips. A little fearful of the clamor and the fact that

Wolfgang was going crazy, she turned to go back to the house and pulled the dog with her. Just as she made her move, someone threw a bottle at the front gate, sending liquid and glass spraying all over her.

Elliot screamed as it hit her in the shoulder and the side of her face. Her eyes stung with whatever was in the liquid and she panicked until she realized it was some kind of alcohol. She could hear shouting.

"Y'all are thievin' wretches!" someone was screaming. "It don't belong to y'all! That's *our* treasure!"

Still cowering, Elliot took several steps away from the gate, wiping at the liquid all over her face and neck and realizing there were glass shards. She stopped wiping for fear she would grind them into her skin, all the while looking to see who tossed the bottle. She could hear more cackling and yelling, and the squeal of rubber as a car drove away at high speed.

Frightened, covered in alcohol, she quickly turned and made her way back up the driveway as the media people yelled behind her.

By the time she hit the house, she was weeping. Dr. Clarke and her young assistant happened to be in the dining room at the time, taking a break to admire the hand-painted wallpaper and heard her come in. Concerned, Dr. Clarke stuck her head out of the dining room in time to see Elliot flying up the stairs, crying, with the dog on her heels. Dr. Clarke ran after her.

"Ms. Aury!" she called, climbing the stairs behind her. "Ms. Aury, what happened?"

She could hear Elliot crying in her bedroom and she followed the sound. Peeking her head inside the open bedroom door, she could see that the big dog was sitting outside of the master bathroom, looking curiously at Dr. Clarke as she timidly entered the room. Dr. Clarke proceeded to the bathroom to find Elliot trying to strip off wet and glass-covered clothes.

"Oh, my God," Dr. Clarke rushed into the bathroom, preventing Elliot from cutting herself as she tried to remove her clothing. "Honey, let me do this for you. You just stand still and I'll pull it off. What happened?"

Elliot was a mess. "Someone threw a bottle of alcohol and it shattered on the front gate," she sobbed. "It got all over me."

Dr. Clarke gingerly peeled off the white top. "Oh, honey, I'm so sorry," she murmured. "Come on, now; get your shoes off and get into the shower so we can get all of this off of you."

Dr. Clarke's soothing demeanor helped Elliot tremendously. The woman helped Elliot peel all of her clothing off and turned the shower on for her. Elliot washed everything away and then some, making sure all of the glass and the booze were gone. By the time she got out of the shower, she was calmer but still upset. Her stomach was roiling to boot and her nausea was making a return. She wrapped up in a towel and, at Dr. Clarke's direction, went to sit on the bed so the woman could check her for any more glass or injury.

Broken glass had cut her collarbone but that was about it. No shards got embedded anywhere else, thankfully, and Elliot let Dr. Clarke put some ointment and a bandage on her collarbone. Exhausted and ill, Elliot changed into a flowing white nightgown and lay down on the bed. She reached her hand out to Dr. Clarke.

"Thank you," she murmured sincerely, clutching the woman's fingers. "That was very sweet of you."

Dr. Clarke smiled and squeezed her hand before letting it go. "Would you like something to drink? How about some tea, honey?"

Elliot shook her head. "No, thanks," she said. "I just want to lay here for a while. My husband will be home soon."

Dr. Clarke left her alone with the big dog lying at the foot of the bed. She and her wide eyed assistant went back to work in the kitchen, continuing their study of Sophie's pristine journal. As the clock neared noon, they heard a car pull up outside and a car door slam.

Suddenly, the front door was flying back on its hinges and Commissioner Aury was storming into the house, flying up the self-supporting staircase in his determination to get to his wife. She could hear the man's voice moving upstairs, full of concern.

Someone must have told him what had happened, she thought. Dr. Clarke returned her focus to the journal before her. She couldn't help but wonder what more was going to happen to this family, and this house, now that the treasure of Purgatory had become national news.

TWENTY-FOUR

THURSDAY, the cavalry arrived.

Penelope, Beck and Shane had come during a cloudy mid-afternoon, fully expecting to house-sit for the weekend but being told by a distressed Nash that the situation had changed. Elliot hadn't wanted the kids to know about the bottle being thrown the day before because she didn't want to worry them, especially Penelope. Nash quietly told them what had happened when they arrived on Thursday. As he knew, Penelope ran to find her mother to make sure she was all right.

Elliot was in the kitchen, a surprising place for her to be considering how volatile her stomach was. She was slow-cooking some beef brisket, Alec's favorite, and the thick smell of barbeque filled the house. She seemed to be able to handle the smell of barbeque but still not chicken. Nash went into the kitchen with Penelope while Shane and Beck went into the ballroom to hang out with Alec.

The atmosphere in the house was casual and relaxed, a far cry from what it had been just yesterday. In the ballroom, both plasma screens were on and blaring as Alec and Shane played Xbox Live against alien zombie invaders. It sounded like a war zone.

In spite of the noise, Nash couldn't ask for anything better. He was determined to have a sense of normalcy around the house as the national news of the Aury treasure heated up. More news media had showed up outside the house and his office was getting calls from national news agencies for interviews. Nash wasn't ready to talk about everything, not just yet. He wanted to wait and see what the scientists had to say.

Nash had a long talk with Dr. Whitney the day before, telling the man that until things calmed down, he could no longer bring a battalion of young people with him to excavate the crypts. No one could blame him, of course, and when Dr. Whitney showed up that morning, it was with two other archaeologists and Dr. Clarke. Gone were the carloads of grad students, at least for the time being. Nash was much more comfortable with the smaller scale activities.

Nash had, in fact, been working from home since yesterday and had told his concerned aides that he wasn't sure when he would come back to the office given what had happened at his house yesterday. The attack on Elliot had scared the hell out of him and he was determined to spend every moment with her, so bloody furious over the thrown bottle that even now, he was still angry about it.

Every time he looked at his wife with the bandage on her collarbone, he got angry all over again. He had no doubt who did it, but no one had actually taken the time to get a good look at the car or take down a license plate number. He had sent the Sorrento police over to The Bottoms yesterday afternoon but they didn't get anywhere. No evidence meant no arrest.

Nash wanted to drive over to the Loreau plantation and burn the place down, but that wouldn't solve the problem. Until he could figure out what to do, he was determined to stick close to home.

He sat down at the kitchen table opposite Dr. Clarke, watching his wife as she interacted with her daughter. Elliot was such a lovely creature to watch and every time he was around her, she had his full attention. As she had since the moment he met her.

His gaze moved over her delicate features, the blond hair

pulled back into a bouncy ponytail, the loose-fitting shirt she wore that couldn't conceal the growing baby bump, and stretchy little black pants.

As Elliot leaned against the counter with an ear of corn in her hand, Penelope put her hands on Elliot's belly and bent down to kiss it, gigging when she caught Nash watching her. He grinned back.

"I do it all the time," he waved her off. "That belly has a lot of lip prints on it and I suspect it's going to have a lot more before the baby is born."

Penelope put her mouth up against her mother's stomach. "Hi, Sophie Elizabeth," she said, her mouth muffled against Elliot's shirt. "I love you, baby girl. I can't wait to meet you."

Nash smiled broadly as Penelope talked to the baby, kissing the belly again and again until Elliot finally pulled her off. Grinning, Penelope took the corn out of her mother's hand and finished shucking it.

"I still think you guys should go to New Orleans," she said. "I mean, why not? What better way to forget about a bad week?"

Elliot's happy demeanor faded. "No way," she said firmly, moving to the refrigerator and pulling out a Mexican beer. "I couldn't relax knowing you guys were here alone. I mean, what if something happened? Things are still too crazy to think about going away."

Nash watched Elliot as she popped the top off the beer and came over to the table to hand it to him. He took it gratefully, kissing the hand that gave it to him.

"I'm going to agree with your mother on this one," he told Penelope. "Until the situation calms down, no one is going anywhere, least of all me."

Elliot leaned against him, putting her arm around his broad shoulders as he wrapped his free arm around her waist.

"You've got to go back to the office sometime," she said with concern.

"I can do everything I need to from here."

Dr. Clarke, sitting in the middle of a family discussion, seemed to be a little uncomfortable. She stood up and started gathering her things.

"If y'all don't mind, I'll give you some room to talk," she said.

"Where are you going?" Elliot wanted to know. "You can stay here. We don't mind."

Dr. Clarke forced a smile. "No trouble, Ms. Aury. I'll go to my car and give you some privacy."

"Wait," Nash waved at the woman. "Go into the library. You can use my desk. I don't want that journal out of the house."

Dr. Clarke understood and she moved her materials into Nash's luxurious man-cave study. Elliot looked down at her husband.

"If she goes in there, where are you going to work today?"

He looked up at her, hugging her against him. "I'm taking the day off," he announced. "I've put in fifteen hour days for the past two months, so I'm taking the rest of the week off to spend time with my family."

Pleased, Elliot kissed him, tasting beer on his lips. Penelope, seeing that her mother and Nash were deteriorating into sweet kisses and soft whispers, found her way into the ballroom where Wolfgang happily greeted her. She lay down on the couch and made the boys turn over at least one television so she could watch regular programming. The dog jumped up next to her, laying its big head on her belly.

Back in the kitchen, Elliot was now sitting on Nash's lap with his hand on her belly. The baby was moving around and he could feel it, grins of delight with every kick. Elliot was talking about a fancy bassinet she had seen, trying to convince Nash that they needed to spend fifteen hundred dollars on it. He thought a cardboard box beside their bed would do just as well, listening to her groans of protest. As he laughed at her displeasure and swooped in to nuzzle her neck, he could hear Shane calling to him.

"Dad!" the boy was yelling. "The weather channel has issued an alert!"

Nash still has his face in Elliot's sweet-smelling neck. "What does it say?"

There was no immediate reply. Then, Beck appeared. "It says that thunderstorms and possible tornado watches are heading over from Houston. At least we know we have a basement now if a tornado comes."

Nash nodded. "When?"

"They said some time tonight."

Nash thought on that, looking up at Elliot to say something and realizing she looked apprehensive. He squeezed her gently.

"What's wrong, darlin'?"

She looked at him and tried to smile, but it turned into a quirky little expression and he laughed at her.

"Give me earthquakes and wildfires," she said. "I don't like tornados or wild weather."

He squeezed her. "That's what we have here in Louisiana. You're going to have to get used to it."

She made a funny face again, shaking her head and exaggeratingly chattering her teeth as if terrified. He chuckled again and stood up, setting her carefully on her feet.

"If rain is coming, then we'd better make sure the archaeologists know," he said. "I'm not sure what they have to do in order to protect whatever they're working on, but that big trench in the backyard isn't going to do well unless they buckle it down."

Elliot followed him into the dining room. "They usually seal it up with tarps."

Nash knew that. He went down into the crypt where Dr. Whitney and the other archaeologists were beginning to bring Paul-Michel out of his marble coffin. They had a portable plastic table set up, covered in a clean white sheet, and they were beginning to lay the bones out on it like a giant jigsaw puzzle.

Elliot had followed Nash down into the crypt. It was the first time she had seen Paul-Michel's remains and she made a face of distaste at her first glimpse.

"Wow," she said, putting her fingers to her nose at the smell. "He's really a mess, isn't he?"

Dr. Whitney was piecing together some vertebra. "He is," he agreed. "I'm wondering if we're going to find the other three in this condition."

On another table, another archaeologist was carefully laying out the pieces of treasure and jewelry they had been able to remove. He had a cleansing station set up and Elliot could see that he had already cleaned about half of the emerald necklace they found in Paul-Michel's crypt.

Fascinated, Elliot leaned over the table to take a look at the nineteenth-century pirate's booty coming to life. The archaeologist noticed her interest.

"Pretty neat, eh?" the older man with glasses smiled at her. "These emeralds are first rate, probably mined in Brazil, as that was along the pirate's coastal travel routes. The big one anchoring the necklace has to be at least thirty carats. There are at least six others that I can see, maybe more. This necklace has to weigh a few pounds. How'd you like that hanging around your neck?"

Elliot grinned. "With emeralds that big, I'd make the sacrifice."

The archaeologist showed her a couple of other things they had brought out, including a gold broach with a fat ruby on it and an exquisite dagger with the blade intact and still sharp. There was also a pair of earbobs, intact and found together, with a giant pearl and ruby hanging off of a long, single strand of solid gold.

They were magnificent and Elliot peered closely over the man's shoulder as he cleaned them up so he could show them to her. Using specially formulated jewelry cleaner and a soft bristle toothbrush, he was able to shine up the dark gold and lustrous pearl to a high sheen. When he was finished polishing them, he held up one so Elliot could get a closer look.

"A queen must have worn this," he told her. "Look at the size of that pearl."

Elliot pointed to the clasp of the earring. "Are they made for pierced ears?"

The archaeologist nodded. "They really didn't have such things as clip-on earrings back then, especially for pieces like this. They're so heavy, they'd pull the clip right off. Do you want to try it on?"

Elliot nodded eagerly, like an excited little kid, and the archaeologist put the earrings carefully in her ears. They were huge and heavy, but absolutely beautiful. By the time Nash finished discussing the incoming weather with Dr. Whitney and turned for his wife, he could see the archaeologist taking pictures of Elliot's ears with the enormous earrings attached to them. He walked up on the pair.

"Hey, what's this?" he demanded lightly. "Where'd you get those?"

Elliot was thrilled with the earrings. "Dr. Bedford put them on," she tilted her head back so Nash could see the earrings. "Look at these things; aren't they beautiful? I wonder who they used to belong to before your ancestor stole them – maybe a princess or duchess. Or maybe a prostitute!"

He grinned at her, passing a glance at the scientist. "You shouldn't have done this," he told the man. "You'll never get them back now. It's going to take both of us to get them off of her."

The archaeologist chuckled. "Well, technically, they belong to you," he pointed out. "If she wants to keep them, that's really your decision."

Nash hadn't thought of it that way but realized the man was right. Everything in this house, treasure included, belong to him to do with as he pleased. He looked at Elliot, seeing such a deliriously hopeful expression on her face that he immediately started to relent.

"Are you serious?" he asked. "You really want to keep two-hundred-year-old earrings?"

Her hopeful expression fell and he caved like an idiot. He didn't even say anything about the fact that they were part of the blood money cache. He didn't get that far.

"Okay, okay," he said quickly, putting his arm around her and kissing her forehead. "They're yours. Merry Christmas."

Elliot giggled gleefully, hugging him enthusiastically and thanking him repeatedly before running over to Dr. Whitney to show him her treasure. The old archaeologist just grinned as Elliot rushed up the stairs, happy as a lark. He shook his head at Nash.

"You've got your hands full with that one," he said. "What do I tell her if she comes back down here scavenging for more jewelry?"

Nash grinned as he began to follow his wife up the stairs. "Give her what she wants," he said. "She's earned it."

Dr. Whitney snorted and turned back for his bones. As Nash entered the dining room upstairs, he could hear Elliot in the library, no doubt showing Dr. Clarke her gorgeous booty. Nash grinned as he followed her voice, glad to hear her so excited about something. She'd been so miserable over the past two months with her pregnancy that he was pleased to see her so happy. Just as he entered the library, she suddenly scooted past him.

"I have to show Penny!" she said.

Nash chuckled, shook his head, and followed her back to the ballroom where one pair of kids were playing video games and the other pair were watching television. It looked, and sounded, like chaos and above it all, he could hear Penelope squealing with delight at her mother's new earrings. He plopped down on the couch between Wolfgang and Shane, settling in to watch television, something he rarely got to do, when Penelope turned to him.

"Nash," she said with hopeful restraint. "I love my mom's earrings. Do you think...?"

He cut her off before she could finish, pointing a finger back towards the dining room. "Go," he told her. "Pick whatever you want."

Penelope squealed happily and gave him a big hug, so excited that she toppled him over onto the dog. Wolfgang jumped off the couch, barked, and then followed Penelope as she ran into the dining room and down the secret stairs. As Nash righted himself,

Elliot sat down beside him and he put his arms around her, snuggling against her.

With the smell of beef brisket in the air and the sun starting to set over the Black Bayou, Nash and Elliot settled down to enjoy the rest of a peaceful afternoon.

————

Nash heard it first, the driving sheets of rain that come on the outside band of a strong storm. It sounded like someone was hosing off the roof. Elliot was snuggled up against him, sound asleep and burrowed deep in their big, comfortable bed. He glanced at her as the rain began to pound, wondering if the noise would wake her up. She didn't move.

Carefully, he disengaged himself from her and covered her back up with the comforter. It was actually chilly in the room, September being unseasonably cool and the incoming storm bringing even cooler temperatures.

They were able to have a fire in their master bedroom fireplace that night for the first time, the embers of which still burned in the hearth. Nash gazed at the fireplace a moment, the glowing wood, and thought of the lovemaking they had done before the fire. The mere memory of it was enough to heat his veins again.

He'd hardly touched Elliot over the past couple of months because her morning sickness had been so bad. She hadn't exactly been in the mood, and he understood, as difficult as it had been for him to restrain himself.

But last night had seen that dramatically change and the woman had come out of her shell. Truth be told, he was a little wary to touch her because he'd never made love to a pregnant woman before, not even his ex-wife back when she was pregnant with Beck or Shane. He'd been afraid to and Julie hadn't cared one way or the other.

But Elliot wasn't shy about it at all; she had stripped off her clothing and literally jumped on top of him. Nash wasn't hard pressed to admit that being beneath her as she made love to him was one of the most wildly arousing experiences he'd ever had. Her gently swollen midsection drew his lust and he found something supremely erotic about making love to his wife as his hands caressed her pregnant belly.

Fertility was a massive aphrodisiac in his book, and they'd made love three times before she fell into an exhausted slumber. Even now, as the rain fell and the fire burned low, he was tempted to climb back into bed and make love to her again. Pregnancy only seemed to make her sexier.

But she was sleeping soundly and he didn't want to wake her, not even to satisfy a semi-arousal from his erotic thoughts. So he pulled on a pair of pajama bottoms and quietly opened the bedroom door, checking the hall door that opened on to the balcony to make sure it wasn't leaking before he moved into Alec's room to make sure his new windows were holding as well.

He went to all the windows on the second floor, checking to make sure they weren't leaking, checking on the kids to make sure they were okay. It was just a habit he had.

Alec was asleep with all of his covers kicked off the bed, as usual, and Shane was snoring so loudly that he had driven Beck into Elliot's writing room, where the young man was sleeping soundly on the couch.

Nash went into Penelope's room to see that one of her windows had a small leak at the bottom because the rain was blowing in sideways, but it wasn't critical. He would be sure and tell his brother about it, though. Moving out of her bedroom, he glanced over to see Wolfgang sleeping soundly next to Penelope on the bed. He was about to shut the door behind him when he heard his name.

"Nash?"

Penelope's head came up in the darkness and Nash paused with his hand on the door. "Why are you awake, honey?" he whispered. "Go back to sleep."

"Is my mom all right?" she asked sleepily.

He went over to the bed and made her lay back down, pulling the covers up over her. "She's fine," he murmured. "Sound asleep. Why?"

Penelope snuggled down and the dog shifted in his sleep. "Because she doesn't like storms. She's afraid of them."

Nash touched her head. "She's fine," he repeated. "Go back to sleep."

Penelope dozed off and he quit the room, shutting the door softly behind him. He made his way back up the hall and into their bedroom, only to find Elliot sitting up in bed. Before he could say a word, she extended his cell phone.

"It rang," she said groggily. "It's Ken Havereau."

Nash's brow furrowed with confusion and some concern as he put the phone to his ear. "Ken?"

"Nash?" Ken was nearly yelling because there was a lot of noise in the background. "Sorry to bother you, but I need your help."

Nash had known Ken for almost ten years. He didn't like the sound of the man's voice. "What's the matter?"

Ken's voice crackled through the phone. "I'm just south of the Sunshine Bridge," he said. "We've got a mess down here, Nash. It looks like a tornado touched down on the west side of the river just east of Donaldsonville then skipped the river and came down again in Union. I can't get a hold of the Matt Jorry; dispatch has been trying to raise him for ten minutes. These people need help, Nash, and the deputies here are looking for direction. I know you're not the sheriff anymore, but...."

Nash cut him off. "I'll be there as soon as I can," he was already up, hunting for his clothes. "Where in the hell is Jorry?"

He was speaking of one of his captains who had taken over the office of the sheriff until the new election in November. Jorry was an intelligent man and a good cop, so it was surprising that he wasn't available during a crisis. Ken sighed heavily.

"I have no idea," he said. "We'll keep trying. Meanwhile, what do you want me to do?"

Nash put the phone on speaker as he put it on the dresser and pulled off his pajama bottoms. "I'm assuming emergency services are already rolling."

"Yessir."

"I want a damage assessment and who rolled where. Watch spreading emergency service thin in case we get another wave of this storm. Contact St. Elizabeth's and Prevost Memorial. Make sure they can handle the casualties and make sure the casualties you send to them are distributed according to their work load. I'll call you in a few minutes to see if you can give me a better assessment of damage and injury so I know whether or not I need to call the governor and ask for state assistance."

"You got it, Nash."

Nash hung up the phone as he pulled on his boxer briefs and his jeans. He pulled a white t-shirt out of the drawer and was just turning around to look for his shoes when he looked up and saw Elliot's expression.

She was sitting up in bed, the comforter clutched to her breast as she watched him get dressed. He was struck by the look on her face, something between sadness and fear. He went over to her immediately, cupping her face in his big hands and kissing her mouth.

"I'm sorry, honey," he murmured. "They got a mess down by Donaldsonville and they can't find Sheriff Jorry. They need help."

She looked up at him with her big, blue eyes filling up with tears. "Nash, you promised. No more call-outs."

She was starting to cry. He sat down next to her and wrapped his big arms around her. His face was against the side of her head when he spoke.

"There's no shooting and no guns," he swore. "A tornado touched down and ripped up some people's lives. Ken can't find Sheriff Jorry and he's looking for help. I can't turn him down, honey. He needs help. Those people need help."

She wiped at her face, laying her head against his shoulder as he held her. "Okay," she whispered. "As long as there are no guns."

"I swear," he kissed her head. "No guns."

He stroked her blond hair and gave her a hug before letting her go and resuming his search for clothing. Elliot sat on the bed, huddled up in the comforter as Nash pulled on a lightweight v-neck sweater and dug into the wardrobe they'd built into the bathroom for his jacket that said "Sheriff" across the back. He came out of the bathroom, fixing the neck on the jacket as he bent down to kiss her goodbye.

"Go back to sleep," he kissed her again. "I'll be back as soon as I can."

She listened to the thunder outside. "I can't go back to sleep if you're not here. Are you taking your phone?"

"It'll be on me every second. Call if you need me."

She nodded, trying to be brave about it. "Okay."

He stopped messing with the jacket, eyeing her. "Are you sure you're all right?"

"I'm sure."

"If you get really scared, the boys are all here. Wake them up and make them sit up with you until I get back."

She wriggled her eyebrows. "I may go in and sleep with Penny and the dog. Wolfgang will protect me."

He grinned. "Yes, he will," he agreed, collecting his keys. "I love you. I'll be back as quickly as I can."

"I love you, too," she said. "Please be careful. It's nasty out there."

He flashed her a smile. "I will."

She heard his footsteps head down the hall and down the stairs. She heard the front door open and close, and then his car start up in the driveway. Getting out of bed, she pulled on a pair of loose pajamas, peering out the window in time to see his car drive off down the driveway in the pounding rain.

Elliot stood in the window long after car disappeared, feeling very alone and very afraid. As the thunder rolled, she collected a blanket from the bed and made her way to Penelope's room to sleep in the company of her daughter and the big German Shepherd.

Somehow the big lick to her face from the happy dog made her feel better as she drifted off to sleep.

TWENTY-FIVE

IT WAS an odd and moist evening, the storm blowing in from Texas turning the sky strange shades of blues and greens. Biffy stood on the crumbling porch of The Bottoms, watching the sky, feeling the weather change. Tulip, her younger and mostly mute sister, sat on an old chair behind her, working on some sewing as the sky above turned ominous.

As Biffy stood and inspected the sky, Will and Ed meandered out onto the porch, kicking dogs aside as they went. They, too, paused to look up at the sky.

"Y'all know we have a right to what they found at Purgatory," Biffy said quietly.

Will nodded, hands shoved into the pockets of his dirty jeans. "We gave them notice," he insisted.

Biffy shook her head. "I don't mean throwin' a bottle and drivin' off," she said. "I mean that our family was founded just like their family, by pirates who robbed and raided to get what they wanted. If y'all think about it, we're still pirates. We still live by the law of the wild and we take what is ours."

Ed was standing on the other side of Biffy. "We can't get on the property now," he said. "They got that big ol' fence up and there's electric wires running underground so we get shocked if we touch the fence. We tried."

Biffy took her eyes off the darkening sky and went to sit next to her silent sister. "Back in the day, our people didn't stop because of fences or fancy *eee*-lec-tricity. Nothin' stopped 'em. Our people used the water to sneak up and take what they wanted. Yessir. Did y'all stop to think that we could do the same thing?"

By this time, Nicky had wandered out onto the porch. He stood there, listening to the conversation, a type of conversation he'd heard daily for months. But this one was different. It sounded as if his grandma was up to something more than the usual.

"Do what?" he asked before his brothers could. "Mam, we need to stop tryin' to get back at the Aurys. Daddy tried and it got him killed. We tried and it only got us into jail. We tried to sue them but that didn't work, either. We need to quit while we can."

Ed and Will were looking angrily at their brother. "Then we have to try harder," Will yelled at him. "You're so 'fraidy, just get out of here."

Nicky frowned. "I just don't want to go back to jail. Y'all are headed that way, the way y'all are goin', and I don't want to go with y'all."

Biffy turned around and shook her finger at him. "Nicky, y'all always did have a cowardly streak," she said. "We are descended from men who used to rule the whole Mississippi River and y'all are shamin' them. Y'all are shamin' what it means to be a pirate, Nicky. It's in your blood, son."

Nicky didn't want to be a pirate. He just wanted to stay out of jail. He wandered back into the house, knowing he wouldn't be included in any further plans. From now on, it was Will and Ed alone.

Biffy turned back to the sky, drawing in a deep breath as she thought on their next move. "They found that treasure but what they found is our due," she said. "Tonight, we're pirates 'cuz we're gonna take a boat across the Black Bayou right into the backyard of Purgatory. They got a fence around the whole place but they don't got a fence across they backyard. It backs right up to the bayou."

Ed and Will looked interested. "What are we gonna do?" Will asked, eager.

Biffy was decisive in her reply. "Get the guns, boys," she told them. "Tonight, we're pirates just like our ancestors. Tonight, we make Jean-Pierre Loreau proud. We take back what is rightfully ours."

Ed went to pull the old tin boat out of the shed while Will went to get the rifles. Tonight, it would finally be decided between the Loreaus and the Aurys.

They would make sure of it.

———

The first sign of trouble was the window shattering in Penelope's room. Elliot was asleep in her daughter's big bed, the dog snoring between her and Penelope, and when several panes of the window shattered, Wolfgang leaped up and ran to the window, barking furiously. Startled out of a deep sleep, Elliot and Penelope jumped out of bed.

"What happened?" Penelope cried, pulling the dog back so he wouldn't step on the shards of glass.

Elliot had no idea. All she knew was that rain and wind were coming in through the window now. She yanked open Penelope's door.

"Beck?" she called. "Shane? Alec? Come and help!"

She could hear feet hitting the floor in various bedrooms as she went back into Penelope's room, looking at the damage. Wind whipped in from the broken window, sending the curtains blowing wildly.

"My new curtains," Penelope lamented. "They're getting wet."

Elliot opened her mouth to say something when more window panes shattered, this time on the window adjacent to the first one. The women hit the floor, screaming, as more glass and water flew into the room. Beck and Shane were already racing into Penelope's room to see what was happening.

"That was a gunshot," Beck said, reaching down to pull Elliot off the floor. "Come on; let's get out of here."

He had a hold of Elliot while Shane grabbed Penelope. They pulled the women out into the central upstairs hall as Alec emerged from his room and went to flip on the light. Nothing happened.

"What the hell?" he flipped the switch a few times. He rushed back into his room and flipped a different switch with the same results. "The power's out!"

Another shot ripped through the upstairs window of the writing room and the women shrieked at the sound. With the wind and rain barreling in, it was loud and frightening. Beck pushed them down against the wall in the upper hallway, keeping them away from any windows.

"What in the hell is going on?" Alec demanded, furious. "Who is shooting at the windows?"

Beck shook his head. "I have no idea, but if they break in downstairs, it's only a matter of time before they come up here and...."

He was looking at Elliot and Penelope, huddled against the wall. When another shot sounded, this time against the side of the house, Wolfgang went nuts and bolted from Penelope's room, running downstairs. They could hear the dog barking savagely somewhere on the first floor. Penelope's eyes welled.

"Wolfie!" she hissed. "They'll shoot him!"

Beck wasn't sure what to say to her. He was more concerned with getting them to safety. He looked at Alec.

"Does my dad keep any firearms in the house?" he asked.

Alec nodded. "In his study," he said. "There's a gun safe."

"Do you know the combination?"

They all looked at Elliot for an answer. Elliot, struggling not to become hysterical, shook her head.

"I don't know it," she said. "We need to call your dad right now."

The group of them scooted back down the hallway in the darkness, staying low to the ground. They could hear Wolfgang barking furiously downstairs but no more shattered windows as of yet. Other than the raging storm, the house seemed oddly silent after the initial burst. It was creepy and ominous, like the calm before the storm.

Once they went into the master bedroom, Elliot and Alec ran for Elliot's cell phone on her nightstand while Beck ushered Penelope and Shane into the master bath. It was a windowless room with two exits, which he figured would be safer than getting themselves boxed into a room with only one entrance. Not knowing what was going on, or who was shooting, he wanted to plan for all contingencies.

Alec and Elliot rushed into the bathroom, Elliot already hitting the speed dial for Nash. The phone rang six times before going to voicemail. Verging on tears, Elliot hung up and tried again. It went to voice mail on the fifth ring this time. Struggling not to panic, she hit it yet again.

"He *always* picks up when I call," she hissed. "He's never not picked up, ever. He must be...."

On the fourth ring, Nash picked up. "Hi, honey," he said, though there was a ton of background noise. "What...?"

"Nash, somebody is shooting out the windows," Elliot started to cry. "You need to come home *now*!"

"What?" he shouted. "What in the hell is going on?"

Beck could hear his father yelling through the phone and he grabbed it from Elliot.

"Dad, someone shot out the windows in Penny's room," he said. "They've also shot out a window in Elliot's writing room. I've got everybody in your big bathroom because they are no windows, but I don't know what's going on."

"Stay there," Nash boomed, something completely uncharacteristic to his manner. He never boomed. "Stay there and get everyone into the shower. Lock the doors and stay put. I'm on my way."

Beck resisted. "Dad, if they break into the house and get into this room, they'll shoot us like sitting ducks. What's the combination to your gun safe?"

Nash was in Donaldsonville, about fifteen miles from home. He was standing in the driving rain, coordinating rescue efforts of the Village Woods retirement facility that had partially collapsed in the tornado. They had at least two dead, maybe more, but the panicked call from his family had him running back to his car.

"Stay where you're at," he commanded again. "I'll be home in ten minutes."

"Dad, listen to me," Beck yelled back. "I can handle a gun. You may not make it back in time. Tell me the combination to the damn safe!"

Nash jumped into his car, hearing the strength and fear in his son's voice. He didn't want Beck getting hurt, but he was coming to think that those boys were the only thing between life and death for his family until he could get to them. He just didn't want to see anyone get hurt. It was his worst nightmare. Torn, yet knowing what he must do, he forced himself to relent.

"1946," he told him. "Beck, please be careful. Stay down and stay low. I'm calling Sorrento P.D. right now, so do what you can until they get there."

"I will." Beck tossed the phone back to Elliot, grabbing Alec by the arm. "Come on. We need to go."

Alec was up, following Beck to the door as Shane stood up to pursue. But Beck held out a hand to his brother.

"You stay here," he said. Then he pointed at Elliot. "Protect her. I don't care if you have to throw your bullet-riddled body over her, but do it."

Shane wasn't happy at being left behind but nodded seriously. Elliot, sitting on the floor with the phone in her hand, struggled not to weep. She could hear Nash's voice on the phone and she put it to her ear.

"Are you there?" she asked, sniffling.

"I'm here, baby," Nash sounded extraordinarily stressed. "I

gave Beck the combination to the gun safe. He'll be able to protect you until I get there."

"Okay," Elliot's sobs broke through. Her arm was around Penelope and they huddled in a frightened mass. "Oh, my God, Nash, I'm so scared. I'm scared I'm never going to see you again."

He could hear her sobbing and his eyes filled with tears. "I'm coming, baby, I swear to God," he said huskily. "You'll see me again, very soon, and we're going to watch this baby grow up, and our kids grow up, and fill that house with grandkids, I promise. You're going to see me every day for the rest of your life."

Elliot was weeping softly into the phone, unable to reply, and Nash blinked, spattering tears onto his face. They mixed with the rain so no one could see how upset he was.

As he was peeling out of the retirement home parking lot, he caught sight of Ken. The man waved him down and Nash slowed to roll down his window.

"Where are you going?" Ken asked.

Nash was pale with rage, with fear. "Something's happened at the house," he said. "I have to go."

Ken's brow furrowed. "What happened?"

Nash was already rolling up his window. "Shots fired. That's all I know."

He was off, tearing up onto the highway. Ken watched him go, thinking that perhaps he should go along, also. Shots fired was never a good sign, especially at Purgatory, a house that had known more than its share of tragedy. As Ken ran to his patrol unit, he got on the radio to other units in the area.

Shots fired at Purgatory.

In spite of the situation in Donaldsonville, more than one unit responded to the call.

———

Beck and Alec slithered down the central staircase because they figured it was the most protected, away from windows. It was very dark, the only light coming from the porch light that sent muted streams of illumination into the front rooms. With the drapes pulled, there was very little light to see by but enough to move around in.

Wolfgang had stopped his ferocious barking, so they didn't know where the dog was at the moment. Still, they couldn't worry about it. When Beck and Alec reached the bottom of the stairs, they crouched low and scooted across the hall and on into the library.

The gun safe was behind Nash's big, antique desk, tucked up against the wall. A floor-to-ceiling window was next to it and as the boys made a move towards the safe, they could see a couple of shadows out on the porch, dark wraith-like figures casting shadows against the drapes. They were moving slowly, whispering to each other, and Beck and Alec froze as they watched the figures move. Beck was pressed up against the wall as a shadow lingered on the window next to him.

Suddenly, the window shattered as the butt of a rifle came through. Beck reacted instinctively and grabbed the rifle butt, yanking whoever it was into the house. Will Loreau's John Deere hat flew off and landed somewhere near Alec as Beck and Will began fighting over the gun. Alec leapt up and clocked Will on the side of the head, sending the man to the ground. Beck yanked the rifle from his hands and turned it on him, pointing the barrel at his head.

Wolfgang suddenly came flying in from the ballroom, barking viciously. He jumped on Will and chomped his arm, snarling and biting as Alec grabbed the dog and pulled him back. He didn't know any of Wolfgang's commands so he just kept yelling at the dog, hoping he would stop and hoping he would not get bitten in the process. Wolfgang drew blood on Will before Alec was able to pull him off.

As Will lay moaning on the ground, Beck spoke. "You asshole," he snarled. "I ought to blow your brains out right now. What in the hell are you doing?"

Will held his injured arm. "Ya...," he gasped, trying to sit up. "Y'all are thieves and murderers. Y'all are bred from the same stock we are. We is pirates, y'all. We take what we want!"

Beck and Alec looked at the man as if he were insane. "Pirates?" Alec repeated. "Dude, you are seriously whacked. Let's see how much of a pirate you think you are when you're in prison with guys who want to make you their bitch."

Will sat up, unsteadily, looking fearfully at the snarling dog. "That treasure y'all found belongs to us," he said angrily. "It belonged to my family and y'all stole it!"

Neither Beck nor Alec had any idea what he was talking about. "You stupid hillbilly," Alec slapped him in the head. "You can't just break into people's homes and steal stuff. What's wrong with you?"

A voice that wasn't Will's answered.

"He can take what he wants. That's what we're gonna do."

Alec and Beck froze at the sound of the voice as Ed Loreau suddenly appeared in the broken window, a rifle pointed at Beck's head. Ed smiled thinly.

"That treasure belongs to us for all of the wrongs the Aurys ever committed against the Loreaus," he told Beck. "Drop that gun, boy."

Beck wasn't about to drop the gun. "If you shoot me, I'll shoot your brother before I hit the ground. Think about it."

"Then I'll lose a brother, but you'll die. Then I'll take what I want from this house, including that sweet little blond-headed girl."

Infuriated, Alec let the dog go. Wolfgang rushed Ed, knocking him to the ground and latching on to his neck. In the chaos, Ed dropped his gun but Will also kicked up, knocking the rifle from Beck's hands. Beck wasn't close enough to get Ed's rifle as Will picked up the gun and pointed it at Wolfgang.

Alec saw what was happening and rushed Will. The rifle went off, the bullet winging the dog and Wolfgang yelped. As Alec and

Will wrestled for the gun, Beck picked up Ed's gun and whacked Will on the head with it, knocking him to the floor.

Wolfgang was still on top of Ed with his jaws clamped on Ed's neck. There was a big, bloody spot by the dog's hind legs and Alec went to the dog, speaking gently to him to see how badly he was injured. Throughout it all, Wolfgang had never let go of Ed, who was conscious and frozen with panic.

Beck, too, was looking at the dog. He happened to glance down at Ed and make eye contact.

"I don't know his release command," he said frankly. "You'll have to wait until my dad gets here."

Ed just made weird crying noises and closed his eyes as the rain from the broken window blew onto his face. Alec bent over him and thumped him on the head.

"Where's your other brother Daryl, or whatever his name is?" he asked. "Is he going to jump out of the walls with a gun now, too?"

Ed didn't reply, but a soft voice from behind them in the darkened central hallway did. More disembodied voices in the darkness made both Alec and Beck jump.

"No, he's not going to jump from the walls," the voice said.

TWENTY-SIX

SHANE HAD LOCKED the bathroom door after Beck and Alec had left, turning to look at Elliot and Penelope huddled on the floor. Elliot was still talking to Nash, or at least, the line was still open and on speaker. Nash didn't want to hang up so they heard the sirens and police radio on the other end of the phone as Nash raced the fifteen miles or so home to Purgatory. Elliot drew comfort from it, at least for a few minutes, until the bathroom door exploded when someone fired into the lock.

She screamed and dropped the phone, cutting off the call. Elliot and Penelope dove for the protection of the shower as a figure came through the door and whacked Shane across the temple with the butt-end of a rifle. Elliot and Penelope screamed, covering their heads as they cowered in the shower.

Elliot was positive she was about to be killed and she kept trying to cover Penelope's body with her own, but Penelope was working against her and trying to protect her pregnant mother with her own slender body.

They wept in fear, waiting for the gunshots, but none were forthcoming. Elliot eventually peeked between her splayed fingers to see what was going on. A cold wave of shock ran through her as her eyes registered the sight.

Biffy Loreau was standing in the bathroom, looking around at all of the new tile. She had the rifle propped up on her hip in a bizarrely casual gesture for someone who had just blown her way into a room.

"It looks like something out of a magazine," she said, finally looking at Elliot and Penelope in the shower. "I seen this bathroom once before, years ago. I used to know this house pretty well. It all looks so different now."

Elliot was terrified as she watched the woman. "You... you know this house?" she repeated dumbly.

Biffy nodded. "Sure do," she said. "Only it 'tweren't like this when I knew it. It were different. Case's mama and daddy had this big bedroom up front and Case had the bedroom back there. He liked it 'cuz he could look across the bayou to see me."

Elliot had no idea what the woman was talking about but she figured as long as she kept her talking, the less likely the woman was to shoot her and her daughter in cold blood.

"Case Aury?" Elliot clarified. "You knew Case?"

Biffy nodded, eyeing Elliot and Penelope in the shower. She held out her hand. "Y'all come out of there," she said. "I hear y'all is pregnant, Ms. Aury. It ain't good for you in there. Come on out."

Penelope moved first, slowly and unsteadily, pulling her mother out behind her. Elliot's pajamas didn't conceal her rounded belly and Biffy alternately eyed the belly, the bathroom, and Elliot.

"Back when I was a young girl, Case Aury and I had eyes for each other," she said after a moment. "Case was older than I was. I was just a girl of thirteen or so. Case was supposed to marry Jewel le Blanc but he loved me instead. His mama and daddy made him leave me alone, but not before I got pregnant with Femmie."

Elliot's eyes widened. "Case Aury was Femmie's father?"

Biffy nodded as if it were no great revelation. She was very matter of fact about it. "Did Nash never tell y'all that?"

Elliot was shocked. "No, he didn't."

Biffy shrugged. "He probably didn't know," she said, disgust and sadness in her tone now. "The Aurys were an uppity bunch.

They didn't want anyone to know that Case got a Loreau girl pregnant. It would have shamed their high and mighty family. They gave me some money so I wouldn't tell anyone, and Case went on to marry Jewel and had Nash's daddy shortly thereafter."

Elliot's mouth was hanging open. She suddenly wasn't so afraid anymore, for reasons she couldn't explain. "So Nash and Femmie....?"

"Femmie was Nash's uncle," Biffy was back to being matter of fact. "Will 'n Ed 'n Nicky are Nash's cousins."

Elliot had to make a conscious effort to close her mouth. "Oh, my God," she looked at Biffy seriously. "Do your grandsons know that?"

Biffy shook her head. "Naw, they don't know," she said. "When the Aurys gave us the money, we hushed up. My mama wouldn't even let me tell Femmie. She was afraid the Aurys would take the money back, so I raised Femmie without the Aury name. I never had a choice 'bout it."

Elliot was starting to feel very sorry for the woman. *No wonder she's such an angry bitch all the time.* "I'm so sorry to hear that they treated you that way," she said seriously. "That wasn't right."

Biffy eyed Elliot to see if she was sincere, torn between anger and gratitude. "No, it ain't," she finally said. "That's why we come here tonight."

"Why?"

"Because we heard about the treasure. We're family, too. It should belong to us, too."

Elliot couldn't really disagree with her. She thought hard on her next course of action, hoping it could get her and the kids out of this situation and perhaps right an old wrong in the process. The terrifying night was taking an odd turn.

"Ms. Biffy," she began. "If what you say is true, and I don't have any reason to not believe you, then I think you should be entitled to a share of the Purgatory horde. Nash and I are going to donate most of it, but I don't have a problem with sharing some of it with you. Maybe you could sell it and fix up The Bottoms, and have money for your grandsons to go to school or build their own homes. I seriously don't have any problem sharing it. But you didn't have to break in here tonight and scare us all to death."

Biffy looked at her with surprise. "Y'all... y'all is willing to give us our due?"

Elliot nodded. "I'm sure Nash will agree once he's heard your story," she said. "But for now, can you please call your grandsons off if they are the ones who shot out my windows? I don't want them to hurt my boys."

Biffy still looked dubious, but she seemed shocked more than anything. The evening wasn't turning out exactly as she envisioned it, but that wasn't an entirely bad thing. Elliot took the lead, trying to give the standoff some direction.

"Let's go downstairs and talk about this, okay?" she said. "I'll even show you what we've found so far."

Biffy thought on the offer, slowly nodding her head. Elliot took her still-terrified daughter by the hand and, together, they went to Shane, who was starting to come around.

Penelope put cold water on a cloth and wiped it over his face, trying to bring him to some level of consciousness. Elliot watched her daughter tend the young man and thought it might be a very good idea to leave those two behind, safe from the Loreaus who seemed to be infiltrating the house. She wanted to keep them out of the line of fire.

"Penny, you stay with Shane," she instructed. "I'm going to take Ms. Biffy downstairs."

Penelope shook her head frantically but Elliot countered calmly. "Yes, please. Shane needs you right now. I'll be fine."

She could hear Penelope's soft weeping as she left the room and led Biffy into the upper hall. She was about to say something to the women when she heard a gun go off downstairs. Startled, she started to run, with tubby Biffy trying to keep pace with her, taking the stairs quickly and running towards the sound of a scuffle.

As they approached the library, she heard Alec ask about the other Loreau brother. Biffy was behind her, seeing the situation that her grandsons had gotten themselves into, and she responded to Alec's question.

"No, he's not going to jump out of the walls," she said, watching a pair of startled faces turn to her. "Nicky didn't make it tonight. But I did, and I just had an interesting chat with your mama."

"Mam!" Will cried. "Tell 'em to pull the dog off!"

Biffy took a few steps forward to see more clearly in the darkness that Wolfgang had Ed pinned and she looked at Elliot, enraged.

"I'm gonna shoot that dog!" she hollered.

"No!" Elliot rushed forward, calling to the dog. "Wolfgang, no! Alec, get him off of that man!"

Alec went to Wolfgang and pulled and yanked the dog back, finally able to force the pooch to release his hold. Wolfgang allowed Alec to pull him away as Ed sat up, rubbing his neck. There was blood on his hands.

"That dog bit me!" he declared. "I'm gonna kill it!"

Elliot threw out her hands to all parties concerned. "No one is killing that dog," she said firmly. "He was just protecting the house. If you hadn't come around shooting out my windows and breaking in, he would have never attacked you. So nobody is shooting that dog. Got it?"

Biffy still stood in the library entry, rifle in hand, eyeing the dog next to Alec who was now licking the wound on his hindquarters. Realizing she probably wouldn't get what she wanted if she shot the dog, she turned away from the animal and moved into the library.

As the rain pounded and occasional lightning lit up the room, Biffy could see what a beautiful room it was. As Elliot moved for Alec and Beck to make sure they were all right, Biffy moved for Ed and Will, sitting up on the floor with blood on them.

"Ms. Biffy," Elliot finally said to the woman, her arms around Alec and Beck. "It makes a lot of sense now why the Loreaus are the way they are. Your family history and the history of the Aurys is so deeply intertwined that it's nearly the same. I realize that saying sorry doesn't make it better but I think in this case, actions speak louder than words, although I sincerely wish you all hadn't broken in here tonight. I'm not sure how Nash is going to take it."

Biffy looked down at her grandsons, bloodied and beaten. She sighed faintly.

"Them boys was only doin' what I told 'em to do," she moved in front of the big window that faced out over the driveway, inspecting Nash's antique desk. "Whatever hate they have has come from me. My hate has come from generations of Loreaus who thought they'd been wronged."

"What do you think now?" Elliot asked. "Ms. Biffy, I'd be happy to welcome you into the family. It sounds like you belong here as much as the rest of us."

Biffy wasn't quite sure what to say to that. She looked down at Will and Ed, who were gazing up at their grandma with an expression between resentment and curiosity. Biffy just shook her head after a moment.

"I don't know what I think," she said quietly. "But I do know that I've missed this house and I've missed Case. I've missed him all these years. Can I get a look at that back bedroom just one more time? It's where I conceived Femmie, ya know."

Elliot smiled faintly. "If you put that gun down, I'll show you the whole house."

Biffy returned Elliot's smile, reluctantly, but it was the last thing Elliot saw before the front window exploded and Ms. Biffy's head along with it. Elliot screamed and threw herself against Alec as glass and bloody tissue blasted into the room.

Suddenly, the front door was flying open and men with guns were bolting in through the door and the shattered windows of the library, shouting and creating chaos.

Elliot huddled between Alec and Beck, terrified, as the men with weapons swarmed the room. Someone rushed up and grabbed her, and she screamed until she realized it was Nash. Bursting into tears, she threw herself against him and he picked her up, carrying her quickly from the chaos of the library. Alec and Beck followed close behind.

Nash made it into the ballroom before trusting himself to speak. He was so wound up, so terrified at what he would find at Purgatory, that he was in shock to realize that Elliot was in one piece. He'd had his doubts.

"Are you all right, baby?" He was holding her so tightly that he was crushing her. "Are you hurt?"

Elliot had her arms around his neck as he held her against his chest. "No," she sobbed. "I'm fine. Beck, Alec and Penny are fine, but Shane was knocked in the head. He's upstairs with Penny."

They could hear more shouting out towards the library as well as things banging about, and Elliot's head came out of Nash's neck.

"Tell them not to wreck my house," she said, struggling to be put down. "It was Biffy, Will and Ed Loreau, and they're all in the library. There's no one else as far as I know."

Nash had his hands on her face, inspecting her to make sure she was all right, indeed. He had to see for himself. "Are you sure?"

She shook her head. "I'm sure," she insisted. "Nash, Wolfie got shot. He was in the library last I saw him."

Nash was concerned for the dog, but not nearly as concerned as he was for his pregnant wife. Seeing that she was sound and whole, he let out the biggest pent-up sigh he could summon and put his arms around her, holding her tightly.

"Sweet Jesus," he breathed, allowing himself to feel some relief after twenty-three minutes of utter terror between the time he got her call and the time he ran into the house and pulled her into his arms. "Thank God y'all are all right. I had no idea what I was going to find when I came home. What in the hell happened?"

Before Elliot could answer, Ken stuck his head into the room. His gun was still in his hand. "All clear down here, Nash," he said, looking at Elliot, Beck and Alec. "We're moving upstairs."

Elliot looked at him. "That's not necessary," she assured him. "It was just those three in the library."

"You're sure, Ms. Aury?"

Elliot nodded. "I'm sure. But someone might want to take Shane over to the hospital. Ms. Biffy hit him pretty hard."

Ken backed out of the room as Nash, satisfied that Elliot was alive and well, turned his attention to Beck and Alec to inspect them as well. The boys shrugged him off even though Alec had the beginnings of a lovely black eye. Nash was so relieved he seriously thought he might cry, but his thoughts turned to the kids upstairs. He took Elliot by the hand.

"I need to see Shane and Penny," he said.

The four of them went upstairs to find it empty and the door to Shane's bedroom locked. Nash pounded on the door, assuring the kids that it was okay to open the door, and Penelope opened the old panel and threw her arms around her mother, weeping. She hugged Nash, too, before he could get into the bedroom to see Shane, who was on his bed with a big washcloth on his head.

Nash checked the bump on his son's head, trying to talk him into having it checked out, but Shane didn't want to go to the hospital. Rather than argue with him, Nash just let it go. He was too relieved to get upset or argue over anything at the moment.

As he turned for Elliot, Wolfgang suddenly appeared, wagging his tail and looking worn out. Penelope saw the dog and ran to him, hugging him and cooing at him as she tried to get a look at the wound on his back leg. Nash held the dog, getting a look as well, and saw that the bullet had just skimmed him. He petted the dog on the head.

"Good boy," he said. "We're going to take you over to the vet in the morning to get that looked at."

"He was really fierce, dude," Alec said with some enthusiasm. "He attacked those dudes who broke in and chewed them up pretty good. He was awesome."

Nash smiled faintly, petting the dog on the head again. "I'm glad he was here."

Everyone agreed and Wolfgang got more pets and hugs. As the kids focused on the dog, Nash took Elliot by the hand and pulled her down onto the second bed.

"Now," he said softly. "Tell me what happened."

Elliot was remarkably calm given the events of the evening. She held Nash's hand tightly as she told him of the broken windows, of no power, and of being herded into the bathroom by Beck and Alec, who took charge of the situation. She was very proud of them. She told him about Beck and Alec going downstairs to retrieve the guns and of Biffy Loreau shooting the lock off the bathroom door.

Beck and Alec kicked in with their version of what happened downstairs, how Will and Ed tried to break in and how they all fought for their lives. It was a vivid and harrowing tale, one that made Elliot sick to listen to. It also underscored their bravery, of young men growing into fine and courageous adults.

The boys told their story until the point where Biffy Loreau lost her head. From there, everything seemed to trail off. Nash turned to Elliot, who had fallen oddly silent through everything. She just sat there, looking pale and tired, and he put his arm around her.

"Well," he said decisively. "I think the best thing we can all do is get back to bed for now. Sorrento P.D. should be here any moment and I'm going to cover up the broken windows with...."

"We'll help, Dad," Beck said, motioning to Alec. "We'll do the windows in Penny's room and in Elliot's writing room. I didn't check to see if any more were broken other than the library windows downstairs, but I don't think so."

"I'll do the library," Nash told them, thinking that it was now a crime scene. "In fact, I should probably get down there to see what's going on."

Shane, with the knock on the head, was told to stay awake by his father, who turned the television on for him before he left the room. Penelope volunteered to stay with Shane, even when her mother insisted she go back to bed. Penelope compromised by climbing into the second bed in the room and covering up, determined to keep Shane awake because of his head injury.

As Alec and Beck went about gathering trash bags, duct tape

and plastic wrap to cover up the broken windows, Nash took Elliot back to their bedroom.

"I'm going to take Shane to the hospital when I'm finished downstairs," he muttered. "I know he hates hospitals, but he needs to be looked at."

Elliot nodded. "I agree," she said as they entered their bedroom. It was dark and she went to light one of her many candles, turning to Nash as the soft glow filled the room. "Now that this is all over, I feel kind of weak."

His brow furrowed with concern. "Do you feel sick?"

She shook her head. "No, not like that," she said, her gaze moving over his face. "Just... wiped out. Ms. Biffy and I had an interesting conversation as she held a gun on me."

Nash set her down on the bed. "What about?"

Elliot lay back on the pillows, gazing up at him as he stood over her. "She said that Case Aury was Femmie's father. Did you know that?"

Nash scratched his head and averted his gaze as he sat down on the bed beside her. "No, not for certain," he said after a moment. "I'd heard rumor of it all my life, of course, but no one would ever confirm it, least of all my granddad. So she told you that?"

Elliot nodded, reaching out to take his hand. He held on to her tightly. "She said that the Aurys paid her money to keep quiet when they found out she was pregnant," she explained. "She said they didn't want the shame of it. Do you think it's all true?"

Nash shrugged. "I don't know," he said. "Probably. I think my dad thinks so."

"He's mentioned it before?"

"Once, in passing. He said something once about Femmie having Case's eyes, but I never gave it much thought. I guess... I guess I probably should now."

Elliot toyed with his big fingers. "Biffy said they came tonight because of the treasure," she told him. "She said she wanted her due. You know, it's funny, but she didn't seem really angry or crazy tonight other than the fact she was wielding a rifle. She seemed calm... like she wanted to talk. She also just wanted to see Purgatory because she said she had a lot of memories about the house. By the time you guys charged in, she was very calm. I think I could have talked her into giving up her gun. I feel kind of sorry that you guys did what you did to her. I don't think it was necessary."

Nash looked at her, almost angrily. "Baby, I wasn't going to take that chance. We could see the silhouette of someone up against the window and they were clearly holding a gun. Knowing my entire family was in the house, I was going to shoot first and ask questions later. I'm sorry if that upsets you, but that's just the way it is."

"I know," she said quietly because he was starting to get riled up. She studied his profile as he looked at her hands, lifting one up to kiss it. "Nash, who fired the shot that killed Biffy?"

He looked at her again. "Does it matter?"

"No," she whispered. "I just wanted to know."

He leaned over her, bracing both arms on either side of her as he looked her seriously in the eye. There was something set and deadly to his gaze, something Elliot had only seen once since she had known him. It was the look of a man who knew when to make a life or death decision.

"I got a hysterical call from my wife tonight telling me that someone is shooting out the windows of our home," his voice was low and steady. "I leave the scene of a disaster to fly home with five other deputies who should be working the disaster scene but are instead going home with me to save my family. I pull up and see someone in the library with a gun in their hand. My entire family's lives are at stake, including the life of my wife and unborn baby. Now, if you were in my shoes, would you have pulled the trigger?"

He was deadly serious. "Without hesitation," she whispered.

He nodded, seeing the sincerity in her eyes. Leaning down, he kissed her soft mouth, tasting her flesh. Scooping her up against his chest, he kissed her fiercely, realizing how close he came to never tasting her again. It scared the wits from him but he reminded himself that she was safe, warm and alive in his arms. That was all that mattered.

"I love you, Ellie Aury," he breathed against her. "I would kill or die for you. Don't ever doubt that, not ever."

"I don't." She held him fiercely. "I love you so much, Nash. Pirate treasure, ghosts and crazy neighbors aside, buying Purgatory was the best thing I ever did."

He couldn't dispute it. In fact, he pulled back to smile at her. "Selling it to you was the best thing *I* ever did."

Elliot wholeheartedly agreed.

TWENTY-SEVEN
FEBRUARY

"HURRY UP," Elliot said. "We don't know when she's going to come tonight, so we need to hurry this up."

It was dark and cold outside, a full moon rising over the bayou. Elliot and Dr. Clarke were standing next to the trench area between the house and the ruined stable block. They were watching Nash, Alec and Shane down in the dark, moist trench with three big, white, wooden boxes. Alec looked up at his mother and frowned.

"Just because you're, like, fifteen months pregnant doesn't mean you can boss us all around like this," he grumped.

As Dr. Clarke grinned, Elliot cocked an eyebrow at her son. Bundled up against the cold February temperature, her enormous belly was evident. She looked like a round, little Eskimo. Before she could respond, Nash put his hand on Alec's shoulder and turned him back to the task at hand.

"Yes, she can, son," he told Alec stoically. "She can boss us around as much as she wants."

Elliot fought off a grin as Alec grumbled. "That's mean," he said. "It's cruel. It's mean and cruel."

"That may be, but if you keep your mouth shut, you'll live longer."

Alec did as he was told as he, Nash and Shane arranged the boxes in the cold and dark trench. Above their head, a full moon was filling the sky and Elliot noticed that the fireflies were starting to come out in force. A soft breeze began to blow and the old spirit bottles in the trees rattled gently. Dr. Clarke looked up from the trench, addressing the sound.

"Hear the spirit bottles?" she asked. "Eudora Welty, the great Mississippi writer, wrote a short story about a spirit in a bottle. It's said that if spirit bottles are hung from trees with a little water in them, they prevent spirits from going into the house. Maybe that is what's kept Sophie from coming into the house all of these years and making contact with her children."

Elliot listened seriously. "Should we cut the spirit bottles down?"

"Not unless you want more ghosts coming inside your house."

Elliot shook her head. "I don't think so." She looked at the men in the trench. "The boxes look fine. Hurry up and come out of there."

Nash deftly climbed up out of the trench, helping Shane out as Alec crawled out himself. As they all headed back for the house, Alec kept turning around and looking at the trench behind them. Elliot, burrowed against Nash as he walked her towards the house, noticing her son's distraction.

"What are you looking at?" she asked him.

Alec shrugged, casting a lingering look at the three boxes in the trench.

"This is kind of weird," he looked at his mother. "Are you sure she'll come?"

Elliot wriggled her eyebrows. "I hope so," she said honestly. "That's why we did this."

"But it's like... like ghost bait."

"Not ghost bait," Elliot countered. "Nash and I have seen the ghost of what we think is Sophie MacGregor during a full moon. She always comes from the direction of the stables and disappears as soon as she reaches the trench. And ever since we opened the crypt, the little ghost comes out...."

Alec lifted a hand to cut her off; he'd heard the story many times. "I know," he said. "You think the little ghost is one of Sophie's children, looking for his mom."

"You don't sound like you believe it."

Alec threw up his hands in a shrugging gesture. "I believe it," he insisted. "I've seen the little ghost. I'm just scared of it."

Elliot laughed, reaching out to put her arm around her son as they reached the porch.

"I just think it's so sad that Sophie's ghost wanders around, looking for her children, just as her children are inside looking for her," she sighed sadly. "We had to wait until all of the bodies were excavated before we could do this, but those three boxes contain the bones of Joseph, Felicity and Saturnine. Maybe if Sophie comes tonight, she'll find what she's been looking for all this time. She never goes any further than that trench, so that's why we put the bones in the trench."

Alec knew that. He paused on the porch, looking out over the yard, seeing the fireflies, the grayish cast from the full moon. He turned quickly and headed for the kitchen door.

"I'm still scared," he said.

"Then go back inside. You don't have to stay out here and watch."

Alec was glad to go back into the warm house and away from the ghost bait. Shane followed him inside as Dr. Clarke, Nash and Elliot remained on the porch for a moment. It was quite nippy outside and Nash wrapped his big arms around Elliot as they gazed up at the full moon. Beside them, Dr. Clarke spoke softly.

"Nowhere in America is the history of the land so rich with lore and magic," she said quietly, her gaze moving over the yard. "I studied the culture of Louisiana because I wanted to understand it, but what I came to realize is that I'll never fully understand it. Tonight, perhaps I'll understand even less."

Nash and Elliot looked over at her. "Why do you say that?" Elliot asked.

Dr. Clarke smiled at her. "Because the realm of spirits isn't meant to be understood. If Sophie MacGregor still walks this earth searching for her murdered children, what torment she must face."

Elliot could only imagine. The wind blew again and the spirit bottles tinkled in the trees again. Elliot looked off in the direction of the trees.

"Those bottles were here when I bought the place," she said quietly. "They're in the front of the house, the back of the house... now I wonder if they were put up because a previous owner, or maybe many previous owners, saw Sophie wandering around, too."

Dr. Clarke could only wonder right along with her. They sat outside in the cold and darkness, talking about ghosts and legends. Eventually, Nash tried to get them to come inside but they refused, instead, sitting on a pair of cushioned wicker chairs that were on the porch just outside of the ballroom.

Nash went inside and emerged with a blanket for both ladies, who accepted their blankets gratefully. Nash pulled Elliot over to the matching wicker couch and shared her blanket, watching the yard, waiting for whatever was to happen.

All of the lights on the north side of the house were off so that no artificial light was cast upon this portion of the yard. Fireflies danced in the darkness as the moon crept higher into the sky.

"It's really too bad we never found Sophie's coffin," Elliot whispered, listening to the night birds call. "I had really hoped we might find it somewhere."

Nash was snuggled up against her, his face on the top of her head as he watched the ghostly landscape.

"It's like we discussed once before," he said softly. "She's either alligator food or she's on unholy ground somewhere. Maybe we'll never know."

Elliot sighed thoughtfully. "Maybe," she agreed. "But I was thinking... she always comes from the stable area. Maybe her body is buried over there somewhere."

As Nash nodded, Dr. Clarke spoke. "Dr. Whitney and I have examined that entire area but we haven't come across any burials yet. For all of the artifacts we've found and the foundations we've excavated, I'm fairly certain the entire area was a bustling support community for Purgatory."

Nash pulled Elliot closer as the temperature seemed to drop. "When I was a kid, there were still a couple of shacks standing out there," he said. "We weren't allowed to go near them, but I do remember that they were there."

Dr. Clarke nodded. "Purgatory has been hugely rich in history and relics. We're learning so much from it on a daily basis. It's been a treasure trove in every sense of the word."

The three of them fell silent again as the night birds sang and the fireflies danced. It was a little spooky over the bayou with the soft wind and full moon, waiting for a ghost to make an appearance. They sat and waited until Elliot fell asleep.

Nash made her move back inside because it was getting so cold, but she wouldn't leave the ballroom because it faced out over the trench section of the yard.

With the new HVAC system blowing warm air throughout the house, Elliot lay on a couch as Nash and Dr. Clarke stood by one of the massive windows that overlooked the entire yard. Weary, and very pregnant, Elliot fell asleep again. She was slumbering deep and dreamlessly when someone shook her awake.

"Ellie," it was Nash, whispering her name. "Hurry, honey. She's back."

Groggy but awake, Elliot sat up with a good deal of help from Nash. He helped her to her feet as she staggered over to the window, rubbing her eyes. Dr. Clarke was there, pointing into the yard.

"Do you see her?" Dr. Clarke whispered excitedly. "She's over by the stable. See the gray mist? It's been there for about a minute. It hasn't moved."

Elliot blinked her eyes, struggling to focus. She could, indeed, see the faint gray mist through the trees, just as she had seen it a few times before. Instantly, she was wide awake and excited.

"I hope this works," she breathed. "That poor woman has been through so much. I really hope this works."

Nash wrapped his arms around her and the three of them stood in the window, watching the gray mist form in the trees. It seemed to mix with the strands of moonbeams piercing the canopy, eventually taking shape and moving towards the house.

Sophie's long dress waved as if being blown by an unseen breeze. It danced and undulated as she moved through the shadows, the strands of her long hair gently blowing as well. She would disappear almost completely in the shadows and then come out full force once she hit the brilliant beams of the full moon.

Elliot, Nash and Dr. Clarke watched, spellbound, as Sophie emerged from the trees and approached the trench. She seemed to ripple as she walked, like the ripples of water across a lake, an intangible visual illusion of moonlight and magic. Everyone watched, wrought with anticipation, as she finally came upon the trench. When she finally touched the rocky edge, she suddenly fizzled away and disappeared.

The three of them stood there, waiting for something more to happen, but the yard remained still and silent. For several long moments, nothing happened. Nash finally sighed, looking to Dr. Clarke, who merely stood there and sadly shook her head.

In Nash's arms, Elliot was wiping away the tears on her face. Nash could see that she was weeping and he hugged her gently.

"What's the matter, honey?" he kissed the side of her head.

Elliot was genuinely sad. "I really thought... oh, I don't know," she sniffled and wiped her face. "I really thought she'd find her children. I wanted her to, so much. It's so sad that they're searching for each other and can never find one another. So we brought her babies to her and she still can't find them? That's just tragic."

Dr. Clarke turned to look at her. "There are two types of hauntings, Ellie," she said. "There's a residual haunting in which the spirit is merely repeating motions he or she did in life, like a tape recorder being played over and over, and then there are intelligent hauntings where the spirit will actually try to make contact with you. Since Sophie did the same thing, night after night, it's just possible that it's a residual haunting and she's just doing the same thing over and over. Maybe she wasn't looking for anything at all."

Elliot shrugged, disappointed. "Maybe," she said. "It's still sad, though. Maybe they're all just a residual haunting and I was just making a big deal out of...."

She suddenly froze, her eyes widening as she beheld something out in the yard. Both Dr. Clarke and Nash looked to see what had her so riveted and in doing so, both of them appeared shocked as well. Emerging from the trench, as if a doorway from another world had suddenly opened and spilled them forth, were people.

A woman in a long and elaborate dress, with luscious dark hair and a beautiful face, emerged from thin air, turning to smile at two teenaged children who suddenly emerged behind her. There was a tall, good looking young man in nineteenth century clothing and a young lady wearing a lovely yellow gown. As the older woman reached out her hand, two more children emerged from the unseen doorway.

The younger children were under ten years of age, both boys, both in short pants and jackets with frilly cuffs on the sleeves. They were dark-haired and handsome, one of them taking the older woman's hand very happily.

As Dr. Clarke, Nash and Elliot watched with shock, these people, as solid and real as living beings, happily walked off towards the trees, gradually turning from color to grayscale, and from grayscale to mist. The older woman picked up the youngest child, hugging him as they both evaporated into the night. One by one, they disappeared near the old stables, vanishing into air as if they had never existed at all.

All but one. The second youngest child was the last one to go. He paused as the others faded away, turning to the house and seemingly looking right at the window where Elliot and Dr. Clarke and Nash were watching them. He was such a handsome lad in his fancy clothes, his dark hair in stark contrast to his very pale skin. He stood there a moment, watching them as they were watching him, before raising a hand.

It was a wave, or a sign of thanks, or perhaps an acknowledgement. It was just a lifted hand, in their direction, before the child turned around and ran after the others who had disappeared in the trees. Soon, he too was gone, vanished like a puff of smoke, and for a full minute after he was gone, no one said a word. They just stood there and stared.

Elliot was the first one to break the spell. She went up to the window and put her hands on it as if to touch the spirits who had just passed on into the next world.

Awed, she swallowed hard as she groped for the words to describe what she had just witnessed.

"Did... did you guys see that?" she finally whispered.

While Nash just nodded, Dr. Clarke actually spoke. "I did," she murmured.

"Really?"

"Really."

Elliot shook her head, slowly, as if she still couldn't believe it. "What a privilege," she said, turning to Nash and Dr. Clarke. "What a privilege it was to witness that. I... I can't think of any other way to describe it. But was I the only one to notice that there were four children with her and not just three?"

Nash was dumbstruck but he managed to understand her question. "Paul-Michel was with her," he said. "We didn't even put his bones in the trench because of what he did, but I'll be damned if he wasn't with her. She found him. I wonder why?"

Elliot was still focused on the shadowed landscape beyond. "Because he was Sophie's first son," she whispered. "She forgave him. Maybe she figured he's spent enough time in the bowels of Purgatory and forgave him."

Dr. Clarke smiled timidly, still quite stunned at what she had seen. She wanted to go back outside and look around for herself but as she moved for the door, she put her hand on Elliot's arm.

"I have always believed in Heaven, but now I know it's true," she said. "Praise the Lord. Sophie and her children have finally found peace."

Elliot smiled as the woman went back outside again, turning to Nash as he stood there in the darkness of the room. She went to him, wrapping her arms around his waist as he pulled her close. The emotions she was feeling from him, from the situation in general, was enough to bring tears to her eyes. The whole scene had been overwhelmingly emotional.

"That was the most amazing thing I've ever seen," Elliot whispered. "Did I just dream that?"

He hugged her. "If you did, I dreamed it right along with you," he murmured. "I have to say, that was the most amazing thing I've ever seen. If someone had told me about that, I never would have believed them. But seeing it for myself... I'm still not sure what I really saw."

Elliot gazed up at him. "You saw *us*," she murmured. "No matter where you are, or how far apart we are, ever, we'll always be together again, forever. I'll never stop looking for you in death or in life. Like Sophie, I'll just keep coming back again and again until someone figures out what I'm looking for."

He smiled and kissed her. There wasn't much more he could say to that except for what he had said to her daily from almost the moment he had met her.

"I love you," he whispered.

When Elliot finally went to bed that night, her dreams were of mists, of lovely dark-haired ladies, and of young boys with ruffles who had finally found peace.

EPILOGUE
ONE MONTH LATER

"DAD, she won't let us hold her," Shane was rightfully angry. "She tells us to be quiet every time we get around her. She won't even let us breathe when we're anywhere near her!"

Nash stood in the entry to the enormous double parlors, his gaze on Penelope as she cradled an infant in one of the fat period chairs that decorated the lavish room. He had just gotten home from work and found a standoff in his own living room. Penelope was very territorial of her prize.

"That's because you guys are too noisy and too rough," she hissed. "She's sleeping now and I don't want you guys to wake her up."

Nash put his hand on Shane's shoulder comfortingly. "Does that go for all of us, including me?" he asked her. "She's my child, after all. I'd really like to hold her."

Penelope regarded Nash dubiously. "Well...," she said slowly. "If you're careful. Mom told me to watch out for her while she took a nap and that's what I'm doing."

Nash fought off a grin as he crossed the room into the protective female's lair. He went to Penelope and kissed her on the top of the head as he leaned down over the baby and kissed her as well.

"Hello, Sophie," he whispered, kissing the sweet, little face again. "How's my beautiful girl today? She looks peaceful, doesn't she?"

Penelope nodded, gazing adoringly at her little sister. "That's why I don't want the boys waking her up. She was up all night and Mom is exhausted."

Nash glanced over at the three frowning faces in the doorway. "I don't think they'll be rough with her," he tried to convince Penelope. "They'll sit right down on the couch and hold her. They won't move her around."

"Shane took her outside yesterday," Penelope accused angrily.

Nash cast Shane a long look and the boy put up his hands as if to defend himself. "I just took her on the porch. The weather was fine and there weren't any bugs. I let her see what it looks like out there."

Penelope was gearing up for a retort but Nash put his hands up to quiet the mob. "She's only four days old, Shane. I don't think being outside right now means a whole lot to her. Don't do it again, please."

Shane made an angry face but kept his mouth shut. In Penelope's arms, Sophie started to stir and Nash reached down to collect his precious, little daughter.

Even as he held her, he could hardly believe she was his. She was the sweetest thing on earth, the culmination of dreams he didn't even know he had. When he looked at her, he saw Elliot. Sometimes the emotion of it was enough to bring tears to his eyes. The night she was born, he'd just stared at her for hours with tears running down his face.

He cradled the baby against his chest, cooing softly to her as the boys decided it was safe and rushed into the room to see her. Penelope stood up and the boys cooled their enthusiasm, eyeing her threatening expression. As the older children regarded each other in various stages of anger and uncertainty, Elliot entered the room.

Exhausted as most new mother's tended to be, she still looked radiant and lovely. Dressed in one of her jogging suits that emphasized her huge nursing mother's breasts, she smiled when Nash looked up and saw her. Love and happiness filled the air between them.

"Hi," he said sweetly. "Did I wake you?"

Elliot shook her head and yawned. "No," she replied, coming up behind Beck and Shane and putting her hands on their shoulders affectionately. "I was already awake when I heard your car pull in."

Nash's gaze lingered on her a moment, conveying a thousand words of adoration, before looking back to the blond little bundle in his arms.

"My mother says we should make her stay awake during the day so she'll sleep at night," he said helpfully. "She says that's what she did with me and Beau. We turned out all right."

Elliot shook her head and pushed through the boys to get to the baby. "I'm a firm believer that babies will make their own schedule," she said, peering at the infant in her husband's arms. "She'll sleep through the night when she's ready. She's only four days old, for Heaven's Sake. Give her time."

Nash just smiled, gently rocking the baby who was becoming increasingly fussy. "My mother also said she sent some gifts for her. Did they come?"

Elliot rolled her eyes while the older children laughed. "Are you serious?" she said. "Nash, she sent more stuff than this baby will ever use. She sent a bed and a bathtub, boxes of towels, more little dresses than I've ever seen, and a gold necklace with her name on it. You should see all of the stuff!"

Nash laughed softly. "Did she send the fifteen hundred dollar bassinet?"

Elliot backed down a little. "Well, yes... but it was the only thing out of all of that stuff that I really wanted."

Nash grinned at her; as long as she got her precious bassinet, she was happy.

"You have to understand that the woman had two boys and then four grandsons," he reminded her. "This is the first girl in two generations, so she's understandably overjoyed. You're just going to have to be patient with her."

Elliot sighed irritably, lifting her eyebrows when he looked at her. "Well, the baby isn't even a week old and already she's spoiling her. She needs to back off a little."

"I'll make the sacrifice," Alec said helpfully. "She can spoil me."

The others laughed at him as Elliot went to Nash and reached out for the baby. "I need to feed her," she said.

Nash didn't want to relinquish his prize so easily. "Let me hold her just a little longer," he begged. "I haven't seen her all day."

"She's going to start crying."

Nash didn't want to see her cry but he didn't want to give her up, either. "*I'm* going to start to cry if you at least won't let me carry her upstairs."

Elliot laughed, putting her hand on his back protectively as Nash, very carefully began to walk from the room, like he was afraid he was going to drop the baby. Elliot called over her shoulder to the grown children.

"Alligator ribs tonight," she told them. "I'm paying. Who's driving?"

Nash took one hand off his daughter and dug in his pocket, tossing the keys for the Lexus back to the group. Alec made a flying leap but was tackled by Shane. Beck caught the keys but his happiness was short-lived when Penelope held out her hand to him and smiled very sweetly. A sucker for a pretty girl, Beck did the gentlemanly thing and handed them over.

Nash and Elliot paused in the doorway of the big parlor, watching the interaction between the four. Nash shook his head and continued walking towards the stairs.

"With the way those four act, you'd think they all grew up together," he commented.

Elliot walked along beside him, still stiff and sore from the difficult birth. At almost nine pounds, Sophie Elizabeth Aury had been a lot to push out for petite Elliot. She had about fifteen stitches down in her nether regions and she was still so sore below the waist that even her ankles were sore. She was moving slowly as they approached the stairs. Nash watched her gingerly take the steps.

"Are you all right?" he asked, reaching out a hand to take her elbow as she moved up the stairs. "Can I help you?"

"I'll be okay," she grunted. "You hold on to the banister so you don't fall."

Nash did as he was told and grasped the banister until they reached the top. They disappeared into their lavish master bedroom, shutting the door softly behind them.

Nash held the baby as Elliot slowly climbed onto the bed, grunting as she tried to make her sore body comfortable. Propping herself up with some pillows, she unzipped the jogging suit and unhooked the nursing bra from the front. Both breasts sprang free and she winced.

"Oh, my God," she breathed, her hands holding her breasts still to keep them from painfully moving around. "I never knew I could be so sore. Every part of my body is killing me."

"I'm sorry to hear that," Nash said softly. "But you're still the most beautiful woman I've ever seen."

She softened, smiling at him. "You're so sweet."

"It's true."

Elliot grinned as he handed the baby over to her. Then Nash kicked his shoes off and stretched out beside Elliot, leaning up against her as she put Sophie on a nipple. The baby latched on and began suckling strongly as Elliot settled down to nurse. Nash lay against her, his cheek against Elliot's arm, his hand on the soft, bare skin of her belly as she nursed their baby.

"I could just watch this forever," he murmured.

Elliot gently caressed Sophie's blond head. "I still can't believe she's here," she said. "It wasn't even a week ago that I was lying in this bed, crying about how I couldn't see my feet. I don't know how you put up with me."

Nash grinned, reaching up to grasp fat baby fingers. "There

wasn't anything to put up with," he said. "You were pregnant and miserable. I understood that."

"You were a saint."

He laughed, remembering back during the nine months of a very moody pregnancy. "I still think eating whipped cream straight out of the spray can was the best," he said, chuckling. "That was the funniest thing I'd ever seen."

Elliot was torn between irritation and humor. "I couldn't help it," she insisted. "It was the only thing I wanted to eat."

He started laughing at the memory. "My poor baby," he kissed her arm. "I know it wasn't easy. But the Jell-O thing was pretty funny, too."

"Don't start that again."

His laughter grew. "Bowls and bowls of green Jell-O. Jell-O everywhere. I can never look at Jell-O again."

Elliot just shook her head, fighting off a grin. Sophie was eating ravenously and she stroked the little cheek.

"She was worth it," she said dreamily. "Look how beautiful she is."

Nash wasn't hard pressed to agree. "She's only four days old and already she has everyone under her control," he said. "What's going to happen when she's a year old or two years old? She's going to have four older siblings who are going to spoil her rotten."

Elliot smiled when she thought on that prospect. She could already see a blond toddler running the household.

"A year ago, did you think your life would be like this?" she asked.

He wrapped them both up in his arms, watching the baby nurse with contentment. "God, no," he whispered. "Sometimes I still think I'm living a dream. This is the most amazing life I could imagine with the best wife a man could have."

Elliot switched the baby over to her other breast, which happened to be by Nash's face. His mouth and nose were buried in the top of the infant's head as she nursed, alternately kissing the blond little head and Elliot's left breast.

"I think she's going to look like me," Elliot said softly. "She's got my nose."

"She's all you, darlin'. I'm not really sure I really had anything to do with her."

Elliot giggled, watching him inhale the scent of their child. "Happy?" she asked.

He closed his eyes, pulling her tighter. "Unbelievably happy."

"Want to try for a boy next year?"

His eyes flew open and she laughed when she saw his reaction. "We've already got three," he said.

She shrugged, looking back at the infant in her arms. "I'd like to have a boy that looked like you."

"I'd like to have another girl that looked just like you."

"So who gets their wish?"

Nash did. Catherine "Cate" Aury was born thirteen months, four days, twenty-two hours and seventeen minutes after big sister Sophie. Nash spent the next few years carrying around book-end, blond-headed toddlers that were the most adorable creatures on the planet as far as he was concerned. The place once called Purgatory saw a new generation of Aurys grow up, love, and thrive.

Sophie MacGregor would have been proud.

THE END

ABOUT THE AUTHOR

ABOUT KAT LE VEQUE

KATHRYN LE VEQUE is a critically acclaimed, USA TODAY Bestselling author (having hit the list over 30 times), an Indie Reader bestseller, a charter Amazon All-Star author, and a #1 best-selling, award-winning, multi-published author in Medieval Historical Romance with over 150 published novels. Kathryn also writes Romantic Suspense as Kat Le Veque.

Kathryn has received praise for her writing and has won several awards for her work, including two nominations for the Holt Medallion. Her books have topped bestseller lists, and she has gained a loyal fan base that eagerly anticipates each new release.

Kathryn is a talented author who has made a significant impact on the world of historical romance fiction. Through her captivating storytelling and meticulous research, she has enchanted readers with her tales of love, adventure, and the enduring power of the human spirit.

Kathryn loves to hear from her readers. Please find Kathryn on Facebook at Kathryn Le Veque, Author, or join her on Twitter @kathrynleveque, and don't forget to visit her website at www.kathrynleveque.com.

ALSO BY KAT LE VEQUE

The Unholy Angels

Hour of Surrender

Trent Chronicles

Valley of Shadow

The Eden Factor

Canyon of the Sphinx

The Eagle Brotherhood

The Sunset Hour

The Killing Hour

The Secret Hour

The Unholy Hour

The Burning Hour

The Ancient Hour

The Devils Hour

www.ingramcontent.com/pod-product-compliance
Lightning Source LLC
Chambersburg PA
CBHW020521110726
47899CB00004B/1192